Joanna Bourne has always loved reading and writing romance. She's drawn to Revolutionary and Napoleonic France and Regency England because, as she puts it, 'l... and sacrifice, daring deeds, cla... clothing.' She's lived in seven ... England and France, the settings of ...

Joanna now lives on a moun... with her family, a peculiar cat and an old brown country dog. Visit her online at www.joannabourne.com, and connect with her via Twitter @jobourne, www.facebook.com/joanna.bourne.5, or www.jobourne.blogspot.co.uk.

Irresistible reasons to indulge in a Joanna Bourne historical romance:

'Joanna Bourne is a master of romance and suspense' Teresa Medeiros, *New York Times* bestselling author

'Bourne is an undeniably powerful new voice in historical romance' *All About Romance*

'Destined to be a classic in the romance genre' *Dear Author*

'Exceptional characters, brilliant plotting, a poignant love story' *Library Journal*

'Unusual, resourceful, and humorous heroines' Diana Gabaldon, *New York Times* bestselling author

'Distinct, fresh, and engaging' Madeline Hunter, *New York Times* bestselling author

'Addictivel...

By Joanna Bourne

Spymaster Series
The Forbidden Rose
The Spymaster's Lady
My Lord And Spymaster
The Black Hawk
Rogue Spy

My Lord and Spymaster

Joanna Bourne

headline
ETERNAL

The right of Joanna Bourne to be identified as the Author of
the Work has been asserted by her in accordance with the
Copyright, Designs and Patents Act 1988.

Published by arrangement with Berkley,
a member of Penguin Group (USA), LLC,
A Penguin Random House Company

First published in Great Britain in 2014
by HEADLINE ETERNAL
An imprint of HEADLINE PUBLISHING GROUP

1

Cataloguing in Publication Data is available from the British Library

ISBN 978 1 4722 2247 3

Offset in Times Lt Std by Avon DataSet Ltd, Bidford-on-Avon, Warwickshire

Printed and bound by CPI Group (UK) Ltd, Croydon, CR0 4YY

Papers used by Headline are from well-managed forests
and other responsible sources.

HEADLINE PUBLISHING GROUP
An Hachette UK Company
338 Euston Road
London NW1 3BH

www.headlineeternal.com
www.headline.co.uk
www.hachette.co.uk

For Douglas

Acknowledgments

I'd like to thank my ever-patient editor, Wendy McCurdy, and my agent, Pam Hopkins, for untiring advice and support in the production of *My Lord And Spymaster*. Thanks also to Mary Ann Clark and Wendy Rome, and the other Ladies Who Drink Coffee, Claudia McRay and Sofie Couch. Finally, I am endlessly grateful to the Compuserve Books and Writers Community, that hatching ground of writers, whose members have offered aid and comfort. Thank you Susan Adrian, Betty Babas, Jennifer R. Clark, Allene Edwards, Diana Gabaldon, Claire Greer, Jennifer Hendren, Carol Krenz, John S. Kruszka, Darlene Marshall, Janet McConnaughey, Jenny Meyer, Pamela Patchet, Vicki Pettersson, Barbara Rogan, Beth Shope, and Karen Watson. The lines "Debts must be paid. The books must balance," are from master storyteller R. A. Heinlein.

ne

Katherine Lane

ONCE YOU GET A TASTE FOR THIEVERY, YOU never lose it. Papa used to say that, clouting her on the side of the head a bit to let her know who he was talking about.

She missed picking pockets. Missed the cool, stealthy slide of fingers into a coat. Slithering away with a purse, wise and secret. She missed the best part—jingling the coins out on the cobbles, squatting down with her mates, and counting out the take. She'd learned to keep accounts, working out a fair cut.

Respectable was flat beer compared to that. Maybe that was why she'd talked herself into running this rig. She was so damn tired of being respectable.

It was a good day for robbery. Fog crawled up out of the Thames and made itself at home on Katherine Lane. It coiled over the drains and lurked in the corners, smelling like the river, which wasn't precisely ambrosia and mead as smells went. Anything could hide in that fog. Probably did.

"Welcome home, Jess," she whispered. She pulled her hood up and kept walking. The afternoon folded in around her, drizzling.

In the fog, on both sides of her, all the length of Katherine Lane, citizens were closing up shop, putting merchandise away, giving the day up as unprofitable. The street girls had moved inside, too, into the pubs, taking their sailors with them and the noise and the bright color of their dresses. More and more, she was passing dark doorways and rows of blank shutters. Pretty soon there'd be nobody in the street but her and that cat picking his way, finicky, across the cobbles. He had errands to run, that cat. You could tell by looking at him.

She'd have lots of privacy to pick Sebastian Kennett's pocket.

The last thing Papa'd said when they were dragging him out of the Whitby warehouse in his shirtsleeves was, "Don't do anything daft trying to get me free."

Papa knew her pretty well. He wasn't going to be pleased when he found out about this.

The alley to the right was Dark Passage—and wasn't that a fine, descriptive name? To the left was Dead Man's Way. Another piece of poetry. When she was a kid she'd run this warren barefoot. She knew these streets, knew every thin trickle of an alley that ran into Katherine Lane. She'd been born in a grim little attic a dozen streets to the north. Time was, she chatted friendly and easy with every beggar and pimp on the Lane. She could have ducked into any of these taverns and been welcome to dry out by the fire. Now she was a stranger. Not Jess. Now she was Miss Whitby. She didn't belong anymore. *I didn't used to be scared here.*

She walked slower as the Lane curved south and slanted down toward the Thames and she watched her feet. The cobbles were slick with muck. Every corner was a puddle. In the old days, she'd have brought Kedger with her, for company. The left side of her cloak, under her elbow, had a pocket sewed for him to ride in. Used to be she'd set him on her shoulder when she had a ways to walk and she was uneasy about it. He'd sit quiet, breathing in her ear, keeping watch.

But this wasn't any place for Kedger. This she had to do alone.

Then she wasn't alone.

She stopped cold, and her heart banged in her chest like a trapped rabbit. A shadow shifted. A hulking shape emerged from the dark of a doorway.

He came toward her, walking out of the gloom, soft-footed for all his size. He carried his lead pipe with the non-chalance of someone to whom this was not a novelty.

"Well now." He slapped the pipe across his palm with a meaty thunk.

He was a thickset man about fifty, graying and weather-beaten. A thin, wicked scar slashed from his right eyebrow to the stubble at his jaw. A soaked and crumpled hat shaded his eyes. Those eyes were his best feature; he didn't look half so villainous when you could see his eyes.

"You going to tell me what we're doing 'ere?"

"Doyle." She let her breath out. "You would not believe how much I enjoy working with someone utterly reliable. Can we go down that alley a bit? If somebody spots you with that pipe, they might just come rescue me. Could be drier in there, too."

"Not much." He lumbered ahead of her, parting the fog as he went. "I been standing here a while, wondering whether I'll die of the ague or some bloke'll come along and slit me throat, just fer a lark. Don't know which I fancy."

"That'll be one of those moot points they talk about."

"Moot. That's the word I wanted." In the alley, he picked a convenient spot, scattered some oddments aside with his boot, and leaned against the grimy wall. "You ain't paying me enough for this, miss, if you don't mind me sayin'."

She followed him and found her own clean spot of wall, companionably face-to-face with him. The overhang of the roof kept some of the rain off. But not, as Doyle said, much. "Impressive piece of pipe, by the way."

"Why thank you, Miss Whitby. I picked it out special when I got your note."

A right old villain, Doyle. She'd been lucky to hire him. He'd been a Bow Street Runner, they said, before he went bad. Now he took jobs an honest Runner wouldn't touch. There was no end of illegal odds and ends to this business of getting Papa free. Doyle was helping her with most of them.

"We're expecting company?" He'd spotted the way she was keeping an eye on Katherine Lane. No flies on Mr. Doyle.

"One man. Largish fellow, by all accounts."

"You want me to hit him over the head?" He hefted the pipe reflectively.

"Would you do that for me?"

"Not on your life." When he smiled, the scar on his face creased horribly. "Leastways, not fer what you're paying me."

A man of principle. She liked that about him. "Happen I don't want you to hit anybody today. Just chase after, with what you might call intent to clout."

"Sounds easy enough. Who do I chase?"

"Me."

"Ah . . . That'll make a nice change from me usual habits. Why don't you tell me about it?"

Doyle wasn't going to like this. She laid out what she had in mind. She didn't go into details he didn't need to know, which kept it brief.

"That's why I work fer you, Miss Whitby. Yer always expandin' me repertoire." The leather of his coat was heavy with the wet. When he wiped his sleeve across his forehead, it didn't dry things any. "Let me get this crystal clear. I waves this bit of pipe about like I was meaning to bash you a couple—menacing, as you might say—an' you runs up and wraps yerself around our coney, quaking with fright. Is that it?"

"Exactly. Wet and sobbing and quivering in every particular."

"That'll snag 'is undivided attention." Doyle tipped up his hat brim and gave her a long, sarcastic study. "I ain't never heard such a cork-brained plan in my life. Except the part about me trying to hit you over the head with this pipe. Plausible, I'd call that."

Always pleasant to work with a man with a sense of humor. She checked the Lane again. Still empty. "I need three minutes to dip his pockets. Buy me three minutes."

That was long enough to find the packet, if Kennett had it on him. Let her get her hands on that, and there'd be no more calculations and lists and guesses. She'd know. *I am so bloody tired of wrestling smoke.*

On the other hand, smoke didn't turn around and knife you when you picked its pocket. "He walks by here regular, late afternoon, going down to the ship. They're off-loading wool goods and furniture and some fancy tilework from Italy he's not paying duty on."

"A smuggler. It just gets better and better. Anybody I know?"

She had to tell him sooner or later. "The ship's the *Flighty Dancer.*"

"God's . . . avenging . . . chickens." He did some muttering she didn't catch the gist of, clanking his lead bar against the brick wall now and then for emphasis. She was right. He didn't like it. "That's one of the Kennett Company ships. Tell me you ain't going after Sebastian Kennett."

"I wish I could say that, Mr. Doyle."

Clank. Clank. Doyle's lead pipe tapped on the wall of the alley. *Clank.* "You ever hear what Bastard Kennett does to thieves?"

"Rumors." They said Kennett cut the fingers off a thief once, in Alexandria. Lopped 'em right off with one of the big knives he kept handy about his person. They told lots of stories. "Exaggeration, most likely."

"I wouldn't bet on it. If you want what he's carrying, send me to get it."

But Cinq could have anyone working for him. Even Doyle. That was why she was out in the rain, cold and wet and scared, doing this job with her own hands. "I can't."

Papa was locked up in that smug, escape-proof house in Meeks Street, waiting for the hangman. The real spy, the man the French called Cinq, was walking around London, free as a bird. He might be strolling down Katherine Lane right now.

I hope Kennett turns out to be Cinq. I hope he's carrying the packet. Hope he doesn't gut me like a halibut when he feels my fingers wriggling in his jacket.

Clank. "I ain't going to talk you out of this, am I?"

"No."

She didn't have a choice. She'd tried bribes, threats,

blackmail—all the old standbys. Nothing worked. Not with the British Intelligence Service. Not with Military Intelligence. Not with the Foreign Office or the Admiralty. Seemed like half the British government wanted Josiah Whitby behind bars.

Hell of a world when bribery doesn't work.

Doyle studied her from under the brim of his hat. "You ain't safe here, Miss Whitby, not being who you are. Not even with me. You go traipsing along the docks—"

"I'm careful."

"—past a line of pimps who got an immediate use for a tasty chit like you. Now you want to go annoy Bastard Kennett. You run mad, or what?"

Not mad, exactly. Sometimes there weren't any good choices.

Back when she was engaging in criminal acts with some regularity, she'd have called this a right pig of a caper. She didn't know what she'd call it now. When she stopped talking flash there was a whole plethora of things she couldn't even say anymore. "You don't have to stay."

Clank. "I earns that pittance yer paying me, Miss Whitby, in case you was wondering."

"You do indeed, Mr. Doyle." He was going to help her. All that low cunning on her side. The knot in her stomach loosened.

"I should jest slit me own throat and save Kennett the trouble." Doyle scratched his thumb along the line of his scar. "Sad way fer a man of my abilities to end. When does he show up for this nonsense?"

"Half an hour maybe. If he's coming."

"Not long then."

It seemed long. She leaned against the wall. In a third floor window, a candle flared into light. That would be one of the girls, working. A wood shutter creaked in the wind. Funny how dry her mouth was, what with all this wet everywhere.

"Doyle . . ."

"Hmm?"

"Stay a good long ways behind me. These knives Kennett's so good with . . . He throws them."

"So I hear. I ain't fond of knives sticking in me gut."

"Always felt that way myself." At the corner, wind piled fog up in a stairwell, pushing it back every time it tried to escape. In a pub down the street they were singing a fair version of "Rule Britannia." They were scum here on the Lane, but patriotic scum.

This was the worst part of a job . . . before it started.

"You do things you're scared of much, Doyle?"

"Time to time. It don't show, miss, you being nervous. Look cool as a clam, you do."

"Thanks. All this water'd cool off a stove." She wiped her share of London's drizzle off her nose and stuck her head out to look down Katherine Lane.

A rude dog of a wind nosed up under her cloak and started her shaking. Just nerves. Even Kedger shook when he got nervous, him being a ferret and coming by it naturally. She'd be fine once she started moving. "I don't like the waiting."

"Me, I ain't delighted with what happens when we stop waiting."

She flexed her hands, pretending she was warming up, trying to fool herself that she was ready for this. A few hours' practice hadn't brought the old skills back. *It's going to be bloody embarrassing if this Captain Kennett catches me fingering in his pocket.*

She heard them before she saw them.

Down the Lane, two men took shape in the fog. The big one on the right was upright but unsteady on his pins. The scrawny-looking cove on the left was holding them both up.

They were roaring drunk, which wasn't an astonishment in this street. They were singing.

". . . A pretty little oyster girl I chanced for to meet.
I lifted up her basket lid and boldly I did peek,
just to see if she haaaad any oysters."

Doyle whistled a long, irritated breath out between his teeth. "That's 'im. Kennett's the big man on the right. Cupshot, the both of them." He wiped his face with the sleeve of his coat. "Just what I need. Drunks with knives."

"If he's drunk enough, he'll probably miss."

"There's that."

Under the wool of her cloak, where it didn't show, she wrapped her arms tight around herself. She'd picked a thousand pockets. She'd be fine.

Kennett was, as they said, a sizable man. Tough-looking, too, for all he was silly with drink. Through the fog she could make out black hair and the lines of a dark, rawboned face. No hat. His coat was hanging open, which was a gilt-edged invitation to getting his pocket picked, if you asked her. She couldn't see much of the bloke on the left with Kennett draped all over him. He was dark and wiry, and he had his head down, watching his footing.

Voices carried in the rain. She knew the song about the oyster girl. It warned a man not to trust a lass he met on the streets. Sadly true.

"Some days," Doyle said, "life is just a bloody great old trial."

"How right you are, Mr. Doyle." She pushed wet hair out of her eyes and waited for the right minute to start yelling bloody murder.

Two

SEBASTIAN KENNETT DIDN'T CONSIDER HIMSELF castaway drunk. He wasn't precisely sober either, of course. There was a wide stretch of navigable ocean between drunk and dead sober. Fine sailing in those waters.

And wasn't it a day for celebrating. Riley, his senior captain, master of the *Lively Dancer*, had come reeling into Eaton Expediters at noon, bringing a cask of French brandy and good news. Riley's son had been born just as the man was setting anchor off Wapping at dawn. Fine brawling toasts everyone had drunk to young Thomas Francis Sebastian Riley. When they'd finished the brandy at the shipping office, they'd spilled into the tavern across the street—him and Riley and the shipping clerks and a dozen of his ships' officers and some total strangers—and taken up drinking there. A noisy strong lad was Thomas Francis Sebastian Riley, according to Riley, who knew something about babies. Baby Thomas Francis would need all the bellowing lungs he could muster, poor mite, with six older sisters. Give him a few years, and he'd probably run away to sea.

A fine day. An excellent day. More than enough reason to raise his voice in song, entertaining Katherine Lane.

"These are the finest oysters that ever you did see.
I sells 'em three a penny, but I'll give 'em to you free . . ."

He tipped his head back and let rain fall on his face. Heaven. He'd been back less than a week, home from the heat and stink of Corfu and points east. The cold pulled the poisons out of his lungs. It was good to breathe weather with some weight to it.

Adrian sang off-key, rapping his cane along the slats and shutters in time with the music. He wasn't drunk. Adrian didn't get drunk, not in his profession. He just couldn't sing worth a damn.

"For I see that you're a lover of oysters."

The brothels were islands of warmth and light floating in the fog. Upstairs, on the second floor, a couple of black-skinned ladies leaned out the window with their long, oiled hair hanging down. The crimson and yellow robes across their shoulders were the brightest thing in these streets. Their little dark breasts were propped up naked on their arms, look-ing chilly. They called after him as he passed, raucous as seagulls, selling themselves. He waved and kept on singing.

"Have you got a cozy room that's empty and nearby,
where me and my pretty little oyster girl can lie
while we bargain for her basket of oysters?"

The street bucked under him in a heavy groundswell. He rode it out. Didn't even stumble. Climbing the rigging taught you to keep your feet. The captain had to set an example. Adrian didn't need to go propping him up. He didn't have to grin like that either.

"She picked my pocket and then off again ran she.
She left me with a basketful of—"

A woman's scream of terror and pain cut the fog.

It came from that narrow gape of an alley. The world snapped into focus around him.

The street was walled at both ends with fog. Sharp, black edges stood out from the gray—a slant of rail, a doorsill, the line of a shutter. A tavern in the distance leaked drunken clamor.

Adrian stepped clear, opening up the fighting space. Ghost in the fog was Adrian. They stood, back to back. He set his hand light on the hilt of his knife. Adrian drew one of his.

Faint and nearby, he heard the brush of cloth on cloth. Somebody stood in that black slash of an alley waiting and watching. Almost, he could hear them breathing.

The next instant feet scraped into a run, starting from a dead stop. A girl rounded the corner, racing as if all the devils in hell were after her. A dark cloak flapped around her, the hood falling over her face, her pale dress revealed, glowing like a candle flame. Head down, arms outstretched, she ran right at him, and hit so hard she staggered.

She clutched his coat. Obligingly, he took hold of her so she wouldn't end up on those hard cobbles. Smoothly done, on both their parts. Damsel in distress was the name of this game. Bad luck for her he'd seen it played out before in a dozen variations.

Right on cue, the alley gave up a threatening figure, huge and male, carrying a two-foot length of pipe. The brute stopped short, staying invisible in the shadows. He held the pose, seeming to weigh odds. Then he lowered the cudgel and rabbited off the way he'd come, surprisingly shy for a fellow that large.

Behind him, Adrian murmured, "This has become interesting. Excuse me . . ." and took off down the same alley, silent as a fish.

His pretty pickpocket stayed fastened onto his lapels, breathing heavily into his waistcoat. There wasn't a man on earth who wouldn't collect her in close, being helpful.

"Please . . ." She panted and dripped, truly pitiful. "Oh, please. He's after me." When she twisted to look over her shoulder, her breasts nuzzled across him like hungry puppies. His groin tightened right up, wanting a share of that.

You're good at this, aren't you? This damp young woman had been standing in the rain a good long time, waiting for the right pigeon to come along. She made a sweet armful. He snuggled her to him, smelling lavender, and the wet wool from her cloak, and some feminine, flowery perfume that came from her skin. There were cooking spices in her hair.

If she was skilled enough, he wouldn't even feel her going through his pockets. He didn't keep more than four or five shillings jingling around loose in there. She was welcome to them. Nobody knew better than he did the chill and loneliness of those rooms on the second floor. Let her buy some coal to warm her toes tonight, or a meat pie, or a day's peace from her pimp, who would be that oversized lout play-acting with the lead pipe.

She'd find a knife or two when she worked her way around his jacket. But she must be used to men who carried knives.

Then her hood furled back. She looked straight at him, and he stopped finding any of this funny.

My God, look at her. Not pretty, was all he could think. *There's nothing pretty about her. That's beauty.* The thought formed clear as the strike of a bell.

She had the face of an ardent Viking. Strands of wet hair lay along the spare curve of her cheek, outlining the bones. Eyes the color of Baltic amber met his. In the weak, rainy dusk, her skin glowed like Greek honey.

All by themselves, his hands reached under the wet cloak and pushed it back. Her cotton dress stuck to her like a second skin. Her nipples had crested up to crinkly nubs, drawn hard with the cold. He circled her body with his hands and stroked downward and pulled her in the last inches till she was against his body. Her back was sleek, supple muscle, trembling some.

"Help me," she whispered, radiating sincerity. Her fingers flirted across his chest, checking for an inside pocket to his jacket and possible banknotes. "He won't come after me if I'm with a man like you."

He was enticed. Utterly charmed. All the time she was

spouting that clumsy flattery, she searched him with an intense, featherlight, touch-by-touch exploration that was incredibly erotic. Did she know that? She was so close she was breathing warm up and down his chest, setting off a little twist in his groin every time he felt the air stir on him.

Her lips shaped some silly story about getting out of her hackney to buy something and being attacked. About running, lost in the fog. But he wasn't listening. He watched her mouth. A man could glide his thumb into that sweet, wide mouth and ease her lips apart and ready her up for kissing. It'd be no trouble at all.

Amazing. He was ravenous for her. He'd gone hard as a rock just looking at her mouth.

She stood straight as a little sapling, taut against him, keyed up and lying through her teeth. Bright, nervous intelligence burned like a fire inside her. She couldn't lie worth a damn.

"They've been chasing me. Feels like miles. I don't know." She licked the rain off her lips. "I don't . . ."

"What is it you don't know?" He didn't fight the impulse. He stroked the pad of his thumb along her lower lip, back and forth, slowly caressing, coaxing it soft and full. Just saying hello to it. She could get away from him any time she wanted.

"I had to . . ."

He kept at it, seeing what would happen next. Her lip was silk smooth and wet where she'd licked the rain off. He followed the shape of it, watching her, keeping at it till she went silent. A shudder passed through her that might have been resistance. Then her mouth slacked open, quivering.

It was a beautiful thing to do to a woman, luring the sweetness of her up to the surface this way. He had her pinned like a butterfly with that single touch. "That's a sad story, sparrow."

"Story?" Her pupils spread wide and black, gazing up at him. She was so responsive. Unbelievable. How had she survived on Katherine Lane, being this sensitive?

"Why don't we forget all that? Let me get you in out of the rain." He hoped he sounded reassuring. What he sounded to himself was drunk. "You'd like that, wouldn't you? I'll take you somewhere warm and safe. Will you come with me?"

No answer. Just that fathoms-deep, velvet fascination in her eyes. He left off tempting her mouth and nestled her chin in the palm of his hand and gave her a chance to collect herself. Rain fell on her face and rolled away across skin that was fine-grained and smooth as flower petals. She was lucky. The life she led hadn't marked her yet.

After a moment, she blinked at him. "What?"

"You don't have to be out here in the wet. Let's go get under cover and talk for a while. Come with me."

"With you?" He liked the way she sounded. Dazed. That was good for a man's self-esteem. "You want me to come with you?" She bit her lip as if she were trying to bite away the feel of what he'd been doing. He wondered if it helped any.

"I'll give you five shillings for the night. Think I have five shillings. M'friend does."

Adrian would lend him the ready. Adrian walked around with lots of money in his pocket, and nobody ever picked it. Where the devil was Adrian, anyway? He should be here, playing the voice of reason, not leaving his drunk friend to be stupid about a pretty whore.

"You'd pay that much?" Laughter sparked in her eyes.

It was a ridiculous price for Katherine Lane. This was a woman worth being stupid over. He surprised himself with how much he wanted to take her away from this market for human meat and that brute of a pimp.

He'd better get her to Eunice before he forgot that he didn't buy street whores. It was a sad, dishonorable business, using these poor, trapped girls, not to mention a fine way to catch crotch beasties.

This one was different. He looked at her and saw himself hurrying her down to the dock, leading her aboard the *Flighty Dancer*, and slamming the door to his cabin. He'd take those breasts in his mouth and open her thighs and slip inside where she'd be warm, even on a chilly day like this. She'd show him all the tricks she could do with those light, clever hands and that soft mouth.

Wasn't going to happen. Instead, he'd bribe her with shillings and take her home with him. Aunt Eunice would know what to do with this bedraggled, larcenous ragamuffin. Eunice might get her off the streets for good. "Five shillings. And I'll give you a meal. Get you warm and dry. I'll take you to . . ." Damn it, he was too drunk and too stumble-tongued with lust to explain.

He couldn't remember the last time he'd wanted a street whore. This one was fresh as a daisy, clean and sweet. She smelled of soap and flowers and spices. Even her fingernails were clean.

Nobody on Katherine Lane smelled of soap and flowers.

Lies. She stank of lies.

Clean and lovely and talking like a lady . . . a woman like this sold herself in a snug brothel in St. John's Wood. She didn't come flying out of an alley in Katherine Lane. She'd been lying in wait—not just for any pigeon—for one man in particular. What did this skillful whore do besides picking pockets and telling lies with her eyes? Did she slip a knife between a man's ribs with those deft hands of hers?

He locked hold of her wrists. "Who sent you?"

"What?" The gold-brown eyes went wide. That was fear. She'd known she might get caught.

She was right to be afraid of him. "Who paid you?"

"I don't know what you're talking about."

More lies. Somebody had set a trap with this pretty, laughing woman. Not a trap for him. Nobody gave a damn about one more merchant trader. It was Adrian they wanted. And Adrian was alone in one of those side alleys, prowling and poking into corners.

He lifted his head and yelled, "Adrian! Watch out! It's a trap."

That set everything off.

"Behind you! Sebastian!" Adrian's shout.

He saw them then. Silent as beetles, two men scuttled toward him. More followed, slipping from doorways and corners. Under cover of the rain and fog, the pack had stalked in, unseen, converging from three directions. They were Irish, from the Gaelic they tossed back and forth. They carried knives and cudgels and chains. These were vermin from the dock-side, deadly and cold as ice. They'd sent the girl as a honey-pot to hold him while the gang closed in. She'd smiled at him while she was planning to watch him die.

"Run from me." He let her loose. "Run fast."

But she backed away, wide-eyed, breathing hard. "How? Nobody knows I'm here." That was shock in her voice, and fear. She turned in a circle, looking for a hole in the net closing round them. And he knew she was no part of this. No decoy.

"More of them down that way. A baker's dozen." Adrian dropped out of the fog into his usual place, taking the left.

Two of them against a gang. Long odds.

He picked a target—one in front, where his friends would see him die—and threw. The bravo collapsed with a sucking, bubbling neck wound. The familiar stink of death rose in the alley. He pulled his second knife.

The thugs hesitated, sending glances back and forth, fin-gering blade and cudgel. Attack or retreat. It could go either way.

Then one man broke ranks and lunged for the girl.

She was fast. Cat quick, writhing, she bit the filthy arm that held her and knocked a knife aside and wrenched loose. She skipped back, clutching a long, shallow cut on her fore-arm. "Not hurt. I'm not hurt."

No tears, no screams. Pluck to the backbone. She was also damnably in his way. He shoved her behind him, be-tween him and Adrian. Protected as she could be.

If this lasts long, she'll get killed. "Mine on the right." He threw, and his blade hit badly and glanced off a collarbone. One man down. One wounded. That would have been two dead if he'd had the sense to stay sober. "Waste of a knife. Damn."

His last knife was in his boot. Not for throwing. This one was for killing up close.

He forced his mind to the pattern the attackers wove, try-ing to spot the leader. Kill the leader, and the others might scatter. Adrian danced a path through the bullyboys, breaking bones with that lead-weighted cane of his.

No way to get the woman to safety. She stayed in his

shadow, using him as a shield, white-faced. *She's been in street fights before.*

Then he didn't think about her at all. Chain whistled past. He grabbed it and jerked the man off balance and drove his knife through a gap in the leather waistcoat, up under the breastbone, to the heart.

For an instant he stood locked, face-to-face, with the man he'd just killed, a redhead with pale skin and vicious, gleeful, mad blue eyes. Outrage and disbelief pulsed out at him . . . and drained away. The eyes went blank.

Then the dead bastard thrashed, rolled with the knife, and took it down with him as he fell.

No time to get it back. A crowbar cracked down on his shoulder with a bright, sour, copper pain. He fell, dodged a boot, and rolled away as Adrian took down his attacker.

The girl screamed.

Up. He had to get up. He was on his feet, shaking his head, trying to see through a black haze. The girl was stretched between two men, being dragged away. He staggered through madness and confusion, fog and pain. Adrian was swearing a blue streak.

Under the chaos he heard a monstrous racket of wheels on cobblestone. A goods wagon turned the corner.

The girl tore loose, leaving her cloak behind. She reeled straight into the path of the horses and slipped on wet cobbles. She had a split second to look up and see hooves. Her face was a mask of raw terror.

He launched himself toward her. Too late. He knew he'd be too late.

The driver wrenched on the reins. Horses reared and squealed. Frantic, she jackknifed away from the striking hooves. She was so close to scrambling to safety . . .

She slipped on the rain-slick cobbles. The wagon skidded. Iron rims shrieked on the stone. The wheel hit the side of her head with a soft, horrible thud. She whipped around, and wavered upright for an instant, and slumped to the dirty stones of the street.

Gaelic broke out. Limping, dragging their wounded with them, the gang retreated.

He stepped over a body and ran to the girl.

She huddled on her side, as if sleeping, covered with blood and mud, her pretty dress torn halfway off her. Her hand lay upcurled on the cobbles, open to the falling rain. For a sick moment he thought she was dead.

Adrian knelt beside him. "Gods. The dear gods. It *is* her."

She was breathing. Sebastian ran his hands across her face and up into her hair.

She opened her eyes, but she didn't see him. "Who?"

"You're safe."

"Hurt. I need . . ." She slipped out of consciousness with her eyes still open.

"How bad is it?" Adrian said.

"The wheel just glanced the side of her head." He pushed her hair aside to show Adrian. "Here. Any harder and she'd have cracked like a melon."

"There's blood all over her." Adrian dug out a handkerchief.

"Scalp wound. All flash and no fire." He touched his way across her skull, trying to sense wrongness, any give that shouldn't be there. In his years at sea he'd seen enough accidents to know what to look for. "Pupils the same size. Ears . . . nose . . . no bleeding. I can't feel a break in her head. I'm drunk, Adrian. They wouldn't have got to her if I hadn't been drunk. Too drunk to do this."

"I trust you, drunk, better than most doctors sober."

She tried to roll. He kept her still. "I need more light."

"Where? That tavern back there?"

She was soaked to the skin, lying in a puddle of water, losing the heat of her body into the ground. She was getting cold . . . a dangerous, clammy cold. "Not here. They might come back and bring friends." He pulled his greatcoat off and wrapped it around her. When he gathered her up, she didn't weigh anything at all.

She struggled when she felt herself be lifted. "Lemme down. I can walk." Before she'd quite finished saying it, her head lolled against his chest.

"Right. You can walk. Bloody likely." He shifted her in his hold so the rain didn't hit her face. "Get me a knife. I'm unarmed. I'll take her to the *Flighty*."

"I'll find you there." Adrian was already wiping a knife on a dead man's shirt. He slipped it into the sheath in Sebastian's jacket. "I have to go. I have to find out who sent them. Take care of her for me, Bastian."

Adrian wasn't just a friend. He was a power in the shadow world of political spies, Head of Section for the British Intelligence Service. It wasn't the first time Adrian had tangled him in his professional disputes. Fair enough. But sometimes innocents, like this poor girl, got hurt.

"You have some nasty enemies in this town."

"I do indeed." Adrian checked thugs as he passed, flopping them faceup, finding them dead. "Didn't you see?" His dark, cynical face twisted in anger. "They weren't after me. It's her. She's the one they want."

Three

The Flighty Dancer

"GET THE DOOR," SEBASTIAN ORDERED. THE CABIN boy scurried ahead, his bare feet slapping the planks.

When he laid her down on the bed, she mumbled, "Where . . . ?"

"She's bleeding, Captain."

"I see that, boy. Get me hot water." The sharp tone sent Tom scrambling from the cabin.

Her braids sprawled in loops over his pillow. Hard to believe this little mite of a girl had armed men chasing her through alleys. What the devil had she got herself mixed up in?

Half-conscious, she rolled away, slapping at him feebly, trying to sit up. "Lemme be . . ."

"Softly, girl." He was gentle when he pushed her to the mattress. "Softly. There's no place you have to go. Lie still."

Did she see him when she looked at him? Probably not. Her eyes were blank. "It's dark. It . . . hurts. Hurts. I can't get *out*."

"You're safe. Where does it hurt?"

"Don't be stupid. Hurts everywhere." She decided to black out for a while. Her eyes slid shut, and she went limp.

"I imagine it does." He eased her down flat. "Let's hope you haven't cracked anything important in your head. I'm damned if I can fix it." There was nothing to do for her but wait. The best doctor in London couldn't do more.

His fault she'd been hurt. The one day in the year he let himself get drunk, this woman needed him. There didn't seem to be enough inventive ways to call himself an idiot.

He unwrapped her from his coat and pulled her shoes off. She wasn't bleeding much anywhere, but she was soaking wet, shivering with shock and cold. That, at least, he could fix. All that filthy, soaked clothing had to come off.

He hesitated, then drew his knife. He set the point under the gilt locket she wore and turned the back of the blade and cupped his hand to shield her skin and cut. Lace snicked apart. That was Alençon lace, seven and sixpence a handspan these days, smuggled goods and illegal. And this was a very expensive whore.

She didn't react when he peeled away damp, clinging cotton. Her breasts slipped free. They were peaches, golden on top where the sun got to them, pale below. They swayed, stippled with goose bumps, the nipples tight.

"No damage to that pair. That's going to make hordes of men happy, won't it?"

Beautiful and beautiful, left and right. Unruly parts of him took note, getting hard and ready. His cock was offering suggestions on the best way to warm her up. He and his cock were just going to have to disagree about that.

"Let's get the rest of this off." He sawed through a bit of silk ribbon, then cut a widening vee of nakedness down her belly, getting less and less dispassionate with every inch. Devil knew how doctors managed. Maybe they were all eunuchs.

Her skin was cold against the back of his hand, smooth as water. Soon enough he brushed a feathering of curly hair. She was blonde down there, too. Blonde as summer wheat. A man never knew till he checked.

A legion of men had plowed that particular wheatfield, and that was a sin and a shame for a woman like this.

Her belly curved down from her hips to the long, soft plain with that vulnerable navel at the center, then rose in a little mound where those curls sprang up. It was territory that called out for a man to come lay his head in the cradle of her, there, and turn and kiss his way up that hill and fill his mouth with the smell of her and the taste . . .

He shouldn't have his hand there without invitation,

He took a deep breath and moved on, cutting away the rest of her skirt and peeling it back.

What was she doing on Katherine Lane, trying to sort through his pocket change? Who left her alone, in the stink and cold of the docks, to get attacked by gangs of Irishmen? That was going to stop.

One last tug. He pulled wet cloth out from under her. She lay on the white cotton covers of his bunk, a little on her side, instinctively trying to curl against the cold, wearing nothing but a locket on a thin blue ribbon.

Naked, she looked small and breakable. She'd seemed more substantial when she was on her feet, telling him lies and kicking thugs.

He'd been wrong about that locket. It wasn't gilt. This was gold, soft and heavy, with the design almost worn off. When he picked it up he could feel the age on it, the years that had rubbed it smooth. The clever hinge was Italian work.

"This trinket doesn't belong on the Lane. Neither do you, sparrow. We're going to have a long talk about that when you wake up." He didn't open it. He set the gold back between her breasts and left his hand there, his knuckles just touching her. "Your heart's thumping along like clockwork. That's good. You keep that up."

Under his fingers, her skin was smooth and unnaturally cool, with the heart beating inside. She might have been a marble statue, just called to life, taking the first breath. He could slide over a few inches and help himself to those breasts. He'd maybe taste them fairly soon. They'd be honey and cream with a rough nub of a nipple tweaking back and forth on his tongue.

Damn. Was he really thinking that way about an unconscious woman?

Yes. Yes. Oh, yes. Let's do that. His cock didn't have any scruples at all.

But then, his cock wasn't in charge. "And I'm roused up like a squad of marines on shore leave." He pulled his hand off the girl and stomped across the cabin, feeling moderately despicable, looking for towels. "That's uncomfortable. Let's wring some water out of your pretty hide and get you covered up."

Blankets were in the bottom drawer, towels beside the washstand. He brought them to the bed and sat beside her and dried her off fast, trying not to touch her skin. "We'll discuss your very tempting wares when you're awake. I like dealing with women who can talk."

He wrapped her in one of the Valletta blankets he shipped, vivid blues and greens in long stripes. Wool soft as a kitten. He cocooned her, head to foot, till he couldn't see a square inch of skin. It didn't help as much as he'd hoped. "Where the hell has that boy got to?"

Unbelievable, the effect she had on him. Had he ever wanted a woman this much? "You're something a man might pull up in his net one night. A mermaid, perfect and chill. Maybe you shed your scales and walked up Katherine Lane right out of the kingdom of the sea. Maybe that's how a woman like you got there."

Without opening her eyes, she said clearly, "It's dark." Whoever she was talking to, it wasn't him.

"The lamps aren't lit. I'll do it soon."

"I can't . . ." Gradually, like a flower closing, she curled herself into a ball. When she hid her head in her arms, she smeared blood across her face. "I can't get out."

"I'm here."

"Dark . . ."

Because her eyes were shut. "I'll make it light in a minute."

Loud thumps in the passageway said Tom was back. The boy slammed the door to the bulkhead, slopping water from the bucket. "Is she dead?"

So much for his private idyll with a mermaid. "She's not going to die. She's going to sit up and ask why I keep a lazy, half-sized baboon in my cabin. Bring that over here."

He sat down on the bunk beside her and wet a corner of a towel in the bucket. He began to clean the scrapes on her hands. Tom, a precocious eleven, craned for a look under the blanket. "Gawd, ain't she a beauty. An' she sells that up on the Lane?"

"Not to the likes of you."

The girl opened brown gold eyes. Her first sight was Tom's face, level with her own. "I fell, Sir. I weren't . . . careful." She tried to focus on him. "Who 'er you?"

"I'm Tom. I'm pleased to make yer acquaintance."

"Tell 'im I can't get out."

"What? Oh, yes, miss, I'll tell 'im. Can I get you something? Cup of tea. The fire's lit in the galley. I could get you a cup of tea, miss."

He could feel her shaking under the blanket. Fear and cold and confusion. "Tom." He thumbed toward the door. "Lose yourself."

The girl's gaze followed Tom as he left. Slowly she blinked her way around the cabin . . . bookshelves, the chart table, a stack of crates, and finally back to him. "Where am I?"

"My ship. How many fingers am I holding up?"

"You think I hit my head." She freed a hand from the blanket and explored into her hair. "I did."

"How many fingers?"

"Three."

"Does the light hurt your eyes?"

"Everything hurts." This time, when she tried to sit up, he helped her. He kept an arm around her while she huddled, hazy-eyed, clutching the blanket to her, looking bewildered. She would have aroused protective instincts in a stone.

"Talk to me, sparrow. Who are you?"

"Jess. I'm Jess."

When she'd been reeling in and out of consciousness, her voice had been pure East London. Now she sounded gentry. Somewhere, his cockney sparrow had picked up an education. She got more and more interesting. "Do you remember getting hit?"

She shook her head. Her face knotted in pain. "I shouldn't do that."

"No, you shouldn't. Do you know what day it is?"

"No. I . . . Stop asking stupid questions."

She'd mislaid a couple pieces of her memory. He'd seen that happen once, when his bosun took a fall from the rigging. It had been a day before the man remembered what ship he was on. He never did remember the fall.

"You're still shivering. Let's get you dry." When she didn't object, he picked up the towel and started unbraiding and untangling, blotting water out of her hair, making every move slow so he wouldn't scare her.

She was thinking the whole time, frowning. After a while she said, "I don't remember everything. What happened to me?"

"You fell under a wagon and got hurt." They'd talk about it tomorrow. That was one of several discussions he had planned.

Done. He put the towel down. Her hair dried up lighter than he'd expected, the color of a new-cut spar. Lovely. A man would keep this woman just for the pleasure of taking her hair down at night.

"I got my brains scrambled up, didn't I?"

"A little, maybe. Give it an hour or two and you'll be fine."

"I don't—" She stopped abruptly and jerked away from him. She pulled the blanket loose and looked inside. Her eyes came up, accusing. "I'm not wearing any clothes. You got me naked."

He was scaring her. He dropped the towel and backed away, holding his hands wide and empty.

THE man retreated, trying to look harmless and not succeeding to any extent at all.

He said, "You're not naked. You're in a blanket."

Oh, that was reassuring, that was. She was wearing damp skin and a wooly blanket. She pulled cloth up to her chin and hid behind it. "We must know each other pretty well, whoever you are."

"My name is Sebastian."

"Se . . . bast . . . ian." She tried the syllables out. She was pretty sure this was a complete stranger. A dangerous stranger. She'd known lots of dangerous men, and she could recognize one at a glance. "You're one of the things I don't remember, Sebastian. I don't remember you at all."

"You don't know me."

"Then I should have my clothes on, shouldn't I?"

He kept his voice soft, talking to her like she was a scared child. "They were wet."

There her dress was, a heap of slit-up rags on the carpet. "My dress got wet, so you cut it off. You must be a right terror in a thunderstorm." A prudent woman in her situation wouldn't embark upon sarcasm.

"You were soaked to the skin and freezing and bleeding at the edges. I couldn't do anything with a bundle of muddy cloth." He made stripping her naked sound prosaic as oatmeal. "And you were leaking mud all over my bed. I sopped a gallon of dirty water off you."

"Mud. That explains it." Her head pounded like a mill wheel. Every muscle in her body hurt, some of them in inventive ways. She couldn't remember how she got here. She was naked. There was nothing good about this situation. Nothing.

She was in bed in the captain's cabin of a good-sized merchant frigate, about a hundred seventy tons. *This isn't a Whitby ship. I'm not safe.* The cut of the cabin and the neat brass fittings said it was from a shipyard in Boston. This man, though, he sounded English, not American.

Most of all . . . it was strange inside her head. Felt like somebody'd taken a big ladle and stirred her brain a few times. Nothing was where it should be. When she went asking why she was sitting frog-naked in the captain's cabin of a merchant frigate, she couldn't dip up a teaspoon of explanation. *I am in a mort of trouble.*

Captain Sebastian stood five feet away, looking large and lethal, with a worried frown. "I'm not going to hurt you."

Well, you'd say that, wouldn't you?

He was young to be captain. Thirty, maybe. He had black hair and a big beak of a nose, and sailor skin, dark and rough, burned by suns that weren't polite and English. Colorful splotches of blood were drying on his shirt. That would be her blood, probably.

I've seen him before.

A memory bobbed up, all in one piece. She was standing against the Captain, so close next to him, they were intimate as a pair of teeth. *Fog swirled past. That inky hair was wet, slicked down over his forehead. He slid his fingers along my mouth, tickling. That's all he did, and I was heat and pleasure and squirming inside like he'd kissed me for an hour.*

He knew what he'd done to me. He wanted to do it.

I said, "Five shillings?" and I laughed at him.

The memory tipped sideways and sank like a stone. She had no idea what came next. She groped in the corners of her mind and couldn't find anything.

His voice rumbled, "You're worrying. I want you to stop that. I'll take care of you."

I don't want you to take care of me. I want to have my clothes on. She huddled up close and tucked the blanket in tight under her. *This is a Greek blanket. We use them for packing the fragile cargo. Papa buys a bale or two on the docks at Valletta, last thing, and we toss them on top of . . .*

Then it was gone. The image of the dock at Valletta rippled into pieces and blew away, taking Papa with it. There was something she needed to do for Papa. Something important. She had to . . .

Chaos and spinning pain in her head. Nothing else. She couldn't think.

She looked down. Her toes peeked out the bottom of the blanket, pink and defenseless and silly-looking. "I don't remember how I got here."

"I carried you in after the wagon hit you. Let me get you some light. It's getting dark early."

I got hit by a wagon? That's a fool's trick. Doesn't sound like me, somehow. She watched him as he walked across the cabin, taking lanterns with him. It hurt like needles to move her eyes. They hurt when she closed them, too. *Sometimes you only have bad choices. Lazarus used to say that to me.*

When the Captain passed the squares of the windows, she saw him in outline against the gray outside.

That joggled loose another little moment.

He had his back to me and he was holding a knife. Men came spewing out of the Dark like demons. He put himself between me and those men . . .

"I was out . . . in that." She looked at the rain and fog outside the window. "With you. And you killed someone."

"There was a fight." He set the lanterns on the chart table. "We'll talk about it tomorrow. You can sort everything out when your head doesn't ache."

He's a killer, then. I know too many killers.

He'd protected her, in some shadowy fight in the fog. She was sure of it. Maybe that was why he didn't scare her as much as he should have. She watched him make fire, sheltering the tinder with his hand. Big hands, he had. He was substantial in general, and being on shipboard made it obvious. A man his size filled up the space, bulkhead to hull, deck to overhead.

He blew on the spark and got the candle lit. All the while he was taking quick glances in her direction. Assessing. Seeing whether she was about to panic or scream or run. She might have, if her head hurt less. Easier to panic when your head didn't hurt.

He hooked one lantern up over the chart table. It swung when he let it loose. Bright and shadow skittered around the cabin. He walked toward her, holding the other lantern, and he bulged out in his breeches, randy as a stallion.

No.

Fear ran down her like water. For the first time since she'd opened her eyes, she was crawly skinned frightened. Cold with it. Shocked and sick with it.

She darted her eyes away and pretended she didn't see. Oh, she was looking at the chart table. She was staring at the carpet on the deck. But she didn't fool him. He pulled up, halfway across the cabin, just stood still, and watched her.

She folded up small, hiding under the blanket.

"Stop that," he said sharp-like.

Easing the blanket with her, she edged back farther in the bunk. No escape that way. The door was on the other side of the cabin. Past him. No escape there, either.

"Don't be a idiot." He looked annoyed.

A flash of memory struck. *The Captain yelled, his face distorted with rage and contempt. "Run from me."*

She was in his cabin. No way out. The world got wavery at the edges. *I am in so much trouble.*

He started toward her, across the cabin, deliberate and slow, like piled-up thunderheads approaching at sea. She jerked the blanket and scuttled backwards on the bed, rucking up the covers till she slammed against the portside hull. Just a startling amount of useless, that was.

He came to the side of the bed. He hung up the lantern on the hook in the overhead and stood there scowling. "Would you calm down? I'm not going to lay a hand on you."

Her memory was full of dark patches of pain and fighting and trying to run. Anything could have happened to her, and she wouldn't remember. "Maybe you already have."

"You think I'd do something like that in front of an eleven-year-old cabin boy, and you cold and limp as a dead mackerel? Don't be silly."

"I'm not being silly. I'm sitting here with my dress off, and you're . . ."

"I'm what? This . . ." he gestured crudely, "doesn't mean a damn thing. This is because you don't have any clothes on and you're female. For God's sake, I don't attack women every time I get a cockstand."

She shook her head. The world went spinning. She was so bloody sick. He could grab her if he wanted to. Just reach out and do it.

"I'm not the kind of sorry bastard who rapes women." His words would have left marks on stone. It chilled her right to the soles of her feet, that soft voice. "Hell."

"My father has money. I can pay you . . ."

"If your father had money, you wouldn't be on Katherine Lane." That hawklike glare never wavered. Unreadable eyes, he had. "It doesn't any good to tell you not to be scared, does it? You'd be a fool if you weren't scared. What do you want me to do about it?"

I should kick him and run. She didn't though. Like he said, she wasn't a fool.

"Do you want me to get out of here? I can go up on deck and let my cabin boy keep you company."

The lantern he'd hung was swinging still, reshaping the shadows of his face. Revealing and hiding. Hiding and revealing. It was deliberate, the way he stood crowding her at the bunkside. He was showing her he could come as close as he wanted and still not lay a hand on her.

He said, "You can try leaving under your own sail. You won't get far before you keel over, but I won't stop you. Take the blanket, if you want."

A minute ticked by. She said, "You didn't do anything to me, did you? You didn't . . . "

"I did not. I don't take sport with unconscious guttersnipes. London's full of willing women. Pretty ones." He pushed the bed-curtains back along the railings and cupped his fingers over the bed frame. "Less grubby, too."

You had to look into that hard face for a while before you saw he was laughing, quiet, underneath. At her. At himself, too, maybe.

"I guess . . . if you wanted to do something, you'd be doing it."

"I would, if I wanted a woman pale as a fishbelly and listing badly to port. A real villain wouldn't let that stop him."

"Fishbelly."

"Fishbelly green. You still are."

She wouldn't have trusted a kindly, reassuring man. This bloke, rude, impatient, and exasperated, though . . .

"Let's make a deal, Jess. I don't touch you, and you stop trying to dig a hole through the portside planking. Those are the terms and conditions. Shake on it."

He wanted her to shake on it. Somehow this made sense. She was pretty sure parts of her mind weren't working.

"I keep my contracts," he said. "Ask anybody."

He had his hand out. It was twice as big as hers and dark with the sun. Bands of callus crossed the palm. He got that reefing sail in high winds when the lines cut into his flesh as the ship bucked and he had to hold on.

She slipped her hand out from under the blanket, into his. It was a shock, touching him. Made him seem bigger and closer and more real. It set off a pulse in her belly, nervous and twitchy like. A little drum, drum, drum started up between her legs. She recognized the feeling, since she wasn't ignorant in such matters. That was her body noticing he was a fine-looking man. Her body generally had more sense than that.

He shook her hand and let go. "That's it, then. I'll keep you safe tonight. Safe from me, too. Your part is, you trust me. For one night."

He was already walking away. He tossed the words at her over his shoulder and picked a wide-bottomed decanter out of the brass rack in the bookshelves. "You're getting the better of that deal. You wouldn't make it twenty yards if you tried to run."

He acts like Papa. Like his handshake's good from Dublin to Damascus, and everybody knows it. I don't recognize his name, but I'll bet I just struck a bargain with a master trader.

"I'll give you a brandy to seal the deal. You're blue as a whelk and shivering. Wrap that blanket tighter."

She watched him pour a glass, not being stingy. He stretched up and took a wood box down from the top shelf. When he opened it, it folded to both sides, like a book, to show medicines. Bottles and jars and paper packets were strapped in, neat and shipshape.

He uncorked a blue bottle and counted drops into the brandy.

Not surreptitious, Sebastian. That meant he was daylight honest or else he was deep as a well. No way of knowing which, just at the moment. She'd assume deep as a well till proved otherwise. "I like the way you're letting me see you doctor that up."

"That's to disarm suspicion."

"You get marks for trying. What are you putting in it?"

"This and that." He set the bottle back in its place and pulled a muslin pouch out of the box. He unwound the string and jiggled the bag open in the palm of his hand. He picked out a pinch to sprinkle over her glass. "The tincture is to dull the pain. These herbs are to stop that fever you're about to get. The gray powder floating on top is to show you it's serious medicine."

"You think I'm going to drink that."

He swirled the glass, letting everything mix. "You can toss it out a porthole. Waste of good brandy, though."

"The fish might enjoy a brandy. It's a cold, wet night in the Thames."

"It's cold up here, too, and nearly as wet." He carried the glass across to her, being casual, like he didn't care whether she took it or not. "Drink this and stop being a fool." His fingers didn't brush hers when he handed it over. "If you're not going to trust me, I can always cart you outside and dump you back in the rain. I might even find the exact muddy puddle I picked you out of."

Empty threats. She preferred them, actually, to the other kind.

She sniffed at the glass. Nothing to smell but brandy and something like smoke. When she took a sip, there was nothing much to taste, either. He was a man of secretive medicines. "What did you say that dusty stuff was?"

"I didn't. That's medicinal herbs from the mysterious Orient. Guaranteed to do everything but raise the dead. Can't possibly hurt you." The Captain busied himself putting his medical gear away.

Hah. But she took a sip. "I don't trust medicine much. It's good brandy, though. My father deals in brandy." *We smuggle it.*

Rain tapped on the deck above. That was a good sound. Familiar. She'd spent a hundred nights at sea with the rain overhead. Funny how she felt quiet inside, steady, being with this man. She felt safe. He had practice taking care of his ship and his crew. That's why his hands were leather, strong and hard. That was from handling ropes and checking cargo and holding onto what he intended to keep. It set prickles of awareness running along her skin, thinking that those hands had undressed her. He'd touched her body, doing that, even if he didn't admit it. It made sense he wouldn't want to talk about it.

She looked out the window, past the reflection of the cabin. Rain slapped hard on the glass and ran down in lines.

The light was going. The wharf was empty of carts and horses. Lamps in the warehouse yards cast long, greasy, rippling streaks of light on the stones of the dock. To the left, midriver in the Thames, dozens of ships anchored—schooners and frigates, lighters, barges—all with lanterns, fore and aft, bobbing in the tide. A jagged forest of masts and rigging glowed eerily against the mist.

It's important what day the ships leave. The sailing dates are half the puzzle. The other half . . . The other half is . . .

And then she didn't know what the other half of the puzzle was. It made sense a minute ago. Now it didn't. Maybe this was what it was like, being mad. "I can't think."

"Then it's lucky you don't have to think."

"One of those fortunate coincidences." She wrapped her arms around her knees, looking at the little gray bits floating in the brandy, trying to decide whether she should drink it. It came down to trust, didn't it? The Captain had risked his neck for her, out there in the streets of London. She'd given him nothing in return but sand and mud in his bed. And she'd made a bargain. She kept bargains. "I haven't thanked you, have I? For saving my life. I almost remember you doing it."

"I spend most evenings fishing women out of the deeper puddles in the port area. I consider them legitimate spoil. It doesn't do any good in the glass, Jess."

He'd been captain a good, long while. He gave orders like a man used to being obeyed. "I haven't made up my mind yet." She yawned, surprising herself.

"I suggest you do so, before you fall asleep again. Or set it aside. You don't have to worry, you know." Captain Sebastian's voice rumbled through her, mild and reassuring, stroking away at the last of the frightened places in her, loosening the knots in her nerves.

He could do anything he wanted to her. Commit any evil. And he didn't. Here and now, because he was such a dangerous man, she knew she could trust him. Paradox they called that. Looking at it from three or four different angles, she still came up with the same answer.

Wasn't it lucky her brain worked well enough to tell her that? She took a deep drink of the brandy.

HE saw the exact moment she decided to trust him. She drank the brandy, and she stopped looking like a cat in a sinking lifeboat.

That was good. He was damn sick of scaring her. "Are you still afraid of me?"

"Some. You're formidable as hell. I suppose you know that." She tilted her head to one side. "I don't know how to treat you, Sebastian. I wish you were some pudgy little chap who didn't scare me to death."

Alone and hurt, totally at the mercy of a stranger, she could say that and give him a little sidewise grin. Courage to burn, this woman had. "You'll get used to me."

He was aroused all over again, seeing that street urchin's grin. She was going to laugh at him like this, when he had her in bed. She'd tease him and play games under the covers. He'd like that.

Since he wasn't going to get her underneath him, squirming enthusiastically, anytime soon, he did some walking around, kicking the damp towels together in a pile, rolling up the coastal charts and putting them away in brass tubes, giving his body a chance to cool off.

After a bit, she said, "You carried oranges. I can smell them."

"First cargo up from the hold." The *Flighty* would smell of oranges for a while yet. He didn't notice, himself. By one of God's small mercies, the crew stopped smelling cargo after the first day or two. "I sold them on the wharf the morning we docked and was glad to get rid of them. Tricky, delicate cargo."

"They stow forward and below the waterline, with air moving around them. Then you tear up the water heading home."

She knew shipping. She had a father or brother or lover who was a shipping clerk or a sailor.

"We leave keel marks on the waves."

"I can see a picture of it in my mind, how you packed the

oranges in. Where they were stowed. How they unloaded. Why do I know so much about your ship?" Panic, just the edge of it, touched her voice. "If I don't know you, why do I know this ship?"

"There's lots of ships on the river, Jess."

She was scaring herself again, thinking she knew *Flighty* and he was lying to her. So he rolled up a map of the Thames estuary and used it to point to the ships at midriver, the ones they could still see in the gloom, naming them one by one, talking cargoes and ports . . . Canton, Baltimore, the Greek isles, Constantinople. He watched fear eddy and slack inside her. But he'd sold goods all over the Mediterranean. She wasn't a match for him. He talked and talked, and slowly she let herself be gentled into trusting him. She trusted too easily. Somebody should be taking care of her.

"Feels like I've been there, some of those places." She shifted inside the blankets. He got a brief glimpse of some anatomy he'd been admiring earlier. It was even more tempting, half covered. "Valletta. Crete. Minorca. I can almost see them."

When she belonged to him, he'd take her to sea and show her Crete and the Greek isles. Why not? She'd take to life shipboard like a seagull. It'd be fine to come on deck and see Jess at the rails, her hair blowing, her bonnet off, and her skin brown from the sun.

Or if she wanted to stay in England, he'd bring the world back to her. He'd drop anchor in London and come home to her and shuck his boots at the door. He'd find her curled up next to the fire, waiting for him. She'd be sleepy, the way she was now, and they'd talk about his trip. Everything he'd seen. He'd bring back baubles from his trading and lay them at her feet. This was a woman he'd enjoy spoiling with presents.

"My brain doesn't work at all." She rubbed her hand over her forehead and into her hair to badger her brain better. It was a bad idea. She winced, and her fingers came away red. "I've got blood on your blanket. I'm sorry."

"I have three hundred in the hold. I won't miss one."

"A third of a percent. Well within normal shipping loss."

And she'd got the number right. Mystery after mystery was wrapped around his Cockney sparrow. He was going to enjoy unwrapping them.

She yawned and leaned back against the bulkhead. "I should go home and feed Kedger. Pitney does it if he remembers. But he doesn't like Kedger. Not really."

Kedger would be her dog, or a cat. Women liked pets. Maybe when he came home from sea, Jess would be sitting waiting for him with a cat in her lap. Hell, if she didn't have a cat, he'd buy her one. He liked cats. "Kedger will be fine. Stay with me."

She was brooding, holding the glass in both hands and looking at the brandy instead of drinking it. "I hate going back to the rooms when Papa's not there."

When he sat down next to her, she'd already forgotten to be afraid of him. He cupped her cheek, turning her till he had her whole attention. "Stay with me, Jess. It's cold out there, and it's dark, and it's raining." In the rookeries, five or six men were waiting for her, hoping for a quiet minute to bash her over the head.

"It is raining."

"And you're drunk as a wheelbarrow. Getting there, anyway."

"I'm drunk?"

"Three sheets to the wind, as we say at sea. Let's finish the job." He tipped up the bottom of her glass and made her drink, hurrying her through the rest of it, getting the medicine into her before she fell asleep. "That's right. Last drop."

"Drunk?" She let him have the empty glass. "I can't think anyway, so it probably doesn't make much difference. You would not believe how strange it is inside my head."

"Why don't you relax and enjoy it."

"I don't do that sort of thing. Get drunk, I mean. I'm a very serious person."

She was a serious person in danger of rolling off the bed in a few minutes, all boneless and relaxed.

She watched him set the glass away on the table. Her topaz-colored gaze was beginning to shift out of focus. "Papa said not to do anything daft. But I think I did." She frowned.

"You ever catch fish in a pool, Captain? The way they dart off when you go after them. It's like that, trying to remember. There's something I have to do."

"Let the fish be for a while. You'll remember in the morning." All that brandy in her, and she was still rummaging through her mind, worried as a conscientious clerk with a misplaced invoice. It was a stubborn woman he had naked in his bed tonight. But she didn't object when he gathered her together and laid her down on the pillows. Didn't object when he stroked her hair and the back of her neck. He watched her thoughts dissolve like snow melting off a roof. After a while, her fingers uncurled their grip on the blanket. The gold locket slipped to nestle between her breasts. Her truly excellent breasts.

"You have lots of women, Captain? You look like somebody who's had lots of them." Her voice was dreamy. She was already lost in what he was doing to her face and her neck.

None like you. Never anyone like you. "Not so many. A sailor can go without when he needs to. I don't grab, if that's what you mean. I ask. Tonight I won't even ask. Are you warm enough? I can get another blanket."

"What? Oh, yes. Toast. Be warm in a snowdrift with you doing that to me."

He leaned over her, looking down, admiring the golden woman he had, half-asleep, in his bed. She put her hand up between them, not pushing him away, just touching him with sleepy curiosity. Accepting him. Her eyelids fluttered when he touched his lips between them and kissed her forehead. She closed her eyes then, for him. It was the first in a long line of surrenders she'd make, and never realize she was making.

He set his lips to her eyelids, breathing across skin tender as flower petals, step by step seducing his professional pickpocket.

This was the beginning for the two of them. Strange, how sure he was of that. Two hours after plucking her out of the mist on Katherine Lane he felt an irrational sense of possession. It was as if the tide had washed her ashore at his feet. He was going to immerse himself in the slow-spun pleasure of winning and loving this woman. He could see the years he'd spend with her stretching out into the future.

"Maybe I'll go to sleep." Her voice closed around him in velvet. That was how she'd feel when he was inside her. When she surrounded him. Like velvet.

She was already his Jess, even if he was the only one who knew it. He intended to hold on to her. Tomorrow, he'd track down that careless father of hers and get her away from him. Or find her pimp. Whoever she belonged to. There'd be no more dangerous work for her, out in the cold, picking pockets for that shadowy brute with the lead pipe. Whoever it was who ran her, he'd threaten them or bargain with them or pay them off. Her price didn't matter. He was a rich man.

Then he'd seduce her into his bed. That would be the voyage of a lifetime, raising her sails to the wind, pulling the lines taut, one by one. She'd started out already, traveling with him.

Within a week he'd have her sweaty under him, not a stitch on her, begging and incoherent. He promised it to himself. She'd open to him like some exotic fruit, achingly tart and sweet, and he'd worship all the length of that sleek body. When she was ready for him, he'd slip inside and explode into her.

He had plenty of time to entice and lure her. He'd be fixed in London a while, seeing to the hanging of Josiah Whitby.

Four

HE LAY BESIDE HER FOR A LONG TIME, KEEPING her covered, watching her sleep. She sprawled with a limp, defenseless abandon he found incredibly touching. He wanted her asleep beside him, like this, tonight and tomorrow and for an endless string of nights in the future. This was no girl for a quick tumble. When a man found a mistress like this, he kept her. Maybe he kept her life long.

He'd be doing her a favor, buying her and seducing her into love with him. She needed somebody to take care of her.

"You're a trusting fool, Jess, whatever else you are," he went on without a pause or raising his voice, "and if men slip by my guards and try sneaking up on me, I'm likely to gut them first and regret it later."

"How is she?" Adrian was in the cabin, silent as if one of the shadows had stepped off the wall and gone walking around. He was that good.

"Drunk. Asleep. Hurting. Not sure where she is or why. That crack on the head has her confused. She'll be better when she wakes up in the morning."

"Good." Adrian's voice was cold. "Now tell me why she's naked in bed with you, you rutting bastard."

Hell. He rolled off the bed fast. His feet thumped to the boards, and he stood, confronting his friend across the dim cabin. There was no trace of amusement in Adrian's expression. He was dead serious. Angry. Very angry. This was Adrian as his enemies saw him.

He remembered Adrian kneeling over Jess in the alley, smears of her blood on his hands. Quick, clever Jess, with the Cockney accent and pockets of surprising knowledge. She was Adrian's match in so many ways.

He should have known a girl like this would belong to somebody. The certainty hit him like a blow.

I've taken Adrian's woman to bed.

Adrian said tightly, "What have you done to Jess?"

There was a time for truth. It was not now. "Nothing. I didn't do a thing to her you couldn't have watched."

"Nothing?" The blanket had slipped. Jess was showing a yard of wanton golden skin. "Why do I find that so hard to believe? Gods in Hades, she's stone cold unconscious." For an instant, Adrian looked as dangerous as he was. "I wouldn't have thought you were a man for complicated revenge. What are you doing?"

"What revenge?"

A stark minute ticked by. Adrian said, "You don't even know who she is."

"Your woman? Tell me, goddammit. Is she your woman or not?"

"You don't know." Adrian's face was utterly unrevealing. "You took one look at Jess and tumbled her into bed. Why didn't I see that was going to happen?"

"I didn't tumble her anywhere. I was keeping her warm."

"How very gullible I must look these days."

The bloody-minded, antic bastard was laughing at him. "She's not yours."

"I should make you sweat, Bastian. I really should." Slowly, his friend's face changed. Unholy amusement gleamed in his eyes. "You can stop looking like I've gut-shot you. She is not, as you so engagingly put it, my woman."

His breath loosened. "She's not one of your agents?"

"Not remotely."

He hadn't realized how rigid he was till his muscles loosened. Relief swept through him, amazingly strong. It was an emotion he set aside to analyze later. "Who is she?"

"Ah. That is the question of the hour, isn't it?" Adrian stood beside the bunk, watching the girl, a complex, unreadable expression on his face. "The last time I spoke to her, she was fourteen, skinny as a lamppost, and flat as a board."

"She's changed. Now tell me who she is."

Jess turned onto her side and moaned softly. They both looked down. Adrian was there first, pulling the blanket to cover her, lifting her hands and tucking them inside . . . a protective gesture, but curiously detached. "Let's take this up on deck. She sleeps light, and I don't want her to see me."

"She doesn't sleep light with a mug of brandy poured down her throat." He shouldered past and sat back on the bed beside Jess. She'd got her hair caught under her arm. He set it free, spread it over the pillow so she'd be comfortable. She didn't wake up. She nestled into his hand, putting her breath into his fingers. "She's not hearing a thing. What the deuce is going on? Who were those men?"

"Let me think about this for a while. Do you have any brandy left, or did you waste it all knocking Jess out?"

"Talk."

"I'm thinking." Adrian picked up the glass Jess had used and sniffed at it. "You drugged her." He held it up in the light. "What did you use? I'm always willing to try new things."

"The powder I picked up in Alexandria. Just medicine." He held on to his patience. When Adrian was like this, there was nothing to do but wait it out. "What was she doing on Katherine Lane?"

"Now that I can tell you. She was lurking with intent, very artfully. Waiting for you."

He stayed sitting beside her on the bed. Her hair was soft and a little damp between his fingertips. She might have sensed him. She stretched restlessly, not waking up. Her head butted his knee, and she sighed and relaxed against him, as if she'd just tied up safe in the shoals of some tricky bay. "What does she want from me?"

"She wants to pick your pockets, of course. Doyle supplies that exciting news. She did not tell him why."

Doyle was British Service, Adrian's second-in-command. "That was Doyle in the alley, with the lead pipe."

"I'm surprised you didn't recognize him. Not many men in London his size."

"I didn't see his face." If the British Service was interested in Jess, she was in deep trouble. "Why does the Service have its top field agent following a Cockney pickpocket?"

"I will amaze you by revealing that she is not a simple Cockney pickpocket." Adrian lifted the decanter and poured, stopping neatly halfway up, as if there were an invisible mark on the side of the glass. "Doyle has the greatest respect for her, by the way. He's managed to inveigle himself onto her payroll. He says he's getting rich."

"Why was she picking my pocket?"

"An irresistible interest in their contents, I'd imagine. She has the most endearingly straightforward mind."

"Why?"

"That, we do not know. She does not trust Doyle with her girlish secrets. It'll be something pocket-sized, one presumes. Shall we investigate? Empty out, and we shall see."

Damn Adrian. "You want to see what's in my pockets?" He coiled off the bed. His greatcoat and jacket were slung over the chair, wet, dirty, and bloody from the fight. He pulled out a coin pouch and spilled it into his palm. "Five shillings. Half crown. Ha'pence." He slapped that on the table. "And in the pockets we have . . . couple of pence . . . another grubby ha'penny. That's seven and nine. We can buy out the store with that. What else? Silver watch." He pulled it out and laid it next to the coins. "If you want my pocket picked, why don't you do it yourself?"

"I'm not the one light-fingering about your person. Jess is. What else?"

"If this is one of your games, I'm going to wring your neck." He turned out the pockets of his coat and added to the pile. "Jackknife. Key to the strongbox in my desk at home. House key. And now we strike gold—a letter from Cousin Penelope in Little Thrushing, Hants. She's putting in roses. You'll find that riveting."

"Enormously. What's the rest of that?"

He'd stuffed a few papers into his greatcoat at the last minute, leaving the shipping office. "Invoice for the sale of oranges. Receipt for 300 yards of rope. Copy of the waybill for some furniture I transshipped to Scotland." He dropped them on the table. "That's the lot. What's going on? I want the short answer."

"With Jess, alas, there are no short answers." Adrian quested with a finger, turning papers over. "This is unpromising, isn't it? What are you hoping to find in my friend's pockets, Jess? He has captured your vagrant regard, and that I find very interesting indeed."

"She's not a pickpocket. Not your agent. Is she a whore?"

"Good heavens, no. Whatever gave you that idea?" Carrying his glass of brandy, Adrian picked his way around the cabin. "I'm sure there are dozens of respectable women walking Katherine Lane. You have crates stacked all over." Three long, flat wooden boxes were lashed to the bulkhead. "I don't call myself an expert, but I'm almost certain these belong in that big, damp pit you've got down below. The hold, you seafaring sorts call it."

"It's a Roman mural from some villa Napoleon sacked near Milan, headed to a collector in Hampstead. It's worth the rest of the cargo put together. I'd sleep with it under my pillow if it would fit. Why is the Service watching Jess?"

"You probably have it listed on the manifest as ballast. The customs evasion practiced by the so-called respectable merchant community—"

"I don't want to talk about customs evasion, Adrian."

Adrian took another long swallow. Liquor never had any effect on him. Hard to know why he bothered. "Doyle tracked down one of the surviving Irishman. They hail, quite recently, from Dublin, where they are likely unlamented. They were hired from the dock two days ago with orders to kidnap Jess.

Hired by—and I quote—'a black-haired cove, all muffled up,' which limits my search to half the male population of London. Sebastian . . . she's Josiah Whitby's daughter."

It was like the long drop when the ship slides down the trough of a storm swell. Only he never hit bottom. He plummeted, feeling sick all the way down, endlessly.

"Jess . . . Whitby."

"Yes."

Josiah Whitby was Cinq, a murderer and a traitor. Nobody knew this better than Sebastian. He'd gathered the evidence that was going to hang the man.

Jess sighed and stirred. The curve of her shoulder emerged from the striped wool like the line of a wave coming to shore.

She was a woman of many small beauties. Cinq's daughter was sleeping in his bed.

They called the traitor Cinq because he signed his messages with the sketch of a pair of dice, the fives uppermost. The offices in Whitehall were his private lending library. Somehow, he helped himself to secrets at the War Office and the Admiralty. Somehow, he slipped them out of England, past the British naval blockade, into France. Napoleon knew British plans before the British army in Spain did.

Two years ago, French frigates ambushed the *Neptune Dancer* in the Jersey straits. She went down with all hands.

His ship. His men. All of them dead because Cinq gave her sailing plans to the French. The first mate of the *Neptune Dancer* had been Sam Carter, a wild, tough Yankee from Portland. The best friend a man could have. They'd sailed together to Ceylon and India, back when they were fifteen.

He'd been hunting Cinq for two long years. He'd found him and gathered the evidence that would send the man to hell. Josiah Whitby would die. The gallows was a quicker death than he'd given Sam Carter.

He walked over to look out at the Thames so he didn't have to see Jess Whitby.

Adrian said, "Josiah isn't guilty, you know."

They'd argued about this endlessly. "He's your friend."

"Friendship has nothing to do with it."

"It does. I'm sorry. That's the whole point." There was too much light in the cabin for him to see past the glass. He shaded a spot with his hand to look upriver. There were still ships moving out on the tide, even with the last light going. Not something he'd let one of his captains do. "You used to talk about a daughter, didn't you? You knew her in Russia. That's this girl."

"She put together the company. That accounting system you like so much. That's her work. When she was sixteen."

"It's . . . remarkable." That splendid clockwork of numbers, precise and clever and subtle. It was impossible to believe a sixteen-year-old girl made that.

"Josiah dickers for goods. But it's Jess who made them rich. When she was twelve, back in St. Petersburg, she used to hold forth at the breakfast table, laying down the law to Josiah how much he could bid for amber or sables. She'd sit there calculating the profit margin on smuggling across three borders, and I'd lean over and remind her to keep her braids out of the butter dish."

"Her name's not really Jess, is it? You called her something else."

"Jessie. It's Jessamyn really."

Jessie. That was it. He remembered hiding in a pigeon loft near Boulogne, waiting for the smuggler's boat to come at dawn, listening to Adrian talk about Jessie in St. Petersburg, who still wore pinafores and long braids and ran her father's business like a top. "Somebody should get her out of England. There's nothing she can do here but see her father die."

"You underestimate her." Adrian emptied his glass. "She's going to find Cinq for me. I gave her the best reason in the world when I arrested Josiah."

"You arrested Whitby because I gave you a mountain of overwhelming evidence."

"I arrested Whitby so Colonel Reams of Military Intelligence wouldn't get his grubby paws on him. I keep saying that, and nobody listens. Can I offer you some of this? It's quite good."

"You go ahead."

"I've always admired your taste in brandy." Careful as an apothecary, Adrian measured out another finger's worth. "I cannot understand why a bright girl like Jess doesn't see my logic for incarcerating her father. Bastian, why is my mad, brilliant Jess going through your pockets, at considerable discomfort and personal risk?"

"I don't give a damn why—" He knew then, suddenly, what Jess Whitby had been up to. "Bloody hell. She wasn't searching me. She was planting something. That's it." He grabbed his coat and dug his fingers into the corners of the pockets.

"I wondered if you'd think of that."

"Next time, say it." He checked the next pocket. "Something small. A scrap of a memorandum from the War Office. Something easy to overlook and damning." There was nothing in the jacket. "They're brilliant, all right. That's how they get Whitby free. They make me the scapegoat. She drops one piece of paper in my pocket, and they get rid of the man who built the case against him."

"How diabolically clever of her."

"Go ahead and laugh. Your Josiah Whitby is a dung-eating pig who sent his daughter to rub herself all over me. He doesn't give a damn about her." He dropped the coat. "I could have raped that girl against a wall instead of bargaining a price. It's not here, whatever it was. It wasn't in her clothes, either. I'd find it back on the ground in Katherine Lane if I went to check."

"I doubt it. I wonder what was supposed to be in Cinq's pockets tonight." Adrian set the glass on the chart table, on a map of the south coast of England. "I will inquire, delicately, at the War Office if anything has gone missing lately."

"Ask what you want. I need to clean up."

Blood from the fight had dried on his skin. His clothes were sticky with it. Jess's blood. And blood from the men he'd killed for her. He unbuttoned his waistcoat and tossed it in a corner—that was ruined—and eased his shirt off over his head, gritting his teeth. He'd gotten himself hit with a crowbar, protecting the girl.

"Need that strapped up?"

He rotated his shoulder, letting loose slashes of pain. "It'll do." The water in the bucket was still warm. He slopped it into the basin. The dried blood washed off, disconcertingly red, as if he were still bleeding. He took a towel from the floor, the one he'd used to dry her hair. It smelled like spices when he washed with it.

He poured the last clean water over his head, getting some of it in the basin, some on the floor.

Jess slept with her hand tucked at her cheek, like a child. The curl of her fingers was as beautiful as a seashell. *I wouldn't have touched her if I'd known what she was. But, holy God, I would have wanted to.* He'd been gut-deep certain this woman belonged to him. He couldn't remember the last time his instincts had betrayed him. "Your brilliant Jess is a fool if she thinks she can play that game with me. She has no idea the kind of man I am."

"She has plans," Adrian murmured. "What? Probably something that involves risking her neck. I've got the only man who can stop her locked up. Even Doyle can't do it. How very much I wish she and I were on speaking terms."

"Save it. Listen." Under the clank and rattle of the *Flighty* and the racket of rain hitting the deck, he heard wheels on the wharf. "Someone's here."

Adrian cocked his head. "That'll be Doyle with the hackney." He studied the girl on the bed with a remote intensity. "You won't ever forgive me for arresting Josiah, will you? I don't generally betray my friends. But then, my dealings with you Whitbys have always been exceedingly complex." He touched her cheek. Her head rolled to the side, completely lax. "Out of the hunt. She never did have a head for liquor."

"A concussion is more to the point."

"How right you are. Between the knock on her head and the potent powders of the East, she won't even remember being here. When I take her away, she won't remember you at all, *mon vieux.*"

Adrian always thought he was being subtle.

Jess Whitby had got herself wound up in his blankets. Her leg was bare to the thigh, long, with a down of golden hair. Erotic images started rolling around his mind like badly stowed lumber.

He pulled on a clean shirt. The linen was salty from being washed at sea, a good, familiar smell. Nothing exotic and woman-scented. "Get her off my ship."

"Oh, I will. I will. Carry her for me, will you? I threw my knee out, fighting." Adrian wrapped the blanket around Jess with a proprietary air. "And no clothes at all. You are so . . . thorough. It always complicates matters when they don't have any clothes."

You're not funny, Adrian. "Where are you taking her?"

Adrian found her shoes. "I'm in the process of deciding that. Let's proceed, shall we? I want her out of here before more gentlemen with knives show up."

It was mostly blanket he felt when he picked her up. But a bundle of blankets wouldn't have shaped itself to fit his arms or leaned, confident and accepting, against his shoulder. Her hair blew back in his face when he pushed through the companionway door and the outside cold rolled over them. He recognized the spice on her now. She smelled of cardamom.

She won't remember me. He wanted to shake her and wake her up and make her look at him so he'd be sure she wouldn't forget him. He wanted to see her eyes dilated, huge and dark, with his image inside. Most of all, he wanted her gone.

The dock was empty. Adrian pulled his throwing knife and went first. They crossed the gangway and headed toward the coach that waited in the drizzle, side lamps lit. If Adrian's knee was playing up on him, it didn't show in the way he leaped up into the coach. He reached down impatiently. "I'll take her from here. Hand her up to me."

All he had to do was hoist her up and walk away. You abandon damaged ware. You mark it off the inventory, and toss it away, and forget it.

He couldn't do it. Adrian, damn him, knew that.

It should have been awkward, climbing into the coach, carrying a girl snuggled against him. But she didn't weigh much. He set her in his lap, wrapped in his coat, keeping her steady when the coach lurched forward. "What are you going to do with her?"

"If I said it's not your concern . . . ?"

"Don't try my patience."

"I can't take her to Meeks Street." Adrian stretched his boots out casually across the strawed floor. "I might as well turn her over to the Foreign Office, neatly trussed. They've hatched several asinine schemes that involve her."

Sebastian wasn't going to ask why the Foreign Office wanted Jess Whitby.

"They don't quite dare to arrest her openly—they are so very discreet, our diplomats—and I've been refusing to do it for them. I am unpopular with the Foreign Office at the moment." Adrian stashed the knife in his sleeve. "Colonel Reams at Military Intelligence is also full of plans for Jess. We're agreed, are we not, that Colonel Reams will not get his hands on Jess?"

"Fine. Forget Meeks Street." He already knew where they were going. He wondered how long it would take Adrian to admit it.

"There's the hotel in Bloomsbury. That's where the Whitbys live when they're in London. I could take her there, I suppose."

"So she can be kidnapped more conveniently."

"Unfortunately, true." Adrian lifted the leather curtain on the window. They were already away from the alleys and warehouses of the docks. Ahead, in the distance, a necklace of tiny bright dots marked Westminster Bridge. "I'm sending her home with you."

It was the logical choice. "I don't want her."

He was cold, except where he was wrapped around the girl. He'd been in the Mediterranean too long. Jess would be cold, too, in this gray fog. He pulled his coat more tightly around her. Strange how distinctly he could feel her breathing.

So much bright, nonchalant courage in this small package. She let herself be her father's tool for betraying England. God alone knew how much damage she'd done.

Adrian pretended to watch the street. "Eunice will coddle

her cracked head, and that motley crew of pirates you call footmen can guard her. Even Military Intelligence won't touch her
if she's under Eunice's wing." He let the curtain fall. "I need
someone I can trust to take care of her. You'll do."

"Do you think I'll change my mind about Whitby because
you toss his nubile daughter in my lap?"

"Toss her in your lap? My dear Sebastian, I—"

"It's not going to work."

Five

Meeks Street

JOSIAH WHITBY LAID COAL ON THE FIRE. A POOR-hearted, stinking fire coal made, but they didn't put firewood in this study they'd set aside for him. You could scrape and strop a scrap of wood to make a weapon, if you were desperate and determined and didn't have much else to do with your time. They didn't underestimate their guests here at Meeks Street.

That was what Jess wouldn't see. She'd never admit Josiah Whitby was a fine candidate to be this traitor. She'd never admit any possibility of it. The Service knew what kind of man he was. Jess had never seen it.

He was cold in the mornings, nowadays. A man got old without noticing it.

He didn't concern himself greatly with his own hanging. He'd been in the East long enough to know a man couldn't dodge his fate by so much as a hair. But he didn't want to leave Jess alone. Not now, when Cinq was taking an interest in the Whitbys. Not in England, where the carrion crows were already circling.

So he worried. There wasn't much else to do here. Oh, Jess brought him manifests and cargo lists to keep him occupied.

A good lass, his Jessie. But the counting house was her baili-wick. He liked goods a man could hold in his hand and sell face-to-face. There was no savor to these numbers on paper.

Hurst—he called himself Adrian Hawkhurst these days—didn't quite apologize for arresting him, but he felt badly about it. They both knew he'd been forced into it. The bars at the window kept Military Intelligence out as much as they kept him in. Without them, he'd be talking to Colonel Reams in a cellar in the Horse Guards. That was something else Jess wouldn't see.

She'd do something daft, his Jess, she was so furious at Hawkhurst. His girl wasn't made for anger. She didn't know how to do it well.

Hawkhurst sent in the newspapers every morning. They were laid out on the desk right now: the *Morning Chronicle*, the *Times*, the *London Gazette*. Good as a coffee shop. In a while the boy would bring buns to eat and stay to chat and drink tea. The other men from the Service would drop by, in and out, all day. They didn't leave him on his own to brood.

But Jess . . . He was damned uneasy. Jess was up to some-thing.

She never could fool him. To give her credit, she didn't try—not till now when he was caged up and couldn't stop her. She brought him apples and sat talking about indigo and porcelains, and then she went out hunting spies. She had her nose to the ground, like that ferret of hers, chasing the biggest rat in London.

Unless he missed his guess, that was what Adrian Hawkhurst had been planning all along.

Six

Mayfair

SHE WANTED TO STAY IN THE DREAM. THERE was nothing but pain out there, past the borders of the dream. In the dream, she was safe and warm.

The Captain lay beside her in the ship's cabin. He had enchantment in his hands, the Captain did.

He said, "You're worrying. I told you to stop that." He stroked her hair and down her neck, down to the blanket. It was a Greek blanket, from Valletta.

There was something she should do. Something important . . . "I'm not thinking very well."

"That's the brandy. Almost guaranteed to stop you thinking sooner or later."

Her thoughts swirled away under those patient, skilled hands. She let him flow over her like a river.

There was something she had to do . . .

The Captain's fingertips slid light, light across her skin and the thought slipped away. It was raining, up on deck. Water falling from the sky, across the ship, into the sea. She was flowing downhill, becoming water.

His hair hung down, straight and black and heavy. Under the blanket, he stroked her back, up and down, where she was naked. He was being careful with her. He was like fire, being careful with her. He said, "Are you warm enough? I have more blankets."

"Be warm in a snowdrift with you doing that to me." It didn't frighten her, the hard, masculine fortress of his chest. Made her feel safe. She'd have been afraid, otherwise, with everything whirling the way it did and nothing familiar around her.

Ned had been solid, like this man. But thinner. Younger. And Ned had been golden, every hair on him. Ned stroked her and made her feel this same way, until he . . .

"What's the matter?" The Captain set the tip of his finger to her forehead. "You thought of something. What was it?"

She didn't want to remember Ned. Ned was gone, eaten up by the sea, and it hurt to think about him.

Wind blew rain against the glass in the cabin windows, chill and dark. It brought memories. She was dizzy with them. Circling and circling. She remembered Ned beside her in the straw, both of them naked, and the door of the barn open with the moon hanging in it.

She said, "He was warm everywhere I touched him."

"Tonight, I'll keep you warm. You're safe with me, Jess."

A sailor would know about being safe. Getting back to harbor.

The Captain breathed in her hair. It set music plucking on her nerves. That funny thing in Russia. A balalaika. That's what they called it.

She seemed to have edged over some point of no return without even noticing it. "Maybe I'll go to sleep."

"I wouldn't be at all surprised."

Milk pails clattered outside, and a dog barked.

Jess opened her eyes and woke up in an attic, feeling bereft. The dark streamers of the dream released and dissolved.

It was a nice enough attic with a slanted roof and white-wash on the plaster walls. The mahogany washstand was Chippendale and held a bowl and pitcher from the factory in

Staffordshire. Whitby's shipped that pattern, the one with the peacock on it, all over the Baltic. The Swedes loved fancy china.

Dream images and knowledges slipped away. This was morning. God alone knew where she was.

The sun in her eyes told her it was early. Her ears told her she was in London. When you hear someone in the street crying, "Milk-O. Fresh milk," in that accent, you're in London. She was in bed, between fresh linen sheets, wearing an old cotton nightgown that buttoned up to her chin and her mother's locket. It wasn't obvious how she'd got here.

She crawled out from the covers, being careful of her head, and padded over to the window. It was open to the morning. The curtains were the sort of pretty chintz that sells for six shillings a yard. When she stuck her head out and looked left, she saw the back of the house, all grass and untidy garden and a kitchen yard with dish towels hanging to dry on a string. Somebody in this house got up early indeed to wash out her dish towels, or else they'd been left in the air overnight. When she looked right, to the front of this big house, she could see a slice of street. Beyond that was a garden with iron railings. She could hear birds out there, having fits of singing. Working that out—and she unraveled harder knots every day—she was in the West End. Mayfair.

Her head ached. She felt like she'd been in strange dreams and been jerked out of them, sudden. She hurt, everywhere. When she lifted the nightgown and took inventory, there were bruises everywhere she could see easy. She had a long cut on her arm.

That's from the fight. I was in a fight. I was on Katherine Lane poking my nose in Sebastian Kennett's affairs, and . . .

He wasn't Captain Sebastian. He was Sebastian Kennett.

Kennett was at the center of that huge knot of dark and pain and fear that she couldn't untie. She was with him in the fog and the rain. Then she was in his bunk, wearing only her skin, listening to him explain why that was sensible as bread and cheese. Kennett was a man who could talk fish into a bucket. She'd fallen asleep beside him at some point.

There must have been just a whole wandering tribe of

incidents after that, because now she woke up here, wherever here was, tucked into this chaste, narrow, reassuring bed. No telling how she ended up wearing a nightgown.

Somebody'd put clothes for her, folded neat on the chair, and her shoes, cleaned and set side by side. That was a piece of delicate reassurance. Whatever she got involved in this morning, she wouldn't have to face it in her nightclothes.

The dog took up barking again, somewhere down the street, being enthusiastic about it. The sound carried crisp in the cool morning air. Made her head hurt in a couple different ways.

Sebastian Kennett had a house in Mayfair. She knew that from the thick file she had on her desk, all about Captain Kennett. Maybe this was his house. She had to wonder what his family thought about him bringing her home.

The comb by the washstand and the hairpins were meant for her, obviously, so she stood in front of the mirror and went to work braiding her hair soft and loose and brought it over her shoulder, the way she would if she was staying home, just her and Papa, and they didn't expect to see anybody.

Kennett had been gentle when he dried out her hair. Like a cat washing a kitten. Could she think this way about that big, rough man? It seemed to fit.

Cinq would have tipped her overboard just to hear the splash.

Or maybe not. Maybe Cinq was laying deep plots. She wasn't a good judge of villains, having spent her youth being one. She lacked that sensitive moral barometer.

I have to get to Papa. He'll worry about me if I don't come.

When she tried the door, it was unlocked. A locked door wouldn't have kept her in, of course, but it was heartening not to start the morning picking locks. The attic corridor made a turn on one side. The wall held a diamond-shaped window.

She went down the steps, keeping one hand on the wall, feeling a little dizzy, off and on. The attic flight was bare, clean wood. The next was covered with cheap green runner. Kennett must have carried her up all this way last night, up three flights, and put her to bed. It had been an evening chock-full of activity for him.

The main upper floor was lush as a peach. She walked through, on soft blue carpeting, heading for the front of the house. These doors were bedrooms. She could have sorted them out by smell—clean linen and flowers and expensive perfume—and known which ones to sack if she was making this little peregrination at night and feeling larcenous. Between the doors they'd hung groups of Persian miniatures, framed in carved ivory. At the far end of the hall was a big, wide, open window with the curtains pulled back.

I never get used to living in a fancy house, owning rich things. It's gentry who live this way, not me.

Even now, she couldn't walk through a house like this without picking out what she'd steal. It wasn't like she laid hands on anything, after all. She was just looking.

She came to the iron railing and looked down the curve of the staircase to the entry hall. The floor was black and white squares of marble, Carrara marble and Dinan, like a chessboard. The house she and Papa owned in St. Petersburg had a checkered floor like this and columns around the sides.

Whitby's shipped Carrara marble out of Livorno when the port was open and nobody was shooting at passing ships. Fine profit to be made on marble, but it was a three-legged sow to stow.

The crystal chandelier must be six feet tall. Beautiful thing. She held her head high and floated down the staircase, running her finger along the banister, letting herself pretend she was making an entrance to some grand party. You couldn't help doing that with a staircase this fine. It spoiled the mood a bit to have somebody pounding away at the front door the whole time.

Likely they wanted to get in, whoever it was. There seemed to be a total dearth of servants in the house. Anyway, nobody come to dub the jigger, as she would have put it in her misspent youth. That was a reliable clue it might be a bad idea to do so and, anyhow, this was none of her business. Surprising how much trouble you stayed out of if you minded your own business. Lazarus used to mention that to her from time to time. Papa did, too.

Could be bailiffs or savages from Borneo or jealous husbands on the other side of that door. No doubt a matter best left alone.

But she'd got curious. When she opened the door, there was a skinny cove in a rumpled suit, three laborers, and five great wood crates with rope handles, all crowded onto the porch. Not bailiffs, at least.

The skinny cove marched right across the threshold. "Tell Standish I'm here." He passed over his hat. "I need tea. Dustcloths. Footmen with crowbars. And Standish." When she stood there, holding his hat, he added, "Shoo. Shoo," and made brisk sweeping motions. "Tell him I've brought the collared-rim urn and the grooved ware. Don't stand there like a goose." He set about haranguing the laborers, who looked bored.

He didn't seem to be dangerous, even if he was about to fill the front hall with large crates. Likely, worse things were happening somewhere in London this morning.

She left them to it and dropped the hat on one of the tables they had handy, probably for that purpose, and followed the corridor to the back of the house.

Standish was the name of Kennett's uncle, so now she knew for sure. *I'm in Kennett's house. One question settled.*

This time of day, she could follow the smell of breakfast and have a good chance of finding somebody. The door was closed. *I never know whether to knock or not. About a million rules, the gentry have.* She pushed it open and walked in.

There were clay pots everywhere. A big, glass-fronted case filled half the room, full of dark brown pots, mud-colored pots, pots with designs scraped on the sides, old Greek pots with people, pots in three-legged stands, and pots lolling on their side showing their bellies, pots stacked up four and five high. Regular armies of pots, with the auxiliaries called up.

An old man and old woman sat at an oval table in front of the window with the light spilling all over them. They were ordinary people. The man was untidy in his brown wool jacket and limp neckcloth. He had a craggy face and wild black hair, getting gray at the temples. The woman was neatly dressed. Nothing fashionable about her. Behind them, the window showed a vivid, bright garden, overgrown with green. The Sheridan sideboard next to the wall held silver dishes, covered, keeping breakfast warm.

The man laid down a book. The woman looked up from a newspaper.

This had to be Kennett's uncle and aunt, Standish and Eunice Ashton. It was all in the files on her desk back in the warehouse. They'd raised Kennett when his father didn't show any inclination to do it. Word was, the old earl wasn't best pleased to have his little mistake brought up in plain sight by his brother and his sister-in-law. Word was, Eunice Ashton never gave tuppence what the earl thought.

The old earl was dying, nastily and at length, in Italy. One of those just retributions, that particular disease.

Everyone in Whitechapel had heard of Eunice Ashton. She gave refuge to women in trouble. Any woman. Whores, too, and it didn't matter who owned them. She'd face up to the devil himself, they said. Even Lazarus let her pass unmolested in his territory.

And here they were . . . decent folks, eating a civilized breakfast. If Sebastian Kennett was Cinq, she was going to smash this pretty, comfortable world into a thousand bits.

"Good heavens, child. You're awake." Eunice Ashton held out her hand. "Come in. Come in." She was no carefully preserved beauty. Her face was wrinkles and deep lines, honestly old, like a countrywoman who'd been out in all weathers and never coddled herself. The steady eyes were bright as jewels. It was a warm hearth on a freezing day, the kindness in that woman's face.

I'm going to hang Cinq, and he's probably your nephew. No matter what you are—decent, kind, wise, loving—it won't make any difference.

She didn't want to talk to them. Didn't want to be in this house at all. She groped behind her for the doorknob.

Eunice Ashton was already on her feet. "You must sit down. You don't look at all steady. I'm sorry not to have been with you when you woke up. I looked in earlier and decided you'd sleep for a good long while yet. There now. Standish will pour tea." The old woman was beside her, taking her hands, both of them, inside her own. "I don't know if tea really helps when one feels precarious, but it does give one something warm to hold on to. A kitten would work just as well, but we don't have one at the moment. They *will* grow into cats. Sit, dear."

Jess found herself guided into a chair. It was like when the pilot takes the wheel in some tricky port. All of a sudden the ship, even a big, wallowing three-master, goes smooth and easy and glides past the breakwater and the sand bars, through the rip currents, tame and docile, up to the dock. It was a magic pilots had. Maybe they signed an agreement with the ocean.

One minute she was at the door, trying to think of a way to leave without being rude. The next she was sitting at the table.

The old man looked at her over a beak of a nose—that was the same nose Kennett had—and smiled vaguely and found the teapot. He poured tea, and added milk and sugar, and stirred, all without looking at what he was doing, and set the cup in front of her.

She saw no guile in the old man. No meanness in the old woman. She might not be the steel-trap judge of people Papa was, but she would have built houses on that assessment. Whatever it took to send Englishmen to their deaths for money, it wasn't in them. If Kennett was Cinq, they had no part in it. That made it worse, knowing she'd be bringing shame and disaster on them, and they'd have no warning.

The man nudged the cup toward her.

Tea. Yes. She could drink tea.

It was South China, good enough in its way. She was used to Russian tea, smoky from being heated over charcoal and blunt-flavored from a caravan trip across half the world. She had a taste for it after living in St. Petersburg so long. Papa always kept a supply.

Her stomach would stop being sick and cold if she put tea into it. Maybe her head would stop aching. She'd take a few sips of tea, and thank them, and leave. And there was something polite she should be saying. Lord, all the money Papa'd spent on governesses, she should know her manners.

"Thank you for taking me in." She put both hands around the cup. They were right. Hot tea was good to hold on to. "I'm sorry to impose myself on you this way. It's . . . I'm not sure what happened, exactly. There were men after me, I think. And I fell. I was standing in the rain, thinking I might get myself hurt . . . And then I did. Get hurt. I'm not sure how." It occurred to her she was babbling. "Sorry. This isn't coming out right. My head's not working well."

"Of course it isn't." A capable hand, thin-skinned, marked with brown spots from age, closed over hers. "You will stop hurting soon. I'm Eunice Ashton. You are not to worry about anything."

"I don't remember it all, you see."

"Of course not. One doesn't, I believe, after a blow to the head. You met with some accident by the docks, and you weren't in any state to tell us where to take you. Where can we send word you're safe? They must be frantic, looking for you. What's your name, child?"

But no one was looking for her. Not a soul. If she didn't show up at Meeks Street, Papa would just think his jailers were keeping her away. Pitney knew she'd gone hunting Cinq and where, but he wouldn't expect her at the warehouse today. Kedger would worry when she didn't bring him his piece of kipper this morning, but a ferret couldn't precisely raise the alarm, now could he? Nobody else would notice if she dropped off the face of the earth. Gave her a chill, knowing that.

She swallowed. "I'm Jess. Jessamyn Whitby. There's nobody looking for me."

The old woman's eyes were wise and unreservedly kind and very practical. "Well then, Jess, you shall drink your tea, and we will decide what is best to do about this."

"Lady Ashton . . ." *Or is it Lady Eunice? Or something else? Lady Standish? Sometimes it's nothing at all. They don't make it easy.*

"Eunice, dear. Just Eunice. Or Mrs. Ashton, if that makes you feel more comfortable. And I will call you Jess, if I may.

Really, the most useless and unpleasant people seem to have titles. So much simpler to discard titles altogether and be just a Jess and a Eunice, don't you think? Have you read Lalumière's *Ten Questions*?"

"I don't think so."

"Or *An Enquiry Concerning Political Justice* by Godwin? Well, I suppose not. I'll lend you a copy when you're feeling better. So eloquent and lucid."

That sounded like books on philosophy, and one of them by a Frenchman. It was probably a mistake to read too many books like that. You believe what they put in books, and who knows what you'll do.

Kennett probably read philosophy if his aunt was fond of it.

Lady Ashton . . . Eunice . . . poured tea and started after the milk jug, murmuring, "Rousseau, perhaps." Strange as three-toed snakes, some of the gentry. What an odd conversation she was having. "Well. Yes. All right."

The old man gave a shy, rather sweet smile. "She won't make you read today. Or do anything else you don't want to." The book propped in front of him had a German title that translated to *A Study of Striation Patterning in the Milo-Archaic Pottery of Bavaria*, which explained the pots cluttering the place. Over the top of the book, his gaze focused on her with a startling intelligence. "You don't have to be worried. Eunice will take care of everything."

"Of course, Standish." Eunice tapped the plate beside his book. "You have toast."

Jess could feel herself relaxing, muscle by muscle. Even her sinews and bones knew these were good folks. No wonder Kennett made houseroom for thirty thousand pots and a battalion of rescued harlots. If she'd had an uncle and aunt like this, she'd have let them keep elephants.

Before Standish got a bite of toast, the door of the parlor slammed back to the wall, shaking every pot in the room. A skinny, untidy maid stood in the doorway. "That professor fellow's brung a bunch of them bleeding great boxes. You want 'em put upstairs?"

Crikey. She'd forgot. The foyer could be three-deep in crates for all the use she was. She clattered cup into saucer.

"Oh Lord. My fault. I opened the door. I was supposed to tell you—"

"Excellent. That'll be Percy at last." Standish used the toast to mark his place in the book. "Pots from Glamorgan. Excuse me." He kissed his wife neatly on top of her head and stalked out like a long-legged wading bird in search of fish.

"More pots," Eunice said. "And not another square inch to put them in." She rose as she spoke. Lightly, she put her arm around Jess. "We'll manage somehow. Now, tell me what has happened to you and why there's no one who knows or cares where you are. That seems a very melancholy state of affairs, if true."

Being held by Eunice Ashton was like having sunlight wrapped around you. She closed her eyes. "It's not like that. My father's careful of me, generally. It's not his fault."

"Where is your father?"

She could say anything to this woman, anything at all. It was no secret, anyway. Half the port knew by now. "They arrested him a couple weeks ago." *Hurst arrested him. Even with everything that happened, I thought he was Papa's friend.*

"Good heavens."

"It's not Newgate or the Tower. They haven't even laid charges yet. It's not that bad."

"It sounds very bad indeed."

"He's 'detained for inquiry,' whatever that means." She was pulled close and held, and it felt like the most natural thing in the world. Cold spaces inside her opened to let the warmth in. "I try and I try, and I can't shake him free. I go to our friends and they try, but nothing works."

"Is your father Josiah Whitby? The Whitby who owns those warehouses and the ships? Whitby Trading?"

"That's him."

"Then he should be taking care of you, arrested or not. He hasn't left you on your own, has he, with no one looking after you?"

"I take care of myself, mostly. I do a better job of it, generally."

"I'm sure you do. That doesn't mean you should be left

alone." Eunice sounded tart, and that was comforting, too. "You must be very frightened."

Frightened? Oh, that hit the nail on the head. There was no end to how frightened she was. Oceans of fear stretched out on every side. She was scared when she jerked awake before dawn, and scared in the office. Scared when she pounded her brains all day, tweaking out the patterns that might show her Cinq. Scared when she went to see Papa in that discreet, sneaky house at Meeks Street. She was scared when she lay down at night, not sleeping, her hands clenched in the sheets, hour after hour.

"I go to Papa every day at teatime. He worries . . ." Then somehow she was talking about the house at Meeks Street. How they listened to her, behind the walls when she was with Papa. How he was acting so bloody calm and cheerful it set her teeth on edge. How she was looking for Cinq.

She was saying things she hadn't said to anybody else. By the time she explained that the British Service wasn't feeding Papa properly, and he didn't look well, not at all, she was doing it all muffled into the cotton print Eunice wore.

"You will solve this. I think you must be very good at solving problems." She felt Eunice wipe tears off her cheek.

Wiping her face. The last person to do that was her mother, dead of fever, ten years back. "I don't know why I'm doing this. I don't cry."

"Of course you don't, child."

"Crying's pointless. It means you can't think of anything better to do. There's always something to do."

"Always. We must simply decide what it is. Not, however, this morning." Eunice sat next to her, still speaking in that unruffled, deep voice. "First, you will drink your tea. It's getting cold." And the teacup was somehow between her hands again.

"Yes." She'd just sit here for a while and hold on to it.

"I think, since your father can't be with you, you should stay here with us."

She couldn't stay here. All kinds of reasons not to stay. "I can't—"

"We have plenty of room, even if we're rather cluttered

with pots. I can't be easy with the thought of you going back home with no one but servants to take care of you. And there's that nasty accident at the docks. So worrisome. Let me give you some toast. The toast is better than the muffins today. The bread comes from the baker, and Cook made the muffins. I'm afraid this is not one of her good mornings. She drinks." As she spoke, Eunice spread marmalade on toast.

She was being managed. It had been a long time since anyone tried managing her for her own good. Maybe she'd let it happen for a while.

The plate in front of her was Sèvres, with roses painted on it. A nice piece of china. Whitby's had to bribe two sets of customs officials and change ships to get Sèvres porcelain. They sold it in Boston. Good markets in the Americas.

Papa wouldn't live to trade with Boston again unless she found Cinq.

"You don't like marmalade?" Eunice said. "There's a lovely man in Hampstead who sends me pints of it on Boxing Day every year. We never seem to get through it all before he sends some more, and he does make it himself. Have some tea first."

She wasn't hungry, but to be polite she took a sip of tea and picked up a piece of toast. She'd get up in a minute and make her good-byes and leave. All kinds of things she had to do at the warehouse. From the hall outside came the sound of something heavy, thumping, and Standish saying, "Do be careful with that," repeatedly.

"He's taking them to the salon to unpack." Eunice filled up the cup. "It isn't so much the pots, you understand, but they send them packed in straw. Straw everywhere, and sand, and sometimes fleas. He won't let me give the pots a good wash. I have hit upon a system, however . . ."

It had been weeks since she'd just sat, doing nothing, not thinking at all. Eunice didn't expect answers or explanations. She was an extraordinarily comforting person to be around. Probably lots of people cried down the front of her dress.

She'd stay just a few more minutes, being polite.

She listened to Eunice talk about pottery. Seemed to be lots one could know about pottery. When she opened her eyes, the light didn't stab in. And her head hurt less. She drank more tea. Then there were two new slices of toast on her plate, and she ate them, too. The tea was good, of its sort, but she'd send some Russian tea to Eunice.

The door opened. A tall man in waistcoat and shirtsleeves walked in. "Good morning, Aunt Eunice." He leaned and kissed the woman's cheek. His black hair was straight and thick as Russian sable.

"My nephew." Eunice picked up a new cup and began pouring. "He carried you in last night, when you were hurt. Bastian, this is Jess Whitby, who's come to stay with us a while."

He sat down and faced her and became Sebastian Kennett.

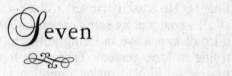

Seven

SHE REMEMBERED HIM STANDING BESIDE HER IN THE rain. He'd set the tips of his fingers, careful and rough-textured, on her lips, and she'd shivered from it.

"Sebastian . . ." The one soft word escaped before she saw what was in his face. His eyes were like the black ice on one of those marsh ponds in Russia, cold and brittle and hard as steel.

". . . Kennett," she finished.

His gaze moved deliberately across her, like he was taking inventory of the parts he'd seen naked. She had the thought that if she reached out and put her hand up to his cheek, her skin would freeze to him, like she was touching cold metal in the winter.

He said, "Miss Whitby. I see you're out of bed."

"Up and about." *We can start a whole new acquaintance, what with me having my clothes on.* There was nothing left of the man she met last night. Not a sign. "I'm pretty much fine, thank you for asking."

Last night, Captain Sebastian Kennett had kept her safe from cold and dark and fear. He'd wrapped her in gentleness warmer than a blanket. This morning, he was Bastard Kennett, who had a deadly name on the docks and no softness anywhere in him. Enough to drive a duck daft, trying to sort it all out.

He was carrying his jacket over his back, hooked in two fingers. He tossed it over a chair and sat down. It was a swell's coat, cut by some expert on Jermyn Street. That was a lot of expensive tailoring going to waste, if Kennett was trying to look genteel. There was too much tough, stringy muscle on him to make a gentleman. Might as well put a tiger in a waistcoat and call it a pussycat. "You came damned close to being dead. Has she eaten anything, Eunice?"

"Yes, dear. Toast. Do try not to scowl in that intimidating way. I believe she has a headache."

"She knocked back a gill of straight brandy last night. That's enough to make her sick, all by itself." He sounded disapproving and Methodist about it, which was a fine attitude from the man who'd tipped the brandy down her throat.

"It's not the liquor." *Or maybe it is. Hard to tell right now, frankly.*

"What are you doing out of bed? You look like you've escaped from a winding sheet."

If somebody'd asked her, she would have guessed nobs were reasonably civil to people they'd had naked in their bed the night before. Turned out they were rude as starlings. She was always learning new things. She took the tip of her knife and began outlining the roses frolicking around the rim of her plate.

"Your color's not good. Are you dizzy? Blurry vision?" Him pretending to be a doctor.

"I'm fine. You were right about what you said last night. I just had to wait patient and my memory came back home, wagging its tail behind." She didn't rub her forehead. He didn't have to know how much it hurt in there. "Most of it."

"It must be frightening, mislaying pieces of oneself." Eunice set the teapot down. "Is it clear now, what happened to you?"

"Dim in some parts."

But she remembered the fight. The alley had been slippery with gray rain. They came for her out of the fog and the chill. Kennett's knife whipped out like red lightning, drawing a line between her and the shadow men. He was fury and wildness, twice as lethal as the thugs who attacked them, a snarling guard no enemy could get past. Impressive. Impressed the hell out of her, anyway.

"Sebastian never tells me what he's been doing," Eunice said. "It's not dull, I suspect."

"Interesting last night, anyway. He convinced about a dozen men not to drag me off down an alley. Very heroic."

"Which wouldn't have been necessary if you'd stayed off Katherine Lane," the Captain snapped.

A few years back she'd have stuck her tongue out at him. She wasn't a gutter brat anymore, so she resisted the impulse. "I don't remember all of it, but I think I may be alive because of you. I owe you a debt."

"You don't have to be grateful."

"If you think somebody who owes you a debt that big is grateful, you aren't much of a trader."

She hit the gold with that one. Kennett clamped his teeth over what would have been a fairly ripe comment, probably, if his aunt weren't sitting there. No telling what they'd have ended up saying to each other if the door to the breakfast room hadn't opened just then.

A man ambled in, tall and dark-haired and handsome in a soft way, complaining. "We've been invaded. That Welshman and his laborers are cracking boxes open and shouting about it. The noise drove me downstairs." The genteel whine didn't pause as he made his way across the room. "Standish has potsherds laid out all over the salon. I told him any pottery that wanders into my bedroom will be used for target practice. He has been warned." He took note of her then, because he was going to complain about her next. "I wish you'd warn me if you're going to start bringing these girls to breakfast. I don't like surprises."

The Captain plucked a muffin from the basket in the center

of the table and passed it back and forth, from one hand to the other. He leaned back, content to observe events, noncommittal, his legs stretched out long under the table.

Eunice said, "Quentin," warningly.

So this was Quentin Ashton. Quentin was somebody else she knew from the paperwork in her office. He was Sebastian's cousin. He was next in line for that earldom the Captain wasn't going to inherit from his father, Kennett being a bastard in every sense of the word.

Quentin Ashton sauntered over. "My dearest aunt, you cannot rescue the poor of London, female by wretched female. I wish I could convince you of that. You're trying to empty the sea with a teaspoon. What we need is a change of government." He stood peering down the front of her dress. "At least this one is presentable."

There was a time, she'd have been tempted to lift his watch, what with his belly pressed up next to her. She was past that now. It was a nice gold watch, too.

He said pensively, "It's a pity. You'll dress her in black serge and put her to some domestic drudgery. She'll be useful and respectable as a tablecloth. Such a waste. I can't help but wonder if some of these girls aren't happier in their natural element."

Up close—he was close—Quentin looked less like his cousin than she'd first thought. He was like a copy of the Captain, but one struck off near the end of the print run so the ink didn't set deep.

"You'll make her a parlormaid, I suppose. She'll do well enough, if her employers count the spoons regularly." He tweaked her chin. Just like that. Tweak. "Would you like to be a parlormaid, young woman?"

On the whole, no.

"You have the look of one," he told her. "I wish you wouldn't spoil her, Eunice, with your Lalumière and Wollstonecraft and the rest. She won't understand a tenth of it. It's not as if she'll ever engage in rational political discourse. You make them discontented when you teach them to read, and you confuse them."

So she said, "I can read, actually."

He pulled his gaze out of her bodice and noticed she had a face. "What?"

"Read, write, add and subtract, and I know all the kings and queens of England, in order."

"Jess, this is my nephew, Quentin." Eunice was tart about it. "And this is Jess Whitby. She'll be staying with us a while. You don't have to eat that muffin, Sebastian. They're rocklike today."

"My years at sea have hardened me to the rigors of home-life." The Captain dunked the muffin in his tea to soften it. "Quent, before you say anything else. This is Whitby of Whitby Trading. She's Josiah Whitby's daughter."

"Whitby? That's ridiculous. How would Whitby's daughter get here?"

Eunice swept crumbs out of Standish's German book with her napkin. "She was in an accident at the docks near her father's warehouse. Bastian, very properly, brought her home to me."

"What accident? What do you mean, an accident? Sebastian, how did this happen?"

"The port's a dangerous place." The Captain was watching her, being thoughtful. Planning, she would have said. "And Whitby should take better care of his offspring."

"For the next little while, I will take care of her," Eunice said. "And you, Sebastian, will see to it she has no more jarring encounters on the docks. I am counting on that. Are you eating breakfast, Quent, or must you run?"

"I can't stay. I'm expected at the Board. But she shouldn't . . . It's not . . ." Quentin started in on a couple more sentences before he finally settled on, "You weren't wrong, Bastian. I'm sure you did the best you could, under the circumstances, but this isn't one of the street sweepings Eunice meddles with. We can't adopt the girl like a stray cat. She has to go home." He took her arm, emphasizing his point. He had smooth hands, hands like a woman, but he managed to squeeze one of her bruises. "Have you thought how it's going to look, keeping her in your house? For her? For us?"

The Captain's eyes flicked across her. "I don't see a

problem." He was the picture of a man used to clearing problems out of his path.

Quentin thrashed his way through a whole thicket of reasons why Jess Whitby shouldn't be in this house. Good enough reasons, some of them, but he wouldn't have persuaded a jellyfish. Easy to see why Quentin Ashton wasn't a force to be reckoned with at the Board of Trade. "People are going to ask why she's here."

"Sebastian hit her with a hackney." That came from the doorway.

A woman had joined them. She was tall and thin and black-haired, about thirty. "At least, that's the consensus in the kitchen." She went to the sideboard and lifted the cover from a plate, letting loose a rich, silver *ching*. "Ah. Kippers. Much can be forgiven a morning that brings me kippers."

"I didn't hit her with a hackney," the Captain said. "I didn't hit her with anything."

"How pleased you must be. I suppose you have some reason for bringing her home with you. Beyond the obvious." She picked up a silver fork to choose among the kippers. "Not that one monkey more or less makes a difference in this menagerie. Do you know, Quentin, if I were you, I wouldn't put my hands on Sebastian's playthings. He doesn't share."

"Really, Claudia." But Quentin stepped away, hasty like.

This was Quentin's sister, Claudia. The family nose was unfortunate on a woman. In Whitechapel they'd have called her homely. In the West End, she was probably distinguished looking.

Claudia lifted another dish cover. Eggs under that one. "How lively my morning has been. There's general agreement belowstairs that she cast herself beneath Sebastian's chariot wheels. The question is whether she took her clothes off before or afterwards. Much heated discussion in the kitchen. There are bets."

"And that is quite enough of that," Eunice said. "Jess, this is my niece, Claudia Ashton. She will eventually remember she was raised a gentlewoman."

"An impoverished gentlewoman, than which there is no more futile creature on earth. *Did* you throw yourself in front of my cousin's coach? How intrepid and original of you." Claudia's attention was all on the eggs, musing. "So few of our guests arrive at the door in their rosy and un-adorned pink skin. I'm sure there's a story behind so very much impropriety."

Half of London saw me carried in here last night. "You could ask the Captain."

"Discreet and silent as the grave, Cousin Sebastian. We'll get no interesting tales from him. What they're wondering in the kitchen is whether he compromised your somewhat problematic virtue. No bets, because impossible to determine. Am I the only one eating this morning?"

Quentin said loudly, "She's Josiah Whitby's daughter."

"And Josiah Whitby is . . . ? Ahhh." Claudia turned and gave her an open appraisal, head to foot. "The merchant. I met him at a party once. A vulgar little tub of a man in the most amazing waistcoat. Your father?"

Everyone seemed to notice Papa's waistcoats. "That's him."

"Quite indecently rich, they said." Claudia sat down, per-fectly straight, and her back never touched the chair. "And yet Sebastian brought you home, naked in his greatcoat. What an adventurous life merchants lead. I am perfectly willing to be shocked, I suppose."

"It is fortunate my presence makes Jess's visit impecca-bly respectable." Eunice filled another cup and offered it across the table to Claudia. "The less said about everyone's state of dress, the better. More tea, Jess?"

She looked in her cup. "No. I'm fine." She was bobbing like a cork in all these undercurrents. Her head ached, of course, but she couldn't have dealt with Claudia if she'd been chipper as a robin.

"You appear distressed. How wise of you." Claudia used tiny silver tongs to pick up a lump of sugar. "You've made a mistake, putting yourself in Sebastian's hands. He's an ambitious man. Aren't you, Bastian?"

"No. But I'm a busy one. Excuse us, Claudia. Eunice. Quentin." The Captain stood up. Something glinted in his eyes and disappeared, fast as a fish in a wave. "Jess, you've finished here." He tucked under her elbow and lifted her out of the chair like she was made of feathers.

Claudia said, "I was just beginning to enjoy myself."

"Don't. Eunice, I'm putting her to bed before she faints in the teacups." He pushed her ahead of him, toward the door.

Eight

HE DRAGGED HER INTO THE GRAND FRONT HALL. The laborers had taken their wood crates away and left the place empty as a platter. Sun lit up the big swag of crystal chandelier above and the silver candlesticks sitting on a side table and the cypress-wood backs of the chairs. Everything rich and fine. She was alone with Sebastian Kennett.

She searched his face for warmth or humor . . . anything to show this was the same man she'd met last night. Not a sign. Just that cold, assessing stare. It was like Captain Sebastian had moved out and left a stranger inside his skin.

She remembered the feel of him. The palms of her hands had learned ten thousand secrets about his bone and muscle last night. She didn't want to know those things. She didn't want to know him at all.

He escorted her, firm like, to the curve under the staircase. Not a soul in sight. It was a wonderment how they didn't have any servants milling about this place. He pressed her to the wall, where the scrolls and flowers and leaves worked in the plaster got acquainted with her back. Lumpy and full of points, that fancy plasterwork.

He said, "You were waiting for me on Katherine Lane."

Pitney warned her to keep away from the Lane. Doyle—canny, wise old Doyle—told her not to play games with Sebastian Kennett. Didn't do her any good asking for advice if she wasn't going to listen to it, did it?

She had lots of reasons for wishing her head didn't ache. "The Lane's free to anyone."

"Anyone who doesn't mind getting attacked and hit on the head. You didn't plan on that when you were out in Katherine Lane, sticking to me like a mustard plaster."

"Not in the slightest particular. You ever notice how life just sneaks up on you? I remember once . . . I was in Cairo, just minding my own business, and—"

"I wish to hell you were back in Cairo right now. I want you out of here."

Well, he would, wouldn't he, if he was Cinq? Cinq would have all kinds of secrets and skullduggery piled up in the corners of his house. "I'd figured that out, being a woman of great natural sensitivity. I was about to embark upon a humorous anecdote pointing up the general uncertainty of life and how we—"

"Stow it, Miss Whitby." Of everyone with the Ashton family nose, the Captain wore it best. Getting glared at over that nose . . . oh, that was a proper spine-chiller, that was. If she'd been one of his sailors, she'd have set about scrubbing the decks, double quick. "The hell of it is, I can't send you home. Whoever's supposed to be taking care of you, isn't. But you can't stay here."

She could, though.

What were the odds he kept private papers in some strongbox within a hundred feet of where she was standing? Had to be letters, maybe a journal. Could be all kinds of incriminating paper lying about. Something in this house would tell her whether he was innocent or guilty. Kennett wasn't going to have enough secrets to upholster a thimble when she got done with him.

Five feet away to the left, on one of the decorative little tables, was a big leather dispatch case, bulging like a pregnant lady. That was Quentin's probably, and he left it out where anyone could get to it. If the Captain was Cinq, he probably strolled through Quentin's papers with great regularity. A man as careless as Quentin was just an incitement to treason.

The bits and points of the plasterwork she was leaning on didn't get any more comfortable. "I'd like to stay. And your aunt invited me. I like your aunt, by the way."

"Everyone likes my aunt. I don't let people take advantage of Eunice."

"I won't—"

"You already have. I don't know what lies you've told her, but you stop that now. No. Don't try to deny it." He bracketed her shoulders, one side and the other, with huge, iron-hard fists, perfectly immobile. Probably he intended to make her nervous. It worked moderately well. "There is one reason, one only, that you aren't out the door this minute. It's not safe for you out there. A friend of mine has a country house in Hampstead. I'll send you there."

Him, making plans for her. "I stayed in the country, once. You would not believe how dangerous it is. Pigs and horses and these huge black crow birds they let go flying loose everywhere. Birds the size of chickens. And cows. I got stepped on by a cow once and it didn't half smart. I'll stick in London, thank you."

She had to admit it was satisfying, prodding him this way and watching him glower. Petty of her.

"You'll do what I tell you," he said.

I don't think so. "Does your aunt know you buy girls up on Katherine Lane?"

Not a damn change in his eyes. Not a blink. A deep file, Kennett.

"You overpay for it, too." She saw a tiny twitch to his mouth. Her point. "Maybe I'll just toddle back into the breakfast room and enlighten her. Then you can tell her what we got up to in your bunk last night. I can't be informative myself, because I lost track about ten minutes after you slipped me that drug."

"Damn it. I did not—"

"You can tell *me* what happened. We'll all be interested."

"I carried you home and dropped you in bed. And put

some clothes on you. That," he bit the words into chewable fragments, "is what I do to women with head injuries. Molesting them is low on my list of amusements. I have a number of bad habits, Miss Whitby, but raping unconscious women isn't one of them."

"Your aunt'll be glad to hear that. Sighs of relief from every quarter. Shall we go back in there and talk about it?" It was dangerous sport, blackmailing the Captain.

His hold got heavy and hard on her shoulders. Heavy as lead. "What did you try to put into my pocket last night?"

Every word of that was English, but strung together, they didn't mean anything. And she was so tired. Tired and dizzy and a little sick. *Into his pocket?* Maybe it was some interesting part of last night that she'd forgotten. "I like riddles, generally. But not today. Try another game."

"Let's try the truth." He gave her a shake, as punctuation. "Your father gave you something to slip in my pocket. What was it? A letter? A document? Do I have to go back and pull it out of the mud?"

Pull what out of the mud? What letter? She had to close her eyes to take the words apart and think about them. *Into his pocket.*

He thought Papa had sent her tippy-toeing up Katherine Lane to stuff incriminating evidence into his smallclothes. He thought they'd send some innocent to choke his life out on the gallows to save her father. Oh, but that was plausible and logical and cold.

That's the way Cinq thinks. "You would not believe how much I'd like to send you out searching the muck. I'm going to rise above it, though. There aren't any papers in the mud. None anywhere."

"Your father doesn't give a damn if he puts you in danger. He sent you after me, knowing . . ." His hold tightened up. "Now what's the matter?"

His dark, predatory face leaned close above her, all sharp angles and blunt planes. What black, black eyes he had. Night eyes, with a fire burning in them. They pulled like a whirlpool of dark water. It'd be almost a relief to let go and just fall in.

He muttered, "Why am I even talking to you? You're swaying on your feet, you're too bloody sick to stand up, and you're not going to tell me the truth anyway." In a swift coil of motion, he reached down and slipped her feet out from under her and grabbed her up in his arms. "Let's get you to bed." He started up the stairs, his boots thumping on the marble, tough and angry.

It was like being lifted up by an ocean wave, like there was no end to the power he had. She gripped a handful of his sleeve. "You can put me down. Right here will do fine."

"You want to crawl your own way back to bed?" They were at the top of the stairs, fast as talking about it. He strode down the long second-floor hall, past bedroom doors and those Persian miniatures and something new—a procession of little brown pots marching in a line against the wall. "Next time, I'll let you try. That'll be amusing. When you collapse, I'll step over you."

Then it was up the back stairs, and he wasn't even breathing hard. The last flight to the attic had a narrow turn in the middle. He went through sideways. Didn't even pause. That was the good balance he'd learned at sea, climbing the rigging. He kicked the door to her bedroom open. It slammed back to the plaster. Made a hell of a clatter.

Then he laid her on the counterpane so careful she could have been made of glass. Complicated as hell, the Captain.

She sat up fast, jerking the bedclothes loose. After a minute, the room didn't spin anymore, and he was standing over her, waiting. It was one of those moments with a lot of possibilities for what came next.

Hard to say what Kennett would do if he was Cinq. Strangle her maybe. Or he might strangle her even if he wasn't Cinq, just from sheer irritation. A woman with a modicum of common sense would get up and run for the door.

"Look at me." He gave one tap to her chin, almost perfunctory. "That's right. Now, hear me well, Miss Whitby. What you're planning to do in this house isn't going to work. You can hide a mountain of evidence in the corners, and nobody will believe it. Scheme you ever so wisely, charm you ever so well, you'll fail."

"I'm not—"

"You stay under these conditions." Oh, but he was angry with her. Not that he'd been all beer and skittles up to this point, but now he was particularly scowling. "You will behave yourself while you're under my roof. No more lying to my aunt. Keep away from Quentin. And don't spar with Claudia. You will lash down that lively tongue of yours when you talk to her."

"Civil as a nun's hen. That's me."

"I should boot your pretty arse out of here so hard you bounce on the front steps. You're part of a foul business, Miss Whitby. You've brought it into my house, touching my family. But there are men out there, waiting to swallow you whole. I can't send you back to that."

"I'm perfectly—"

"I know exactly what you are." He slipped his fingers to the back of her neck, twining into her braid. It gave her a shiver all up and down her spine, feeling him delving deep in her hair, warm and intimate, and not even thinking about it. They seemed to have skipped a couple steps in getting to know each other. "This room belonged to the governess in the old days. It's quiet and private up here. The door has a bolt. My aunt keeps the women here, the ones she takes off the street, because they need to feel safe. Do you know why I put you all the way upstairs, Miss Whitby?"

"You've run out of guest rooms downstairs? Always makes me feel so crowded and inhospitable—"

"You're as far from my bedroom as you can be, with the whole house between us. No matter how tempted I am, I'm not going to come sneaking along, knocking on your door in the middle of the night. You can sleep easy, knowing I won't come to get you. If you're an honest woman, this is your fortress. But you're not an honest woman, are you?"

Nothing she could say to that. She'd never had the luxury of being honest. It was too late to start now.

"My bedroom is two flights down, fifth door on the right. How long before you come to me?"

"A century or two." She licked her lips. Wrong thing to

do. She knew it as soon as she did it. He was looking at her mouth. "Never."

"And there's another lie from you, Miss Whitby. There's not a speck of honesty in you, is there?"

He left his hand nestled loosely in her hair. It had plans for her, that hand. She could feel it begging to slide down her back and slip over her, everywhere.

"I don't like you touching me." But she didn't pull away, did she?

"I don't like any of this. It's vibrating across the room between us right now. Me wanting you. You wanting me. My hair's standing on end there's so much lightning built up in here." His fingers, just the tips, stroked the outer curve of her ear. The warmth between her legs went answering back. "Don't pretend you don't feel it. You're no innocent."

She wished she was innocent. She'd have given a lot, right then, not to understand him.

She'd wondered, sometimes, if she'd ever find a man she wanted to bed with. She never had, not in all these years since Ned. She couldn't count the nights she'd spent, tangled in the sheets, twitching, climbing a pillow, pretending there was a man touching her. She'd met a parade of bankers and merchants and handsome young soldiers, with hot smiles and insinuating hands they tried to sneak over her when they could get her alone.

Not all of them were after her father's fortune. Some of those men she'd liked. Not a one of them she wanted to wrap up close to her and take inside her.

Tonight, in bed, her dream would have Sebastian's face. She'd finally met a man who got her teakettle whistling. One of those cases of being careful what you wished for.

Light, light, he stroked down her neck and her body played a chord of music for him.

He whispered, "Remarkable. You are remarkable. Did you know that? Last night I thought I'd netted a mermaid out of that muddy alley. Something magical." Black fire writhed in his pupils. If she relaxed, even an instant, she'd slide right down into him, into all that fire, and get burned up. "You came to the Lane to throw a net around me, using your eyes and your hair and that wet dress sticking to your skin. By God, you caught me. But you caught yourself, too. That wasn't part of your father's scheme. You didn't plan on feeling anything, did you?"

I didn't plan on any of this.

"There's no limit to what you'd do, following his orders. You'd risk your neck on Katherine Lane. You'd connive and blackmail yourself into my household." He put both hands on her now, tilting her head to look at him. The touch was gentle, but his voice was hard as iron. "You'd lay on your back right now, as sick and hurt as you are, and let me have you, if it would give you a place under my roof." He held her head, and his thumbs ran along the underside of her jaw where the skin lay thin over the bone, sensitive. "Not a magical creature of the sea after all. You turn out to be someone who'll crawl into my bed whenever that old bastard tells you to."

"My father is not—"

"When you come to me, make sure you come with hunger in your belly. I want you to ache for me. Everything else between us is a lie, but the wanting is real."

"I don't know what you're talking about."

"Yes, you do." His whisper was liquid music, trickling through her body, pooling between her legs. "You're doing it now. Wanting. See how easy it is?" That frightening, focused intelligence studied her, inches away. Slow as if he were moving through water, he picked up the long braid from her shoulder and ran it between thumb and forefingers. "Do you wonder what we'll be like, the two of us?"

Yes. "No."

He wrapped the braid in his fist, oh so gradually, and wrapped and wrapped like he was taking up towline. "Two flights down. Fifth on the right. You'll open my door. I'll be waiting for you, thinking about what I'll do to you. You'll slip out of your nightclothes, out of every stitch on you, and come to my bed. You'll be hungry and needing, and I'll be on fire for you. We'll neither of us be able to stop it, once you walk through that door."

He pulled, slow and persuasive, reeling her in a little

closer, a little closer, using the length of the braid, till his hand rested next to her throat. A sailor's hand. She could feel it there where she breathed, hard as deck wood along his knuckles, smooth as polished teak.

"You'll lean to me, and you'll ask me to touch you. You'll tell me what you need. I'll do it all. I'll do everything."

His voice sent a tremble up her spine. It wasn't fear. It was anticipation. Stupid, stupid, body she had.

Gently, the back of his fingers stroked the path that carried her heartbeat. He was caressing her pulse, there at her throat. "See how your breasts are crinkled up already. They're imagining my mouth on them, the way it's going to be. That's how strong the pull is between us. Your body is already thinking about me."

"I—"

"We'll be magic. We'll turn into gold. Slippery gold fire, melting into each other. Hush." That rasping, velvet voice crawled right under her skin. "We both know what's going on."

His eyes were black wells of infinite possibility. She got fascinated, looking in. Probably this was how those fish felt when men came after them, night fishing, with lanterns. They hung in the water, staring and dazzled, waiting to be speared. Dim-witted as a fish, that was her.

"Half of me wants you to stay in my house," he whispered. "Because I want those nights with you. If you don't want that, too, then I suggest you get out of here. I can have you out of London in an hour, to Hampstead, and that old captain of mine. Will you go? Or will you stay here with me, knowing you'll be in my bed in a day or two?"

"You're trying to scare me off."

"Clever Jess. That's exactly what I'm doing." There was a fraught little pause. He might have been a shark, deciding whether to circle in widdershins or t'other way round. "Be wise, sparrow. Run from me."

She held perfectly still. Not because he had hold of her. Because she couldn't have moved if her life depended on it. "No."

"Wrong choice, Jess Whitby." He let go of her. Took his

hand away and let her free. "Wait a day or two before you come to me. Neither of us would enjoy bouncing on those bruises."

"I liked you better when you were a ship's captain named Sebastian."

"I liked you better when you were a street whore." He smiled, enigmatic as an oyster, if oysters smiled. "Stay then. Be polite to Claudia. And if you ever look at Quentin the way you're looking at me now, I'll make you regret you were ever whelped."

Outrage chopped off any speech she had in her.

Kennett didn't even stay to see the effect of that grenade. He lobbed another as he walked out the door. "You'll want to send for some dresses. I can see all the way down your tits in that one."

Nine

Dorset Street, Whitechapel

CINQ WORE BLACK—A BLACK GREATCOAT THAT fell to boot top and a black, low-crowned hat with a wide brim. A scarf of raw wool, colorless in the streak of light from the high, barred windows, covered nose to neck and hid what the gloom didn't.

"Liam's dying." The Irishman sounded more annoyed than anything else.

Good, Cinq thought. If that hag in the corner didn't kill him with her nursing, Lazarus would slit his throat. Lazarus didn't allow outsiders to hunt in his territory. "Your share will be that much larger."

"You're a cold one."

"I can be." The voice was low and deliberately unmemorable. "Get me the girl."

"Not so soon. It's too dangerous altogether."

"You will take her now, before they hustle her out of town. She'll leave the house sooner or later to go to that warehouse in Garnet Street. I'll send word. Grab her there."

"And isn't it brave you are, when it's my neck." The Irishman took a final look at the figure laid out on the pile of straw. Watched the labored breaths that kept the corpse an inch this side of death. "I need more money for this. Fifty pounds."

"We keep to the agreement."

"Sean and Fergus are dead in their blood. Cut down like dogs, God help them."

"Then they've no need of money. Deliver the girl."

"Ye said it'd be easy, damn yer eyes. There's five men dead, and Liam's on his last. Bastard Kennett's after our necks. This ain't the job we was hired for, not at all. Fifty pounds more."

"Ten. For your losses."

"Fifty, I say. Fifty now and the hundred when we bring the girl."

"And I say you're a bungler and a fool. I handed her to you on a silver platter. I told you where she'd be, and even then you lost her. There's men upstairs who'd take this work and be glad of it."

That was bluff. These Irish scum were the only men stupid enough to lay hands on Whitby's only child. She was protected by Lazarus, too. And now Sebastian. It was simple suicide to touch her, and every thief and brawler in London knew it.

All the more reason to secure the girl before this fool found that out. "Follow her. Take her. And don't hurt her again. Dogmeat's no good to me."

The man spat on the dirt floor. "She'll be alive. The money better be waiting when we bring her to the boat."

He wouldn't live to enjoy it. Lazarus would see to that. Or Sebastian would. Really, it was laughably easy to eliminate witnesses.

"One more thing. Hire some harlot and get her into the house. There's always a new slut cringing and whining at the door. They'll take her in. She'll tell you what the Whitby girl's doing. Use her to bring the girl to you, if you can. This is five for the whore." Cinq dealt pound notes onto the rough table. "It's enough. Don't tell the pimp, then, if he's greedy." More pound notes joined the ones on the table. "Five for you and the men. And five goes to . . ." a nod toward the dying man, ". . . his care. Or his family, if he dies."

"I'll see to it." The Irishman scraped the money up. It was that easy to ensure death, muffled and swift, to the man in the pile of straw. To him and the crone crouching in the corner. Two more people who'd seen Cinq would be tidied away.

When the Revolution swept through London, this rabble would be washed away with the rest of the Old Order. Napoleon would find a use for them in the army of the Revolution.

Cinq pulled the scarf higher and climbed the steps out of the cellar, walked through the tavern, out to the wretched street, and stepped into the crowds of workmen, sluts, beggars, and thieves hurrying to work.

Ten

Douglas Hotel, Bloomsbury

"HELP ME WITH THIS." GRUNTING, SEBASTIAN lifted the corner of the bed. Adrian slipped an edge of carpet under it.

"Well, that was a waste of time." Adrian straightened up, brushing his hands.

"We had to look. Let's get the chairs back."

He set a wide bergère chair in front of the windows in a patch of late afternoon sunlight. The other chair, a big, soft armchair, belonged by the hearth. The table went beside it. The lamp went on the table, then the bowl of roses. When they finished, it would be like nothing had been moved. They'd done this before, when they were gathering evidence in France.

The Whitbys lived in unobtrusive comfort in this hotel when they were in England. A suite of bright, high-ceilinged rooms overlooking Russell Square were kept for their exclusive use. Whitby owned the hotel.

If Jessamyn Whitby was part of her father's treason, the proof might be here, in her bedroom, away from the prying eyes in the Whitby offices. He found himself hoping he wouldn't uncover anything. What did it mean that he was already looking for ways to make her innocent?

"You're not going to find stolen papers." Adrian stood in the center of the Aubusson rug, turning slowly, considering possibilities. "If she's keeping anything here—which I doubt—her hiding place will be obvious. Diabolically, cleverly, unfathomably obvious. Once I find it, I'll kick myself."

"You do that. I'll start on the bookcase." He pulled stacks of books from the top shelf and began going through them. Jess wasn't keeping letters from the War Office on an open shelf in the corner of her bedroom between *Curiosities of Greece* and *By Mule Through Serbia*, but it'd be obvious enough to suit Adrian.

He might not find stolen papers, but he was going to discover Jess. Parts of her were scattered here, everywhere, in the place she lived and the things she owned. This room was going to tell him who she was. "What does Doyle say about the Irishmen?"

"Five dead on Katherine Lane, where they have become the magistrate's problem." Adrian strolled over to poke into the dressing table. "One Irishman is hors de combat somewhere in Whitechapel. Lazarus has picked up another. Lazarus is not amused when men come to his part of town to maim and kidnap, that being his prerogative. That leaves four walking around loose."

"More than I'd want after me." Four men, hunting Jess Whitby.

"And Ireland is not yet emptied of villains, alas. I'm glad she's sleeping in your house tonight." Adrian lined up the comb and brush on her dresser. "Among other things, it lets me search her bedroom." He made faces in the hand mirror, laid it down, and sniffed at a scent bottle. "Jasmine. From Houbigant in Paris. I used to buy that for her when she was twelve. She has not quite rooted me out of her life. What else . . . ?" He slid a drawer out. "No powder. No pots of rouge. No arcane aids to beauty. From this we will infer there is no man she wishes to entice. A welcome breath of simplicity in this convoluted affair."

"There's nothing simple about Jess."

"On the contrary. There's no one more candid. She is a veritable tutorial in how not to tell lies. How is she?"

"Frayed around the edges. In pain, and trying to hide it. She's probably asleep now. Eunice will let me know if she gets worse." He went down the stack methodically, unfurling one book after another and replacing it on the shelf. "I put her to bed. Maybe I can intimidate her into staying there for a day or two."

"Good luck on that. We're all behind you." Adrian began to set the contents of the drawer on the dresser top. "Handkerchief. Always useful. A fan. Ivory and lace. That's very pretty. Pound notes. Coinage of the realm. One glove. Where do all those lost gloves go, I wonder?" He opened the next drawer. "More of her feminine mysteries." He drew out a cuff pistol. It was small, German-made, with fine engraving on the barrel and grip. "Nice." He inspected. "Not loaded recently. She feels safe in London. I cannot help but feel that is unjustified."

"She's safe with me."

"Thereupon I do rest my constant hope and reliance. Would I feel better if Jess went about armed with small but accurate pistols? I must think upon that."

Her books were in French, German, and Italian. One by one they turned out to be somebody's travels in Greece, Arabia, and Macedonia, by foot, camel, and donkey. No account books. No codes. No marking on any of the pages. No secrets stolen from Whitehall.

Next row. He thumbed across the titles. *Tell me about Jess* . . . and the books did. These were stories from lands at the edge of the map, halfway to fable. *I was right to see the Viking in your face. Samarkand and Timbuktu and Persepolis. What are you looking for, Jess? Or what are you trying to run away from?*

When he left her this morning, she'd been pale and shaken, holding herself together with pure bravado. That was courage, straight and simple, and it drew him as much as the beauty of her.

One moment burned in his memory like a live coal. He'd

taken the curve of her cheek in his hand. Jess stared back at him. He could have seduced her, gently, carefully, taking account of that collection of bruises. She was so bloody desirable, and she wouldn't have stopped him.

But she could be that beautiful, and still be part of her father's filthy business. So he'd snarled and let her go. The other choice was laying her down in bed and stripping that borrowed dress off her.

Not wise, laying hands on that woman. It made him want more.

A Voyage Through the Crimea to Constantinople proved to be a trip through Crimea, and went back in place. Next came Pope's translation of the *Odyssey*. It was the only poetry in the bookcase. Bold writing on the frontispiece read, "Find time to read this while I'm gone. Ned." The pages were uncut. She kept the book, but she'd never opened it.

And who is Ned? He'd find out. "I want that woman out of my house."

Adrian shrugged. "I want reliable mail service to St. Petersburg in the winter. We must both live with disappointment."

"If you care about this girl, you'll get her out of my house. I may not have gathered all the evidence, but I'm the one who examined it and laid it out. When we hang her father, she's going to know I was part of it. It's going to make her sick, knowing she sat at the same table with me." *Knowing I had my hands on her.*

"If Josiah hangs, Jess will be an indescribable mess anyway. I intend to see it doesn't happen." Adrian slid the empty drawer out and upended it, searching every side. "Nothing. Some more nothing. Ah. This is promising."

From the bottom drawer of the dresser, Adrian pulled a slim lacquer box, half full of letters. He laid them in a row and flipped through the envelopes quickly, deliberate and engrossed.

Even from here Sebastian could see those were personal letters, and not recent. "She doesn't keep state secrets tied up with a blue ribbon."

"An excellent point. I shall take you along every time I ransack a bedroom." Adrian sat on the wide bench and opened the first note.

"Then why are you reading her letters?"

"Incurable nosiness. Let me concentrate."

Which left him to do the search. Last shelf. Still no packet from the Foreign Office, pretending to be *Jottings from Arabia.*

On a stand next to the bookcase was a wire cage with water dish and bedding, clean, but empty of any animal. She didn't just have a dog or a cat, then. She kept something small and furry in there. Maybe something exotic she'd picked up in her travels.

Above the cage hung a small, bright painting, very old. A maiden stood in a garden, her hand resting upon the arched neck of a unicorn, a white hound at her feet. Jewel-colored birds perched in the branches around her and her long, golden hair was unbound, flowing like a river. "I didn't know this was out of France."

"Hmmm?"

"I've seen copies. This is the original." He barely let himself touch the edges as he lifted it and checked behind. "It's thirteenth century, from Arles." That's how powerful the Whitbys were. They owned something like this and hung it in a girl's bedroom. "That other one, over there next to you, is a Bartolomeo Veneto. We could retire in luxury on the sale of these two."

"Help yourself." Adrian, cross-legged on the bench, had immersed himself in the next letter.

A Hepplewhite tallboy came next. The bottom drawer told him Jess's taste in nightwear ran to soft batiste, silky as wind, so smooth it felt warm to the touch. Her shifts were threaded with bright, frivolous ribbon and expensive lace. But he already knew about her shifts, didn't he? She didn't keep stolen papers or account books among her underthings.

A jewelry box sat on top of the tallboy, in plain sight, next to the night candle. It was acacia wood with ivory, a work of art in its own right. He lifted it down and brought it to the bed. "Why doesn't she lock up her jewelry?"

"To save me the trouble of hauling out my lockpicks."

Jess didn't bother with locks in her bedroom. Any thief who made it this far wouldn't be stopped by locks.

He opened the case. Dozens of rings and necklaces rested in small, blue-velvet compartments. The stones were clear, intense in hue, set in gold. Jess liked her finery bold, and she preferred glow to sparkle.

The top tray in the jewelry box lifted out. The one below held earrings and bracelets. Antiques and exotics. Baltic amber set in the Russian style, Persian turquoise, old, old Turkish enamel work, a bracelet of small cabochon citrines—everything in rich colors that would complement Jess's honey-colored beauty. The best piece was a star sapphire, Ceylon blue, about fifteen carats. All first quality goods, but nothing remarkable. He traded a hundred stones this good every year.

He lifted out the second tray. He'd open Jess's mind like this, layer by layer.

Below, in the last secrets of the box, he met magic.

In a black velvet nest, dozens of pale moons glowed, not white, but the most fragile golden pink. Here were pearls the color of dawn. *Mushajjar* pearls, from the Gulf of Persia. The largest was the size of his thumbnail. He cupped them in the palm of his hand and they weighed no more than dreams and sea foam. You had to know a lot about pearls to realize just how astonishing this necklace was. It should have been locked in a vault.

"Something else we could retire on?" Adrian was intent on reading, but, as usual, he knew everything going on.

"You could buy Yorkshire." He coiled the magic back into place. Beside that amazing necklace, in the next compartment, was a red brown seashell and a dried daisy chain, both of them wrapped up safe in white silk.

This is private. This is her heart. I should feel guilty about seeing this.

"What the devil would I want with Yorkshire?" Adrian tapped the letters together and looped the blue ribbon around them and made a jaunty bow. "Gods. I was never that young. I'm glad Jess was, for a while."

"It wasn't tied like that."

"I'm showing her somebody's been in here." He set the letters carefully back in the box and closed the lid. "Not a sparkling correspondent, young Ned, but I don't suppose she noticed."

That was the name written in the *Odyssey*. "Who's Ned?"

Adrian was up, wandering the room. He stopped at the fireplace and peered in. He waited just long enough to be annoying. "The Honorable Edward Harrington, Lord Harrington's third son. Ned. She was fifteen. He was bright, likable, ambitious, and quite sickeningly in love with her."

"A paragon."

"It has given me considerable satisfaction, over the years, to think of Jess, out in the straw in a horse barn, bestowing her virginity on that boy." He shifted the fire screen. "He had the face of a young Apollo."

Jess's lover. The one who'd put knowledge in her eyes. "What happened?"

Adrian ran his thumb along the carving of the fireplace. The mantel was black marble and the design was scrolled leaves. "Genuinely bad luck. Josiah shipped him out as supercargo, to see what he was made of. Ned died heroically off the Barbary Coast, saving the lives of two of his shipmates. He was seventeen." Adrian rolled up his shirtsleeves and knelt on the bricks of the hearth. "Jess spent the next year constructing Europe's best accounting system. I don't think she slept at all for a couple months."

"I see." He wasn't sure what he saw, except that he was jealous of a boy, half his age, and dead.

"He was a better man than either of us." Adrian twitched a knife from its sheath on his left forearm. "And I think Jess has left us something . . . Yes. Here we find bits of ash on top of a newly laid fire. You burned paper the last time you were here, didn't you, my girl? I neglected your education, if you can make a mistake like that." The point of his knife slid into wispy gray ash, separating layers. "I have writing here. Hand me a piece of that paper, will you? And the quill."

They'd done this before. Stationery and quills were in the little desk. He stroked a quill back and forth across the wool of his sleeve and handed it to Adrian. They both held their breath while Adrian used the feather to tease up a fragment of ash and transfer it onto a clean sheet of paper.

"Got it. Good. See what you make of this." Gingerly, Adrian passed it up to him. "It's her writing."

The fragment was dull brown and charred around the edges, the writing barely legible. A word leaped out at him. Another word. Five or six letters in a row. He could read some of it. "It's a list of ships. *Mary Jane* . . . something. The *Prosper* . . . That's either the *Prosperity* or the *Prospero*. There's dates next to them. *Lady of Swansea*. The *Lively* . . . That has to be the *Lively Dancer*. One of mine."

"She burned this just before she came to Katherine Lane yesterday." Adrian probed in the ash again and shook his head and stood up. "Nothing else usable." He pulled out a handkerchief and began cleaning his hands. "Ships. Why? What does it mean?"

It means she's looking for Cinq. "She's tracking ship movements. I'll know more when I've looked through the papers in her office."

How does the woman who created Europe's best accounting system hunt Cinq? She makes a list of ships. Then she comes after me. Why?

Outside the window, fifty yards away, a streetlamp grew a pinprick of light, then became a soft, round glow. The lamplighter was on the far side of the square, working his way around. It was almost dinnertime. He'd go home, and see Jess.

If she's trying to trace Cinq, she's innocent. No matter what her father's done, she's not part of it.

There was nothing more to be read on the burned scrap. He let it fall back in the hearth. "We're through here. I'll head back home and see how she's doing."

If she's innocent, I can have her.

Whitby was guilty of so much foulness. Jess was clean. He had to separate her from her father before the bastard dragged her down along with him.

Adrian joined him at the window. "I'll see you in Garnet

Street at midnight, outside the Whitby warehouse. What does one wear to ransack a warehouse? Black, I think, and the charcoal waistcoat. Tasteful, yet understated."

"I wonder what she'll do when she finds out we've searched here and in her office." He pulled the curtain closed.

"Something drastic." Adrian sounded pleased.

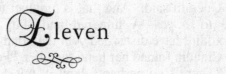

Eleven

Kennett House

"Take this slowly. You're more badly hurt than you realize." Eunice had put her firmly into a wide, soft chair in the parlor. "Like that. Yes. We will wrap you up, if you don't mind. You're cold at the edges."

So Jess slipped her shoes off, and leaned back, and let herself be cocooned in a big shawl. It was a wild tartan of royal blue and scarlet and dark green. They'd see you coming across the heather in this one.

"We'll have dinner in an hour," Eunice said, "unless Cook gets distracted. You are not to worry and make your head ache. Everything can wait till tomorrow."

Then Eunice plunged back into the turmoil in the kitchen and left her to Quentin and Claudia. There was a new woman to take care of, down in the kitchen.

This new one had come to the back door, crying and terrified, running from her man. According to Mary Ann, who came to build up the fire and clear away the teacups, the latest girl was a pretty thing. "But soggy as a wet March. Enough to keep bread from rising, the way she takes on."

Quentin and his sister were at the game table, playing

piquet. They made an elegant pair, like something in a painting. Him, in his evening clothes, fine enough for any party in Mayfair. Her, in dark plum silk. Ten thousand bolts of cloth in London, and Claudia picked that color. No accounting for taste.

Quentin said, "And that is repiquet for me, which brings me to . . . yes. A hundred and sixty points. You really shouldn't have discarded your diamonds."

Claudia folded her hand together. "Perhaps."

"There's no perhaps about it, my dear." Quentin led an eight of spades.

The big bow window of the front parlor looked out over the greenery in the park in the middle of the square. The curtains were flowered Spitalfields brocade. The secretaire and the cabinet were Chippendale, and the carpet was a Kashan. Old stuff everywhere. That was pure gentry, that was, buying old things, when there was new work just as good and cheaper. Five or six of Standish's pots were lurking around on tables; old Greek pots, orange and black, very fine. The one closest to her showed a naked man skewering somebody with a long spear. She'd asked her governess, once, why the Greeks didn't wear clothes in the old days, but she never got an answer.

A book lay open, facedown, on the back of the sofa—another of those wild-eyed political texts they favored. This morning's newspaper was folded on the side table. A bag of needlework was tucked among the cushions of the sofa. This was where the family sat in the evening, reading and talking, playing cards.

Quentin said, "The play is all in the discards, Claudia. I don't know how many times I've told you that."

Kick him in the shin, Claudia, and pretend it's an accident. But it wasn't going to happen. The gentry didn't act that way.

Sitting quiet, eyes half-closed, Jess could hear distant comings and goings in the kitchen. Eunice would be down there, calm and competent and matter-of-fact, dealing with problems, blunting the raw edge of fear. This latest woman, whoever she was, had fallen into good hands.

If things had gone a hair different, it might be her downstairs. It scared her, sometimes, thinking how close she'd come to ending up in a brothel. Lazarus saved her from that when he made her a thief.

She hadn't planned to stay in bed all day. It would have felt too much like obeying the Captain's orders. Besides, she had work to do. But somehow she'd fallen asleep, fully dressed, stretched out flat on top of the covers, as soon as he left. She had a dream of women coming in and out of the room, touching her forehead, covering her with a quilt, walking with quiet feet. When she woke up, it was almost sunset.

Outside, night was taking over the neat trees and scythed grass of the park. Shadows bled into shadows till they made one big darkness. She didn't want to be out in that.

I'll see Papa tomorrow. I'll tell him what I've been doing. Papa's going to yell at me till my ears fall off.

The bright, strong fire in the grate kept her knee and her shoulder and the side of her face almost too hot. She laid her cheek against the nubbly brocade of the wingback and watched Quentin and Claudia play piquet. It was an interesting game. Quentin cheated.

Claudia didn't glance up from her cards. "Ladies do not remove their shoes in the parlor, Miss Whitby."

"I know. It's your aunt's idea. Maybe you can say no to her, but I haven't managed it yet."

"Eunice is a law unto herself. She is also the daughter of a duke." Claudia chose a discard. "You, Miss Whitby, are in no position to copy her eccentricity."

"Lord, no. Prosaic as a hen's egg, that's me."

"Ladies also do not use barnyard metaphors. I suspect you are capable of considerably more decorum than you practice." Claudia selected a card carefully, played, and lost again. No surprise, with Quentin dealing.

The wingchair Eunice had put her in was sturdy as a tree. This would be the special property of the Captain. She could see Kennett coming home from business at the docks, tossing his hat on that table next to the front door. He'd shed his coat and leave it draped over the banister. Then he'd walk in here in shirtsleeves and drop into this chair with a sigh and stretch his boots out to the fender at the fire. She could almost feel the imprint where his body had relaxed, day after day. Curling into this chair felt like being held safe in a big hand.

Kennett's rich house folded around her, giving her shelter the same way it protected that poor woman down in the basement.

In Egypt and the dry countries of the East, they took hospitality seriously. A guest didn't root through his host's saddlebags, planning betrayal and death. A man's own family would boot him out for being contemptible. She didn't like to think what Mahmoud and Ali and Sa'ad would say if they could see what she was planning. They'd turn away in disgust, most likely.

There was no virtue in her. If there had been, she'd have traded it for the sailing date of a ship or a stray rumor from France or one scrap of proof against any of the men she was watching. There was nothing she wouldn't do to save Papa.

Quentin felt her eyes on him and looked up. "You must be bored, watching the play. You should join us."

"Not today. Maybe when I'm feeling better." *Maybe when the moon turns green and jumps up and down in the sky like a frog.*

"Soon, then. We'll try a bit of whist. Claudia might have more luck with whist." He did a top shuffle of the cards, leaving the bottom quarter unchanged. Planting the book, they called that where she came from. He wasn't clumsy exactly, but she'd learned from experts.

She'd given up cardsharping forever when she was fifteen. It was a promise to Papa—her present to him on her birthday—that she'd never cheat at cards again. Papa was just determined to reform her.

There was no flavor to card games when you couldn't cheat. "I don't play much."

Quentin finished his deal, smiling secret and superior. "I'll teach you. It's not too difficult for a woman to learn. I promise I won't be too hard on you." He'd lined five little towers of copper up in a neat row in front of him. He was raking in his sister's pin money, ha'penny by ha'penny, cheating for farthings. What was she supposed to make of that? There were men living in round, black, goat-hair tents in the desert she understood better.

He dealt for himself and Claudia, taking some from the top of the deck, some from the bottom.

Claudia picked up the hand and studied it, selecting her discards, looking glum, as well she might. "I'm sure she knows how to play, Quent. She probably does it with a vulgar avidity."

Why can't I ever think of insults like that? She snuggled into the shawl. "It's vulgar then, winning at cards."

"To a lady," Claudia sniffed, "winning or losing is a matter of indifference."

"Ah. My governess never said a word, and she was supposed to be cousin to some marquis or other. I've long suspected that woman diddled us finely."

"My trick." Quentin helped himself to the cards on the table, neatened the corners, and stacked them in from of him.

For an instant she saw—what?—in Claudia Ashton's eyes. Sardonic humor? Anger?

Claudia wasn't a fool. She had to know her brother cheated. Did the Captain know? It must make for absorbing evenings, them at the card table, congratulating each other on being well-bred, and Quentin cheating nineteen to the dozen.

I'm not going to be bored here.

"Greed, of course, is the bane of the mercantile classes . . ." Claudia kept talking.

But Jess didn't hear. She was listening to the silence. Downstairs, it had got quiet.

Silence, where it doesn't belong, terrifies. Sets the hair on end. There's the silence when the ship is still, all at once, in the eye of the storm. Silence in the woods after the distant *yip yip yip* of wolves. Silence in a tavern when somebody pulls a knife.

In the kitchen, at the back of the house, the murmur of voices and muted clatter suddenly stopped. She was already on her feet before she heard the crash and the sudden sharp scream that came up through the floor.

She took off, running.

JESS skidded down the kitchen stairs, full tilt, in her stocking feet. The treads were worn smooth from servants trotting up and down. *Hold on. Grab the railing. Hurry.*

The big cavern of the kitchen was lit like a stage. Whitewashed walls blazed under the bright lamps. In a single glance, Jess took in the gray flagstone floor, copper pots boiling on the stove, blue-and-white crockery, long, brown wood tables with a white landscape of flour.

At the back door, Eunice faced a beefy, red-faced beast of a man, bellowing and drunk.

The cook and two kitchenmaids huddled in front of the fireplace. A girl in cheap red satin cowered on the floor, bawling her head off. There were no footmen down here. Nobody to help Eunice. The place was full of terrified, shrieking women.

"Gimme what's mine!" He was unsteady on his feet. Savagely, brutally half-witted with drink. Only a born fool would walk into this house and threaten this woman. "I been good to her. Girl belongs ter me."

Eunice was alone, confronting twenty stone of drunken brutality. Her body said, *You don't get past me.* Said, *You can't have her.* Just by standing there, she said it.

I didn't realize how small she is. How old. She has bones like a bird.

". . . sticking yer nose inter me business . . ." He raised a clenched fist.

He's going to hit her. He's drunk enough to hit her.

Stupid, stupid, stupid to touch Eunice—somebody Lazarus protected. Stupid to invade the West End to retrieve a girl. Drunk and stupid as dirt.

Jess rounded the bottom of the stairs. She yelled, "Look at me! Hey! You! Dogface. Look at me, you bloody pig!"

He didn't hear. He wouldn't hear if she shouted it up his nose. Mindless drunk. He'd batter right through Eunice to get what he wanted.

". . . wring your neck. Yer got no rights to what's mine . . ." Staggering, he drew back, prepared to swing.

The cook and the maids screeched like parrots. *Why isn't Quentin here?*

Pots bubbled on the stove, giving off steam and the smell of onions and chicken. She grabbed a big one by the handle, using both hands to pick it up. Heavy as hell. Sloshed all over the floor. Soup. Something full of vegetables, anyway.

The handle was hot. *I'm gonna spill it on my bloody feet.* Soup splashed over the edge. Too hot to hold. *It hurts, it hurts, it hurts*—Past Eunice. *Don't slop it on Eunice, for God's sake.*

She swung the pot and sent an eruption of lumpy, hot soup into the drunk's face.

He howled like a banshee and clawed at his eyes.

I need—What? What? To the side, by the door, shawls and coats hung. She grabbed a big black cloak off the hook and threw it over his head. He doubled over, yowling, and plunged across the kitchen, charging from side to side like an enraged bull. He crashed into the table. Dishes skittered and toppled to the flagstones, shattering.

"Run, for God's sake."

The kitchenmaids did. The girl who was the cause of all this sat with her arse glued to the floor, mewling like a cat, while Eunice struggled to pull her to her feet.

God save me from fools. "Get her the bloody hell upstairs."

The pimp fought free from the cloak. He came out roaring like a fiend, brick red, dripping vegetables. The swollen, half-blind eyes were holes of madness. He shook his head and saw her . . .

Never hurt a man, Lazarus used to say. *Kill him or run. Never just hurt him.*

He charged. She had no chance to run or dodge. Eunice was still behind her. She needed something to fight with. Anything. Her hand found a big pitcher on the table. She heaved it at him and hit him square on the nose.

He didn't even wince. He just kept coming.

Twelve

ROUGH HANDS GRABBED FROM BEHIND AND pushed her out of the way. Cold panic drenched her. She started to hit out.

The next instant, she knew. She knew the size and shape and the brusque sureness before she had a good look at him. It was the Captain. She'd never been gladder to see anybody.

He put himself between her and all that mad rage. He stood between her and the vitriol dribbling through those thick, blistered lips.

". . . sodding bitch . . ."

"Out." The Captain cut through curses like a knife. He knocked aside the fist aimed at her, grabbed the upraised arm, and twisted it backwards. "Out of my house."

The table shuddered as men knocked against it. Plates and bowls crashed. A howl trumpeted from the drunk as Sebastian's knee connected with his groin. He bent over, gasping and bleating.

The Captain gripped the man by his leather coat and spun him around and sent him stumbling out the kitchen door. He fell, sprawled on the sharp corners of the entryway steps.

A last housemaid, ducking and bobbing in the shelter of the pantry, shrieked like a whistle. The drunk groaned and hugged the bricks. When the Captain followed him outside, he frantically crawled his way up the stairs on his belly, yowling. Before he got to the top, Kennett picked him up by the scruff of his neck and tossed him bodily onward, down the path, to land flat on his face on gravel.

"I didn't do nuffin'. I didn't do—"

The Captain hauled him up. "If I ever see you . . ." The Captain slammed his fist into the man's ribs. ". . . near my house. If I see you . . ." He took the jerking, spasming body by the throat and shook him like a dog shakes a rat. ". . . near my family. If I see you near any woman in my household. If I pass you on the street . . ." He held the figure upright and punched a final, short jab. "I will kill you."

This wasn't a fight. This was Kennett punishing a man. He threw the bloke away like offal and turned his back on him. He didn't even bother to watch as, shambling and weaving and crying, the man staggered forward and fell against the back gate and fumbled it open and fled.

She'd followed the fight out of the kitchen, up the areaway stairs, just to see if the Captain ended up twisting anybody's head off. Always better to know what was happening than to try to figure it out later. In the garden, she laced her fingers into the iron railing and held on, taking it all in.

Behind her, in the kitchen, sobs receded in stages. Eunice was finally getting that damn, damp parcel of misery upstairs.

When he was through with the pimp, the Captain came up to her and stood, looking past her.

A pair of footmen jostled up against each other, trying to get out the back door and into the garden. The footmen in this house were wiry and muscular old sailors. These two would have been helpful a few minutes back.

"Where have you been?" But the Captain didn't wait for excuses. He dressed these fellows down with a few dozen choice words and sent them slinking back to the kitchen. Pure ship's captain, he was, doing that. All he lacked was flapping sailcloth in the background and a wide open sea.

Then he turned his attention to her.

She told him what he wanted to know, first off. "He didn't touch Eunice. Not a hair on her head."

"I saw." He walked towards her. "He got within ames ace of knocking the hell out of you, though."

"Didn't he just." She pulled back against the railing and made space for him to walk past. She was giving her attention to the knotty problem of whether she should sit down, careful, on the stairs till she got over being dizzy or if she should shortcut the process and just collapse in a heap.

The Captain surprised her with a gentle hold that kept her upright. "Here we go. That's right." The garden, green and brown and gray in the dusk, swam by as he guided her along for ten or twelve steps, across the garden, walking on the grass, till they got to the bench at the side. "I've got you." His voice slicked along her nerves like a warm touch. Then she was sitting on the bench and he was next to her.

She closed her eyes and considered slipping off onto what looked like fairly soft grass. There was a big patch of it to the left here.

"Don't faint." He fitted his arm around her, over her shoulder.

"I'm not going to." But maybe she would. Cold pricked all over her body. Even her lips were numb.

He turned toward her on the bench and she felt his hand on her cheek. Calloused fingers, warm and smooth, ran over her eyelids, touched her mouth. "Damn. You're cold as ice."

Absently, as if he'd had practice at it, he smoothed down her hair. "I won't ask why you're wandering around the house barefoot."

He took her left hand and put it in her lap, palm upwards, so he could study it. "Did you get burned?"

"Burned? Oh. From the pot handle. No damage done. That bloke, though—" She swallowed the rest of what she was about to say. She didn't talk flash anymore. Not for years now. "That man. He's not going to be pretty when he heals up."

"He wasn't pretty to start with." The Captain had turned her hand up to the light from the kitchen windows, searching it like the lines on her palm held the secrets of the universe.

"Some pink maybe, from the burns you tell me you don't have. And here we have the scrapes from last night, when you were dodging Irishmen. I cleaned those for you." He pointed here and there. It tickled, even though he wasn't touching at all.

"All part of my catlike retreat. Always puzzled me cats don't seem the worse for wear more than they do. I suppose it's all that fur."

"I'm sure it is. And this." He trailed a fingertip along the edge of her hand, where the old scars were. "You acquired before you met me. Looks like you put your hands through glass."

"A reasonable guess." They were tooth marks, actually. She remembered how she'd got those bites, and it was a bad, cold memory.

Maybe he felt her shiver. He didn't ask again. He closed her fingers up, wrapping her hand inside of his. Then he let go. "You keep getting hurt, Jess. I'd like to put a stop to that."

"Me, too."

He didn't say anything for a while after he put her hand away.

This was the Captain in a different mood. He wasn't angry with her, which was one of those small pleasures in life you had to be careful to enjoy when they went swinging past. He'd been stiff and furious when he stomped out of the attic this morning, full of bite and sarcasm. He seemed to have gotten over that. No telling why.

The kitchen was filling up again with a twitter of women's voices, high-pitched and excited, discussing at length and deploring in depth. They were sweeping and putting things away and cleaning crockery up. Making the world right again. Doing what women always did when the men were through rampaging. It was reassuring to hear, but she didn't want to join them. She leaned her head back and felt him behind her. Felt his arm, strong and solid, under a layer of wool and one of linen.

She shouldn't just relax like this, on a man's arm. She didn't know him well enough, and she didn't like him, and he might be Cinq.

Though it was hard, just this minute, to make herself believe Kennett could be Cinq. She'd try again later and see if she did a better job of it.

He didn't seem to notice she was leaning on him. He just looked up at the sky, musing like. "I get indications, Jess, that you've led an eventful life. Didn't anyone ever warn you not to square up against charging madmen?" Her shoulder was against his chest, they were so close. When he spoke, she could feel his voice with her body.

"Wasn't like I had much choice. You can't talk to a man that drunk. He would have broken Eunice like kindling. Then he'd have torn that weeping tribulation of a girl into scraps."

"So you waded in, armed with a saucepan." With his arm still around her, he settled back and stretched so his boot heels dug into the gravel . . . a man at ease in his back garden, watching the last light ebb out of the flower beds and weeds. He curled his arm to pull her closer. It seemed rude to complain when he didn't mean anything by it. He wasn't even looking at her.

"That was a damn fool stunt," he said. "Thank you."

"I didn't do it for you."

"I know that. You did it for her. I was at the top of the kitchen stairs when I saw you heft a soup pot and go for him." The hold around her tightened. "It took me a century to get across the kitchen. Every second I was telling myself you were strong and smart and you wouldn't let her get hurt. I trusted you as if you were my own hands." He sounded . . . She didn't know what he sounded like. Like he was talking to an old friend, instead of her. "When I left this morning, I planned to come back and start prying you out of here. I'd worked out some strategies. I still thought I could scare you, for one thing."

"You'll have to wait your turn. I'm not finished being terrified of that last fellow."

"Oh, you're terrified all right. You're quaking with fright." Amusement burred, low in his throat. "I'm not going to evict you. Stay. You've earned a place here. Move in, bag and baggage. Bring your cat."

"I might." She should bring Kedger. That would teach him to go offering hospitality wholesale.

He'd shifted around on the bench again, making himself comfortable, and she ended up leaning against him. Where they touched, side by side, was a long strip of warmth, and the rest of her was chilly. His fingers moved idly, tapping at her arm where he had his hand wrapped around. She felt the touches land on her, one by one.

It was strangely companionable, sitting beside him, watching the night creep into the garden by inches. She let herself soak up his heat where they were sharing it. She could almost relax. It was like sitting next to a wolf. One who'd just eaten. A wolf with a full belly and his tongue lolling out. A wolf in excellent good humor.

Still a wolf, though. "I thought you'd kill that man. When you picked him up and started hitting him, I thought you'd pull out a knife."

"Not in front of Eunice."

"I figured that out, afterwards. Whatever you do to that man, you won't do it in front of her. You won't even tell her about it." She'd learned something else about the Captain. He played a role when he was in the West End. He kept the violence inside him, secret and controlled and he didn't bring the dangerous parts of his business home. "You never show your family what you are."

"Not if I can help it."

"They'd be shocked, I guess. Would you have killed him, if it'd been just me watching?" She couldn't believe she asked him that, straight out. Probably it wasn't wise, asking the wolf questions, even when he was in a good mood.

"I already killed a man in front of you, didn't I?" He ran his eyes over her before he went back to admiring his garden. "I won't make a habit of it, Jess. You've seen the worst of me. Most days, I'm a respectable trader. I don't murder everybody I get angry at."

"That's moderate of you." He had family inside the house, his aunt and uncle and cousins. But he was out in the evening talking with her. Maybe he didn't have to hide what he was so much. Maybe he could say things to her he couldn't say to the others. "Anyway, you don't want dead men in your back garden. I mean, who would?"

"Good point."

They could sit like this as long as nobody brought up any awkward topics of conversation. Neither of them said anything. *Complicity* was the word that came to mind.

The dark corners and clumped shadows under the bushes didn't make her uneasy tonight. Nothing would dare to lurk in the dark with the Captain here. He held her in a friendly way, like they got along fine. Like they'd done this a hundred times. Like they always wandered out here into the garden whenever the weather was good and that bush over in the corner was in bloom. If it bloomed.

They sat for a while, and he stroked her arm the way a man might pet a cat, not thinking about it. A buzz slid under her skin. Not quite innocent, not quite sensual. Building bit by bit. Just a little heat. She let herself enjoy it, because he wasn't noticing.

She wasn't an expert on gardens, but this one looked neglected. There was a pair of matching bushes at the back garden gate with something overgrown and exuberant running wild next to them and a scraggly row of roses against the wall. Somebody'd left a garden rake leaning there.

"A clear night." That was the Captain, taking in the sky. "There'll be rain tomorrow, late in the day."

"That's going to amaze the populace. Rain."

"See over there." He drew his free hand across the sky and showed her a swipe of thin cloud, red in the sunset. "The mare's tail. The rain's following that, coming in from the north. Heading our way at about fifteen knots."

"I'd like to do that. Predict the weather. I have weather records from all over Europe in a storeroom at the warehouse. I play with the numbers and try to make sense of it, but I never can. They'll have books of weather tables, someday, the way they have tide tables."

"Maybe. Then we won't have to set our wits against it."

She watched his face while he watched the sky. He and the weather were honorable adversaries, looked like. A lot of sailors felt that way about the weather. He smiled, liking the challenge.

And she was lost. She could feel the twist inside her as it happened. The stark, masculine beauty of his mouth reached out and grabbed at her chest. Her breath caught with a chirrup in her throat.

Lazily, he turned to her. "There's a witch down in Portsmouth who keeps the wind in her sock. The sailors bribe her to give them good weather."

There could have been a bell inside her that struck little soft chimes when he talked. Every feature of his face stood out exact and distinct, like he was the only thing lit up with the last of the day's light. She wanted to move close and lick the corner of his mouth with her tongue. She wanted to suck on him there and taste him. The shudder that gripped her had nothing flowery and soft and girlish about it. It was a roar and a buzz and an ache between her legs, vulgar and explicit as hell.

She knew what it was to enjoy a man, flesh on flesh. She hadn't forgotten what it felt like to kiss from lips to eyelids and along his ear, and down to his mouth again. She wanted to suck and lick everywhere on the Captain's face till she knew him with her mouth. Till he was part of her.

She was so bloody unwise sometimes. It didn't need Papa to tell her that. She was in Sebastian Kennett's house, with what she'd call dire intent. He might be deadly and dangerous—beyond the obvious deadly and dangerous he wore like a jacket for everybody to see. He was no one she should be licking the cheekbones of.

She squirmed toward her side of the bench. "About Eunice. I wanted you to know. It wasn't stupid, what she did."

He eased her right back next to him, casually, without making a fuss about it. "No, she's not stupid."

That was from being at sea so much, that gesture. He was used to being where everything shifted around him all the time and needed to be nudged back where it belonged. She did that kind of thing herself. He was keeping her warm as the evening cooled down. Just that. She was the one with the vivid imagination. "Some people walk up to danger and pat it on the snout because they're dead ignorant. Your aunt's not like that. She knew what could happen to her when she stood in front of that girl. I didn't expect to find a woman like her in a house in the West End."

"You won't find a woman like her anywhere." The Captain ran his fingers in a smooth line on her arm, up and back, casual about it. He dragged every particle of her mind along with it.

I don't want to like you, and I'm beginning to. I don't want my body to go jumpy and soft where you're touching. I don't want to feel anything at all for you.

"I'll tell you a story." He shifted and tucked her head against his shoulder and pulled her in close, taking back the two inches she was absconding with. "Stop jumping around like a rabbit. Lean back and relax. I was seven. I was standing in mud, next to the Thames."

"I'm not really—"

The muscles of his arm had gone unyielding, like tree roots or hawser rope. He was casually strong and immensely careful with her, and she wasn't going to get loose easily. "Quiet, or I won't tell you. You came to Katherine Lane because you want to know about me. This is your chance."

"Are you leading up to something, holding on to me like this?"

"Maybe."

"Because the last time we talked, you were going to wait till I ambled down to your bedroom one night. I think you called it inevitable."

She didn't recognize it just at once. That rumble in his chest was him laughing. "Give me some credit. Nothing's going to happen on a hard bench in the night air. And I'm busy tonight." Suddenly, startlingly, he put his lips to the top of her head and kissed her there, on the part of her hair. He was too fast to stop. Just there and gone before she could think.

"Look, Captain—"

"Damn, but I want you. I should be getting used to that. Now listen. This is interesting." His deep voice flowed across her. "I was seven and it was in the winter. December. Maybe January. I don't remember after all this time. The riverbank wasn't frozen. It's the worst time, when the bank isn't iced hard and the mud seeps with water so cold it burns. You never get warm, not day or night. All the boys who are going to die, that's when they do it. That and the spring."

Unwillingly, she saw the picture he was painting. She remembered that kind of cold. The year Papa left for France and didn't come back and there was no money at all, she'd been out in the cold at all hours, stealing a living. But even then, she hadn't been a scavenger on the Thames, picking up what fell off the barges. A mudlark. Even at the worst, it hadn't been that bad. *I don't want to feel sorry for the boy you were.*

"My basket was about half full of coal. I'd hit on a good spot—picked up a dozen pieces within a foot of each other—and I was looking around for more. A carriage pulled up on the road. A lady got out and began walking down the bank to the river. Mad thing to do. She had a wool cloak on. I remember thinking that if I were bigger I'd go knock her on the head and take that cloak from her. Not to sell. I'd keep it to roll myself up in and sleep warm. If I could have got away with it, I'd have killed her for one night of sleeping warm. That's what I was."

He didn't say anything for a long time. This close to him, she felt every breath moving in and out of him. Maybe he was thinking about what he could have become. She had thoughts like that herself, sometimes. "That was Eunice?"

"That was Eunice. She walked right out onto the mud flats, sinking in and getting filthy. She staggered her way up to me and said, 'Are you Molly Kennett's son?' And I said, 'What if I am?' She said, 'You're to come with me. I've been looking for you for a long, long time.' "

The last sunlight had leached out of the sky and the strongest of the stars were showing through. He had his head back, looking at them. The profile of his face was like the outline of some mountain. Granite and cliffs. But he wasn't rock hard inside. She would have been able to deal with him if he'd been simple and hard inside.

"The lady undid the tie on her cloak and took it off and put it around me. Then she just slopped her way back to the carriage in her wet dress, not even looking behind to make sure I followed."

She'd known Kennett was abandoned by his father after his mother died. Thrown out like garbage. She hadn't known the rest of it. That earl, the man who was his father, should have been knocked on the head and drowned, quiet like. "Why are you telling me this? It sounds private. You're telling me because I helped Eunice?"

"Partly. And I owe you some secrets," he opened and closed his fist, deliberately, watching himself do it, "in fair exchange."

Fair exchange for what?

"And it's a warning," he said. "About me. About what I am."

I watched you kill a man yesterday. You half killed another, just now. How many warnings do you think I need?

"I used to stand under the bridges, so hungry it clawed the side of my guts, and look up at their carriages driving by. All those fine, fat gentlemen. I hated them." The grating sound she heard was his jaw clenching. "I stole from anyone weaker than me. I would have become a murderer in another five or six years." The Captain's face was all shadows. "That's why I understand your father. We both grew up with that kind of hate. I know why he turned traitor."

He thinks Papa would kill men for money. She pushed away from him and sat up straight. "You don't know anything about my father. You don't know the first thing. He's—"

"Not guilty. You have to believe that because he's your father." His eyes picked up some spark of lantern light in the kitchen and glittered. "I wonder what you're willing to do to prove it."

Whatever he was thinking, he was wrong. And it was probably insulting. "There's nothing I wouldn't do. Not one thing. I already—"

"Later. We'll finish this later. Come inside and eat." He stood up and reached down to take both her hands and pull her to her feet. "We'll have dinner and listen to Quentin explain why the perfect social order doesn't coddle the poor. Walk on the grass, unless you want me to carry you. This gravel will tear you to shreds if you walk around without shoes."

Thirteen

Garnet Street, the Whitby Warehouse

". . . ABOUT A DOZEN OF THEM. THEY CAME IN after midnight. They locked the guards in the high-value storage." Pitney, sweating and frustrated, led the way down a row of oak barrels. Jess followed. "We didn't know anything till the morning shift came on and found them. I sent you that note the minute I got here."

"It's not the guards' fault. Not your fault either."

"I'm supposed to be in charge here. God's bleeding damn, Jessie." Pitney slammed his fist down on a bale of broadloom cloth and stumped on with the familiar drag and thump. He'd taken a bullet in the knee, running Whitby cargo near Dieppe. It was old and accustomed, walking along with Pitney, limping and fuming, at her side.

Nothing had been disturbed on the open shelves of the main floor or in the transient racks next to the loading dock. This wasn't thieves. This was His Majesty's God-Save-the-King government. Hell of a thing when you couldn't trust your own government. "Did they get into the safe?"

Pitney's bald, freckled scalp was turning red the way it did when he got agitated. "They picked the lock. It's the German safe we got last year. It came with a sheaf of guarantees."

"If you want to get into a safe, you'll get into it. There's always a way. Makes it kind of pointless, really."

"MacLeish is counting out the money, but it's all there. The banknotes weren't even touched. Everything else . . . Jaysus, Jess, they tossed the jewelry in a pile on my desk, just heaped up." He glared at the shelves they were passing. "The clerks are checking inventory in the main hall. Most of the small stuff is accounted for already. We should get a new safe."

"Least of my worries, I expect. What else?"

"They broke a few locks in high value. Trunks and crates got crowbarred open, but it looks like they didn't take anything. MacLeish is squawking like a wet hen, wishing something had walked off so he could complain. Whatever they wanted was in your office."

"No surprise. I should have . . . Oh, devil and blast it. Kedger." She took off at a run. Pitney struggled behind her, swinging his stiff leg, cursing.

The door to her office stood open. Kedger was safe. Snarling and unhappy with every inch of fur on end, but safe. They hadn't touched him.

Thank God. She went to him and put her hands right down on the cage so he could sniff at her and know everything was fine.

"Bloody traps. We might as well not have any law in this country, the way they ignore it." Kedger clung to the bars, upside down, furious, bristling, and red-eyed. "They scared Kedger. Sodding mudsuckers."

"I didn't let him out last night. He was . . ." Pitney absently picked at the bandage on his index finger, ". . . cross. Jess, your father don't like you swearing."

"What? Oh, yes. Thank you, Mr. Pitney. I'll watch that."

Kedger started up a long, impassioned aria about the previous evening, full of squeaks and snarls and threats of ferret vendetta.

"I couldn't agree more, Kedge. All that and then some." She slipped the bar and opened the cage door. He looped back and forth, wriggling under her fingers. "That's my fine boy. Finest ferret in the city."

She knew who'd invaded in her office in the dead of night. Mr. Bloody Adrian Hawkhurst of the bloody British Service and Captain Bloody Sebastian Kennett. They just waltzed across town and ambushed her guards and ransacked her office when the fancy struck. Pirate waters, she was in lately. Always something new and unpleasant on the horizon.

Kedger scrambled up her arm to cling to her shoulder and continue his complaints from there.

She found the soft place behind his ear and scratched it. "Sorry you didn't get to bite anybody. My advice is, stick to rats. You take a chunk out of the British Service, it's going to disagree with you, sooner or later."

Pitney said, "This is why they came. They spent their time looking here."

He was right. Her office had been searched to the bone, then put back to rights. More than put back. All her clutter was tidied up. Every pile of notes was lined up, square-cornered and exact. Next to the samovar, the six cups were stacked, upside down in a pyramid, nice as ninepence.

They'd made themselves cups of tea and cleaned up afterward. Neat bastards.

She picked up the top cup, the one painted with jasmine flowers. This was the one she always used. She ran her finger around the rim.

Pitney cleared his throat. "You sure it's the British Service?"

"Who else?" She put the cup back. She'd leave them stacked this way for a while so she'd get angry every time she looked at them. "It's Adrian Hawkhurst who did this with the cups. It's Sebastian Kennett who left my papers shipshape and Bristol fashion."

The Captain had said, "I owe you some secrets in fair exchange." He'd sat next to her on that bench last night and talked to her easy and friendly and thanked her for helping Eunice. He'd put his arm around her and kept her warm. All the time he was thinking how he'd break into her warehouse. It just didn't pay to trust anybody, did it?

Kedger curled around her neck, touching up under her hair with cold little nosings. He knew how scared she was.

Pitney said, "Why, Jess? The Service don't have to sneak around at night, wearing masks."

"It's some game they're playing. The British Service against the Whitbys." She put herself into her chair, the one Papa bought her in Milan, with the arms carved into lion heads. "Them against Military Intelligence. Them against the Foreign Office. They like their games."

The wood on her desktop was smooth and cool. A big, rich desk. A merchant's desk. So much work she'd done here. She'd felt important. These last years, she'd pretended to be more than a scruffy thief from Whitechapel. *Hubris*, the Greeks called it. Bad things happened to folks who engaged in hubris, according to her governess.

She never changed inside. She was still a thief. It was always just a matter of time till the beaks came for her. "We're losing the game, in case you wondered."

"They can't—"

"They can do anything they damn well want to. Look at this." Every drawer in her desk was open, just a crack, so they made a little set of steps. "They could pry these drawers out in two minutes. Instead they go picking the locks and take an hour over it. A mind like that just strikes fear into sensible people."

Inside the drawers, everything was neat as a bishop's wig. Nothing missing.

No. Take that back. One bit of inventory was unaccounted for. The sack of lemon drops she kept hid behind the cashbox was gone. They'd helped themselves. If that wasn't rampant abuse of power, she didn't know what was.

In the back of the bottom drawer was a bundle of dark clothes and a lumpy, black burlap bag. In a couple small ways, the lumps were shaped different than when she last handled it. They'd pawed through her old burgling bag. All these years, nobody touched her burgling tools but her. Nobody. "They're making some point with all this. I hate it when people get subtle with me. I'm not good at subtle."

Lately, life just teetered from disaster to disaster, didn't it? Enough to make a clam dizzy.

She wished, right to the pit of her belly, that she was still a kid, out in a fishing smack with Pitney, pulling in bales of smuggled lace, keeping an eye out for the Customs. Someplace ordinary, doing something simple.

In the middle drawer, her correspondence was sorted out by size. "They got into the letters from France. That's a dozen men they can send to the guillotine any Wednesday morning they're feeling bored. I should have burned this lot as soon as I read it."

"You couldn't expect the Service to show up," Pitney said.

"I should have. Lots of things I should have thought about. It's never bad luck. Always bad decisions." Lazarus told her that a hundred times. Too late, now, to remember. She started sorting the letters out, picking the ones that had men's lives in them. "Will you shovel these into the stove for me? I held on to to them, thinking there might be something I missed. All I've done is put more necks on the chopping block."

"I'll do it." Pitney took off his jacket and rolled his sleeves up. The government jackals had pulled the Kedger's cage six inches out from the wall, wanting to take a glim behind.

Kedger slipped down to her desk and sniffed at the letters. He grabbed a quill and launched off and plopped to the floor with a little grunt. He didn't make any sound on the rug, but she heard him skittering as soon as he hit the bare boards. He took the quill under the bookcase to devour it.

"It's time for you to leave England." Pitney rocked the cage back into place, one edge, then the other, bit by bit. He had practice moving awkward loads, all those years smuggling with Papa. "Time to cut anchor, Jess, and run."

"It's too late for that."

THE porter at the front door of Whitby Trading offered him an errand boy as a guide, but Sebastian shook his head and walked by. He knew the way. He took the main staircase upward and walked a long corridor permeated with the smell of spices. On the right, arches gaped open to the lower floor, with ropes hanging and winches and a sheer fall to the receiving area twenty feet below. There were hundreds of yards of storage down there in the main warehouse, and this was only one of their buildings. Whitby's was a huge operation.

Jess was the prize at the center of this maze. He passed empty rooms and an errand boy in a hurry. No one challenged him. Not a guard in sight, and the clerks were out on the main floor, checking inventory. Anyone could walk in, wrap a woman up in a rug, and make off with her. They didn't protect Jess worth a damn in this place.

He didn't keep a warehouse in London. His cargo sold out of rented space at the docks. His agent—Eaton Expediters— kept two desks for him and dealt with the customs paperwork and his invoices. Kennett Shipping was lean still and growing. Someday he'd have what Whitby had here.

The main clerks' room was thirty feet long, high-ceilinged, lined with account books and cluttered with files. Jess's office was at the far end. A wide pair of plate-glass windows let her keep an eye on the clerks. On the other side of her office another window looked down into the warehouse below. Nothing moved at Whitby's she didn't know about. This was the heart of the kingdom.

She was in her office. She sagged at her desk like a jib sail with the wind spilled out. He headed for her, past rows of desks punctuated with quills and ink bottles.

She wasn't entirely unprotected. The man with her—it was the Whitby London manager, Pitney—stopped rearranging the ferret cage and came around to the desk so his burly body partly shielded her from view, giving her some privacy. It looked like he was in the habit of taking care of her. A small point, but telling.

She wore sober dark green today. Her wheat-colored hair was pulled back ruthlessly from her face, leaving it ascetic and pure as a Byzantine icon. There wasn't a way he'd seen her—not stark naked, not muffled head to foot—that she didn't make him hungry for her. He took one look at her down the long stretch of the office and got stiff as a boy in his first brothel. Stupidest muscle in the body. Distracting as hell. He stopped, halfway down the room, and calculated costs of replacing rope on the *Lively Dancer* for a minute, till he'd put jack back in the box.

Coming closer, he could see she'd left the cups stacked up beside the brass samovar, cobalt blue, blood red, and canary yellow. On the shelves all around the room, the lines of ledgers showed gaps, like missing teeth. That was where the lads from the British Service had helped themselves to her account books.

She'd left her door a crack open and he could hear her talking. That was careless of her. Taking it slow, acting as if he belonged here, he came up close and stopped, still as a tree, and listened.

"I don't even know what they're looking for." Jess sounded tired and subdued, not like herself. "They have enough proof to hang Papa three or four times over. They don't need more."

"Josiah's a rich man. He'll buy his way out. They won't—"

"It's not Papa they're after." When she lifted her head, her face looked fragile as blown glass. The bruise on her cheek stood out starkly. "It's me. They want me to take the drop right next to Papa."

"For God's sake, Jessie."

"It's easier for them if I'm scared. They want me to panic and make mistakes."

"I can have you offshore with the tide. You can wait this out in Amsterdam."

"They aren't going to let me go. They got men following me, making sure I don't wriggle out of the net." He saw the shrug, a quick rise and drop of her shoulders. Her voice dropped so low he could barely hear her. "Doesn't matter anyway. I can't leave Papa. They should know that. Funny, in a way. I never thought the English would be so hungry to hang a woman."

That was nonsense. He'd put a stop to her thinking like that.

"Nobody's going to hang," Pitney said. "Not you. Not Josiah. I swear it, Jess."

"Maybe. Look at this." She held her hand out, palm

down, showing it to Pitney. "Shaking like an aspen. If Hawkhurst wants to break my nerve, he's about done it. That's the worst of having an old friend as an enemy. He knows me down to the hinges on my soul."

"*Northern Lass* is still in the Thames, waiting for the tide. I'll take you out the back way. Don't pack. Don't go back to the hotel. I'll—"

"They say it doesn't hurt much, if it's done right." She shook abruptly, like a cat touched by a drop of water. "I need the names of the ships that sailed yesterday, and everything that sails today and tomorrow. Everything, down to the coastal scows and the fishing boats. Get me a list."

"I'll send some boys out. Jess, we can't find one ship out of—"

"We can. We have to." Her voice was steady, her face grave and grimly intent. Even if he hadn't seen proof after proof last night, he'd know she was hunting Cinq. "Did *Northern Sun* bring reports from France?"

"Two new ones. You're in no shape to read them."

He agreed with Pitney. She shouldn't be working. She shouldn't be out of bed. There was nothing holding her together but spit and stubbornness.

"I'm fine. Maybe Leveque pinned down the—" Then, between one second and the next, she knew he was there. Her chin lifted. Their eyes met through the glass. "Or maybe the Captain'll join us instead of skulking around the doorsill."

Caught. He pushed the door open the rest of the way. "The Service isn't trying to hang you."

"I guess you'd know. How long have you been a jackal for the British Service, Captain?" Anger straightened her spine and ratcheted her voice tight.

"A few years. The Service knows me pretty well. If they were trying to hurt you, you wouldn't be in my house. I don't let anyone touch the people in my house."

Pitney stomped over to put himself in front of Jess, legs braced. The tense, open right hand, held low, said he had a knife, probably in his boot top. It should have been ridiculous, a man that age squaring off against him. But it wasn't. Anyone who came at Jess would have to kill that old man to get to her.

He wouldn't like to face Pitney in a fight. "We need to talk, Jess. Call him off."

She considered him levelly, then murmured to Pitney.

"I'll be outside." The old man walked past, stiff-legged, and hitched himself up on a desk in the clerks' room, guarding Jess through the plate glass. Ready to charge.

There was no reason to repeat Jess's carelessness. He pulled the door tight. Jess's bulldog didn't get to listen in.

She was wary and angry. She didn't like being caught off guard this way. He was walking on her territory uninvited, and she resented it. She knew he'd pillaged through her papers. They were both angry, and he was going to give her orders she didn't want to hear.

He circled in toward her, slow and indirect, taking the tour of her office. They both needed a minute to calm down.

Old cargoes hung in the air, the smells of raw wool, Russian tea, and spices. Under it was something musky, probably the stink of the ferret they'd found. A ball of twine sat on the shelf, scissors still thrust into the middle. Red leather chairs were pulled up to the long worktable, cluttered with files and papers.

He'd spent five hours here last night, sitting at her desk or standing over this table, going through her papers. Adrian was right—Jess ran this company. Her accounting system was an amazing machine of numbers, wheels within wheels, intricate as a snowflake. She gave orders to a man like Pitney, and they were obeyed. This big, central office was hers, even though the Whitbys might only be in England one month out of the year. This wasn't the dollhouse of some favored daughter. Merchants worked here. They opened bolts of cloth on that long table and sifted handfuls of loose tea. Men rolled up their sleeves in this room and ran a trading company. A dozen men and one woman.

"He'd purely like to take a swing at you." Jess looked small behind the big desk. None of it showed. Not the brilliant mind. Not the courage. "Pitney, being protective. I wish he wouldn't do that. At his age, he should know better. You'd take him to pieces."

"I don't fight old men."

"Prefer a challenge, do you? You can argue with me, then." She shuffled papers, scowling at them, shimmering with anger. She was so damned lovely doing it. *She must ambush every merchant who comes in here. They don't know how to deal with her.*

I do. He didn't make a sound, walking the last of the way toward her. The Isfahan carpet was soft as moss on a forest floor. "I was going to tell you about it this morning, what we did here, but you took off at the crack of dawn. I didn't want you to see this without any warning."

"A warning? Well, that would have made it all right then. A warning. When we were talking in the garden last night, you were planning to break in here." She glanced up long enough to see the answer in his face. "Must have been amusing as hell for you, sitting there, fooling me."

"It wasn't like—"

She slammed the drawer closed. "It was exactly like that. I see why you're such a canny trader. You never said a word that wasn't true, and all the time you were lying up a storm. You made me like you. That's clever, doing that."

He'd done more than make her like him, and they both knew it. He'd made her want him. He intended to keep doing that. There wasn't much he wouldn't do, binding this woman to him.

He had other crimes to admit. He'd drag them all out and get it over with. "I was in your hotel in Bloomsbury yesterday."

She didn't understand at once. The long, straight brows drew together.

"We went through every drawer, every book, paper, every box. Everything you own." How did a man apologize for that? Especially since he'd do it again, if he had to. "I'm honestly sorry. I had to know if you were part of your father's treason. I needed proof you were clean."

"Then I hope you got it." The letter she'd picked up

crackled in her fist. "Good-bye, Captain Kennett. You can find the way out, I imagine." When she looked up, he saw the fear underneath the anger. It was a deep, well-practiced fear that looked like she'd been working on it for a while.

He'd earned that anger. But he wouldn't let her be scared of him. "I'm not your enemy."

"Of course not. We're cordial as a pair of nesting doves, you and me. My father's an honored guest down at Meeks Street. Those are purely decorative iron bars all around him." She got up slowly and leaned over her desk, her fists knuckle-down on the wood. "What do you want?"

"I want you to step back from what you're doing. Your father's guilty. You can't help him. You're risking your—"

"My father is innocent. I'd stake my life on it."

With her, it was literally true. "You're careless with your life, Jess." *I'm going to put a stop to that.* The long wood table held files and the loose papers and the notes she'd pinned everywhere. "Do you have any idea what you're doing here? Why don't you light a keg of gunpowder?"

She didn't meet his eyes. "Sometimes, everything's dangerous."

He was going to put an end to this, to Jess playing ducks and drakes with her life. Last night, he'd gone through every paper on her worktable, getting angrier and angrier.

He picked up the nearest stack and pulled out a file. "Do you want me to tell you what you're doing here? You're following . . . who?" He read the name. "Right. He's a rare son of a bitch." He dropped that and took the next file down. "And this ugly bastard—I'm pretty sure he scuttled one of his own ships. Who else?" He flipped his way through. "A simple embezzler. He's wandered into bad company, hasn't he? Here's a sterling citizen who started out as a wrecker down in Cornwall."

"They're not the choir at St. Paul's."

"They're the scum of the docks. Including," he slid the last file across the table, "this one. Sebastian Kennett. You must like him particularly. He's the one you followed down to the docks." He was furious all over again. She'd set her office clerks to trailing him. Asking questions. Poking into his business. They'd followed his family.

She looked back at him, stern as a carved statue. "One of those men is Cinq. I'm going to find him."

"What you're going to do is walk out of your warehouse and disappear without a splash. Shall I tell you what's in all these files? Insurance fraud, shipping shortages, a taste for catamites, one act of piracy, and multiple cases of outright theft. Have I missed any little vices in that list? You have copies of their bank accounts. How the damn hell did you get hold of that?"

"Bribery, mostly. It's a business expense, and we budget for it. Look, I don't know about you, Captain, but I have work to do this morn—"

"No wonder you were attacked on Katherine Lane." He dropped the papers back on the long table. "They must be standing in line to knock you over the head."

"I'm not—"

"You've been risking your neck for weeks." *You could have been dead before I ever met you.* He'd yell right in her face, since he didn't seem to be making an impression. "I'll ship you right out of London in a barrel, if I have to—"

A deadly ripple of fur shot out from under a bookcase.

"Hellfire! What?" He jerked back. Reflexes, honed by years of dodging exotic threats, kicked in. He went for the knife.

It was the ferret, out of its cage. Snarling jaws clamped to his boot, tearing into the leather. "Watch it, Jess! Get back. They bite."

Before he could stop her, she was on the floor, pulling the claws and snarls loose from his boot, clutching the animal against her. "Bad ferret! No!"

Twenty inches of malevolent fur wriggled and cheeped and stretched to lick at her face. She choked out a laugh and settled, tailor-fashion, onto the floor, unselfconscious as a child. "Bad Kedger."

He let his breath out. "Bloody piping peace." He'd seen the thing in its cage last night, hissing and snarling. He'd wondered what a vicious beast like that was doing in her office. "It's a pet. Your pet."

She gave him a sideways glance and the edge of a grin. "This is me mate. Been with me a while, the Kedger. Kedger, meet the Captain."

He tried not to be obvious, slipping his knife back into the sheath in his jacket. His heart was still banging in his ribs. He'd thought the beast was going to take her eye out. "Some women keep spaniels."

"So I hear." She pressed her face into the length of hostile, undulating animal and blew gently into its fur. "Quiet now. That's the beautiful Kedger. Fine boy."

That husky voice insinuated itself into his imagination. The silk of it twined through his body, pulling and stroking. He could almost feel Jess with her face pressed to him, blowing against his skin, murmuring.

He was going to bewitch this woman and intrigue her till she was sleepy-eyed and willing and their mouths got up to all kinds of mischief on each other's bodies.

But not now.

He hardened up instantly, imagining that. This wasn't the time or the place. *Stop it. She's so close to being frightened of me. Think about something else. Think damn hard.*

It was impossible to think of anything but Jess. Out in the clerks' room, the whole length of the room, the blinds were up, letting the morning light in. Sun glared off every desk and cabinet and streamed through to light Jess up from behind. Wisps of hair escaped around her head and glowed like Venetian glass. A gilded girl, in a halo of dazzle.

From under her coiled braid, a black button of a nose emerged, then a gray, pointed snout, then sneaky black eyes. Lips drew back, showing fangs, upper and lower. If it bit her, he'd strangle it. "It's tearing holes in your dress, hanging on that way."

"He's excited. His life's been replete with incident lately." She spread her fingers and let the beady black nose explore between them. "It's kind of unusual, the way he went for you. He doesn't bite just anybody."

"He doesn't bite me either, if he knows what's good for him. Why don't you put that son of a . . . ferret where it won't do any damage."

Her smile widened. She'd enjoyed seeing him dance around, avoiding teeth. He didn't begrudge her a little vengeance. The vermin sneered over the crook of her arm, clicking like a demented clock. She said, "He doesn't fancy you, does he? They say animals always know."

"That's what they say."

"Sees unplumbed depths of infamy in you, I expect." One-handed, cuddling the ferret, she fumbled with the latch of the cage. The ferret ran down her arm, upended, and took a stand on a bit of rolled-up carpet, cursing, tail puffed out like an angry cat's. "He seems nervous today. You would not believe how sensitive ferrets are."

The door of the cage closed. Steel grated between ferret jaws as Jess's sweet, sensitive pet tried to gnaw its way out. Death threats whirled behind its beady eyes.

He thinned his own lips back. *You can be a fur muff by sundown, chum.* He met the glare with one of his own.

The black paws scrubbed together in quick, tiny jerks. Then the vermin turned its back and began grooming itself. He and the ferret understood each other precisely.

"I let him loose down on the main floor after business hours." Jess fiddled with the water dish, poking her finger through the bars. "He spends the night running through the freight stacks, terrorizing the cats. Kedger's always in a good mood after a night rollicking around the warehouse."

She pushed a strand of hair back from her face with a quick circling of her forefinger. It flowed down the shy crevice behind the shell of her ear, unwinding like dribbled honey.

She knew he'd come up close behind her. She was buzzing with annoyance inside, but he felt—he could almost smell—her awareness of him. She wanted him. Jess was a woman, with a woman's knowledge. The heat in her wove through the air between them, to him, and back to her, tying them together.

He'd had lovers, wise and skillful women who'd used every secret of the courtesan's art to arouse him. Jess did that with her smallest gesture, not even trying. She stayed absolutely still, with her back to him and her hand resting on top of the big cage, pretending nothing was going on.

She was lovely, and she drew him like the tides. What the hell was he going to do about it?

Metal *tick-tick*ed on metal. She was playing with the lock. "Pitney's another one Kedger likes to bite. No telling, is there?" She was reminding him Pitney was twenty feet away, glaring through the glass, motionless as a gargoyle. All the time, he could feel the nervous energy radiating off her. Every inch of her skin was gathered up, anticipating, in case he touched her.

Not today. Not tonight. But soon, he'd touch her entirely and everywhere. He'd plunge into her and feel her come apart with pleasure. He didn't plan to make any secret of what he had in mind. Let her anticipate that for a while.

"Jess." Not startling her, he set his fingertips on her shoulder. She was no coward. She turned at once. Her lips were uncertain, full of that pull between them that she didn't like at all. Her brown gold eyes were unflinching.

He could have cajoled a response out of her, even here, even now, when she was angry at him. That was the weakness in a woman like Jess. She couldn't take a good grip on hate. Not the way he did. It didn't burn and broil in her innards like a ball of acid. She couldn't hold a grudge with a pair of fire tongs.

"I'm sorry I ransacked through your things." Give him enough time and he'd talk her into forgiving him, because he was a manipulative son of a bitch and she was a warm-hearted woman.

He wouldn't do it in this fishbowl of an office. Not with Pitney on the other side of that glass window and clerks walking around. He'd do it when he had her alone, and there wouldn't be any interruptions.

I'm going to keep you alive, Jess.

"You're poking a stick at a bear. At thirty-seven arrogant, wealthy, dangerous bears. One of them is going to swat you like a fly."

She shrugged. The soft, dark cotton of her dress slid under his hand.

"Stop baiting those men, or I'll see you locked up at Meeks Street, right next to your father. I'll do that to you, if that's what it takes to keep you safe. Call the hunt off."

"No." She stared at him steadily. That old cur, Josiah Whitby, didn't deserve one-tenth this loyalty.

When he let her go, it was like letting go of sunlight in a dark room. "Find another way."

THE Captain walked out, leaving that little minnow of an apology behind. He was sorry. Hah.

She should have said something clever and cutting. That's what a proper lady would do. A proper lady thought up insults beforehand and kept them ready. Kept a list, like.

Pitney grumbled his way from one side of the room to the other, glaring at every place Kennett had been, thwarted because she hadn't let him start a shoving match in her office.

She plunked herself down at her desk and sat sorting her thoughts into stacks, like letters. "He says he's going to lock me up if I keep hunting Cinq."

Pitney picked up some files the Captain had pushed onto the floor. "He'll do it. Kennett's a man of his word."

"That's an admirable trait, generally."

No matter how she rearranged the quills and paper and ink in the top drawer, they wouldn't look natural again. Damn him.

He'd been in her bedroom. He'd held her trinkets and keepsakes in his hand, studying them with those shrewd, shrewd eyes, picking out tidbits of her mind like he was a scavenging crow. *He saw all me bits and scraps. All my shabby, little memories. They've seen everything, him and the other men. It's like the wind tossed my skirts up and showed off me nether parts to a pack of sailors.*

Next time, I'll let Kedger bite him.

This was how it felt when somebody broke into your house. All those years she'd gone burgling, she'd never known.

She really was a villain, wasn't she? Not just joking with herself and a little proud. She'd done harm and never once noticed. *I wonder how many bedrooms I've rummaged through. A hundred? All those people felt like this.* That was a ledger full of debts she should be paying back.

One of the clerks was at the door, striking a pose so he'd be noticed. She recognized him, vaguely. Even big as Whitby's was, she tried to remember the men, and this one was always underfoot. She caught Pitney's eye. "That clerk, Barnaby. No . . . Buchanan. That's it. Could you see what he wants?"

Pitney went to intimidate a clerk.

Her burgling bag was still in the middle of her desk blotter. She took it down into her lap. It felt comfy there, familiar from all the times she'd carried it. "Dangerous, is it?" Now he had her talking to herself. The Captain's fault. "He can't even imagine dangerous." She ran her fingers over the burlap. "He should see what I'm not doing. The part I'm too scared to do."

This was rope on the side here and hooks and her burgling tools. Souvenirs of the old days. It was organized inside so she could find everything by touch. Nothing jingled or clanked, no matter how much you shook it. "None of his business, anyway. I don't know why I keep this. I haven't used it in years."

Pitney was back. "I told him what to do with his signatures." Pitney'd probably been earthy and explicit. Buchanan, if that was his name, was retreating, posthaste, down the clerks' room.

She got up and let the Kedger out of his cage. He circled the room, his tail perked up high and his fur ruffling.

Pitney said, "Jess . . . What are you planning?"

The Captain should find out what it feels like when somebody paws through his goods and chattels.

She hadn't admitted it to herself, till he asked. But she had her burgling bag out. Part of her had known what she'd do.

"We're going to take a stroll, me and Kedger. I need to look into a few things."

At this hour, Mr. Doyle would be sitting in a public house near Covent Garden, the Crocodile. She'd invite him along. She might even surprise him. There wasn't much that surprised Mr. Doyle.

She clicked her tongue to call Kedger. He swarmed up her chair and began sniffing at the bag. It'd been a while since they'd gone on the stroll together, but he remembered.

"Jess, don't do this. Stop and think. Josiah's going to have my liver and lights if I let you get into trouble while he—"

"While he's in quod and can't stop me. Right you are, Mr. Pitney. He is not going to like this at all." She slipped her bag of tricks over her shoulder, just seeing how it felt. It went home under her arm, all the knobs and bumps feeling right. "The Captain paid us a visit. A polite woman would return the favor."

"The Service has men—"

"Following me. I know. Never lonely when the British Service takes an interest in you. I'll go out the back way." She picked up the bundle of clothes. Kedger, knowing the drill, launched through the air to her shoulder. When she put on her cloak, he scrambled into the big pocket. His place. "You would not believe how much I'm going to enjoy giving them the slip."

THREE men loitered beside a black hackney carriage drawn up to the curb. They could have been Irishmen from one of the work gangs trundling cargo from wagon to warehouse. They might even have worked for Whitby's. Most of the men on this end of the street did. And these three kept a close eye on the front door of Whitby Trading.

Across the street from them and fifty yards down, a lone marine had his back to the wall, waiting stolidly. He was set in place by Military Intelligence. He was Colonel Reams's creature.

Sebastian Kennett's men were inside, in the lobby. The pair sat on the wood bench, under the eye of a disapproving porter, deciphering their way, word by word, through the *London Times*.

The British Service was there. Invisible. A street sweeper. A waiter smoking in front of the tavern. Two men checking

Fourteen

Eaton Expediters

SHE'D ALWAYS LIKED ROOFS. SHE LIKED BEING UP high. There was a whole city up here nobody knew about but chimney sweeps and thieves. Miles of slanting, topsy-turvy roads ran over the gables, across balconies, and up and down chimneys and fences. It was quiet here. Peaceful. Safer than the streets, if it came to that. Her own private London. This was one more thing she gave up when she went respectable.

She'd left her cloak and her woman's clothes with Doyle, at the bottom of a drainpipe two houses down. Might as well lay a ladder up to a house as run a drainpipe. Doyle said if she was going to climb that, why didn't she just jump off Tower Bridge and spare him the apprehension. A fine man to work with, Mr. Doyle.

It was a regular turnpike for cats up here. A fair treat to crawl across.

She squatted on the cornice, keeping low to the roof so she didn't make an outline on the sky. She wore a black scarf wrapping her hair and soot-colored trousers and shirt. If somebody spotted her, she was small enough to pass for a sweep.

Over there, on the other side of the alley, was Eaton Expediters. The jump across was seven feet, give or take.

A solid company. The Captain was only one of the shippers who ran paperwork through Eaton, using them to keep records instead of hiring clerks of their own. He should set up his own premises, though. Kennett Shipping had got to be the size it needed a general manager who stayed ashore and looked after the cargo. Somebody should talk to Sebastian about that.

"It'll be interesting to see his books, anyway. He's highly profitable."

The bag at her back wriggled and listened.

"I might clear him. I have four of the dates secrets were lifted from the War Office. If he didn't have any ships sailing out of London right then, he's clear. Cinq ships his secrets to France, fast as he can peel 'em loose from Whitehall."

Eaton's roof was a steep bit of slate. Nothing more slippery than old slate. And she couldn't rig up a safety line. Everywhere here was rotten stone all through and mortar crumbling like cheese. Disgraceful, really, the way people neglected their chimney pots.

Seven feet. She'd made hops worse than this when she was a kid. Of course, she'd had a partner then, helping out, handling the rope. It was harder, doing this alone. That last time, the time when she fell, she'd been alone, going home after a job.

She wasn't going to think about that.

"Trouble is, the Captain's got just a mort of ships. Always some Kennett ship in the Thames. It's not going to be that easy."

He's not going to lock me up. The British Service isn't finished playing games with me.

The Captain thought the scum of the dock were dangerous. Did he want her dealing with Colonel Reams? That was the other choice. Reams slicked his way in and out of her office, promising to help Papa, promising to give her that list of dates the secrets walked out of the War Office. If she married him.

"I can deal with Reams," she told Kedger. "If it comes to

that. I have a plan." But it was chancy. She didn't like to take risks.

And Reams was a woodland violet compared with what she'd have to face after that. "Always a challenge, innit?"

It was a fine day for burglary. The sky was blue, with clouds piled up way off to the west, looking thwarted. She could see a slice of the Thames from here, raw gold, bright as a mirror. South-facing windows flashed squares of light back to the sun.

Everybody thought burgling was done at night. A fair amount was, of course, but folks are particularly unwary in the daytime. They leave the world unlocked and simplify matters for thieves.

"Time to get going. Those clouds aren't going to hold off forever."

The black bag she had slung under her arm gave a squirm and a wiggle. Kedger's nose peeked out. A ferret at work, sniffing the air. Silent though. He knew to keep quiet when she was on a job.

"If Kennett's Cinq, the money's going to show up in his books." She skritched the top of Kedger's head. "And I'll find it. I am England's expert on skullduggery in accounting."

Right. Kedger nodded.

"I don't think he's Cinq. I wouldn't feel like this, if he was Cinq."

She stretched, loosening up her muscles. That was enough to startle a shirring of sparrows into the sky. The soffits and railings were always full of sparrows, hopping back and forth, changing places for no reason. The dozen she'd roused took off and headed for the river. Higher up, another sort of bird was whooping around in the sky. Martins? Maybe those were Martins. No telling why Martins and Robins had a human name and the rest of the birds didn't. The air could be full of Georges and Clarences and Prunellas if they gave birds proper names.

Whatever birds they were, the five of them were making free with the air, dancing on the wind, practicing their art. Grabbed her breath away, it did, they were so beautiful.

It'd been a good few years since she made a jump like that. "I can do this. I used to do it all the time."

A squeak from the bag at her side. Kedger agreed. Not being a toady. Really meaning it.

She should have spent more time watching birds. Cheerful little buggers, birds. They enjoyed themselves when they flew. They loved it.

She paced off her running space. Four strides. Left, right, left, right. Easy enough. She kicked an old pigeon nest away and watched it fall, end over end. A long way down.

The last time she'd been on a roof, she'd been headed home, working her way down a line of old warehouses, when the slates broke. She slid down into an old airshaft and it collapsed in on top of her. It took them two days to find her. The rats found her first.

Don't think about that.

A clear and beautiful day over the roofs. Almost no wind at all. Couldn't be nicer weather.

Kedger was getting impatient. Not a ferret who took the long view, Kedger. She closed him in and slung the bag to the center of her back, where he'd be safe. She tightened straps here and there. Nothing flapped in the breeze. She looked across the alley. No hurry. No hurry at all.

It hurts when you fall. Hurts like the end of the world. She'd been alone, except for the rats. And the Dark. Toward the end, the Dark started talking to her.

Don't think about it.

Papa never let her climb roofs after she went to live with him, not even for fun. She used to sneak out sometimes. She admitted it afterwards, of course, and he about yelled her ear off. Probably fathers were always strict with their daughters. She should have left him a letter in case she . . .

It was bad luck, leaving that kind of letter.

There's only the sky and the wind and where to put your feet. Nothing else.

Lazarus used to say, if you don't enjoy burgling, you should give it up. No reason to do it if it wasn't fun. *I'm going to enjoy breaking into your books, Captain. Oh, yes. Show you what it feels like.*

She felt light, at times like this. Felt like she was floating inside, clean and empty, and the sky was made of crystal. This was what the birds had.

She gathered herself together and set her eyes on the other side. She rocked, like a cat getting ready to spring. The moment snapped into place. She uncoiled.

One. Two. Three. Four. Her last step struck square and hard on the overhang of the cornice. She threw herself.

And slammed into cold slate on the other side. A narrow, black instant of pain split the sunlight. The slate trembled and beat beneath her. She held on to the slant of the roof.

With a cold, terrifying ripple, she slid.

And stopped. Her bare toes caught and held.

Her skin sucked into the crevices of the roof. *Don't think. Don't think. Don't think.* The roof was promontories of slate, valleys of shingle. She grew like moss. She was part of the roof. The wind swept past her with a cold whistle.

Don't think. Pigeons flapped inches above her head and she didn't blink.

She held on to the roof with her breath and the curve of her cheek. Inching slow as a snail. Slow as the crawl of the sun. No hurry. All the time in the world.

All the time in the world. All the time . . . And at the end she stretched and cupped her fingers over the lip of the fine, sturdy, ornamental pediment of Eaton Expediters and turned her grip to iron.

Got it! A handhold. Give her one solid handhold and she could climb Buckingham Palace.

Time started again. She dragged herself up and over the parapet and dropped onto the damp leaves that collected in the angle of the roof. Safe now. She put her forehead on her knees and hugged herself together. She'd just sit for a while. *I am out of practice.*

"Cut that one close, didin I?" she whispered. "Lazarus would've boxed my ears."

The sack at her back grumbled and shifted, calling itself to her attention. The Kedger was miffed at her. Got miffed easy, Kedger did.

"All rug now. Sorry for the rough ride." She jerked the knot on the drawstring. "Off you go, chum. Enjoy yerself." Kedger was an arc of scuttling gray, up and over the roof peak, galloping down the other side. When they got inside Eaton's, he'd tell her what rooms were empty and which ones had somebody behind the door. He'd warn her if anyone was coming. No surprises when she had Kedger for a lookout.

She crawled to the edge to look over. Four stories down, hats and bonnets meandered along the pavement. No one looked up. They never did. Thieving was all about being in plain sight where folks never looked.

"Most jobs have a bad patch in them." She said it soft, to the scratching of distant claws. "That was our bad patch. The rest'll be easy."

No answer, but she was sure the Kedger agreed.

Eaton's roof was a lengthy business of up and down, up and down, over a row of dormers. Good British workmanship everywhere, with an Italian influence in the molding.

"If I get the Captain crossed off my list, I'll clear out of his house." There were lots of fancy handholds here. A fair treat to crawl across. "Before I wind up in his bed. I feel myself slipping in that direction. I'm not between the sheets yet, but I'm thinking about it more than I should be."

Kedger trailed behind her, just out of sight.

Being righteously angry at the Captain didn't make as much difference as you'd think.

She avoided some guttering. Nobody secured guttering the way they should.

The Kedger's head popped up over the roofline. He poured toward her, carrying something in his mouth. She accepted a button. A little spit and a quick polish on her sleeve revealed it was brass. Amazing what Kedger came up with, even on a roof.

"You're going to make us rich if you keep this up." To please him, she dropped it in the sack. He sniffed after it a minute, then climbed up her arm to investigate her braids. Sniff . . . nibble . . . tug . . . tug.

"Anything in there I should know about?"

The Kedger responded with a comment on women who bounced ferrets around in burlap sacks.

"Sorry, mate. I'll be more careful next time."

He chirruped, still grumpy.

"Are you going to pull all my braids out, or just that one?"

He'd made his point. He took his place on her shoulder and dug his claws in, stretched up tall, and pointed his nose to the wind. *South,* he ordered.

"Fine with me. Let's go visit Captain Kennett's account books."

Two floors down, Eaton's clerks were emptying out of the main room, going to the tavern for lunch. She'd enter through the attic and slide right through an empty building. Lord, but she loved burgling.

ifteen

Meeks Street

IT WAS RAINING IN A SULKY, ENGLISH WAY WHEN she paid off the hackney driver. It wasn't night yet, but windows glowed up and down Meeks Street. There'd be warm fires and bright lamps in all these big, comfortable houses and folks sitting over cups of tea. Cheery.

Meeks Street was a complacent row of stucco houses. They built walls around the gardens to keep the grass and trees from wandering. More trees, with small round leaves, grew in a thin line of garden that ran up the middle of the street. The air smelled wet and green.

Here she was. British Service Headquarters.

As soon as she turned in the gate, the dog started barking inside, deep as a bronze gong. No sneaking up on Number Seven.

It was a dry pain, knotted in her belly, how much she needed to be with Papa. When he was through yelling at her, they'd sit together and talk about Russian sable and brandy and the price of indigo and pretend to each other that everything was going to turn out fine.

The brass plate beside the door read "The Penumbral Walking Club." The British Service, having their little joke.

Yanking the bellpull was one of those pro forma actions. They knew she was here. She could feel somebody watching her from the windows upstairs, from behind the curtains. They'd send Trevor to open the fool door when they felt so inclined.

She waited. The rain settled down to the task of making her miserable. She had time to renew her acquaintance with the green-painted front door and the bars on the windows. There were bars on every window in the house, upstairs and down. The old man who did the cooking in the kitchen downstairs kept a shotgun propped near the window where she could just see it. You'd have to get by him before you even tried for the windows. Then there was the dog. This had to be the least crackable house in London. Not an amazement, considering.

Papa was going to ask about her recent activities. If she didn't tell him, he'd just ask Pitney. Peach on her in a minute, Pitney would.

The lock scraped and the door opened. But it wasn't Trevor who'd come to let her in. It was the Captain. "Are you trying to kill yourself?"

Some days it doesn't shower luck down on you. She'd counted on having a little more time before she had to face him. "Good afternoon to you, too, Captain. Mucky weather we're having."

"You were on the bloody *roof*. Have you lost your mind?"

"There's a school of thought that holds that opinion." Somebody from Eaton had trotted over and told him his books had gone missing. He'd figured out she'd been on the roof. Canny as a parliament of owls, the Captain.

"It's fifty goddamned feet up. One slip, and they'd have scraped you off the pavement into a bucket."

"That's a vivid bit of description. I put your books back before I left. Did they tell you?" When it started raining, she'd nipped back inside and dropped the ledgers off in a corner office, stacked on the desk in a neat tower. "Look, am I going to stand out in the rain till I get old and gray or what?"

He pulled her over the doorsill like he was taking in lobster pots. "You think this is funny? You think I'm not going to lock you up."

"I don't have any idea, actually. I'm disenchanted with locks, lately. Everybody ignores them."

The front parlor at Meeks Street was formal and ugly and damp and stone cold, about as unwelcoming as it was humanly possible to make it. They did it on purpose. She pulled off her cloak. At least it wasn't raining on her in here. They'd do that, too, if they could figure out how.

"Sit. Over. There." The Captain clenched his teeth. If she was his cabin boy, she'd find herself something to do at the other end of the ship, right smart.

"I'm here to see my father, not you."

"Do what I say and you'll see him a lot quicker."

The Captain was going to be a stone wall when it came to reasoned argument, so she went over and sat, tame and polite, in the chair he'd picked out for her and let him take her wet cloak and bonnet and throw them over the arm of the sofa.

He went down on one knee to toss coal on the stingy, midget fire in the grate and poke at it like a demon on duty in hell. Oh, he was in a champion snit, he was.

The fire, what there was of it, felt good on her face. "You were right about the weather, now that I think of it. You said it was going to rain today."

"You could have killed yourself, getting to my damned account books. Don't do that again. Don't do anything like that again."

So they weren't going to talk about the weather. "Fine. Next time I'll sneak in at night and tie up the guards and ransack the place. That's the way it's done. And I'll steal the boiled sweets."

The fire wasn't going to get her warm, not if he poked at it till doomsday. She leaned her head against the back of the scratchy, red velvet chair and closed her eyes. She was always cold and tired these days, and she'd been up since dawn. The glow she'd brought back from milling Eaton's had worn off. The joke didn't seem funny anymore—just desperate and scary and moderately pointless. "You'd think it'd put a crimp in this rash of housebreaking we've been having, the amount of rain that falls in this town."

"Don't fall asleep on me."

When she opened her eyes, sure enough, he was standing over her with his let's-keelhaul-another-hapless-seaman expression, trying to intimidate her with his size and his muscles and being enraged. Old tricks, but they worked fine.

"You sneaked out the back of Whitby's. You dodged the men I put there to take care of you. You crawled up Eaton's like a damned monkey. You're shivering. You're filthy." He reached out and found a spot of grime she hadn't scrubbed off her cheek. "I could sink a barge in the circles under your eyes. You actually think I'm Cinq."

"You could be." She shouldn't have said that, not straight out. She was too tired for this.

"You think I'm Cinq." He grabbed the back of the chair she was sitting in. She jerked awake. "You think I'm a murderer and a traitor, and you don't have sense enough to get out of my house."

"Nodcock, that's me. You would not believe how many people have pointed that out."

That hatchet face was close, jaw clenched. If half the rumors were true, he'd flattened men with those efficient, sledgehammer fists in every port around the Mediterranean. The other thing they said about him was true, too. He was soft with women. He never thought of touching her when he was like this. In the years that lay between that boy in the cold mud of the Thames and the man he'd become, he'd changed into someone who couldn't lay angry hands on a woman. The chair was having a hard time, though.

"Did you find anything, Miss Whitby? Did you find one solitary jot of proof worth risking your neck up among the chimney pots?" She had a furious, just fit to be tied, angry Captain here. "How is it you've survived in the world as long as you have?"

"One of life's mysteries. I—"

"Did you find one word that says I'm a traitor? One syllable? One line in a ledger?"

Found out you're making a roaring profit on Greek sponge.

"I didn't find anything marked 'payment from the French Secret Police' in among the red coral and carpets, if that's what you're asking. Nobody keeps illegal profit in their company accounts. You'd have to be naïve as a daffodil to go looking for it there."

There were twenty thousand thoughts in back of his eyes. "You're talking about the evidence we have against your father. You've seen—"

"I've seen what your tame forgers planted. You couldn't nick Papa for smuggling, so—"

"This isn't about smuggling."

"You think not? Papa used to thumb his nose at the Customs cutters and sail home with bullet holes through the hull. He's been an itch in the breeches of His Majesty's government for twenty years. Now they're scratching him."

"The British Service doesn't play cat's-paw for Customs."

"They work for the Foreign Office." *I'm going to regret making him this angry.* "And the War Office, and the bloody lord high admiral. They all want to pick the bones when Whitby's falls. So the Service jiggery-pokeries up the proof."

"Bilge."

"You arrested Papa on *nothing*. On lies."

"Don't call me a liar, Jess." An inch from her cheek, his hands bunched and strained. His tendons hardened into iron.

But it wasn't just anger. Anger wasn't the half of it. All this time he was yelling at her, he wanted her so much he was shaking. He kept his hands clenched on the chair so they wouldn't get loose and drag her over to that cold, lumpy red sofa. That was how much he wanted her. The force of his self-control crashed on her like high tide on a breakwater.

"You should back away," she whispered. They both knew what was going on. There wasn't enough ignorance in this room to cover the palm of her hand. "You don't want to do this."

"You're talking to a bastard sea captain, Jess. Let me tell you exactly what I want to do." Soft words. Soft words. He didn't move an inch. "I want to haul you over to the nearest flat surface and flip your skirts up. I want to climb on top and lace my fingers right down into the marrow of your bones and cast off and fly. I want to sail you like a kite in the sky. I want you holding on to me for dear life."

"Oh. Well." A kite. Flying in the sky like a kite. It might be like that with him. Everything south of her brain wanted to go tumbling through the sky with him.

He said, "I spent the last three hours waiting for somebody to knock at that door and tell me you were dead."

She could see him, waiting out the hours while she'd been enjoying herself on the roof. Him, pulling back those thin curtains upstairs every time a carriage came down the street. Him, pacing the room. Plenty of time to get angry. She'd walked into all that anger. "You don't plan to actually try any of that, do you? The flying part. I thought you were leaving it up to me. I don't like the looks of that sofa."

"Hell." He lowered his great dark head. "Bloody hell." His hair fell forward over his face, shiny and black as poured ink. She wanted to reach out and slide her fingers right into that. A shiver ran through her, everywhere under her skin, when she thought of stroking his hair, smooth as water and warm from the fire. She was a fool.

He let go of the chair, deliberately, finger by finger, and pushed away from her. Everything about him was leashed power. Everything disciplined. "Go see your father."

He stomped across the room. His shoulders and the back of his neck kept right on being expressive. When he ended up in front of the ugly sideboard next to the parlor door, he looked in the mirror and their eyes met. Lord, but he was hungry. He could have been a wolf howling down the whole length of the cold night sky and she was the moon or something. Not paltry, the Captain's appetite.

Time to get out of here, before he came up with new ideas. A kite. Hah.

She had to pass him to get to the door that locked off the rest of the house. She wasn't surprised when he put out his arm to block her path. Part of her had been waiting for that. Maybe she'd walked by him this near so he'd stop her. The little jar of touching him, light as a leaf falling, shocked her breath away.

He said, "One more thing."

The fine, white Irish linen of his sleeve stretched out in front of her. She stared past him, at the door, barely breathing. But he didn't move. Of course, he was too canny to touch her, here, where the Service might be listening and Papa was locked up down the hall. That was why Sebastian Kennett was so good at destroying her peace of mind. All that cleverness.

He might be Cinq. Or he might be a reasonably honest man who just wanted to hang her father. No way to tell. Being this close to him felt like running along a dark coast at night, five or six miles out at sea, and not knowing whether that line of land was friendly or about to reach out with cannon and grappling hooks and claw the ship down into the sea.

He took over the space between them and filled it with his breath and his heartbeat and the heat that was coming off his body. He smelled of sweat and anger. Totally male. She kept having these awkward moments with the Captain.

"I wouldn't keep black dealings in the company books," he said. "You know that. You went up to the roofs, trying to clear me. Because of what's between us."

"There's nothing between us." And that was a right old lie.

The gather of her dress brushed his arm when she shrugged. That set off another shudder. It behooved her to walk away from him, some time or another, and get through that door there. Soon, like.

"You didn't find what you were looking for, did you? As far as you're concerned, I could still be Cinq."

She could have told him, to the shilling, his return on capital for every ship in his fleet, and she didn't have one idea in her head how to go on with this particular conversation. "You could be."

"I'm not. You're going to prove it. While you were larking about on the roof, I went through your charts and calculations—"

"The ones you stole from my office."

"The ones I borrowed."

"You—"

"Put it aside." He made an impatient sweep of fingers

against her cheek, half caress, half comment. "Would it do any good if I apologized? Would you be less angry? Would it wipe away what I had to do? We're finished with that."

No, we aren't. "You took my damn lemon drops."

"And we all enjoyed them. Now listen. You have four dates the War Office lost secrets. You cut your list of blood-thirsty, murdering scum in half, because most of them didn't have ships in London all four dates. I take it Kennett Shipping did."

He was waiting for an answer, so she said, "Yes."

"If I get you all those dates, the dates the secrets went missing, can you find Cinq?"

That's half of what I need. Only half. Sometimes at night, in her dreams, she saw ships slipping across her maps—black ships the size of her thumb, headed for France, carrying secrets, snickering at her.

"Jess . . ."

"The Service doesn't have those dates. It's Military Intelligence. Colonel Reams." Reams wore bright scarlet regimentals and had a big office at the Horse Guards and he made the dregs of the docks look like gentlemen. *Reams will eat me alive if I make one tiny mistake.*

"I know. We'll deal with Reams. Think about how to do it." He took a minute to read her face. "You've already come up with a way to get to him, haven't you? Fine. You'll tell me what you're planning and I'll help you."

I wish you could. I wish I had you at my back, holding the ropes, keeping me safe. "I don't know why you'd help me."

"That's something else for you to think about." He turned and took a long step to pound on the door, telling Trevor to come open it and let her into the rest of the house. "You're going to trust me, Jess. You're halfway to it now." His voice rumbled and buzzed in her bones, clinging to her senses like toffee. The very last of her anger leached away. What topped up the foam on the beer was how much she wanted to do just that. Trust him.

The key turned in the lock. Trevor hadn't been far away.

"When you talk to your father, tell him to get you out of

England. You're not safe here. And stay next to the fire so you don't freeze to death."

PAPA stomped around the study they'd given him, expressing himself. He'd been at it a while. Seemed like it was her day for getting yelled at by angry men.

"Does tha ask me? Does tha? Am I in the Bay of Bengal that tha' can't send word?"

"I—"

"What use is it to me or to anyone, thee dying in thy blood on Eaton's doorstep? Eh? Where am I then, when tha breaks thy neck like a chicken?"

"I was careful."

The windows held a streaky view of rain at sunset, seen through iron bars. Pretty soon, they'd draw the curtains and keep the night out.

"Careful? I swear by God, if I hear tha's been skiperting across the roofs again, I'll put thee on the next ship out of England. I won't have it."

"Yes, Papa." He'd about finished yelling at her, which was a relief to both of them and likely everyone else in the house.

"Pitney don't need another idiot to look after, him having the whole London office for that purpose and half the fools at Customs and the Board of Trade." She was sitting on the low stool by the fire. Papa put his hand on her head, as if she was still a child. "Tha's to stop taking daft risks."

He was worrying about her. Papa was locked up, and any hour of any day they could take him off to Newgate Prison and lay charges against him. He wasted his time worrying about her. "I'm careful."

"Oh, that's a reet comfort, that is. My Jess says she's careful. Where's thy common sense, lass? If tha' need must break into Eaton's, *hire* a man. There's sneak thieves on every street corner. It's not like we don't have the brass."

Might as well shout her business from the rooftops as hire a thief. Not a one of them honest. "Yes, Papa."

"Or bribery. There's a mort of trouble saved in this world by simple bribery. Happen that's how someone got his fingers into our books to plant the poison. It'll turn out to be one of the clerks and a little bribery."

"Happen you're right."

He set his knuckle on her cheekbone, telling her all the things he wasn't going to put into words. "Tha's a gradely bruise forming here. Very fetching."

"I've been avoiding mirrors. But it's not important."

"Not important to tell thy father tha'd been hurt? I must hear it from Pitney. He comes and tells me and looks ashamed the whole time. Tha's put him between two loyalties, Jessie. It wasn't well done of thee."

That was another of the demons clawing at her. She had to see Pitney get grayer and more haggard every day he walked into the office. Pitney worried about her. "I'm safe enough. Did you know I have bodyguards trailing after me? I swagger around town like that Roman emperor everyone was aiming knives at. Caesar."

"That'll be some of that expensive education I bought thee."

"So it is. I'm hoping for a lull in folks attacking me, what with these vigorous men following me everywhere. And I moved out of the hotel. I've gone into hiding, like." She didn't mention she was hiding in the Captain's house and that he might be Cinq. A delicate omission, her governess used to call that sort of thing. "You wouldn't believe how cautious I'm being."

She'd made him smile. "Tha hasna taken care since the day tha was't born." Papa squeezed her shoulder and let go and walked across to close the curtains. "The Foreign Office came by again."

"Ah."

The Foreign Office had got worried about the Whitby holdings in the East, afraid Jess Whitby might absentmindedly marry some Frenchman or Russian. It was all nods and winks and nobody saying anything right out, but the bottom line was, if she married some reliable Englishman they picked out and gave him half the company, Papa walked free. How long he'd live after that was anyone's guess. Nobody more ruthless than diplomats.

Except the military. Colonel Reams didn't wink and hint. The colonel made his proposal right to her face, all hoarse and threatening and spitting a little when he got excited about the whole business. He was another one promising to set Papa free, the minute the ink was dry on a marriage license.

They must all think she was a right idiot. "Colonel Reams dropped by the warehouse."

"Ah." Papa settled the curtains, one against the other, closing off the draft, making it snug. "Bidding, then."

"Bidding." On her. The Military and the Foreign Office were watching each other, and both of them watching her.

Papa said, "Don't be alone with Reams. Keep Pitney by." A wise man, Papa.

They'd been in less comfortable prisons. This was a good strong fire at her back. The *Times* lay open on the desk. An old pewter chocolate pot was set by the hearthback to keep warm. Papa's clay pipe had its rack on the mantel. The Service took care of Papa, if you ignored the bars on the window and the fact they were about to hang him.

She wouldn't tell him she planned to burgle Kennett's study tonight. They could find other things to talk about.

"I took Kedger with me today, when I visited Eaton." Good. Her voice was steady as a rock. "He had a grand time, just like the old days. He must have brought me every quill in Eaton's, one after the other. A right muck he made of it, too. Got himself spotted like a leopard. Ink everywhere."

SEBASTIAN found Adrian in the stuffy little room the Service used as a listening post, leaning on the wall, tilting a black-bound notebook to the lantern light. "We need to talk."

"Don't snarl at me, Bastian. I don't send her crawling around on roofs."

"You didn't stop her."

"I am not, all evidence to the contrary, omniscient. I had

no idea she planned that particular idiocy." Adrian put a finger in the notebook to mark his place. "If you keep your voice down, the Whitbys will not hear us and be distracted from what is doubtless an illuminating conversation."

In the room next door, Jess was catching hell from her father. The walls vibrated with a bass voice, bellowing. Then came an interval of quiet that might be Jess, answering softly. Then Josiah, yelling again. Fine. Let the entire Coldstream Guards harangue her if it would keep her off the roofs.

Trevor, square, serious, and young, was taking notes. He hunched at the table to the side, his ear pressed to a brass ear trumpet that curled up out from the wall. His pencil cast a twitching shadow in the white oblong of light that came from the open side of the dark lantern.

There wasn't space for three men in this cubbyhole. Sebastian flattened himself against a rack of pistols. "I'm going to stuff her in a damned crate and ship her to China."

"Will you?" Adrian gave him the same meditative consideration he'd been using on the book. "Welcome to the select band of men who want to ship Jess somewhere distant and inaccessible."

"She's going to break her neck trying to save that old hyena. Or somebody will break it for her." There were a dozen ways for Jess to kill herself. She seemed to be trying them out, one after another.

Trevor kept writing. He had a smirk on his face, as if he enjoyed eavesdropping on Jess.

"*Enough.*" He slapped his hand on Trevor's notes. "This stops."

The boy shoved to his feet, fists bunched at his side. "I don't take orders from some—"

Maybe he'd take this pup outside and teach him some manners. "They know you're listening."

"Trev." Adrian waited till the boy scowled and opened his fists. "Take Whitby his tea. Put some sausages on the tray for Jess. She forgets to eat when she's engaged in lunacy."

"We should keep her here, where she'd be safe. Captain Kennett," the boy crammed a barrelful of derision into the title, "just wants to get her into bed. It's obscene, letting him put his hands on her when he's the man piling up evidence against her father. We could make her comfortable, and she'd get to be with her father. We could put her in the second guest room."

"How snug," Adrian murmured. "Our very own collection of Whitbys."

"He's not taking care of her. Besides—"

"Besides, you want to run around holding the key to her bedroom. Having beautiful women in your clutches isn't nearly as much fun as you'd think, Trev."

The boy was young enough to blush. "It's not like that."

"You disappoint me. Take your notes with you, and this," Adrian held up the book he'd been studying. "Galba wants the summary by tomorrow morning. Translate the Russian for him. It's not one of his languages." When Trevor didn't move he added gently, "Now."

A muscle twitched in the boy's cheek. "It'll get done. You're making a mistake handing her over to him." He slid pencils into the pencil case, taking his time. "She's said all along those are forged entries in the Whitby books. Maybe the Captain did it. He's the only man who's had them." He clicked the door closed behind him. Quietly.

What the boy needed was a year scrubbing decks on a merchant schooner. Fortunately, Adrian's apprentice spies weren't his problem. "Is that the British Service theory now? That I'm Cinq?"

"That is Trevor's working hypothesis. But he's fifteen and smitten. And he's never shared a filthy French pigeon loft with you." Adrian sat on the edge of the table in front of the lantern, blocking most of the light. "If you feel the need to discuss that with him, don't break the bones in his right hand. I need them. Why am I talking to you instead of eavesdropping on Whitbys?"

"Common decency."

"A virtue in short supply hereabouts. Did I explain to you that we're spies? Surely I mentioned that at some point."

"Give her some privacy with her father. She doesn't have many more hours with him before he hangs."

"I'd rather not hang him at all, thank you."

I wish we didn't have to. I wish he wasn't Cinq. "You're scaring her. I want you to talk to her, face-to-face."

"She won't see me."

"Do it."

"There are very few things I can give Jess at the moment. My absence is one of them." Carefully, because the metal was hot, Adrian turned the dark lantern, lighting up a different portion of the room. "I'm playing jailer here. I'm not going to force her to be polite to me to get to her father."

"She thinks you're going to hang her."

A fierce, impatient shake of the head. "She can't think that."

"She does." He let the silence lie.

"I suppose I deserve that." Adrian rubbed thumb and forefinger together, looking at them. "How very far we have come from St. Petersburg. You will convince her she's being ridiculous."

"Not while you're sneaking around behind the walls, peering and taking notes. She's afraid of you. Talk to her, for God's sake."

"She would appall us both by spitting in my face."

The door opened inward. "There you are." Doyle, wet-haired, radiating cold, stood holding the knob. "And the Captain. Good. Is that damned unrestful woman going to stay put for a while? I want to send the boys home and call in a new lot."

"You should have an hour." Adrian gestured to the wall behind him. "Trevor's bringing food. She'll stay to see Josiah eats."

"I'll get some food, too. No telling what she'll decide to do next." Doyle's greatcoat dripped lines of wet onto the hall carpet. "I would very much like our girl tucked up safe in bed tonight. All night. Can you see to that, Captain?"

Doyle had a lot to answer for. "Why the hell didn't you stop her?"

"Now that's exactly what I keep asking myself." Doyle reached up easily, hooked his fingers over the door frame, and leaned into the cubbyhole, looking from one man to the other. "The whole time she was climbing the side of that building like a fly I asked myself why I didn't talk her out of it." He snorted. "Next time you two come along and try."

"No, thank you." A slim black knife appeared in Adrian's hands, tossed from palm to palm. "I kept her out of mischief for three nerve-wracking years. If you think she's bad now you should have known her at twelve. Is the Irish contingent doing anything interesting?"

"Hanging around Kennett's place, pestering the servant girls when they go out. Watching the Whitby warehouse. Following Jess. Fletcher's boys and girls are keeping an eye on them, but there's no sign of Cinq. Not yet." Doyle glanced both ways in the hall. "I'd like Trevor on duty, if you can spare him. He needs time on the streets, and it'll get him away from Jess." There was no trace of Cockney in Doyle's voice. "He's unreliable when it comes to the girl."

"We all are." Adrian stilled. In the dimness, the knife was nearly invisible. The thin silver line of a razor edge seemed to hang, suspended. "Let Trev be gallant. We get so few chances."

If he annoys me, I can always send him to Madras. "She's making you into a bogeyman. Face her."

"It's not that easy."

"Because you arrested Whitby?"

"Mostly." Adrian tossed the knife and caught it, two-fingered, by the blade. He'd done that a thousand times in the years Sebastian had known him. Toss and catch. "There's more to it."

Doyle said, "Just tell him."

Adrian laid the knife on the table beside him. "The last time I spoke to Jess . . . I'd managed to get Josiah shot through the lung. We were old friends, and he let me use the mansion in St. Petersburg as a base of operations. A mistake on his part, as it turned out."

"Josiah knew what he was doing," Doyle said.

"There were three or four dead men in the salon and I was carrying one of those vital documents we always seem to have. The fate of nations depended on it, of course." His voice was bleak as sea water. "So I walked out. I left Jess in the front hall, with the tsar's men breaking down the door and her father's blood running out through her fingers." Adrian's face was in shadow. Only his eyes picked up a gleam of light. "He lived. Jess and Josiah spent a month in a Russian prison and Jess never forgave me."

"You never forgave you," Doyle said. "You saved twenty, maybe thirty men's lives. If the Russians had got that memorandum back, it would have been a thousand dead."

"I shall wrap that warm thought around me in the long reaches of the night. She was fourteen."

He didn't want to see what was showing in Adrian's face. "It's been years. Whitby's alive and snapping. Jess can get over being annoyed at you. I'll set up a meeting at my house."

Adrian picked up the knife again. "I'll think about it."

"You do that."

The brass listening-funnel that extended from the wall was filled with wisps of Jess's voice. He could almost understand. If he stayed here, he'd keep trying to. "I'll be upstairs going through Jess's papers. Send somebody home with her when she's through with her father." He put his hand on the door. "Not just a guard. She needs company, so she's not alone." It galled him to say it. "Send the boy."

"Trevor?" Adrian gave a spark of amusement. "He will manfully protect her through the wilds of Mayfair, hoping for brigands. He's green with envy that you got to kill men for her. I am very glad she is *not* locked up here. Sebastian . . ."

Trevor could daydream all he wanted to. "What?"

"Subdue your gentlemanly scruples for a minute. I want you to look at this." Adrian pulled aside the curtain on the wall to show a panel set at eye level.

"I won't spy on her."

"But you pass the idle hour pawing through her dainty underlinens. These distinctions escape me. To be hair-splittingly accurate, I am spying on him, not her. They know I'm watching. Think of it as a sort of game. Be quiet now. They can hear us when I open this."

Adrian closed the lantern and threw the room into darkness. The panel opened smoothly to show a square of light, filled by mottled fabric. The other side was a bland landscape on the wall of the study. He doubted it fooled the Whitbys for a minute.

Jess sat on a low footstool in front of the fire, her hands clasped together, her forearms resting on her knees. Her hair was loose from the long braid, drying. Josiah Whitby, short, barrel-bellied, heavy-shouldered, and bald, stood beside her, his hand spread on the cascade of wheat-gold hair.

Faintly, he could hear the man say, ". . . a job lot of woolens. MacLeish can do the bidding. There's space on the *Northern Light* for the next St. Petersburg run."

"I can buy tea," Jess said. "I don't know why everyone thinks I can't bargain for tea."

"Tha's a fine, wise lass and I wouldn't send thee to dicker for soap in a bathtub."

Whitby wore the dun-colored worsted coat and old-fashioned breeches of a stout countryman and a poppy-red silk waistcoat. How had that squat, brown toad sired a woman like Jess?

After a minute, Adrian closed the panel. "That's what I wanted to show you. Them together. Do you think he could be Cinq, and she wouldn't know?"

It was easier to hate Whitby when he didn't have a face. "She isn't going to let go of him, is she? Whatever happens."

"She won't let go. There is no end to her loyalty, Sebastian. She might even forgive me."

"The evidence says he's Cinq."

"Forget the evidence. I spread my own entrails over the rocks and took auspices. My guts are never wrong. Think about this. Just think," Adrian said. "Would a man who wears waistcoats like that commit treason?"

ixteen

Kennett House, Mayfair

IT WAS MIDNIGHT WHEN SEBASTIAN PAID OFF THE hackney. The house looked quiet under the rain, with one light in the lantern at the front door and another in Eunice's room, upstairs. It was pouring down, cold and harsh, but he made the round of the house, unlocking the gate to the garden and checking everywhere, just to be sure. Nobody was lurking in the areaway or the stairwell. Nobody in the wet bushes in back.

There was no trace or track of Doyle's men out in the dark. He didn't expect to see them.

At the side of the house he shaded rain off his face with his hand and looked up. Jess's bedroom window was dimly lit. Eunice had found a night candle for her. Good. He hoped Jess was sleeping, not lying awake, worrying.

Nobody could get to her tonight. He climbed the steps to the house that had once been his damn-hell father's and was now his and let himself in with his key.

The foyer was piled with merchandise of some sort. He threw his sopping greatcoat over the bannister. Eunice, carrying a candle, walked around stacks of boxes toward him.

"There you are, dear." She steadied herself with a hand on his shoulder and stood on tiptoe to kiss his cheek. "Such a night. I wondered whether you'd come home or sleep on the *Flighty*. I told them to leave lights in the hall, just in case. Jess is tucked up safely."

"Thank you." He didn't have to say what he was thanking her for. For taking care of Jess. For telling him Jess was safe. For knowing that it mattered. It was good to be home.

"I sent for her pet, by the way, and we've installed him in her bedroom. That should steady her. She's promised to keep it upstairs, so it won't bite Quentin again."

Now he was giving hospitality to the vermin. He'd known it was going to happen sooner or later. "Good idea."

He dropped his hat on the side table, next to Quent's big dispatch case. It was half-open, with fifty papers ready to slide out and get lost. Tomorrow, Quent would swear he'd locked it tight as the Bank of England. He had a mind like a sieve. God only knew what damage he did at the Board of Trade.

"That young man who works for Adrian brought her home. Trevor Chapman. I asked him to stay for dinner, and he stared at her over the lamb cutlets as if she were the Holy Grail. Very bracing for her, I should think, to have an ally there. I gave her a whiskey after supper instead of tea, so perhaps she'll sleep. What does Adrian intend for her father?" After a pause, she said, "I'll ask him, if you can't say."

"We don't know yet. We just don't know." He rubbed the back of his neck and looked around. He was used to wood crates arriving, but these had an ominous shape to them. "Why is the front hall full of coffins?"

"Armor."

He must have looked blank. She said, "Full body armor. Medieval."

"I don't object, but why is someone sending us armor?"

"Historical Society meeting."

He'd forgotten. Another damn thing to worry about. "The last Friday of the month."

"Which is tomorrow. Teddy Coyning-Marsh is giving the lecture. He's very solid on German mercenaries, I believe, but he does tend to ramble. The men are coming tomorrow morning early to assemble the upright figures. We will arrange vambraces and gorgets and couters upon tables in the drawing room. Far too many people are coming, of course, and they'll chatter through the lecture. I wish some nameless fribble hadn't decided the Historical Society was fashionable."

"If you'd stop feeding them, they wouldn't come."

"It's not as if the food was reliable. They come to see what the next culinary disaster will be. I've bullied Jess into coming on the grounds that a minor annoyance will distract her from more important ones. You needn't attend if you don't want to, but I'd feel better if you were taking care of her."

His house would be packed with rich dilettantes and socially ambitious matrons. They'd eat Jess alive. Or she'd eat them alive. Either way, likely to be an interesting evening. "I'll be there."

"Good. Standish is going to display the Agamemnon krater in the front parlor. For the armament on it. And Windham will be here. He has promised faithfully not to discuss the Reform Bill. You look tired, Bastian. When did you last sleep?"

He'd spent last night rummaging through Jess's office and today going through copies of her papers. "I'm headed up to do that now."

"A few weeks ago you told me you'd found the man responsible for sinking the *Neptune Dancer*. You said you knew the name of the traitor. You meant Jess's father, didn't you?"

"Yes."

"I spoke with him several times, three years ago. Standish was shipping pots to that German collector. Your Whitby impressed me. An astute man. Straightforward, unpretentious, very hard underneath. Honest, I think. I find it difficult to see him as a traitor."

Here was one more person, telling him Whitby was innocent. Just about a clean sweep. "There's evidence."

"So I should imagine. Sleep. We'll talk in the morning." Eunice pushed him in the direction of the stairs.

He didn't take a candle with him. Upstairs was black as a coal pit, but he navigated darker decks every night at sea.

Jess was in the attic. Not far away at all. She'd be under the covers, wearing one of those soft, pretty nightdresses she favored. If he knocked on her door, she might invite him in. They hadn't finished talking.

But neither of them was interested in just talking. "The hell with that." He undressed in the dark and lay down in bed. He could feel Jess in his house, as if she were a sound just out of the range of hearing. As if she were a spinning top somewhere, humming.

JESS heard the night watchman calling two o'clock and woke herself up. She was in bed, in the chill of a rainy night, in the middle of the sleeping city, in her room in the attic. A tiny lamp burned dim and yellow in one corner. The curtains were pulled to shut the Dark out. It was raining steady now, a muffled tapping on the roof just a foot or two away. Made her think of being shipboard. She'd spent a lot of nights at sea, listening to rain on the deck above.

Kedger slept in a ball at the bottom of the bed, picking the one spot where he'd get kicked every time she turned over. He had a wide streak of perversity, that ferret.

Time to be up and doing. It took half a minute to pull her working kit from under the bed, Kedger nosing and sniffing at it the whole time. She didn't want to get caught roaming the halls with these useful toys, so she folded them into a shawl and put it in place, secure and unobtrusive, around her shoulders.

Carrying a candle, she went down the stairs, stealthy as thin soup, with Kedger loping along behind her.

Dark closed in behind her as she passed. Dark waited everywhere outside the circle of light. She knew about Dark. Dark is huge. At night it slithers out of the cellars and rears up, solid and powerful, big as half the world. It stretches out on every side, all the way to dawn. Dark was hungry for her. She could feel it staring at her back, every step she took. If she stopped and held her breath, she'd hear the rustle of it in the corners.

Pitiful, when a woman her age was scared of the dark.

She was on the second-floor hall now, where the family slept. She set her feet down softly. She knew—somehow she was absolutely certain of it—that Sebastian was a light sleeper. She had to be, as she used to tell her old thieving cronies, quieter than an army of mice.

Down the hall. This was Claudia's room. It smelled faintly of violet pastilles. Quentin's room. That was soap and leather polish. Then she was outside the Captain's bedroom, just across the hall from his study. Kedger sniffed along the bottom of the study door and passed it as empty. She jiggled the skeleton key in the lock. The tumblers turned over, silent as water, and she slipped through the door and closed it behind her.

She lifted the candle, shielding it with her hand. Captain Kennett's study. Hers for the taking.

His office was like him, practical and shipshape and—if she was going to be honest—intimidating. His desk sat foursquare in the center and commanded the place. Rolled maps were in the rack in the corner, ledgers in a bookcase at the wall. Newspapers were piled up and tied with string. She did that, too. She saved newspapers and journals and took them on board. Mornings, when the sky was clear and there was nothing but blue water to the horizon, she'd haul a chair on deck and put her feet up on a coil of rope and drink coffee from a mug and catch up on stale old news.

Kedger wandered off to investigate the desk, looking for quill pens. She padded over to take her own intelligent interest in the Captain's affairs.

There'd be evidence here, if Kennett was Cinq. Not a letter signed with a pair of dice, but names and places and numbers that didn't add up. There'd be a whiff of corruption in the accounting. She was hoping not to find anything.

A big folder sat in the middle of his desk. When she untied the ribbon and opened it up, she found a nice collection of lithographs and watercolors, and some maps. Maps so old they crumbled at the edges. She couldn't judge art, not the way Papa did, but these looked very fine. They'd have been a temptation to her, some years back, when she was still thieving. She retied the ribbon, getting the bow exactly right.

"More like it was than it was to start with," Lazarus used to say.

Then she sat herself down comfy in Sebastian's chair to do some invading of his privacy. Sebastian's desk smelled like the ocean. He carried the sea home with him in his pockets, rolled it up in his maps, buckled it into the leather telescope case. Salt water smell.

She lit candles on his desk—there were five of them in the lamp under the green shade—and blew hers out. It was quiet in the West End this time of night. Under the wind, the house creaked like a ship. If she listened hard, she'd hear the Captain breathing. He wasn't that far away.

He struck her as a man who'd sleep naked. He'd be stretched out long and lean in the sheets, relaxed, rocking a little with his breath, like a ship at dock. If the Captain had been a ship, he'd be one of those Revenue cutters. He'd be all prow and proud lines and boards lapped down tight. Deft and shipshape. Implacable, the way Revenue cutters were. Skillful in motion. Wise with the sea. Powerful.

He was strong and fierce and sleek-bodied. She wasn't thinking about coastal vessels anymore. She was imagining his body above her. Herself, rocking under him, being the sea that held his ship. Opening to him. Rising up to meet him.

And that was a waste of time and a frustration and just a blatant invitation to madness, thinking like this.

The first three drawers in his desk slid out easy as butter. Citadels of dullness. When honest folk had something to hide, they locked it up. Saved a thief endless trouble.

If she just went and got into the Captain's bed and didn't make any more fuss about it, she'd stop lying awake at night. She'd stop jerking out of sleep, sweating and gasping, her body twisted around her pillow. She'd stop dreaming about him. She'd sleep like a rock in the Captain's bed, after they were through with each other. There was nothing like the sleep after lovemaking. That was sleep of some profundity.

Morals that would make an alleycat blush, that's what she had.

What she wanted was in the bottom drawer. Well, well, well . . . Eureka, as one of her governesses was fond of saying when she found her knitting bag. *We have found something worth locking up.* She pulled out the metal box.

The little felt packet was wrapped up in her shawl. It unrolled to reveal the whole sweet set of lockpicks, each resting in its pocket. Her charms, she'd called them in the old days, when she used them fairly often. They were accustomed and friendly as her own fingers.

She crossed her legs and cradled the strongbox into her lap. Not heavy. That was good. That meant she wasn't about to waste her time breaking in on jewelry or coin. And look what a delightful lock was adorning this pretty box. Louis Girard made these in Lyon, every one sneaky and excellent. Had to be something interesting hiding behind all that intricacy.

What are you hiding, Captain? What do you care about this much?

She closed her eyes to pick, the way she always did. Lord, but it was satisfying to be busy with something she loved. Back when she used to go a-stealing, the men she worked with told her she whistled under her breath when she picked a lock. She never noticed it herself, but it used to make them nervous as hell. They were always breaking her concentration to tell her to shut up.

She never got annoyed at locks the way some people did. It was such a joy when your fingers finally saw how the tumblers fitted together, and the whole sweet mechanism lay in your hands, ready to swing open.

Maybe this was how Sebastian felt when he was trying to seduce her . . . like he was opening a complicated lock. Except he was more like that Greek cove who just cut the whole business in half with a sword. Her governess had been right. There was more to those Greek stories than you'd think.

The clock marked the half hour. Kedger balanced up on his back feet and stood up and watched her. The lock made tiny, contented, burring sounds, like a pigeon, as she eased the picks around.

She'd learned lockpicking from Lazarus. He'd stolen dozens of locks for her to practice on. He didn't let her pick pockets, not from the day he bought her. It made sense, of course. It had to be more profitable robbing a strongbox than a pocket, and it was no more dangerous, since you got hanged either way.

Nothing in London was safe when she'd been Hand. Damn, but she'd been good.

The lock clicked open. She let her breath out, long, slow, and contented. The box was hers. Captain Sebastian Kennett could just stir that in his tea. That would teach him to put his trust in expensive ironmongery.

She chucked the banknotes out. Lots of them. The Captain liked to be prepared, didn't he? Funny to think of banknotes as something to clear out of the way. Time was she'd have fetched that home to Lazarus and counted this an evening well spent.

What the Captain had here was letters. Lovely, lovely, letters. She lifted out the stack and flipped it, starting from the bottom.

Letters from other shippers and traders. Letters from his agents in Greece and Alexandria. He gathered up news, just like Whitby's did. Politics, cargoes in and out, shaky banks, and suspect merchants. And some letters of credit Kennett had issued. He wasn't earning as much return as he should be. He needed a business manager, really, to tighten up how he handled liquidity. Kennett Shipping was large enough to afford one.

In the middle of the stack she came to a thin blue notebook, the sort of thing a schoolboy might write his Latin exercises in. But this was Arabic. And in Kennett's blue black ink. A diary maybe? Had to be something important if he kept it in Arabic and locked up.

He probably thought he was safe, keeping his secrets in Arabic. Thought he was being clever. Hah.

She might not read Arabic, but she could copy it. She pulled writing paper from the top drawer and unstoppered the ink, let the book fall open where it wanted to, and started.

Kedger came over to sit in her lap, helping by nudging her hand every so often.

She'd filled six pages with loops and squiggles and dots when the clock chimed the hour. Time was just scampering along, wasn't it? That was writing from two places. That should be enough to find out what it was.

Time to hurry. Never overstay your welcome. That was
another thing Lazarus had taught her.

More letters. More gossip. Kennett really did run his business well. Statues from Greece. Good profit in that if you
knew what you were about, which the Captain seemed to.
Here was his agent in Marseilles, talking about troop movements with a candor that'd get him shot by the French. Kennett pulled that kind of loyalty out of his people. Some likely
trading ventures into the Balkans. Fascinating, but nothing
she should be looking at.

Then a letter in Italian . . . *"The sale of plans and maps
was completed with only trivial difficulty."*

Plans. She skipped to look at the signature. Giovanni Reggio. She knew the man. A short, untidy, dark rogue who
smelled of garlic—that described half of Minorca—but this
one was shrewd and treacherous and a direct pipeline into
France. Her father used him, too.

*Your merchandise arrived safely in Paris. You may expect
payment from LeClerque to your American brokers within
the week. I have been the soul of discretion, of course, as
always, and the principals in Paris are entirely satisfied.
My correspondent is most anxious for the next shipment
from London. After my oh-so-tiny commission . . .*

Maps and plans. She changed francs to pounds in her
head. The sale had been for 800 pounds. A small fortune.

The letter sank down to her lap, feeling too heavy to hold
up. She sat for a long time, staring at it.

This was how you felt when the ship crunched up on
rocks in the night. Shock and helplessness and nothing
ahead but cold, dark water closing over you. Lots of struggle
you were going to lose at.

She'd worked so hard, looking for this proof. But it had
been almost a game, these last few days, searching his house.
She'd been so sure she wouldn't find anything.

"It's not proof. It's just paper." Kedger nudged under her
hand and she reached to hold him. "It's just paper."

She'd thought she understood the Captain. He was stern

outside. He walked around looking at the world like he was about to board it with a cutlass between his teeth. But she'd felt warmth glowing out of the center of him, like a sun. Cinq would be cold and selfish as winter. Not like the Captain. Could she be so wrong?

Kedger nudged again. She whispered, "It could mean anything. It's no better than what they have on Papa."

She knew what she had to do. She had to give Sebastian to the English authorities. They'd let Papa go. Her father would live, and Sebastian would hang, and she'd crawl away into a hole and be sick. She was sick now.

The clock chimed. She packed everything away neat into the strongbox and closed it up and put all the lights out, except one to carry with her, and went out into the Dark.

HIS bed was next to the window. He liked to turn his head and look out at the sky over the trees in the square when he was falling asleep, losing himself in the stars the way he used to do when he was first mate and took watch. Sometimes, when he was drifting off, he caught himself trying to chart the course of the house, calculating its latitude from the height of the North Star.

He'd fallen asleep to the sound of rain. But he'd passed too many nights in dockside taverns to ever sleep deeply. Stealthy footsteps woke him instantly.

That was light in the hall. That would be his sneak thief, Jess, plying her trade.

She'd crept past Quent's room, not even pausing. Good. He didn't have to go out there and knock his cousin endwise.

She'd stopped outside his door. No. Outside the door across the hall. She was not, unfortunately, coming to share his bed. She was breaking into his study. It took her half a minute to get through the lock. A woman of varied and interesting skills, Jess.

He'd listened to her putter around his office, making rustles and clicks he could barely hear. Then there was no noise at all. Jess was comfortably ensconced, going through his desk. He could almost see her, working away at it when she should be resting.

He lay with his hands clasped behind his head, looking at the night, fighting an absurd impulse to go in there and help her ransack his office. She hadn't slept, had she? Not more than an hour or two. When she was through with this bit of burglary, she'd stumble out into the dawn and start running Whitby's.

He slept off and on, waiting for her to be finished. Keeping watch, in his way. At last, his study door opened and closed quietly. Barely a click. He heard the swish of cloth on skin. She was headed back to her room.

He'd go flush himself out a thief.

He didn't make noise getting out of bed and grabbing a banyan, wrapping it around himself and walking to the door. When he opened up, they were expecting him. Her foot-high gray lookout was reared up, snarling silently. Dozens of tiny, menacing teeth gleamed in the candlelight.

She wore a white nightgown, long-sleeved and high-necked, with a big, dark shawl close around her. Her hair was in two long braids that hung down over her breasts.

"Miss Whitby and escort," he said. "A little restless tonight?" Then he saw her eyes, and it wasn't funny anymore. "What's the matter?"

"I didn't mean to wake you," she said dully. "I went down to the kitchen. I wanted . . . tea." It was a poor, limp, amateur job of lying.

"You were in my office."

She wore the pale, overwhelmed look of somebody who'd been punched in the stomach. "I have to get back to bed."

"What did you find in my office? What?" She'd come across something that shocked her. He couldn't imagine what.

She started away, and he stopped her. He made his hand soft on her shoulder, but he held her there, letting her know he was twice her size and willing to hold on indefinitely. The ferret made a sound like pebbles boiling. "Tell me what you found."

"Nothing." She brushed her face, as if she'd walked through cobwebs. "I can't talk."

"There's nothing to find in that study. What did you see?"

She didn't answer. Her candle was shaking. The candle-light on the wall shivered and swirled like the lights at sea.

He'd come a long way, luring trust out of her, little by little. He'd lost all the ground he'd ever gained. If he let her go, she'd bound off like a gazelle. If he didn't, the damned rodent would take his foot off.

A door opened. Quentin stuck his head out into the hall, wearing a nightcap and blinking like an owl. "Is that you, Bastian? What's the matter?"

"It's just Jess, looking for something. I'll take care of her."

"Miss Whitby? Jess?"

"Go back to bed." He didn't give orders to Quentin often. He didn't remind him whose house this was and who was in charge here. It was hard enough on Quentin, living on another man's allowance. Tonight, he didn't have time to worry about Quentin's delicate sensibilities.

His family would get used to seeing Jess in his bedroom. When she was ready for it. When she wanted them to know. Not yet, though. Not now.

"Sebastian? This won't do. I'm sure this is perfectly innocent, but it presents the appearance of impropriety. I have to say, this won't . . ." Quent stayed ducked behind his door. He wouldn't want to be seen in his nightshirt, showing his skinny shins. He'd always been vain as a monkey. "This is extremely unwise. I strongly suggest you wake Eunice. She is the voice of reason. I don't expect you to take my advice, and maybe you'll—"

"Please. You don't have to bother." Jess squirmed, but quietly, not wanting to call the whole brigade out into the hall. "I didn't mean to wake anyone. Really."

"I'm afraid I must insist. Your situation here is delicate enough without the suggestion—"

The ferret stopped sniffing and clucking. Suddenly, it dropped to all fours and darted down the hall, making a dead set for Quentin. Quent slammed his door just in time.

"I wish he wouldn't do that." Jess shook in his hands and her skin was cold.

Quentin was probably leaned against his door, ear pressed to the wood, listening.

"I'm taking you up to bed. No. Hold your tongue. Or else shout real loud and wake Eunice up so we can discuss your visit to my study." He pushed her down the hall in front of him. The ferret kept pace, slinking close to the wall.

"I don't want to do this," Jess whispered.

"I don't give a damn what you want right now. Go. Upstairs."

He followed her, watching her heels swish in and out of her nightdress. Through that thin cotton she was wearing, he could see her legs outlined by the candlelight. When she twisted to look back at him, her breasts made beautiful shadows, swaying. The nipples were delicate pink, like dainty, round seashells. Yes. Pressed up against the embroidery on the bodice. There were his little friends.

He was going to want this woman when she was a wrinkled hag. Want her everywhere, every day, under every conceivable circumstances. Tonight, when she looked like this, she stunned him.

The ferret scuttled half a staircase ahead, then looped back to look, then ran ahead again, playing chaperone.

She stopped when they got to her door and set a hand out, braced on the doorframe. As if that would make a difference. She was prepared to dig her heels in and discuss this at length. Stiff, nervous, rebellious, she breathed out, "I don't . . ."

"You don't. Not tonight." He'd made his point. "You're going to trust me, one of these days. You're going to trust me more than any evidence you think you've found. More than your own eyes."

He gave her a little shove towards her room, sending her in there alone. "Put the bolt on. I won't leave till I hear it click. And for God's sake get some sleep."

She didn't sleep though. She looked at the plaster ceiling till she'd about memorized it, then decided that, no, she wasn't going to sleep. She got up and took a pencil and paper and went over to the hearthrug.

Time to settle accounts.

The last thing she'd stole had been those jade figurines. There'd been twelve of them, slick to the hand and kind of glimmery green and heavy for their size. She'd had them on her when she fell. For all she knew they were still under the rubble of that old warehouse.

She wrote, "Twelve pieces of jade. White house on Slyte Street." Carved jade from the Orient. She had no idea what that kind of thingumbob was worth. "Ask Kennett about value," she wrote. She'd set Doyle to finding out who'd lived in that house, ten years ago.

I won't believe some damn letter. Especially not a letter from that worm, Reggio.

Three days before the jade, she'd stolen banknotes and gold coins across town in Mercer Street. "Banknotes and guineas. Mercer Street."

Even if I lie to Reams and get the list from him, that's not the end of it.

Thirty gold guineas, more or less. Banknotes. She chewed on the pencil. A hundred pounds? She couldn't just knock on the door and ask them, could she?

Wish I wasn't such a bloody coward.

Better say a hundred and fifty to be safe. She should work out the interest, shouldn't she? Because she wasn't a thief anymore. The books have to balance. Debts must be paid. It was a good thing Whitby's had lots of money.

$\mathcal{S}$eventeen

Garnet Street

SEBASTIAN FOUND HER ON THE LOADING DOCK, moodily watching Irishmen and blacks file past, wood frames on their backs, straps over their shoulders and across their foreheads. They were lugging sacks of rice from the warehouse out to the wagons. A cool wind nipped through the streets, but the stevedores hung their coats along the railing outside and worked in shirtsleeves.

Jess wasn't checking inventory. She stared blankly as the men walked around her. He wasn't the only one watching, wondering why she was there. Her floor manager kept an eye on her in between checking off cartloads.

Her color was better and the bruise under her eye was almost gone. She'd heal a damned sight faster if she didn't spend her nights creeping around his house, breaking into his office. She'd gotten up at the crack of dawn and left for work before it got light. She'd done it to avoid him.

"You missed breakfast," he said.

"I bought a bun at a shop." She acted as if she'd been waiting all morning for him to show up. "I invested in hot cross buns all round, actually. One for me and a dozen for the bodyguards to share among them. And I sent the boy from the front desk to get coffee for everybody. Between you and the Service and Pitney, I'm putting together my own private army. The buns are a line item in the books under 'military supplies, miscellaneous.'"

Light, easy words. But it wasn't the contingent of guards that put that desolation in her eyes.

What are you thinking, Jess? What did you find in my office last night that sent you scampering out of my house this morning? "Interesting cargo?"

She looked at the rice as if she'd just noticed it. "Not particularly. Thirty tons of Carolina Gold, out of Charleston. The contract reads June, clear as day, but that still came as a surprise to some people. It's been on my hands a week. The buyer is Bennet Brothers."

"You're a trusting soul."

"Not really. I have their rice, after all, and I charge them penalties and stowage. Pure profit, since I had to inventory anyway. I wonder sometimes why God made so many idiots. I really do."

"Letter of credit?"

"From Bennet Brothers? You have a sense of humor, Captain. Pound dealing only for Messieurs Bennet. I collected the last of the demurrage this morning, along with the usual bushel of whining. Now I'm getting their rice out of my warehouse before it attracts rats. I hate storing foodstuffs."

Her warehouse was cleaner than his kitchen at home. Maybe he should put a woman in charge of his warehouse storage. "You run a tight ship."

"No profit in being slovenly. There's a whole long list of things I won't keep in this warehouse at all." Two men came out of the stacks, carrying a heavy trunk between them. She flattened to the wall to get out of the way. She still hadn't looked directly at him. "We strip the burlaps off at the loading dock and shake out the vermin. You would not believe what travels with tea and silks."

"I took at look at you yesterday, through the peep, when you were talking to your father. There's a listening post, off to the side of the study."

"I know about it. They watch us. There's actors at Drury Lane who attract less of an audience."

More laborers passed, carrying rice. "Let's walk. I'm making MacLeish nervous, standing here watching his loading."

One of the advantages of being so much taller than Jess was she couldn't get ahead of him without actually breaking into a run. They covered half the length of her transient storage before that occurred to her. She pulled up beside a consignment lot of fifty wood boxes stenciled Pezzi Meccanici . . . Thessaloniki all over the sides. Machine parts for Thessalonica. That probably meant they were guns being smuggled into north Italy. God alone knew what the customs clerks made of the Whitby shipping documents.

"We had a little cobra bite one of the boys once." She lifted a hanging slate with the ship name and a date marked on it, then let it swing back. "Crawled out of a bale of India printed cotton. About thirty men beat it to death out there on the loading platform."

You're afraid I might just be like that cobra. He didn't like to see her haunted and unsure. It didn't suit her.

She picked at a splinter on the corner of the closest Thessalonica crate. "He lived—the boy who got bit—but he lost his foot. MacLeish trained him as a clerk. He's in Sweden now. I know about the spy holes at Meeks Street. Why are you telling me this?"

Because she was his. Nothing and no one would keep her from him, not even the hurt he'd done her. "So we know where we stand. I don't want lies between us."

"Bit late for that." She'd found another jagged piece of wood and started niggling away at it.

"I won't spy on you again."

"Forthright as a sunny day, that's you." She gave him a quick, searching, worried glance, then looked away.

"What did you find in my study?" *Tell me, Jess. Stop brooding about it and tell me.* "I went through it this morning, and there's nothing I wouldn't have shown you if you'd asked. Not a thing." He let a minute pass with her not answering. "If I were Cinq and I thought you'd found something important, you wouldn't have made it to work this morning, alive and free." He watched her pull more splinters out of that crate. "You're not good at being prudent. There's no point in trying to start now. What did you find?"

"I'd have to be frothing mad to talk to you about it." Belatedly, she tried some caution. "If I'd found anything at all, which I'm not saying I did. If it's all the same with you, I'd rather get back to work. I'm busy this morning."

She pulled away and took off, her long strides kicking her skirts in front of her. They turned corners at random, surprising men busy at inventory or restacking cargo. They passed a neat stack of boxes, huddled together, marked Fragile in five languages and slabs of white Carrara marble, stored at a slant, separated by blocks of pine. She saw none of it. She'd withdrawn wholly into herself, her face set and resolute, her eyes distant.

They ended up in the far corner where the staircase led to the upper floors. She stopped with her hand on the wood railing, muttering, ". . . if he lets me go. No guarantees of that."

She was steeling herself for the next stupidity on her list. She'd probably thought of something more dangerous than crawling across the roofs to Eaton's. Trevor was right. She should be locked up someplace.

It was easy to block the stairway. It always surprised him, that he was so much larger than her. "You'll work with me. You need my help. You don't have to trust me to make use of me."

"You're eloquent, Captain. I can't tell you how much I distrust eloquent. I'm just sure to my toes that Cinq is eloquent as hell."

It was time to tell her. She had to know what lay between them. "My ship, the *Neptune Dancer*, sank with all hands, two years ago. Men who belonged to me died because Cinq passed the sailing information to the French. The first mate was an old friend."

He watched pain stab though her. Every merchant and shipper had friends who'd never come home. She was remembering Whitby ships, lost, and the men on them. Maybe she was remembering that boy, Ned, who didn't come back to her.

She said, "I'm sorry. I am so sorry."

"That's why I'm not Cinq. Why I couldn't be."

Her eyes were shadowed. "The world is so damned full of things that just happen. Maybe you could even be the spy and sink your own ship by accident. I don't know. But my father isn't guilty."

"Then find out who is. Find Cinq, and I'll destroy him."

"I'm trying." The rest of it hit her then. "You think my father killed your friend and your men. Every time you look at me, you think about that. I'm surprised you can touch me at all."

"When I look at you I see nothing but Jess. It's a cosmic joke that you're related to him. You're not your father. You're nothing of his."

The straight, slashed eyebrows pulled together. The gold eyes hardened. "I'm Josiah Whitby's daughter, blood and bone."

"Jess—"

"He's the most honorable man I've ever known. He'd die before he'd betray England."

When he tried to put his hand on her shoulder, she chopped his wrist. "Don't." She hit hard enough to let him know she meant it. "You don't touch me. Not at the warehouse."

"I don't?" He kept his voice mild.

"Look around, Captain. There must be a dozen men who can see us right now. Up there, to the right. See that? That's the clerks' office behind that window. You want to bet there's six or eight of them watching us this minute?"

He glanced up. She was right.

"I can work in this warehouse and run this business because I got a hundred chaperones. I'm not a scandal because I'm always in plain sight, morning to midnight. A dozen men can swear I'm behaving myself proper. I can give orders here because I'm Whitby Trading to these men. They don't think of me as a woman."

Which showed even smart women could be fools. There wasn't one of these laborers or clerks who hadn't imagined pulling her skirts up and laying her back on one of these bales of cloth and having her. They were men, not capons.

She was so protected by her father and Pitney and her warehouse managers that she didn't even know.

So wise a Jess. So practical and clever, and so naïve. Fairly soon, he was going to seduce her.

She turned and walked up the stairs. Saffron today. He smelled it on her as she pushed past. That would be smuggled goods from the south of France. It sneaked up on him every time he got close to her, this knowledge he had of her, this intimacy he felt. He knew how she ran her business. How she estimated demurrage on contract goods. How much sugar she took in her tea.

He knew what she looked like with her clothes off. He knew that.

She shook herself, as if some of his hunger had brushed across her. "I need a cup of tea. Come up to my office, and I'll fix you some of the black we bring in through Kyakhta, into Russia. I might even find a sweet bun for you. Must be my morning for being hospitable to the British Service. And I figger we're about finished with the mauling-Jess-Whitby part of the day."

I doubt that extremely. He followed her. "Jess."

Impatiently, she waited at the landing for him to catch up.

He was level with her now. "You can do it, can't you? When we have the list of secrets stolen, you can match it to the ships moving in the Channel."

"Yes." She didn't move, but deep in her eyes, a part of her went distant from him, into some abstract place he couldn't follow. That unique, ingenious mind of hers was plucking away at the problem. "I could do it with thirty dates. I could sort through every tub that floats in the Thames. Twenty dates would work if they're stupid or have only the one ship."

"You'll find Cinq."

"I have to, don't I?" She looked haunted. She turned her back on him and started climbing again.

"I'll help. You'll trust me to help you." At the change in his voice, she turned around, right into his arms. Nobody could see them here at the turn in the stairwell. "Think of this as one of my arguments."

She fitted neatly up against the curve of the staircase. Her mouth tasted of surprise and honey and black tea from the hills of China. She put up no fight after the first quick intake of breath. God, but that felt good—feeling her not fight. She was ignorant and shocked for the first second. Then she was ignorant and willing. The edges of stubbornness softened.

"This isn't convincing me," she muttered, when he let her mouth free for a second.

"Then I'm not doing it right." He stroked up and down her back. "Let's try again."

Tension and urgency pulsed in his groin. Demand and hunger. Oh, but he had endless desire for this woman. No point trying to fool himself about that. Evil or virtuous, good or bad, whatever she'd done, he was going to have Jess. She'd figure that out pretty soon.

He'd had years of experience caring for women and loving them. He knew how to control his own need. He put that knowledge to use, tempting Jess.

"I wish you'd stop this." But she was holding on to him. Deliberately, he used his mouth to seduce. He felt her trying to think. He breathed into her ear and murmured. Nipped at her earlobe. Took her with little bites, suckling and tonguing all over her face. All of it was to distract her, to chain her to this moment and what he was doing to her. She never had a chance.

When she quivered in his hands, when he knew he had her, he brushed her nipples through the fabric of her dress. One rasp. Another. Scratching with his thumbnail. Gently. Gently. Already there was no shock left in her, no defense, just that cry and thrash. And another thrash and another, till her legs were open and she rubbed herself against his thigh.

His beautiful Jess. He'd toss her into the sky and let her soar. He'd give her joy, again and again, with his body. This was her first taste of it.

So he kissed her for a while. It was a fascination, to feel the vibrating begin in her, like an echo of his own feeling. He could almost reach into her and touch the butterfly of heat that fluttered so unwillingly into life and then spread its wings inside her and beat rhythmically.

He wished he could take her the whole way to the end.

That would be something—Jess turned into pure sensation and burning under his hand.

But this wasn't the time or place for it. Not here, in the heart of her own citadel. He wouldn't take away her pride like that. So he only warmed her a little, to remind her there were other things to life besides worrying and risking her life and trading spices. He stayed at her lips and her breasts and took her no further than kisses would take her. Well, maybe he made a few excursions. He set his mouth on her at the base of her throat and sucked against her skin and made marks, two or three of them, so the men working here would know he'd been there and keep their distance.

Then he stopped and just held her, and let her come down slow. He'd raised only a small heat in her, so it shouldn't be too hard. "Later. There's more, later."

She rubbed her lips on his jacket, trying to hold on to what he'd been making her feel. Then she breathed out and put her head down and let it all go. Some of that tension she carried around went, too.

She was going to remember this when she was in her office with her paperwork, when she sat across from him at dinner, when she lay in bed. She wouldn't be able to keep herself from thinking about it.

He propped her against the handrail. If he'd let go, she would have tumbled down the damn stairs.

"That was a mistake." She lifted her head, looking stunned. "I'm going to pretend I didn't just do that with you. Mistake. Mistake. Mistake." She combed through her hair with her fingers, bringing a lot of it down around her face. It was late to worry about what her men thought, if they saw her now.

It was too complicated to find the words, so he just reached out and stilled her hands. "Let me. And no, that wasn't a mistake. That was damned deliberate." He guided strands of hair over her ears and tucked them in at the nape of her neck.

He traded artwork halfway round the world—statues from Greece, Byzantine Madonnas, old carved figures from the deserts of Egypt. Not just for profit. It was for the joy of it. For the length of a voyage, he could hold beauty in his hand

and marvel. Touching Jess was laying claim to that kind of beauty, but warm and alive. She took his breath away.

"I liked that," he told her. "So did you."

"Get out of my warehouse." But she didn't have her breath back yet, and she didn't stop him when he coiled up loose hair and curled it away among the braids.

"We'll continue this another time."

"Not this side of hell."

"Be home in time to change for this Historical Society meeting tonight, or I'll come get you. Are you steady enough to walk the rest of the way? Those clerks of yours are going to start wondering."

"Those clerks of mine have it figured out by now. They're not fools."

Grimly, she climbed ahead of him and swung around the iron ball that topped the staircase and stalked down the hall, snarling. A messenger boy took one look and hastily backed into the nearest doorway.

He watched her all the way into her office. When she strode down the center aisle of the clerks' desks, every man was in place, quill raised, eyes on the paper in front of him, industrious.

$\mathscr{E}$ighteen

Ludmill Street, Whitechapel

JESS KNEW A DOZEN PEOPLE WHO SPOKE ARABIC, but only two who could read it. One was Papa, and she could hardly bring this question to Meeks Street, could she?

The other was the Reverend. She wanted to see him anyway, so it all worked out tidy. Life did that sometimes.

Ludmill Street was a bad, ugly place. The lane was barely wide enough for a cart to get through. Cobbles sloped steeply to a gully in the center, stinking and clogged with garbage. Not even grass could grow here, only lots and lots of people. Laundry hung crazily from lines out of every window, crisscrossing above her, blocking what sun made it past the roofline. The tenement windows were blind, dark squares with no glass in them, just boarded shutters that kept out thieves. One door stood crazily ajar, showing men and blowsy women sprawled on the floor in piles of straw. The sign outside read, "Gin. Drunk for a penny. Dead drunk for three pence."

The kids were out in force, filling the street, tumbling down the stairs, screaming. Mean, snapping mongrels these kids were. Curs on four legs ran among them and stopped to sniff at her skirts when she went past. She kept a rock in her hand to shy at any dog that took it into its head to bite. You did that where you were a stranger, in places like this. Some of the kids might have tried for her purse, if she'd been fool enough to carry one.

It had been different when she was a kid. Maybe she'd been tougher. She'd gone anywhere and never been afraid. The whole East End had been her playground, every dirty, rat-infested alley of it. Everybody knew her. There was a time she must have called half East London by name.

The Service had followed her in here. She got glimpses of them from time to time, being persistent behind her. Maybe they'd get their pockets picked. She hoped so. Her little contribution to the thieves of Ludmill street.

The soup kitchen was open, serving dinner. Jess put a limp in her step as she headed for it, walking like a tired little Covent Garden whore who's back from a long, hard stroll and doesn't want to discuss further business with anyone.

"Bad day, dearie?" the woman at the end of the line asked her.

She lifted a shoulder. "Bleeding 'orror what some men want."

"Ain't it the truth, luv. Ain't it the truth."

The meal today was cabbage soup with beans in it and hard brown bread. She let the man at the pot fill a wooden bowl for her and stuff bread into the soup. She sat down with the other women. They were joined soon enough by a family party, a woman who smelled of gin, with her baby and two boys.

"You gonna eat that?" the older boy demanded.

She looked at the soup and decided that, on the whole, no, she was not going to eat that. She shook her head, and he took the bowl, gobbling it down fast, not sharing with his brother.

She picked a little piece of bread into smaller and smaller pieces, thinking about the Reggio letter she'd found and about Sebastian. *He can't be Cinq.* But she kept adding it up, and sometimes she thought he could be.

A man like Sebastian wouldn't steal secrets for the money. It'd be politics and idealism and believing in the republic over there in France. Being drunk on fine words and the dreams. Ignoring the reality. Likely he caught all kinds of notions from his uncle and aunt, growing up. They were wild-eyed radicals, Eunice and Standish, but they were good people and harmless as mice, whatever nonsense they believed.

Sebastian wouldn't be harmless. He'd never be just harmless.

She had friends in France who thought Napoleon turned a crank and the sun rose. Nothing wrong with that, she supposed, if you were French, but no way for an Englishman to think.

Sebastian would run for France, probably, when she laid information against him.

"Whotcher done wif yer 'ands." The boy—he was seven or eight—had finished her soup and was looking at the little white scars on her hands. Those were the old rat bites she got when she fell, way back when. Most people didn't notice. Sharp fellow. If she'd still been with Lazarus, she'd have marked the boy down as somebody to watch. He might make a Runner in a year or so.

"Ah," she said. "Story behind that, there is."

The other boy, the younger one, stopped tormenting his little sister and leaned forward to listen. "I was about yer age, I guess, out taking the air in St. James Park one day, sauntering like . . . when what does I see but as nice a pair of duck as I ever clapped oglers on, jest sitting there in this pond. Crying waste of a foine dinner, says I to meself. So I takes this bit of pannam I had in me pocket . . ."

She went on from there for a bit. The woman fed herself and gave the baby a mouthful of the soup broth, letting it suck from the side of the bowl. Jess had both the boys giggling. ". . . set that bracket-faced she-duck a-squawking like a landlady come fer the rent. So anyways, I . . ."

The Reverend was walking the tables, talking to folks. He had a good crowd in here today, most of them getting ready for a night's work of the illegal variety. He was heading her way, so she finished up, ". . . never did get holt o' that bleeding bird. And that's how I come by them scars. That was the day I near got meself nibbled to death by ducks."

That set both boys off again, their mother, too, and some other folks who'd stopped to listen.

The Reverend came over to see what people were chuckling at. She never knew why, but he seemed startled to see her every time she showed up. You'd think he'd learn.

"Jess." He sounded annoyed. "What are you doing here?"

She batted her eyes at him. "What, Rev'rend? Donn'cher like me no more? Yer said—"

"Into my office, if you please." He took her elbow and pulled her away from the table.

"Keep yer truss on, guv'nor. Yer sure in a bleeding 'urry fer it, ain'tcher?"

She heard one man say to another as she walked by, "That's Whitby's daughter. They say she belongs to the Dead Man, she do . . ." So she supposed she wasn't doing Reverend Palmer's reputation much harm.

The Reverend clumped across his office. "Will you please not come here? It's not safe."

She took one of the straight-backed chairs. "I was thinking that, myself, as I came in. I'm going to have to be more careful."

"I heard about your father. If there's anything I can do . . . Well, of course, there is something I can do, and I'm doing it, but I very much doubt you've come here to hear about my prayers." He had a pot of tea on his desk, nearly cold, already mixed up with milk and sugar in the pot. He poured her some, and she set it down to one side and didn't drink any. She'd taken tea with the Reverend before.

"I'll send somebody reliable with you to walk you out of this place." He ran his hand through his lank, thin hair. "Though I don't think anyone's going to bother one of Eunice Ashton's household. Or anyone claimed by Bastard Kennett. Or your father's daughter, for that matter. But not everyone may recognize you. Now, what are you doing here?"

"I come for the food, of course. Must it be beans and cabbage? Are you determined the poor of London won't sneak up on anybody?"

"Cheap and nourishing, just as you directed. Come to inspect the books, have you?"

"That's what you have a Board of Governors for, to harass you about your bookkeeping. Oh, that reminds me. I've spent the last week making solicitors rich. There's going to be a trust, starting a week from Tuesday, so you don't have to be polite to me anymore. Or you can start being rude next Tuesday when the paperwork goes through."

"A trust?"

"Nothing you have to worry about. The money comes in all the same. It just means it doesn't come from Whitby's. It gets managed by grim Quaker gentlemen from Hoare's Bank. Isn't that the devil of a name for a respectable bank? One of my clerks will send you a long, incomprehensible letter about this eventually. Ignore it, is my advice."

"Is it a lot of money you're giving away?"

"Middling. There's not much else to do with it, past a certain point. It's fun making it, though."

This place, and twenty others like it across East London, would be protected if Whitby's fell and the government confiscated everything. It was a cheerful thought, cheating His Majesty's government to feed the scum of the earth. A chuckle in a dark world, charity was. "I came for help, actually."

"Anything I can do."

She grinned, flipped her skirts up to the knee, and pulled folded papers out of her garter. Didn't shock the Reverend though. She'd never found anything that shocked the Reverend. "I got secrets. Seal of the confessional?"

"The Church of England doesn't do that sort of thing, as you very well know. But if you'd like me to spit and cross my heart . . ."

"How about telling me what this says?" She handed over the bits of Arabic writing she'd copied from Sebastian's desk.

The Reverend raised his eyebrow. "Of course. Just . . ." He patted around his coat and eventually found his glasses on the desk and put them on. "So. What have we here?" For a long time he studied the symbols she'd copied, turning page by page till he'd read the lot. He was frowning when he finished. He shuffled the pages into a pile and took off his glasses, closed them, and tapped them against the desk.

"Jess, where did you get this?"

"Found it in a desk I was cracking," she said promptly.

"Where else? None of my business, anyway. I can't possibly translate these for you."

"Not Arabic?"

"Not . . . seemly."

"What?" First time in a while she'd been dumbfounded.

"I recognize this, of course. I was fortunate enough to come across a copy at Cambridge. It's rather famous among Arabic scholars. I don't believe it's been translated into English. These are quotes from an ancient . . . erotic manual. Lyric, classical Arabic. Your first passage deals with the man discussing a certain activity. The second is a description of one of the physical attributes of a woman."

"A dirty book." In Arabic. She leaned back in the chair and laughed. Oh, but she'd fooled herself proper, hadn't she?

Reverend Palmer shook his glasses at her in a minatory fashion. "I cannot imagine where you acquired this, and I don't suppose you're going to tell me. But it's not the sort of thing you should be reading."

"It's Arabic, so I'm not likely to be reading it." She had to wipe tears out of her eyes, from laughing so hard. "And here I thought it was some deep, dark secret. All that sneaking and prying to get me fambles on a dirty novel. Lord, I've outfoxed myself. That doesn't happen to me often."

"I don't suppose so." He squared up the edges of the papers. "You were immensely capable, even as a child. I found you impressive."

"I'm not feeling all that capable lately." She watched him lay those pages of Arabic aside, thriftily, in the box of scrap paper. She folded her hands up, one inside the other, and set the pair of them against the edge of his desk. "This business with Papa . . . It's not a problem I can solve. Not like filling up a hold with cargo. It's slippery. I keep adding seven and twenty-two and coming up with the color red."

"Can I help?"

"You are. You're one of about three people I've talked to in the last week who isn't lying to me all the time." She chewed on a strand of hair. "Reverend." There was one more thing she had to ask. It was hard to put it in words. "I came here . . . I do have a problem. I wanted to ask you . . ." She stuck there.

"Yes." He had some papers on his desk that needed rearranging all of a sudden. It kept his eyes busy.

"What do you do if you like somebody and you're afraid he's done something real bad?" She hadn't known she was going to ask it that way, till she did.

"What do you think you do?"

She'd never been able to fool the Reverend. "I guess I know what to do." She switched her hands around and put the left inside right this time. "It hurts a lot. Hurts every way I play it. I really . . . I like him."

He picked up his glasses and unfolded them, then folded them back up. "I'm sorry, Jessie."

"That's all I get from you, isn't it? Just, 'I'm sorry it hurts.' All these years, you never once told me everything's going to turn out right." Her lips twitched, not making the smile she was trying for. "I may have to peach on him, Rev. You can guess how I feel about that."

"I think you'll find it hard. Is he a good man, this friend of yours?"

"Not very. About like me, that way. And I don't think we're friends, actually. I'm fibbing about the friend part." She felt discouraged, thinking how profoundly impossible it was. "Doesn't matter much. It's not something that could have worked out, whatever happened."

"Then I'm very sorry indeed. I always hoped you'd meet a fine man someday, someone who was a proper match for you. I'd like to see you happy."

"I don't think I get happy out of this particular consignment." She lifted her eyes and let him see all the misery inside her for a minute. He was maybe the only one in the world she could show it to. The Reverend wasn't going to talk about happy endings. Seen a lot, had the Reverend.

She looked away and shrugged. "Maybe he's pure as a spring lamb gamboling on the green, and I'm just being unnecessarily suspicious. He keeps telling me to trust him."

"Do you?"

"Sometimes. I catch myself doing it and try to stop."

"Or you could listen to yourself."

"That's not such a good idea. I'm . . . stupid about him." It was too late, really, to tell herself not to love the Captain. "It's funny, innit, what folks do for some idea in a book. It's not like there's a paradise over in France. I been there, and I know. Secret police, for one thing, and the bribes get higher every year. More paperwork, too."

"You have a way of seeing very clearly, Jess." Raucous laughter came from the main room. The Reverend ignored it.

"I should know the difference between a good man and a bad one. I seen sterling examples of both." She stood up. "Why is it you never tell me what to do, and I always end up doing it?"

"I'm not sure. What did I not tell you to do?"

"Get to work. Prove he's not guilty."

"Sounds like I'm giving good advice these days. Do you need any more of it?"

"That should hold me for a while. Lead me to this safe, reliable escort of yours, Reverend. You would not believe how much work I have to do today."

"You always do." Palmer took her untouched cup of tea, lifted the lid off the teapot, and poured it back in. "Are you safe in that house, with Bastard Kennett? He's a grim-looking man, from the glimpses I've had of him."

"He's that." A piece of her hair had come loose. She stood, twirling it around and around her finger.

Palmer sloshed the teapot around thoughtfully. "I've heard he's a man of his word. An honorable man."

"It's not that simple."

"I didn't think it would be, with you. I'll send you out of here with Mrs. Trimble. Nobody in his right mind would attack Mrs. Trimble. Even I'm afraid of Mrs. Trimble."

He opened the door for her, and they were back in the noise and confusion of the crowded dining room, with kids squalling and women talking loudly. One man rolled on the bench, shouting about the imaginary bugs crawling on him. The Reverend looked it over calmly and turned back to her. "God keep you in the hollow of his hand, Jess."

"God's got better things to do with his hands, I'd say, looking at this crew."

SHE'D do what she had to, to get Papa free. She didn't have the luxury of being a coward.

The Russian teacup with jasmine flowers on it was at her elbow. Every time she set it down, it left a little cup-sized circle marked on the blotter. There were dozens of little circles.

The first time she went on a roof, she'd hung onto the chimney, whimpering, telling Lazarus she couldn't do this. Wouldn't do this. And since Lazarus wasn't a man you said "wouldn't" to, he pried her fingers off the bricks and kicked her loose to roll down the slates till she hit a gable and stopped.

When she inched her way back up to him again she wasn't inclined to snivel quite so much. Eventually, she got over being scared. He'd been right about that.

I can do this. She tucked a sugar cube in her cheek and drank some tea. Then she wrote,

> *I will see the list and assure myself that it is exactly as promised. I will examine the details of one instance of theft. An instance of my choosing.*

Russian samovar. Russian tea. Russian way of drinking it. And she liked the cheap brown Barbados sugar, the kind Mama bought when they were flush with money.

What was the point of being rich if you couldn't drink your tea just as you liked it.

Clerks were putting on their coats and hats, getting ready to end the day. She'd told the messenger boy to wait, though. He was sitting on one of the high stools, playing the game with the little ball and cup.

And there was the clerk Buchanan, peering through the window into her office. He was beginning to get on her nerves.

> *You will produce this document the night before any contract is signed. There can be no compromise on this.*

Pitney was going down the line of windows in the outer office, closing them up and locking them. There was no job in this warehouse he wouldn't put his hand to. He took care of Whitby's like it was his own. Pitney would stay till she left and put her in the hackney himself and stand on the front steps of Whitby's, watching, till she was out of sight.

She drank another sip of tea. Her nib was drying up. She took more ink.

> *I would suggest you bring the paper to the meeting at Kennett House tonight. The ceremony, if you wish, can be scheduled for tomorrow. The settlements are ready to sign.*

Lies, lies, and more lies. But it would get that list out of the Horse Guards. It might not be a bird in the hand yet, but at least it was a bird in the bush instead of a bird locked up safe with a squad of marines guarding it.

Sebastian is not going to be happy when he finds out what I'm up to. Papa neither. And Pitney won't be delighted. Then there's the colonel. Reams is going to be poker-hot furious.

She signed the letter and sprinkled sand on it. She was displeasing men right and left today.

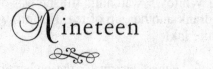ineteen

Kennett House, Mayfair

IT WAS EARLY YET, BUT VOICES BUBBLED UP
from the salon downstairs like oatmeal boiling in a pot. Historians talked a lot, apparently. Every candle in the house
was lit. The front hall smelled like baking and beeswax and
perfume. She walked down the curving stairs, checking the
fiddly clasp on her necklace one last time. The crystals in
the chandelier sparkled like a waterfall in sunlight.

They'd stationed suits of armor around the walls in the
black and white entry hall, eight of them, at neat intervals,
like footmen, but armed with sharp points. She'd attended
scientific meetings in Paris and Vienna—Papa loved that
kind of thing—but she'd never ventured among historians
who took an interest in pikes and poniards. There was Colonel Reams to lie to. Later on, she'd sneak out and visit his
house. A busy night. She should probably be more nervous
than she was.

The Captain was waiting for her at the bottom of the
stairs. He followed her with his eyes the whole way down.

Evening dress looked good on him. His breeches were
the color of the desert in North Africa. His coat like night

over that same desert, rich and black. He tied his cravat plain, the way they did in Paris. He'd put himself exactly where she'd have to walk right to him. A man who seized his opportunity, the Captain.

"Miss Whitby." He was being polite. Of course, he would be polite in the open hall of his own house, with these scholarly nobs milling about. He had a different set of behavior at, say, four in the morning in the upstairs hall, or in her warehouse. Or on his ship, for that matter.

"Captain." She stopped a step up from the bottom of the stairs to see if Sebastian Kennett looked less formidable when she met him level and eye-to-eye. Turned out it didn't make any difference at all. "Eerie, all these blokes standing around in steel plate. I'll be just as glad when they leave."

"They'll pack up and take off tomorrow morning. That dress is from Paris, isn't it?"

"Madame Claudette, on the Rue de Rivoli."

"I would have hated to go through life without seeing you in that particular dress. I don't suppose there's a stitch on you that isn't smuggled."

"The dress fabric's from Lyon. Illegal as hell in England. I'm not going to talk about the rest of it, sparing your modesty and all." Impossible to be distant and cool to the man. She never seemed to manage it past the first couple words. She touched the pearls. "You'll be interested in this, since you trade in baubles."

The Captain knew what he was looking at. She could tell from the way he slid his fingers under the pearls, reverent. But then, he'd seen them before. "*Mushajjar*. The veil of sunrise, pierced by ivory."

"They're a lyrical people, down on the Gulf."

"I've seen pearls like this, once, at a reception in the palace of the doge in Venice." He drew his fingers down the line of pearls, touching them above and her skin below, caressing both. "Not this fine. I admired these when I searched your bedroom yesterday."

There he was, at it again, rolling the conversational wagon off a cliff.

"I like the way you have your hair up in those braids, all

swirled together like that. It looks simple. Then you study it, and it gets more and more complex. Like you. Every time I think I have you sorted out, I pick up another line of complication."

He was the devious one. She was a pat of plain butter compared to him. "I admire a man who knows what these beads are and still has something nice to say about my hair. I was expecting to get your trading instinct roused up with the bauble, you dealing in decorative rarities and all."

"Not rarities like that. Beyond my touch."

"Mine, too, if we're being candid about it. Every time I fasten them on, I think about the unholy amount of capital tied up and shudder. Anyway, you make your money on loose stones more than decorative pieces. Thirty percent net profit. I admire that." She'd pulled that out of the ledgers at Eaton's. Not that she'd gone looking for his profits, but she couldn't help seeing. "Lightning-fast turnover, too."

"Thank you. Jess, has it crossed your mind it's not tactful to remind me you've been going through my ledgers?" But he was laughing at her. He did it entirely in his eyes, not twitching his lips at all.

"Roight you are, guv'nor. A flapping gob's been the downfall of many a foine prig and ruffler."

"And you will refrain from shocking my aunt's guests with your mastery of the vernacular. Lean a little closer. Yes. Just there." He traced the course of a braid around her head, following the path of it with his index finger.

"Am I coming apart? I have about a million pins in. Will you just stop playing with my hair? Crikey, what if someone comes by?"

"They'll be shocked witless. Let's draw you in a mite closer and we'll truly astound them." He nudged her down the last step, and she was looking up at him again. Inevitable, wasn't it? He said, "I'm trying to figure out how it all works." She felt his breath on her forehead. His finger brushed her earlobe.

"It's magic. You're not supposed to look too close." *I like it too much when he touches me. I'm getting used to it. Pretty soon, I won't be able to do without it.*

She set her hand in the center of his chest, but she didn't get to the pushing-him-away part. She just stood with her fingers mixed up in his cravat, acting like they were standing on the edge of some cliffs in a desert with nobody to see but the camels. The house was crawling with historians and Sebastian's family and there was a maid—the woman with the murderous pimp, actually—holding a tray and peering at them from a corner. The Captain didn't let go.

Well, to be fair about it, neither did she. She was being stupid. He was probably being clever. Life was odd like that.

She looked past Sebastian's shoulder. Colonel Reams had arrived. She could see him reflected in the black glass of the parlor windows. His regimentals made a broad, blurry-red pillar in the middle of the dark coats and pale dresses. Pretty soon she'd go tell lies to him. "It's time I went off to snag myself a couple pastries." Eunice had cakes and tarts laid out on the table in the dining room, next to a display of iron codpieces. "If I leave it too late there'll be nothing left but liver and turnip."

"I recommend the apricot ones." He ran his fingers along the shoals and reefs of her elbow, and there was nothing else in the world she could think about. Perverse on his part, and a revelation to her of why her governesses said to keep a goodly distance away from men.

I don't have time for this. I have to go cheat the colonel. She couldn't think of a time she'd bargained in bad faith, but she was doing it with Reams. It didn't make it any better that Reams was a pig and planned to cheat her, up, down, and sideways, the minute she signed a marriage contract.

Three men and a tiny, white-haired woman strolled out of the front parlor and across the hall, headed for the food, arguing about Greeks. And Claudia appeared out of nowhere.

"There you are, Sebastian." Claudia must have been scouting along from column to column like a Mohawk slipping through the primeval forest. "You're needed. They've mixed up the topknots on the suits and Coyning-Marsh is having fits. Eunice requires oil on the troubled waters."

"I don't know anything about plate armor."

"You're an expert on troubled waters. I want to talk to Jess. You're in the way."

He just grinned. In a good mood tonight, the Captain. "All right. Keep it above the belt. And you . . ." Right in front of Claudia, not caring what anybody thought, he reached out and trailed his index finger from her temple to where she'd been bruised on the cheek. "Behave yourself. I'll find you later. Try not to draw blood with that tongue of yours." Then he walked off, leaving her to Claudia's tender mercies.

Claudia said, "My cousin can afford to make a spectacle of himself. You can't. I advise you to be discreet in public." She had to look up and up to Claudia. All these Ashtons managed to make her feel like a small dab of paint.

"Now you see . . . I agree with you. We probably have lots in common once we get to talking."

"My brother tells me you were in the hall last night, outside Sebastian's door. That was unwise."

"That's another thing we agree about. Look, why don't we go snabble a few of those pastries before this crowd goes through them like a flock of locusts. Somehow or other I missed dinner. It's been a trying day and the number of sharp objects lying about just fills me with trepidation. I'll just—"

"You're out of your depth in this household, Miss Whitby, however clever you may be in the shop. I would tell you to leave, but I doubt you'd listen. You're filled with the scrambling self-confidence of the parvenu class. It is sadly misplaced."

That was one of those veiled threats, very probably. Claudia was the kind to issue veiled threats. "I won't say no to any of that. Especially not the part about being out of my depth. I feel like a shallow water craft tonight."

Another pack of historians wandered by. A shabby man with a German accent and frayed cuffs limped along between a pair of dandies right out of Upper Brook Street. They were talking about disemboweling. Not in favor of it, as far as she could tell. Just talking.

Daunting, she'd call this lot. And she still had to deal with Claudia.

"Your pearls are a bit showy." Claudia just went right on

being critical. "They're . . . yellow. Do you have a dozen sets, dyed to match your dresses? So very clever."

Had to be on your toes with Claudia, didn't you? "More pink than yellow, but I see your point. I do it the other way round, though. I buy the dress to match the pearls, being thrifty. This," she pinched up a bit of her skirt, "is *couleur d'aube* from DeMile Frères in Lyon. We keep a few bolts of their silk in the warehouse in Broad Street, under the counter, for special customers." She was letting herself get carried away, but nobody with ebony-black hair should wear the shade of blue Claudia had on. "You might go by and see. Give my name and tell them to show you the bronze lustring."

"Always the shopkeeper," Claudia said. "That's admirable in its way."

"It is when I'm picking out silk."

The front door opened and closed while she was talking to Claudia. More historians. Three women, very stern-looking. And a man who came in alone. Sometime, as he was walking across the foyer, she realized who he was.

Then he was in front of her. Unwillingly, Claudia stepped aside. "Sebastian is in the front room. I'll take you to him." When he didn't move, "I suppose I should introduce you to—"

He said, "Hello, Jess."

Claudia said, "Do you know Miss Whitby? I suppose you meet all kinds of people—"

"Go away," Adrian Hawkhurst said.

The rudeness silenced Claudia. Neither of them really noticed when she turned on her heel and flounced off.

He was Hurst, her old friend. Even now, knowing everything he'd done, half of her leapt up, thinking, *He's going to make everything right.*

He looked at her steady, waiting till she decided what to say. He was dressed . . . She didn't know how to put it. Not more prosperously. He'd always worn beautiful clothing. But . . . fashionably. That was it. He dressed like a nob, now.

"Hurst." She held on to the newel post at the bottom of the stairs.

"I'm calling myself Adrian Hawkhurst these days." He

took his hat off and held it, all stiff and grave. How strange to see him with a high-crowned beaver hat. All that time in St. Petersburg, she'd never seen him with a proper hat, only that furry sable thing with earflaps. For years she'd thought that was proper attire for a butler.

"Did you get the letters I wrote? I always wondered."

He said, "I got them. I kept in touch with Josiah, but I thought it was better to leave you alone."

He still acted like he was Papa's friend. He'd sent his dogs to pull Papa out of the warehouse in his shirtsleeves. He'd locked Papa up at Meeks Street and he was talking to her like they were friends. There'd be all kinds of plausible excuses. None of them worth the spit it took to say. If she'd been a woman given to crying, she would have taken the time to do some, right then. She sat down abruptly on the stairs and wrapped her arms tight around her.

Hurst came and sat down next to her. The two of them, side by side. It was all so familiar. Her stomach hurt like she had an animal trapped inside, clawing at her. She could have doubled over and moaned with the pain of it.

After a long time, she put her hands into her lap. "Remember the way we used to sit like this, in the house in St. Petersburg? That big marble staircase. The Russians were so fond of all that cold marble, but it about froze my arse off."

"I remember." He put his hat on his knee and watched it.

"You used to scold me for talking like that. Said it wasn't ladylike. I wouldn't have done it half as much if you hadn't scolded."

"I know."

"I was almost grown up by that time. Twelve, maybe."

"Thereabouts."

"Papa would leave for a party with one of his mistresses, and we'd sit on the stairs and talk about the party and the mistress, and then we'd go down to the kitchen and the babushka would fix me little pancakes. I haven't had one of those in years. Blini with honey."

"There's a place in Soho you can get them."

"Is there?" She turned her hands over and looked at the

crescent-shaped marks where her nails had bit in. "We'd sit in the kitchen and eat pancakes and drink cups of tea from those painted cups Papa had made for me. And play chess. You taught me to play chess. Papa never had the patience."

"I thought you should learn to play one game you couldn't cheat at."

Hurst always talked like that. He'd understood how hard it was for her, being so very respectable all the time. She'd been able to say anything at all to Hurst. She'd felt safe with him. Even when Papa traveled all up and down Russia, she never minded because Hurst was there.

"Did you always let me win, right to the end? Or did I really get so I could beat you?"

"I let you win."

The feeling of doubleness overwhelmed her, a sense of one man fitting over another. Hurst, the butler, who was her old friend. Adrian Hawkhurst, the spy. She would have trusted Hurst with her life, and he'd never even existed.

She said, "Remember the time you caught me sneaking brandy in Papa's study? You took the bottle up to your sitting room and let me drink the rest of it, and I sat in your lap and told you I was in love with you. And then I got so bloody sick all over you."

"I remember that." He turned his hat so that it faced the other way on his knee. "Do you know, you are absolutely the only woman who has ever said she loved me."

"Was it true what you said that night about loving a Frenchwoman? Or was that lies, too?" When someone is composed entirely of lies, it made no sense asking him questions, did it?

"That was the truth, Jess. Every word of it. You are one of three people in the world who know that."

For what it was worth, she believed him. Even now, Hurst could lie to her and make her believe it. He was very, very good at lying. "I still can't drink brandy. I like it. I can judge it and buy it, but I never did get a head for drinking the stuff." Her voice flaked off in pieces around the edge.

"I know."

"I guess there's nothing you don't know about me, is there?" The inside of her head ached with not crying. "Papa never came out and told me you worked for the British. Not till the end. I don't know why I didn't figure it out."

"You were very young, *devochka,* and you didn't want to know about it. I ran the entire British Service operation for Russia out of your kitchen. Every so often your father's spies and mine would bump into each other in the hall. You have something in your eye, I think." He handed her a handkerchief.

It was the kind he'd always had. He bought them in Jermyn Street—cambric, dead simple, fine sewing, and the hem deeper than usual. She pressed it to her eyes so she wouldn't cry. When she was twelve she'd have blown her nose in it. She'd acquired all sorts of airs and graces, hadn't she?

He said, "That last day . . . Josiah wasn't supposed to get shot. None of that was supposed to happen."

"Did, though." She folded the handkerchief up in a square, neat like. "Papa tells a story about the time he was in a storm off Majorca. Every penny he had in the world was tied up in cargo. They were going onto the rocks, so he threw the whole lot overboard, down to the last box and bale. He said it was a sacrifice to the God of Luck. When you call on the God of Luck, you have to scrape down and give up everything, or you don't get his attention."

She looked him straight in the eye. "My life's like that. I keep having to throw everything overboard. Push. Splash. And there goes Hurst the butler. When did the Foreign Office decide they need our depots in the East? About last year, wasn't it? They're the ones who sent you after Papa."

"Jessie—"

"Must have been a year ago they decided to destroy Papa. That's when the garbage starts showing up in the account books."

He didn't move. Didn't make a sound.

"It's too bad you turned out to be a spy instead of a butler. You can't be much of a spy if it took you a whole year to bring down my father. But you were an excellent butler." She stood up and threw the handkerchief in his face. "Bugger you anyway," and headed back to hide in the dining room.

Saying all that didn't make her feel any better. She hadn't thought it would.

Twenty

SEBASTIAN WAITED AT THE DOORWAY TO THE front parlor in the shadow of a knight's armor. He'd engineered this meeting. If it was a disaster, at least he'd watch.

"She's sitting on the floor," Claudia said. "Like a gypsy."

He put out his hand before she took off in that direction. "You don't want to go over there. Let them talk."

"I rather thought I was rescuing Adrian." Claudia gave an abrupt, sharp-edged laugh. "*Such* an intense little tête-à-tête. There's a history between those two, obviously."

"Don't interfere."

"Your friend and your little heiress. If you have interest in that quarter you should intervene before he snaps her up himself. Are you sure you don't want me to interrupt?"

"I want you to leave them strictly alone." There was malice in Claudia. But once upon a time, she'd taught a fithy-mouthed, resentful bastard boy from the docks how to use a knife and fork. She'd had a sharp, nasty tongue then, too.

Quentin pulled himself away from a discussion with two clerks from the War Office and strode across the parlor with the weighty and distinguished tread of a statesman, face serious, his hands clasped behind his back. He frowned upon the pair sitting together on the grand staircase. "I don't like this. What the deuce is that man doing with Miss Whitby? We stand, as it were, in *loco parentis* as long as she's under our roof. He's upsetting the girl."

"Miss Whitby is upsetting him right back," Claudia said tartly. "I don't believe I've ever seen Adrian ruffled. I didn't know he could be."

There he is, sprawling on the steps beside her. "Whatever her background, that's ungentlemanly behavior."

Then Jess got up, grim-faced, and stalked off. Not a successful first meeting. Adrian had been wrong about one thing, though. She didn't spit at him.

Quentin puffed his cheeks out. "How much do we actually know about this Hawkhurst fellow? He's a friend of yours, of course. That counts for something. Accepted everywhere. Presents a good appearance. But does anyone know his people? Does he even *have* people? When one moves, as I do, in government circles, one hears stories . . ."

"They say he's a Romanov bastard. Perhaps Jess met him in Russia." Claudia tilted her head. "Look. She's gone off crying. How very affecting. I feel called upon to offer womanly sympathy."

The mood she's in now, Jess will flay you to shreds. "I don't advise it."

Claudia said, "Nonetheless . . ." and left.

"I'll go talk to the girl, too." Quentin took his watch out and fidgeted with it. "I should drop a hint in her ear. Hawkhurst is exactly the sort of plausible rogue a girl like that is likely to fall prey to. And she is in our house, after all. She's not in a position to judge a man like that. I can only imagine what he wants from her." He put the watch away without looking at it. "I hear things, y'know. There are whispers about this Mister Adrian Hawkhurst that are not to his credit. I wouldn't trust that man. No, indeed I wouldn't. Not that I expect you to listen to me." He ambled in the direction of the dining room.

And that was another Ashton, off to track Jess down and harass her.

THE parlor filled up as more and more historians arrived. Coyning-Marsh, Standish, and three dons from Oxford argued, fiercely and volubly, passing a gauntlet back and forth, examining it with a magnifying glass from the library.

"I gather I have you to thank for the latest excitement in my household," Eunice said. If she noticed Adrian was looking particularly bleak, she gave no indication of it.

"Ah." Adrian smiled. Quite his usual smile. "You've found out I'm supplying Standish with opera girls."

"Of course I have. How many of the little darlings does he have lately? A dozen?"

"At least."

"Thank you for having sense enough to send Jess to me. Adrian, what the devil are you about, arresting that girl's father? I expect better of you."

"All the evidence says he's guilty as Judas. Very convincing evidence, some of which your nephew brought me. And Military Intelligence was closing in. I had no choice. If it helps any, I didn't enjoy it much."

"I'm sure everyone is very interested in your feelings in the matter."

"Since you mention it, no."

"I don't suppose you could just let him go, could you?"

"Not until someone hands me sole control of intelligence operations at Whitehall, no."

Sebastian, looking formidable and alert, even in evening dress, stood in the parlor doorway, arms folded, watching Jess. In one corner, Quentin lectured a pretty young girl about heraldry. Jess stood alone at the front window, staring out. Her face was composed and distant, like someone sailing out of a port they didn't expect to return to. She didn't once glance at Adrian.

Eunice said quietly, "Do you think they'll hang him? I very much doubt he's guilty."

"We hang innocent men every day in this country." His

mobile mouth twisted. "Right now I am working hard not to arrest his daughter. This is made possible by the War Office's complete failure to believe she runs the business for him."

"I see."

"Eventually, some bright lad from one group or another, very junior, will try to haul her in on some pretext or other. My men will stop him. And the fat will be in the proverbial fire." Adrian snagged a glass of punch from the tray a sullen, preoccupied maid had maneuvered through the crowd. "Why do I drink this? I know better than to eat or drink anything served in your house, but I am a slave to my curiosity. The punch is always bad, but it is never bad the same way twice." He eyed it. "Military Intelligence is snapping at my heels. I'm running out of time, Eunice. This may be the one I lose."

Eunice made a derisive sound.

"Am I sniveling on your shoulder?" he said. "I suppose I am. Why should everyone else have the fun?"

"I do not suppose you fail very often."

"No."

"Then you won't this time. You are proficient at what you do, Adrian. Perhaps the most skilled in the world. How are you planning to get her out of England, if the worst happens?"

"With dispatch. Sebastian has the *Flighty* anchored off Wapping, with the crew aboard." Adrian took a sip from the punch cup. "If some idiot from the War Office decides to pick her up, I'll have an hour's warning. Time enough. I don't suppose Sebastian will dawdle."

In the salon next door, metal crashed and clattered. Voices rose in consternation. Coyning-Marsh and the three dons led a general exodus in that direction.

Adrian said, "Then there is the matter of Colonel Reams."

There were other military men in the room, other regimentals, but the gaudy scarlet uniform of a Guards colonel stood out. Reams looked at home in the company of medieval armor—brutal, direct, muscular, unimaginative.

He'd come up behind Jess. He waited, not saying anything, till she sensed him and turned around. If he'd succeeded in disconcerting her, she didn't show it. Gravely courteous, holding herself straight as a rapier, she nodded.

"It would make more sense to send her out of England now," Eunice said. "She shouldn't have to face someone like Colonel Reams, alone."

"She isn't alone. She has you. And Sebastian. And me. And a growing contingent of the British Service dedicated to protecting every hair on her head."

"Why are you keeping her in England, Adrian? If you're planning to use that lovely child against her father—"

"I'm using her to help him, strangely enough, though I doubt she believes me. And that lovely child has killed three men that I know of, one of them before she was ten. She can deal with Colonel Reams."

The colonel put a hand on Jess's elbow and gestured toward the archway into the hall. Expressionlessly, she shook her head. She listened, with that same stiff lack of response, to a fast, close-set, hectoring string of words in her ear. His bulldog body pushed close, bullying with muscle and the barking voice.

Across the room, Sebastian watched, looking more and more menacing.

"That is blackmail the colonel's trying, or possibly threat." Eunice's mouth set in distaste. "Or he may be asking for a bribe. Can Reams arrange for her father's release?"

"No. You see everything, don't you?" Adrian said. "I hope Sebastian doesn't kill him on the premises. There are miles of dockyard and alley available for the purpose. And I want to help."

"Can Reams arrest her?" Eunice answered herself, "I think not. Not with Bittern so interested." On the other side of the room, the second secretary of the Foreign Office, Lord Bittern, held a cup of punch and watched Reams, his face even less revealing than Jess's. "She's being very determined and resourceful, playing one off against the other. All the same, it would be best if you found this traitor of yours rather quickly. I will not have Jess kidnapped and married off to some Foreign Office nonentity to secure our interests in Turkey. And Sebastian would have to live abroad if he killed someone important."

"The only consideration that keeps several men alive today." Adrian kept an eye on the colonel. "I will intervene be-fore Sebastian commits mayhem. Do you know, there is no conversation so private as one in the middle of swarming multitudes. I wonder which of them arranged this? Jess, I think."

"She's not surprised to see him here."

"The world of espionage lost a great master when you decided to devote yourself to good works. So Jess meets the offensive Reams under the civilizing influence of many pairs of eyes. And what does he have to say that Jess finds so interesting? If he will just turn ever so slightly . . . Did you know one can make a very good guess what people are say-ing by watching their lips? It takes some practice. Reams says, 'I don't see any reason why you won't . . . something . . . something . . . it will cause difficulty . . . good faith.' And why would the colonel be talking about good faith? No. Look back this way, you abominable lump of offal."

Men crossed Adrian's line of vision, moving from armor to armor.

"Out of my way, good people. Ah. There we are. He's saying, '. . . influence to get your father . . .' I can guess what that's about. '. . . the special—'" Adrian's voice cut off abruptly. "I don't like this. That was 'special license.' Jess, my very dear, I cannot believe you have allowed the colonel to talk you into anything that stupid."

Eunice said, "I'll get Sebastian."

"THERE'S no hurry, anyway." Jess had learned that from Papa. The man in a hurry always lost the dicker. "We can do this another day."

"I've already made arrangements." Reams had to keep his voice down—men nearby were already looking in their direction—so it came out a low, thick growl. "The minister expects us early tomorrow morning. Everything's settled. I have friends coming."

You have your friends coming, to twist my arm if I get re-luctant. "I guess we're all disappointed." She left it at that. Hurst always said, let the other fellow do most of the lying.

Hurst taught her about lying. He taught her to fold napkins into fancy shapes and how to fire thirty different kinds of guns. Hurst thought he could just walk in and look miserable and she'd forgive him. Hah.

He was watching her, him and Sebastian. It made her feel safe, knowing they were there. She was just neck-deep in irony tonight.

"Are you daring to doubt my word?" Reams turned red, all mottled, and shuffled his boots back and forth like he was about to stomp on something. "You'll get the list when we're married. That's soon enough."

"I'll have it in hand then. But I see it the night before."

The veins in his neck stood out. "I am an officer and a gentleman and I give you my bloody, damn word. Don't cross me."

And there was some gentlemanly language for you. "It's a big step. Marriage. That's a contract. I need to see if you keep your contracts." Of course, he wasn't planning to keep a particle of any agreement. Did he think she didn't know?

"You want to see this? It's so important you'll insult me to my face?" He twisted around and pulled the paper out of his coat. "Then you can see it. What date? What? Tell me."

He'd brought the list. He'd been planning to keep the bargain all along, if he couldn't intimidate her. Bluffing.

She said, "Show me May fourth, last year."

That started off a crackling and snapping search of the two pages of notes, him twisting the pages and stopping to glare at her. "You shouldn't know that date. Just saying that date makes you guilty." He spread his lips, showing yellow teeth, and it didn't look at all like a smile. "You're lucky I don't haul you in myself."

Bluffing again. If he could have laid hands on her, he would have. Men who bluffed were the easiest ones to bluff right back.

"I shouldn't show you any of this." He said it just loud enough for her to hear.

When Papa traded cloth, sometimes he'd signal her to make a shuffle like she was getting ready to leave. Helped to speed up the bargaining. She'd give a twitch and maybe put her hand on her reticule. Just a glance at Papa and moving barely enough to startle a fly.

She did it now. She let her attention drift . . .

"Here." He thrust the list out at her. He'd clamped the page up tight, then pinched and creased it till only the one thin entry showed. He pulled it away before she could see it.

She waited, not saying anything or budging an inch, till he brought it out again and held it up in front of her and gave her a chance to read. He was seething the whole time. He'd go off in an apoplexy, one of these days.

The line he showed her was genuine. This was the date, place, the memorandum stolen. It matched what she knew, and the colonel had no way of knowing which date she'd want to check. This was a list of the secrets stolen. This was what she needed.

"Thank you." One bit of truth in this soup made out of lies. She didn't look him straight in the face because, given her luck lately, he'd read her intentions written on her forehead.

"You'll get this tomorrow. My first present to you, when we're man and wife." And he was lying through his crooked, tobacco-stained teeth.

It didn't matter. She'd have that list out of his house tonight, while he was sleeping. That was the reason the good Lord put windows in houses. So thieves could go through them.

She said, "Tomorrow, then."

Her lie was shorter, but it was a lie, just the same.

"It is always edifying," Adrian said, "to watch a talented amateur at work. That will be the Military Intelligence list of missing documents. Jess wanted to get her hands on that list, so she asked Reams to bring it to her. Still the most remarkably straightforward mind of my acquaintance."

Sebastian didn't take his eyes off her. She was remarkable. "She's trading. Look at her." A dozen feet away, with thirty men and women as spectators, Reams was trying to bully Jess into some concession. Whatever those two were negotiating, she wasn't going to budge an inch.

Adrian watched the two with steady attention, not even blinking. "The words 'special license' have been mentioned. I am filled with trepidation."

"She's not going to trade herself for that list."

But he wasn't sure of that. Jess, committed, was Jess committed heart and soul with no regard for common sense or her own safety. There was no telling what she'd consider reasonable. "If Reams gets his hands on the Whitby heiress, Whitby won't live out the summer. She has to know that."

"No fool, my Jess."

She wasn't Adrian's Jess. She was his.

Reams inched up closer to snarl in her face. He was short, broad, and heavy and she looked delicate beside him. That was deceptive. Jess was steel. That blustery wind Reams was raising would cut past her and around her and blow itself out. *I wouldn't like to negotiate against her, right now.*

Reams had retreated from his point, huffing and snarling. The paper, folded small, was shoved in Jess's face. She nodded. The colonel put it away again in the uniform's coat pocket.

It was easy to see what Jess planned. "It's too late to go back to the Horse Guards. He'll bring the list home. She plans to go after him and steal it tonight." Just exactly the kind of scheme she would come up with. Clever. A good chance of succeeding. Risking her neck as if it were nothing. "He probably lives on the top floor somewhere, three stories up."

"A pretty townhouse in South Audley Street, but the principle's the same." Adrian grinned. "Three floors. A rather steep roof. I have scouted it out."

"So we take it away from him now."

"Before she does. Yes. Excellent idea. Hold this, if you will." Adrian handed over the punch cup, still full. "We shall foil her little plot with one of our own. The list is neatly back in the colonel's pocket. We will now wander across this room, separately, and you will pour that punch down the front of his dress uniform."

"My pleasure." Oh, yes. It would be. "I'll wait for your
nod. Are you coming up on the left side or the right?"

"Left. If you can contrive to spill just a little on me as
well . . ."

"No problem at all."

CINQ held a cup and strolled from one chattering, yammer-
ing, silly group to another, dropping a word here, correcting
some misapprehension there, being sociable and helpful. It
was surprising how few of these so-called scholars knew
what they were talking about.

The merchant's daughter flaunted herself through the room
with a fortune in pearls hanging around her neck. Ridiculous
opulence. The mushroom class betrayed itself every time.

Money-swollen peasants. Pigs in silk. They were the worst
enemies of the revolution. They worshipped nothing but
money. The true defenders of the poor always arose from the
ruling class.

*I have men on the streets to take her. A woman in this
house to watch her. The ship's ready. It will all fall into
place, any day. It could happen any day. And she'll be on her
way to France.*

She was rude to Colonel Reams, snubbing a man twice
her age, a decorated war hero. The chit might wear pearls
and silk, but she didn't belong among her betters. She never
would. *She'll be small and humble-mouthed when I get her
to France.*

*When her father hangs, whoever controls Jess Whitby,
controls the money. She will be my gift to the Great Cause.*

Sebastian tramped across the parlor, graceless and aggres-
sive, pretending to be a captain at sea. A leader of men. And
everyone believed it. Men perked up, turning his way as he
passed, trying to pull him over to talk, asking his opinion. He
ignored them all. Tonight he was cock of the walk, and he
was scurrying to protect his guinea hen. Maybe he didn't
trust the chit with a man like the colonel.

Sebastian had it all his way tonight. When Napoleon's
Grande Armée marched into London, the bastard would lose

everything. Kennett House—no, call it by its proper name—
Ashton House, would be the reward for long and faithful service.

"I was going to steal this from under his pillow or something,"
Jess said. She turned the list over. Names, dates . . . all the details. Hurst, giving her presents. He'd always found exactly
what she wanted.

"You stole it for me," she said.

"Sebastian helped," Adrian said.

She spent so much of her life dealing with people who
were more larcenous than she was, she felt almost honest in
comparison. "I had it all planned."

Sebastian glowered. There was a conversation in him, just
bursting to get out.

"If I may . . ." Adrian flicked the list out of her fingers.
"This is rather a lot of secrets for you to be carrying around.
I will take charge of it for the moment. And, yes, you will
see it again any time you express the merest soupçon of an
interest. It is yours, child. I bestow the secrets of Military Intelligence upon you. Use them wisely."

Sebastian said, "What will Reams do when he finds out
it's missing?"

"Which he is doing at this very moment, perhaps. What a
pleasant thought."

"Will he suspect Jess?"

"Most certainly. He will suspect Jess, who is, accidentally,
in this case, innocent. He will suspect me. Suspect you. Suspect his doltish and muscular bodyguard. Suspect Standish,
who saw him firmly and disapprovingly to the door. What he
will not do is make open accusations in any direction, since
this piece of paper should never have existed. Existing, it
should never have left the Horse Guards. In fact," Adrian
folded it into a long flat pleat, "within an hour or two, it will
never have existed at all."

They both looked so pleased with themselves, like boys
who'd done something clever. And they had. She was very

glad she wouldn't be headed over any roofs tonight in the dark.

The hard part was still ahead.

"Don't think this makes me forgive you," she said to Adrian.

Twenty-one

Spitalfields.

THERE ARE MANY WAYS TO GET TO LAZARUS. IF
he hasn't sent for you and you intended to reach him alive,
you come alone and on foot. Jess knew as much as you could
know about approaching Lazarus. This was the first time
she'd come uninvited.

She'd nipped out of the warehouse, quiet like, in an
empty furniture crate, which saved a lot of discussion all
round, and caught a hackney as far as Quaker Street. Then
she got out and walked.

Lazarus was in Spitalfields these days. Exactly where,
she didn't know. An apple seller and the first crossing
sweeper she came to ignored the sign. When she stood in
front of the blind beggar and told him, "I'm looking for the
Dead Man," and held her thumb and index finger in the
shape of an *L*, he looked her over and said, "Bell Lane."

So Lazarus had set himself up near Artillery Passage. Not
a long hike. She didn't have anything more important to do
this afternoon, did she?

Spitalfields was full of pushcarts and pie sellers and
shabby men lounging about the streets—Jews and Irish, a

sprinkling of Germans and Italians, Lascar sailors and blacks. She blended into the polyglot crowd well enough. Her dress was dark cloth that could pass for ordinary. She wore no jewelry but her mother's locket on a ribbon, and that looked like trumpery till you got close. Nobody'd guess she had a fortune in rubies in her pocket.

Scared the spit right out of her mouth, it did, going back to Lazarus. She might be doing something fairly unwise. But he was holding the last piece of the puzzle. No other way to get it but to go to him and ask.

She strolled past a church and up the next street. There were trees in the churchyard. Maples or oaks or something like that. The leaves weren't just one green. They were lots of different greens, like different dye lots of silk. The birds on the iron railings were sparrows, with little brown bibs on them.

She kept walking, not thinking about where she was going. She'd just fool herself along, bit by bit.

For years, Papa kept her out of England so Lazarus wouldn't take her back. Even now, Papa paid blood money to Lazarus—she didn't even know how much—to leave her be. Today, she was walking right back into Lazarus's hands.

She heard footsteps behind her. She was committed now. No turning back.

"Whotcher want with the Dead Man?"

Lazarus's Runner was twelve or so, dressed in a miscellany of oversized clothing. He had the face of a choirboy and eyes devoid of humanity. She gave the sign again.

"The Dead Man don't see every trull what ask 'im," the boy said with heavy sarcasm.

She gave the second sign, the secret one, drawing her right finger on her left palm, crossing the lifeline. Then she showed him the cut on her thumb, the one shaped like an *L*.

The old eyes in the unlined face weren't impressed. "I don't know you."

"Tell him Jess Whitby asks to see him."

"Cooey . . . Jess the Hand. A flash mort." There was ancient evil in that grin. This one would enjoy tearing her to pieces if Lazarus pointed his finger in her direction.

He left, running. She stopped worrying about the bauble. From here on, she was either under Lazarus's protection, or she was his meat. Either way, it made her untouchable. Somebody would come soon to show her the padding ken. Lazarus wasn't far now.

She slowed to watch boys knocking a stone back and forth with sticks. She was almost sure Lazarus wouldn't kill her. Almost.

"This way." It was the evil-eyed boy. She followed him down one street and up another. These big old houses had been rich once. They were cut into mean apartments now, with shabby folks sharing rooms. Everything here was makeshift and meager, a life of skimped meals, and patched clothes, and hanging on to respectability by a fingernail. Before she'd sold herself to Lazarus, she and Mama had lived like this.

The padding crib was in a sizable brick house, the biggest house on this part of the street. A pair of bullyboys sat on the front steps, enjoying the sunshine, throwing dice against the wall. She recognized them from the old days. They were brutal animals, just intelligent enough to be surprised and speculative as she went by.

Nothing had changed from when she'd lived in places like this. In the big front parlor Turkey carpets crisscrossed up and down the length of the floor. Lamps glowed through a haze of tobacco smoke. In untidy heaps of bedding in the corners, men, boys, and a few women slept in a litter of bottles and old cookshop meals.

This was where Lazarus held court. On a long table, silver platters and candlesticks, watches, chains, furs, purses, and even jewels were piled up, awaiting division. This was spoil. This was a demonstration of his power, if anyone who reached this point needed one. The best plunder of London passed through the lair of Lazarus.

There had been a Lazarus in London for three hundred years. When the old one died, a new one took his place. Lazarus was the Dead Man Risen, the Cunning Man, the King of Thieves. He was the master of the London underworld. When she was eight, he'd bought her soul.

Lazarus knew the moment she came in, even if he was pretending he didn't. He sat in his big chair, talking to a couple of men. He'd be over fifty now, but he didn't look it. He dressed simple—a belcher neckcloth and leather vest. Workingman's clothing. He had a broad, brown, steady, reliable face. He was the kind of man you'd hire as coachman, till he looked straight at you, and you saw his eyes.

The Hand, nowadays, was a boy about ten, ragged, wiry, and keen. He sat, tailor-fashion, on the floor next to Lazarus, smoking a pipe. Back by the wall, a pregnant woman hunched on a sofa. Hair the color of cream fell down over her shoulders. Her arms hugged her swollen belly. Black John stood to one side, looking somber and scarred and intimidating as ever. His eyes were remote. At one time, she'd have counted him as a friend. No way to tell now.

Her horrid young guide evaporated. She walked into the room alone. Lazarus didn't look up.

Well. What had she expected? She sighed and walked all the long way down the room to a spot a few feet from where Lazarus sat. Then, very simply, she knelt.

SEBASTIAN sat on the arm of the red velvet sofa and wound his watch. It kept his hands busy so they didn't slam into Mr. Horace Buchanan, clerk at Whitby's, snitch for the British Service.

". . . that smelly animal rubbing itself all over the desk. I brought her the Morpeth papers to sign and she snapped at me. Told me to get out." Buchanan lounged in his chair, expansive and at ease. "Well, I did, of course. But not before I saw she'd just finished writing a letter. And . . ." he paused significantly, "it was something she didn't want me to see."

"Did you manage to read any of it?" Adrian was politely attentive.

"I didn't *then*, since she practically pushed me out of there. And naturally, I had to chase over half the warehouse to find MacLeish, since he's never in his office when you want him, so I . . ."

Buchanan was a slender man in his thirties, with a well-starched cravat and gentlemanly hands. He'd paid for the expensive coat he wore by selling Whitby's secrets.

Sebastian didn't trust clerks who dressed better than he did.

". . . supposed to do with the Morpeth contract since our esteemed *proprietress* was too busy playing with her pet to give me approval on the final terms. It isn't as if I have nothing better to do."

Adrian's sober nod implied this was a world-shaking disclosure. Doyle, looking bovine and harmless, stood at the front window of the parlor, watching Meeks Street.

"When I got back from that, Pitney was in her office, helping himself to a cup of tea. He's one of the favored few who stroll into her office anytime they want. They were talking cozy as turtledoves, the two of them. Then all hell broke loose. Old Pitney's pounding the table, snarling like a dog, and little Miss Jessamyn's laying down the law like a fishwife." Buchanan pursed his lips. "Fine doings in a business office. Pitney kept telling her Josiah would forbid it. That's all I could hear. He said Josiah would absolutely forbid it."

"What was that, I wonder," Adrian said.

"I don't know. MacLeish came over and sent me back to my desk." Buchanan brushed the sleeve of his coat. "But I *do* know Pitney got overruled. After a while he toddled off to open the safe, looking unhappy. It's no work for a man, taking orders from a woman. I don't know how Pitney and MacLeish stomach it."

Sebastian put his watch away. Someday soon he'd find an hour to beat Buchanan to a pulp.

The clerk gave a wide-lipped smile. "Pitney came creeping back like a whipped dog. He brought her something—a little wrapped-up packet. Something from the safe."

"What do you think Pitney brought her?" Adrian said amiably. "That little package. Did you see what it was?"

Doyle extracted an ivory toothpick from his pocket and began to pick his teeth.

"Something valuable." Buchanan pinched the knit fabric of

his pantaloons between thumb and forefinger and adjusted the fit over his knee. "That is, I didn't actually *see* what he brought, but I watched Pitney come creeping by with it, clutching it to his bosom. He might as well have been wearing a sign, 'I am carrying something immensely important.'"

"And then?" Adrian prompted.

"Well, she left, don't you know? Just took her hat off the peg and left, right in the middle of the day, without a word to anyone. I . . . ah . . . took the opportunity to drop a few small matters on her desk. Receipts and so on. There was nothing on her blotter except for . . ." He swished the tail of his coat aside and drew a small letter from his pocket. ". . . this."

Adrian held out his hand.

"It was what she was writing earlier, obviously. The letter she didn't want me to see. You can see it's addressed to her father. Normally, she'd hand letters over to the messenger boy." Buchanan's pale blue eyes slid from one man to another. "But she left it there on her desk. I thought that had to be suspicious. Since I was coming here anyway to drop off a few papers for Mr. Whitby, it was quite natural to pick this up and bring it along."

Adrian kept his hand out. Buchanan held the letter tight, plucking at the corners.

"She meant for it to be delivered, and it had Whitby's name on it. It could have been that she just forgot to give it to the messenger. She left in a hurry." Jerkily, he laid it in Adrian's hand and stood up. "I'll just go ask Mr. Whitby if he has commissions for me. I'm not . . . Mr. MacLeish may ask me why I was out of the office."

Adrian inspected the seal of the letter. "You opened it. That was not strictly necessary, Mr. Buchanan."

"I thought it best. If it had been quite innocent, I wouldn't have bothered you with it." Buchanan wiped his fingertips against the cloth of his jacket. "It pretends to be a polite note saying she'll be late, but the name she mentions is *not* one of our customers. I've never heard of him."

"Thank you," Adrian said. "We'll study it carefully."

Doyle laid a huge, friendly hand on Buchanan and pushed him toward the door. "We'll take care of it."

"If I could talk to Mr. Whitby—"

"Not now. They'll be wanting you back at work, I expect."

"I knew you'd want to see this at once. If there's anything else you need from the files, I can—"

"We'll let you know. You just keep an eye open."

The door opened. Buchanan found himself speaking from the front porch. "It's a French name. I find that significant. She receives letters from France. I'm sure of it."

Doyle said, "I wouldn't be surprised if you weren't right about that, Mr. Buchanan. Here now, watch yerself on the steps. They just been washed." He closed the door.

Sebastian waited till Buchanan was down the steps and walking toward Booth Square. "Do you have to use that pig?"

"Men of sterling worth do not spy on their employers for pay. He sells Whitby commercial information to several interested parties." Adrian frowned and turned the letter over. "I wish he'd stop opening mail."

"I don't like the idea of him close to Jess."

"I doubt she notices his existence. If he ever annoys her, she'll crush him like a bug. I wonder what devilment she's up to now?"

"Something mad. She's out there alone." Doyle came back to sit heavily on the sofa, his big, solid frame taking up most of it. He looked worried. "I thought I had all the exits watched. I don't like this."

Sebastian didn't like it himself. "She cleans her desk and leaves one letter behind, addressed to her father. She dodges your men and mine and disappears. Do you think she's leaving England?"

"Wouldn't that be nice? But I doubt it." Adrian held the letter up to the sunlight and squinted at it, then unfolded the sheet across his lap. "Let us see what she has to say. 'Cher Papa.' That's Jess being suspiciously French for my benefit. You do like to get in a sly dig every once in a while, don't you, my girl?"

Probably the letter didn't mean anything, but right now it was the only clue they had to where she'd gone. "Just read."

"Her writing's improved. One of the governesses must have finally accomplished that. When I was being their butler in Russia, she wrote chicken scratches in four languages. *'Cher Papa. Just a note to let you know I may not be free to see you this afternoon. I go to visit our old friend to seek his advice and aid. He may urge me to stay, and you know how persuasive Monsieur L'Hommemort can be—' "*

Adrian's voice cut off, like a knife had slashed through the word.

"Monsieur L'Hommemort?" Sebastian took the letter. "Nobody's named that. Let me see."

Adrian whispered, "Oh, damn you, Jess. Why?"

"L'homme mort. The Dead Man." Sebastian stood up to read the rest. " *'I will see you soon, one way or the other. Jess. P.S. Please do not be angry with Pitney.'* L'Homme mort. It can't mean what I think it does."

"It means exactly and precisely what you think it means. She's already on her way. Damn the girl."

"She's going to Lazarus for help? She's going to wind up held for ransom." Jess might come from Whitechapel, but that didn't mean she knew how to deal with a man like Lazarus.

"It's worse than that. Sebastian, wait. She was Hand."

"What?"

"She was Jess the Hand, with all that means."

Pretty, elegant Jess working for Lazarus? The Hand was one of the inner circle of Lazarus's gang. "It doesn't make any sense. She would have been a child when she left London."

"They are kids, generally. Lazarus picks the young ones. They can be trusted. She went to work for him when Josiah disappeared from England. Then Josiah showed up again, years after everybody thought he was dead. He took Jess back, away from Lazarus and out of the country." Adrian stood up and pulled his coat off the back of the chair. "Lazarus takes money to leave her alone. But he never gave her up and never forgot. In his eyes, she's a deserter."

"And she's walking right to him."

"Right down his gullet."

Doyle took his pistol out of his pocket to give it a check. Adrian was half into his coat.

"Not you," Sebastian told them. "Just me."

Doyle understood first. "Because you can get in alone."

"We can't fight Lazarus on his own ground. I have to talk her out of there."

"He's not going to just let her go." Adrian picked up the note and began folding it and unfolding it, running his fingernails down the crease again and again. "You have to understand. You and the other captains pay the pence and Lazarus leaves your ships and men alone. It's different with Jess. She took the shilling from him before she was nine."

He felt his stomach harden to heavy, cold rock.

"He owns her, Sebastian, body and soul. Remember that when you go charging in there. He owns her."

Twenty-two

THERE ARE MANY WAYS TO GET TO LAZARUS.
Sebastian didn't have time to waste, so he tracked down his
shipping manager on the deck of the *Scarlet Dancer* and
dragged him off to the tavern where Kennett Shipping paid its
pence. The introduction was made. Sebastian held a brief col-
loquy with the lean, avaricious youth who sat in the back receiving payment and marking it off in a book. He described,
exactly and pungently, what he intended to do to the boy's
anatomy if he wasn't taken to Lazarus immediately.

He felt no surprise when a thin blade came from behind to
rest against his throat. The avaricious youth had a friend. It
was the etiquette of these encounters. He repeated his request,
and the threat, this time tossing a roll of banknotes on the
dirty table. A half-grown girl, filthy and cunning as a rat, was
his guide through the maze of streets. Had Jess ever been as
miserable and dirty as this child?

He followed her toward what was either the current lair-
ing place of Lazarus, or else a convenient spot to kill someone and dispose of the body. Choose one.

That was how he came to Lazarus.

* * *

BEING scared turned her muscles to water, but she was kneeling, so her legs didn't give out. She wasn't going to think about men and women she'd seen, kneeling like this, petitioning Lazarus. She wasn't going to think what had happened to some of them. They'd been scared, too.

Lazarus finished talking to one bloke and sent him off. He motioned another over, ignoring her. That was fine. Likely he was deciding what the hell to do with her, now he'd got her. She didn't want to hurry him while he was thinking that over.

Time passed. Word had gone out. Men trickled in, in twos and threes, and sat on the benches or stood along the wall. She knew most of them from when she was a kid. Friends, she would have called them.

These were Lazarus's thieves. Some of them were clever with their fingers or specialists in cracking houses. Some were evil brutes who beat men senseless in alleys. They wore rags, or cheap flashy jackets, or dressed respectable as Quakers. One or two wore the fine clothes of gentlemen and brocade waistcoats.

They were clearing the room for what was coming. They kicked the whores awake and hustled them out. The rabble of little kids and pickpockets and sneak thieves got cuffed out the door, too. It was quiet, except for a low, gritty whisper that rose and fell in the room, like dirty waves breaking on pebbles. It was men left now, men and a few hard-eyed women. This was the Brotherhood. They'd come to see what Lazarus would do to her.

Lazarus finished conducting business and exchanged a word with Black John. He motioned, and the pregnant girl brought him a string bag of walnuts and scuttled back to the sofa.

It looked like Lazarus had finished mulling things over. The whispers died away. The room filled up with expectant silence. She knelt where she was and waited. For a while, Lazarus cracked walnuts, one against the other in his hand, and picked out the meat, and dropped the shells on the floor.

He said softly, "Do you happen to remember the penalty for deserting the Brotherhood, Jess?"

"Yes, Sir."

"What is it?"

"Death."

Mutters ran through the men watching. Lazarus cracked another nut. He had very strong hands.

She knew Lazarus as well as anyone. Once, she'd obeyed his orders, the way all these men did. She would have died for him, if he'd asked it. Ten years ago Papa came back from France and took her away. She hadn't seen Lazarus since.

"Did you get tired of breathing?"

"No, Sir." Life seemed very sweet, just at this moment, on any terms whatsoever. She'd seen a man executed for deserting. The Brotherhood had done it with knives and it had taken all night.

"Then explain why you're here."

Once, she'd sat behind him, where that boy was, and watched Lazarus amuse himself like this, tormenting people, a good few of whom ended up dead. "You know why, Sir. If anybody in this town knows what happened to Papa, you do."

"You think I give a rat's fart what happens to Josiah Whitby?"

"No, Sir," she said quickly.

Lazarus got up and walked toward her. She heard his boots, going past, circling her. She'd forgotten what it was like, being afraid of Lazarus. Been years since she was scared of him.

"You turned out pretty." He was standing behind her, talking quiet. "I wouldn't have expected it. You were ugly as a monkey last time I saw you."

Nothing to say to that. She swallowed and didn't move.

"It took you a long time to find your way back. I guess you were busy making money in all those foreign places."

She felt his hand on the bare skin of her neck, and she froze. Ice speared inside her, everywhere. He killed men this way, with his bare hands, with a sharp twist to the neck. She'd seen him do it a few times when he was making an example of men who peached to the law or fools who tried to cheat him. She'd watched them dragged in, pleading and explaining.

He played with them before he killed them. He let them beg. For her, he'd do it quick. No warning. With her he'd be merciful. It was faster than hanging, he told her once.

"You've been back in London a time or two, haven't you?" His fingers touched the side of her jaw. She flinched. Terror squirmed in her belly like long, cold snakes.

"I been 'ere from time to time," she said. "Everybody knows that."

He was just stroking back some hair that had fallen loose, tucking it behind her ear. His hand dropped away. "You've gone soft, Jess. Soft skin. Soft clothes. Soft inside, too, I think. I hate to see that happen to you. You weren't soft ten years ago."

"I'm here. That's not soft." She concentrated on breathing. If she didn't keep her mind on it, she'd probably stop.

"No, Jess. That's stupid. You weren't stupid ten years ago, either." He stood, looking down at her. "You're a rich woman, I hear."

That was bad. Lazarus loathed the gentry. The blonde girl against the wall there, the pregnant one, was one of his toys. He kidnapped girls from rich homes, kept them a few months, and sold them back to their families. Evening the scales, he called it. Generally they went home pregnant.

"Bloody rich," she said. "Scares me sometimes."

He walked around her and finished up in front. "I never had one of my own people turn on me. Not one of my special ones. Only you."

"Yes." Nothing she could say.

"You were one of my favorites. The best I ever had in some ways."

No excuses to give. Nothing.

"Now you've come waltzing back. You always did take chances with yourself. Never could break you of it. You'll get yerself killed that way, sooner or later."

She risked glancing up. He used to smile when he said that to her. "I been lucky. So far." She got it out past the pain in her throat. It was the old answer, from when she was the only one who dared to joke with him.

Something glinted behind the opaque eyes. "One way you haven't changed. You still have more backbone than brains." He nudged her knee with the toe of his boot. "Oh, for God's sake, Jess, get up off the floor. If I wanted to break your neck, I'd have done it years ago."

He turned his back on her and stomped over to his chair and sat down heavy. He sounded bloody exasperated, just like the old days, back when she was Hand. The tight coil in her stomach loosened a notch, hearing him sound so familiar. When she struggled to her feet she was clumsy with it, her muscles cramped up like she'd been sitting there a week.

"Tell me what's happened to Josiah. Report to me," he snapped.

Lazarus used to send her out to follow men he pointed to and listen to everything they said. Used to send her into shops and houses he was planning to rob, telling her to list up what was in them worth stealing. She'd reported back a thousand times, standing in front of him, setting words out neat and organized the way he taught her. Felt strange, doing it again.

She stepped up close and spilled it out, talking low so no one heard but Black John and the Hand. She told him about Meeks Street. Cinq. The British Service. Reports from her agents. What she'd figured out so far. She knew what Lazarus would be interested in. She gave him facts. Speculation. Everything.

He always liked knowing more than anyone else. He collected secrets the way the other men collected silver and gold.

She talked till her voice hurt. Around her and behind her, the Brotherhood shuffled and spat and coughed. There was a clicking sound that might have been coins. The door opened and closed. A dozen gruff conversations filled the background. Nothing was going to happen till Lazarus finished talking to her.

Eventually he ran out of things to ask her and she ran out

of things to say. She waited to see what he'd do to her. She kept her hands behind her back, grabbed into each other. Lazarus picked up a pair of walnuts in one hand and rolled them back and forth between his fingers, changing one over the other. "Why have you come to Lazarus, Jessamyn Whitby?"

That was the formal question. He asked it a dozen times a day. She could have been any petitioner. It was like she'd never been Hand. Like she'd never been anything at all. She'd counted too much on an old fondness. Looked like it'd been too many years since Lazarus had been fond of her.

So be it. She'd be a petitioner. She'd do whatever she had to. "I come 'ere . . ." Her voice shook.

"Yes?" Damn him for lazing back like none of this mattered.

"I come to buy a service, Lazarus. I need your records from the docks." Lazarus collected his pence from the captains of every ship that put down anchor in the Pool of London. From every sailor who stepped ashore. And it was all writ down. "I brought payment."

She dipped in her pocket and pulled out the bauble and tossed it to the Hand, sitting on the ground beside Lazarus. It was an unexpected throw, but the boy snagged it, sudden and swift. He was as good as she'd been, when she'd held that place. Soundless, he opened the pouch, checked what was inside, and passed it over to Lazarus.

Lazarus poured the necklace across his palm, a web of quivering, blood red drops. Even in the dimness, the Medici Necklace showed its quality. It looked like queens had worn it.

"This is beautiful." He turned it over reverently. "Completely, exquisitely beautiful." Fire sparked and danced in his hand. "A rare payment for your father's life. You brought it with your own hands. You understand the art of these things."

"Artist. That's me." Her mouth was dry as hardtack.

"I accept the contract."

Her eyes squeezed closed all by themselves. She had it. Whatever the cost, she had what she'd come for. A list of every ship—scows and coal barges, Baltic schooners, every East Indiaman and American sloop, all the coastal vessels.

Ships that didn't even have a nodding acquaintance with the Customs House. The lot.

Lazarus said, "Tell me where and when, Jess. I'll send them." In the same quiet, contemplative voice, he said, "We're not finished. Face the Brothers, Jess Whitby. You're on trial. It's time we got on with it."

She was so shocked she went dizzy. The strength that had brought her this far just drained away, like it was her blood running out. Right till this minute, she'd been expecting him to claim her and keep her safe. Lazarus was right. She'd got soft. She'd been telling herself stories. Believing them.

He stood. Gentle, he put his hand on her shoulder and turned her around. He pushed her forward, away from him, so she stood alone. That was all. Not a word to defend her.

She wasn't the only one surprised. A murmur of speculation rumbled out of the men along the wall, growing louder, till it sounded like a dog growling, low in the throat. Some of them were arguing. Nobody was sure what to do next.

"Kill 'er," a coarse voice said, loud and clear, from the back.

"Kill 'er."

Sebastian heard that. He pushed his scrawny guide out of his path and walked through the open door.

He was in time. She was still alive. Jess stood alone in a cleared space at the center of the room. Unhurt. Her face glowed like a pale beacon in the smoky dimness. A pace behind her, a dark pillar of threat, Lazarus stood. Dozens of men crowded the walls, pressed elbow to elbow, buzzing like a hive of hornets. This was the inner circle of Lazarus's vast gang, the deadly aristocracy of the underworld. Thieves, pimps, and murderers, men of unparalleled brutality. They'd kill her—and him—in the blink of an eye.

The Brotherhood was holding trial. Generally somebody wound up dead when they did that. He pushed his way through.

A squat, dark thug had separated from the pack. "She broke the oath. That's death."

"Shut yer gob, Badger."

"Bloody loudmouth."

Another man called out, "Let 'im say 'is piece."

"I ain't 'ere ter listen to the Badger yap."

"Say what you have to say, Badger." Lazarus hooked his thumbs in his waistband.

"She's a traitor." Badger had the slanted forehead and sloping, heavy arms of his namesake. He sneered once at Jess, rounded, and faced the men. "She come prancing in wif 'er flash clothes and 'er fancy talk, thinkin' she's better 'n us. She come 'ere with no respect. No proper deference. Tryin' to buy 'er way in."

Somebody growled, "Jess ain't no traitor."

"She were Hand, fer Gawd's sake."

"She ain't Hand now," Badger shouted. "She ain't shite to us."

"Sod you, Badger." A gangling, redheaded boy, widestanced, fists ready, was hauled back by his friends.

"She turned her back on us." The sly whisper came from a bent, frail man in shabby black. "It's our law. Nobody's above the law."

"And I says we leave 'er be."

Sebastian looked the mob over, taking in the brutally intelligent faces. Two or three echoed Badger's resentment. One man had mad eyes, avid for pain and death. Anyone's death. But Jess had a dozen supporters. The older men, the canny ones, watched Lazarus.

"We cut traitors." Badger drew a blade and held it up, flat side out, to the men. "That's the law."

Jess dropped back a step. Not toward Lazarus. She must know she wasn't going to get any help there.

"She said, 'If I break this oath, ye may carve it out o' my belly.'" Badger gloated. "That's what she said. That's what we all say."

How the hell was he going to stop this? Jess could be dead in two minutes.

He didn't pull his knife and hack a path to Jess, leaving bodies writhing on the floor. He didn't howl and break necks. He stiff-armed one man, shoved another aside, and shouldered to the front, past men intent only on the drama playing out in the center.

Lazarus had spotted him. Eyes, brown as agate, cold as marbles, sardonically amused, met his. They'd dealt before, haggling over women Aunt Eunice wanted rescued. A hard and devious man at the bargaining table, the Dead Man.

Lazarus raised an eyebrow and glanced at Jess and waited. Oh yes. Lazarus knew what he'd come for.

He nodded back. Acknowledging. *Yes. Jess.*

Badger postured for the mob. "And I'm the man te gut the bitch." He swung suddenly, backhanded, with his empty fist.

And stumbled stupidly into the empty space where she'd been. She glided past him, smooth as a fish. "Missed," she said.

"Yer gonna die, rat."

Her voice rang clear. "You speak for the Brothers, do you? That'll come as a surprise to some of 'em."

There was a rumble of laughter.

"Gonna cut you, bitch. Gonna carve you like a pie."

"Never used to be a killing offense, working for the smugglers." Jess flitted just out of reach. "That's a new rule you made, right? Speak up, Badger. Cat got yer tongue?"

There was a joke in that, one everyone knew. Laughter scattered the tension. Badger glared around, the back of his neck turning red. "I got me rights, I do. I got things ter say."

"Spit it out, then. I ain't here to dance wif yer."

Catcalls and whistles broke out from every side. She was turning the crowd in her favor. It might be enough to save her life. If Badger didn't cut her. If Lazarus didn't want her dead. There were a hundred possibilities, most of them bad.

He stood at the front of the crowd, one leap from Jess. Picking his time.

She was all Cockney now—a tough, vulgar, vibrant street urchin. Back in the offices of Whitby Trading, they wouldn't have recognized her. She skipped over the welter of scattered rugs. "Nice knife, Badger. Use that for picking yer nose wif, do yer?" This was the fierce little animal she'd been as a child in the rookery. "Or maybe yer scratch yer arse."

On every side, cutthroats grinned appreciatively.

"Never could catch me, could yer, Bugger?" She dodged again, lightning and laughter. "Oh, sorry. That's Badger, ain't it?"

Rough jeers rang out. Rattled, Badger swung in a furious half circle. "We make an example of 'er. She dies."

Argument bubbled up everywhere.

"She loped orf. We all know the law."

"She didn't pike it 'erself. Went wif 'er da."

"She owes us." That was a dangerous judgment, more so because it came from a sober, middle-aged villain. "Jobs went sour because Jess weren't here, planning 'em. She were ours, and we needed her."

A woman spoke up from the back. "Oh, hold yer bluidy tongue, Jack. She were a kid. Take it out o' Whitby's hide."

"If yer dare . . ." Furtive laughter.

"You tell 'em, Cat."

The red-haired boy said, "She didn't peach. She never peached on us."

"Worked for Whitby, didn't she? It ain't like she went honest."

"I say, she dies."

The most degenerate killers in London squabbled over what Jess was guilty of. She waited, sweating, wary eyes on Badger's knife. And Lazarus watched without taking sides. He looked calm, almost bored, his eyes half-closed. Whatever game he played with Jess, it was unrolling to his satisfaction. Lazarus wouldn't interfere.

If she'd cringed . . . if she'd whined . . . they'd have been on her like a pack of dogs. That hard, bright grin, the spectacle of her sheer, raw courage, held them off. But she was dancing on a knife edge. As long as Lazarus stayed quiet, the mood wavered and shifted. Sebastian had to stop this before they killed her just for the sport.

It was time. He stepped deliberately into the clear center of the room, where Jess faced Badger. Voices quieted. For the first time, Jess looked up and saw him. She whitened. The fool girl should have known he'd come for her.

He used the voice he'd learned on the quarterdeck. "I say, she lives."

Ripples of murmur and silence spread around the room. He took another step and he was where he belonged, between Jess and that damned knife Badger was waving around.

"What's he doing 'ere?" Badger glared suspiciously from face to face. "Who's 'e?"

There were men who did know him. In undertones, his name was handed back and forth around the room. Even here, his reputation meant something.

Jess whispered, "Gonna get yerself sodding killed." But she moved into his shadow, shielding behind him.

Lazarus said, "Gentlemen, this is Captain Sebastian Kennett, come to visit."

"The sea captain?" Badger bared his teeth and tossed the knife from one hand to the other, spinning it, showing off. "Kennett ships. We don't like rich coves what stick their noses in where they ain't—" Badger feinted suddenly, slashing toward him, "wanted."

He ignored the blade like it didn't exist. It cut the air two inches from his cheek. He'd read bluff in Badger's eyes before the blade twitched. Bluff . . . and he'd called it.

They understood nuances, this council of cutthroats. He had half of them on his side, that instant. An appreciative murmur rose, and a laugh.

Badger yelled, "You got no rights 'ere. Yer can't walk in orf the street and—"

"Jess is mine." He made sure everyone heard that. "You have my woman. That's my right here."

Badger's low forehead creased. Events were getting away from him.

"I'm not—" Jess began.

He snapped, "You are," and she swallowed whatever was hovering on her tongue. Something better unsaid, certainly.

There wasn't a man here who wasn't watching Lazarus, waiting to see what he'd do with that claim. Nothing, it seemed. Thirty men saw Lazarus being impassive.

He surveyed the pack, meeting eyes, looking into faces. "Jess is my woman. I say she didn't run. Is there any man—besides Bugger here—" there was a stir of appreciative humor, "who says she did?"

"She been gone a while," one plump rogue pointed out amiably. "Ten years. Ain't like she stepped out for a spot o' tea."

Chuckles.

"Oh, I dunnoh, Blinks. I smuggled me a fair old spot o' tea, when all's said and—" She'd turned toward the voice, taking her eye off Badger. She didn't see the raised fist coming at her.

Badger's mistake. This was the opening he needed.

He blocked the punch. Cracked forearm to forearm. Badger spat a stream of filthy words and dropped into a killer's crouch and brought his knife up.

This fight had been inevitable when he walked through the door. The huge black, the bodyguard, earned his gratitude by snagging Jess and yanking her, protesting, to the sidelines.

Badger didn't mind attacking an unarmed man. He charged, thinking his knife was important, counting on the reach of those long, freakish arms. That left him wide open for a fast punch just below the heart. Speed beat reach, any day. When Badger hunched over to gag his belly out, Sebastian booted him in the groin.

There wasn't a man there who didn't wince. In the absolute silence, Badger swayed in place, gave a womanish whimper, and collapsed in on himself like a rotten melon. The knife clattered to the floor.

Because he knew his audience, because he was making a point, he kicked that vicious animal one more time as he crumbled. It felt just as good the second time. This garbage dared to raise a hand against Jess.

It stayed quiet. He didn't have to raise his voice. "You were rude to my lady, Badger."

No answer from the carcass on the floor.

He picked up Badger's knife, flipped it, and leaned down to press the point to the man's throat. He did it hard enough to send a trickle of blood running down to the rug. "I don't like it when men are rude to my lady."

Badger didn't wash his neck. It was a throat that would be improved by slitting. No loss to anyone in the room, if he read the crowd right. But he'd made his point. He held the pose one second longer, then straightened up and tossed the knife away. That was the kind of gesture Englishmen loved. Besides, holding it was just going to get him in trouble.

This was what he'd needed. Not just a fight. A display of skill they'd talk about for weeks. He'd given the Brotherhood something to think about besides butchering Jess on these carpets.

"I don't like brawls in here." Lazarus's voice slid like a snake between rocks. "This is not Donnybrook Fair."

Jittering currents of expectation swept the room.

"Not much of a brawl." Coolly, he prodded Badger with his boot. "Unless you want this killed."

"A handsome offer. Not today, I think."

He stared into the seamed cruelty of Lazarus's face. "Then it's time we talk." He added, low enough that no one else heard him, "You've played with her long enough. End this."

Lazarus nodded. He looked around the room, collecting every eye, taking control of his gang. "Is there anyone here," he said calmly, "who doubts that Jess belongs to me?"

Dead silence.

"I tell Jess when to come and go. I tell her when to breathe. I decide when she stops." He waited another minute while the silence stretched out. "Nobody else touches her."

Lazarus hitched his jacket closed and walked past what was left of Badger. The talking started behind his back. Speculation, approval, and relief. Jess had her life back. For the moment.

"Step into my office, Captain Kennett," Lazarus said.

Twenty-three

⊷⊶⊷⊶

IT ENDED WITH BADGER FLOPPING ON THE FLOOR and the Captain adjusting his neckcloth, calm as a cucumber. Everybody enjoyed the show. Just another of Lazarus's bloody spectacles. Never a dull moment in the padding ken. That was something else she'd managed to forget in the last couple years.

When Lazarus jerked his head toward the back room and invited the Captain to talk, Jess was glad enough to follow and get away from all the eyes watching her. She'd known Lazarus would keep her safe. Known it all along. He'd taken his bloody time getting around to it, hadn't he?

The back room where Lazarus conducted his private business had been a fancy parlor once. The wallpaper was peeling and most of the plaster had cracked off the ceiling. The place reeked of piss and onions. She wouldn't have noticed that ten years ago. The table held an oil lamp, unlit, and a wine bottle and glasses. Ropes with climbing hooks were hanked up neat and stored in the corner. The tools of her old trade. One chair held an open book and a stack of newspapers. Lazarus read everything he could get his hands on. A crowbar leaned against the hearth. They'd use that for milling kens when they weren't poking the fire with it.

"My pied-à-terre, Captain. Make yourself at home. Jess . . . you two . . . in here." As he walked, Lazarus pulled his jacket off and let it drop. The current toy, that girl he was tormenting, bent and picked it up and folded it over a chair-back. She went to curl up in a chair near the curtained window, looking pregnant as hell. Generally Lazarus sent them home when they got pregnant.

She couldn't help that poor woman. Nobody could. Not till Lazarus got bored with her.

Black John took up a place at the wall where he'd have a good line of fire. The Hand slid in and crouched down in the corner, being alert and inconspicuous. And her, she didn't know what to do. She didn't know how to act with Lazarus when she wasn't Hand. So she stood there feeling sick and shaky, getting cold where her clothes stuck to her skin.

Lazarus stretched and yawned and took the chair beside the fireplace, kicking his boots up onto the empty grate. She'd got reasonably good at guessing what Lazarus was thinking, back when she was Hand. Just now, he was cold, bite-yer-arse-off angry. She wouldn't have crossed him for any money.

She finally made herself meet his eyes. He said, "Welcome home, Jess."

That was him telling her she was staying. He must have been planning to take her back ever since she walked into the padding ken. Always had to do things complicated, Lazarus did.

"Yes, Sir." She rubbed her face and tried to think of some way out of this. Her brain had gone numb as a potato.

"Don't get comfortable, Jess. You're not staying." The Captain prowled the room, working off the fighting edge he hadn't been able to use on Badger. This was another man she didn't want to cross right now.

There was no one like Sebastian. No one. Lazarus could beat him to a pulp, or slit his gullet and have him dumped in the afternoon tide. Kennett acted like he was on the deck of his own ship with fifty men at his back. All those years with

Lazarus, and she'd never seen anyone stroll in so insolent. You'd think he wanted to get killed.

"Is that what you think?" Lazarus said.

Kennett helped himself to the other chair and sat, confronting Lazarus. There was nothing conciliatory anywhere in either of them. He said, "We have things to say. Clear these ears out of here."

"My people don't have ears unless I tell them to." Lazarus was pretending to be genial. A king cobra, being genial. "Sorry to spoil your fun with Badger, but I can't let you kill my pimps for being stupid. We'd be knee-deep in carcasses."

"You let him raise a knife to Jess."

"She could outrun that clod when she was six." Lazarus gave a lazy, malicious smile. "Generally. I showed the Brothers she hasn't gone soft. They'll accept her now. Fluffy, I have a guest." He snapped his fingers impatiently. "Wine. For God's sake, girl, anybody'd think you were raised in a barn."

The toy scrambled to her feet and went for bottle and glasses. She carried the silver tray balanced over her protruding belly and offered first to Sebastian, who took a glass, then Lazarus. She didn't offer any to Jess. Even the toy knew Jess wasn't a guest.

"I wonder if you made a mistake coming here, Captain." Lazarus must have been holding the Medici Necklace all this time. He held it up next to the Burgundy in his glass, comparing color. "You have the reputation of being shrewd. You're sure you won't try the wine? It's excellent."

The Captain wasn't playing the game at all. He was grim as a rock-bound coast. "Let's talk about Jess."

"You're always wanting some woman from me. Can I interest you in Fluffy here? I'm about done with her." Lazarus took a sip and gestured with his glass. "A little close to whelping for some men's taste, but a lively bit. Do you know how I pick these girls? Every one of them's done something a poor girl would get hanged for. Every one. Shall we hear what Fluffy did?" He motioned the woman to him.

She came, stiff and unwilling, ducking her head behind a curtain of hair. "I had a maid. She was fifteen. I . . ." No telling how often she'd had to confess this.

Lazarus was showing off how evil he could be. She hated it when he did that. He wasn't like that. Not really. You'd think he was doing it on purpose to see how far he could push the Captain.

Sebastian stopped it. His voice would have sawed through hardwood. "Do we have to waste time with this? I get your point."

"As you say, you get my point." Lazarus touched the blonde girl. "Go. Did you own women, out in Turkey and Syria, Captain? They say you can buy any color or shape of woman in the East. Women of infinite sexual variety."

"I hear the same about London." Sebastian finished the wine in a single, long pull and tossed his glass to the Hand. "What are you going to do with Jess?"

Lazarus smiled. "Whatever I please. That's the joy of it."

They glared at each other like hawks or eagles or something. Made her feel like a mouse trapped between them. She didn't know what this Fluffy was feeling like. Yesterday's catch, regurgitated into the nest, probably.

Sebastian said, "She lives in my house. I pay the pence. The agreement is, you don't molest my people."

"Captain . . . Captain . . . she was mine before she grew hair between her legs. I own her right to the bottom of her miserable soul. Look." Lazarus made the hand sign. She was beside him before she thought about it, feeling surprised to be there. Habit. She hadn't lost it, seemed like. He snapped out, "Who do you belong to, Jess?"

"I belong to—" She caught herself. Damn. Almost, that had been, "I belong to Lazarus." She must have said that ten thousand times. When Lazarus first made her move into the crib, he asked that fifty times a day, and she had to give that answer. In the end, she'd believed it. "It's been a long time, Sir."

Lazarus wasn't looking at her anyway. He was watching Sebastian. "Do you know what my people have to do? My special ones? The ones I own. They have to kill somebody for me, even pretty girls like Jess here. Isn't that right?"

"Yes, Sir." He had to bring that up, didn't he? The worst night of her life, brimful of death and terror and having nowhere to run, and he had to keep harping on it. After all this time, it didn't matter why she'd sold her soul to Lazarus.

But Lazarus was just reveling in it. "She came to me with the blood still on her. She's one of us. She's mine. Men who come asking for what's mine get hurt."

Sebastian didn't look impressed.

"I don't need rescuing, Captain," she said. "Clear off and leave me to—" Crikey. Now she'd got Lazarus irritated at her. She'd made it worse. She knew better than that.

Lazarus said mildly, "Jess, do you have advice on how I should deal with the Captain?"

She shook her head quickly. Stupid. Stupid.

"I didn't hear you, Jess."

"No, Sir. Nothing to say. Not a word."

"I didn't think so."

He turned back to the Captain. "It took me months to teach Jess silence. For a long time, whenever she begged me to leave someone alone, I was forced to be especially loathsome to them. It was a difficult time for both of us."

The Captain's eyes glinted like sharp knives. "That was a long time ago."

"Was it?" Lazarus held the bauble up. "Report to me, Jess. The necklace."

The Medici Necklace. Easy. "Eleven rubies, perfectly matched. All flawless, except the central stone. That one's twelve carats and historic as hell. Legend is, it dates to the Rajput in the ninth century. The upper right-hand quadrant holds a crystal inclusion, visible to the naked eye. The third on the left is from the twelfth-century diadem of the princess of Navarre. The necklace was assembled in 1480 for Lorenzo de' Medici. Louis Bolliard lifted it from the Romanov treasury two years ago and fenced it in Geneva, where Whitby's bought it. Intact, it's worth eight thousand on the gray market in London. Its white market breakup value is less than six, after three identifiable stones are recut."

The Captain's face was stony cold. She stopped, abrupt like, having caught on to what Lazarus was up to. This wasn't about the necklace.

Lazarus whispered, "I took infinite pains with her, Kennett.

One of my most valuable possessions. I never found another like her."

That made her sound like a pocket watch. But it wasn't like that. Hours, they used to spend talking, in the old days. He'd taught her everything. How to pick locks. How to rope her way down a building. How to plan a caper. That last time, when she'd fallen so bad and got herself trapped in the dark in the old warehouse, it had been Lazarus who came in for her. He'd crawled in the whole way and pulled her out, with the building collapsing around their ears and bricks and timbers hitting them. He'd risked his neck. She hadn't been a bloody pocket watch. He was goading the Captain, pure and simple.

The Captain and Lazarus stayed, eyes locked, not making any sudden moves. It was like they were two men on a tightrope, neither of them shaking the rope.

Then Sebastian leaned forward. "I've taken her to bed. She's my possession now."

Oh, bloody hell. The Captain expected her to lie to Lazarus. She couldn't do it. Lazarus could read her like a newspaper.

"Jess?" Lazarus poked her.

The Captain swung round and ran his eyes up and down her, looking like a man who'd tumbled her, maybe a couple dozen different ways, and enjoyed all of them. She remembered lying beside him in his bunk on board ship with the rain hitting the deck above—him dark and strong as a black angel, smelling of salt and sweat. She'd wanted to bite into him, like bread. She'd wanted to open her legs and tell him to touch her there . . .

Damned if she didn't blush like a schoolgirl.

"I see. Oh, yes, I see. She has grown up, hasn't she?" Lazarus laughed, a great bass rumble that came up from his belly. "Makes 'em just about useless." He gestured impatiently. The Hand jumped up and Lazarus coiled the Medici Necklace down into the boy's cupped palms. "Take that and put it away someplace."

"Sir." The boy gave a cheeky grin, stuffed fifty carats of rubies in his breeches, and sauntered out.

Lazarus watched him. "You can't get good help. On her worst day, Jess was worth thirty of that one. She doesn't strut when she carries valuables. That astonishing object in her pocket, and even I didn't know she had it on her till she tossed it to me." Without changing tone he said, "She thinks you're the spy, Kennett. The whole time she's warming your bed, she's fingering you for the drop. Interesting bedsport, even by my standards."

"I enjoy it." Sebastian just kept on lying to Lazarus. Nobody lied to Lazarus.

Lazarus took a last swallow of wine and held the empty glass out. Fluffy scrambled to take it from him just before he let it drop. "Josiah Whitby can rot in hell. And I leave spies to Adrian Hawkhurst. But Cinq came into my streets and hired Irishmen to kidnap one of my people. That I don't allow. Where were you when Cinq almost grabbed her?"

"Protecting her."

"You're doing a damn poor job of it, you and Josiah. My Jess walks in here, covered with bruises. She's so scared she came to *me* for help. Why should I let her go? At least I protect what's mine."

"By keeping her . . . here?" With a flick of his fingers, the Captain said what he thought of the padding ken. "She's not twelve years old anymore. Let her go before you have to hurt her."

They did more of that staring and talking back and forth without saying anything.

The Captain laid out another line of words, like hard pebbles. "If you don't kill me, I'll come back for her. If you kill me, you can't hold on to Jess. Look at her."

They both did. What was she supposed to do with her face? Flummoxed her.

"Come here, Jess," Lazarus said. That was when she noticed she'd been edging over toward the Captain all this time.

So she went over and stood square in front of Lazarus, not trying to talk. He hadn't changed much in the years between then and now. There were more lines in his face.

"You should have told me you were coming," he said at last. "Weren't you paying attention all those years? You *tell* me when you're going to pull one of your damfool stunts. What am I supposed to do with you, anyway?"

"I don't know, Sir."

"Since you're mine, I should probably keep you here and try to make something of you."

It was quiet, for the padding crib. She couldn't hear anything but the blood pounding in her head. She didn't say anything. Couldn't.

"Ten years ago, I tried to get you back from Josiah. Did you know that? He got you out of England too fast for me. I sent men after you a few times when you were still young."

"In Athens. And Oslo. And again in St. Petersburg. You almost got me in Athens."

"You were remarkably hard to kidnap."

"I tried to be, Sir."

"And you're still not scared of me. You're so clever in every other way, but you were never scared of me." Lazarus turned to the Captain. "It has a certain attraction. It's like owning that bloody necklace—the finest thing of its kind in the world. If her father hadn't taken her away, I'd have made her the best thief in Europe." He brooded on it a bit more and added, "I still could, but I'd have to train her all over again. When I think of the trouble she was last time . . ."

"You have the power to keep her. Or you can let her go. That's absolute power, if you want it."

"Don't push me, Kennett. An hour ago I didn't expect to ever see her again. And bedamned if I'll give her back to Josiah. Where does that leave me?"

More silence. She didn't even try to think.

"Sell her to me." Kennett said it so calm and reasonable she couldn't believe she'd heard right. "We can settle on a price."

The unreality of this was so dense she could have gone floating in it.

"Sell her? Sell Jess Whitby?" After a long minute, Lazarus began to chuckle. "Oh, that's a sweet thought. That is a beauty of a thought." Lazarus was on his feet, tromping around the room, looking at her, looking at Sebastian.

Sebastian stood up, too, ignoring everything but Lazarus.

She'd swear they were both blazing amused. She didn't see anything funny, herself.

Lazarus murmured, "Sell Josiah's daughter to a sea captain. That'll make the old bastard mad enough to spit nails. That is a beauty of an idea, that is. Damn. I could get ten thousand pounds for her."

"Easily."

"Or double that. I could get his damned warehouse. We just need to agree on an appropriate amount, don't we? Does there happen to be a shilling on you, Captain Kennett?"

Sebastian was already fishing in his pocket. He held up a shiny new Dundee shilling between thumb and forefinger. Tossed it. She watched it flip through the air, spinning silver.

Lazarus caught it. "Done. She's yours. And may God help you. Jess!"

"Sir?"

"Who do you belong to, Jess?"

"I belong to . . . I . . ."

"Exactly. You're not mine. Don't call me 'Sir' again. Get her out of here, Kennett."

Sebastian gripped her arm, applying somewhat more than necessary force, pulling her along.

She dug her heels in. There was one thing she had to say. "Lazarus." She'd been eight, the last time she called him Lazarus. The people who belonged to him called him "Sir." "I didn't just leave. Not willingly." It'd been the week after she fell so bad. Papa hired men who just picked her up and walked off with her, right out of the padding ken. She'd been knocked out with opium for the broken arm. Broken couple of things. Her ribs, too. "I didn't even wake up till we were two days out at sea. That first year . . . I tried to get back to you."

"But not later."

"No. Not later."

He considered her from under heavy, sleepy-looking eyelids. "You'd better get her out of here before I change my mind, Kennett. The challenge of it alone. If holding on to her wasn't so damned complex . . ."

The Captain gave her a fine, hearty shove in the direction of the door.

"One more thing," Lazarus said.

The Captain was carrying a knife somewhere on him. That featherlight change of balance was him thinking about pulling it and using it. "Yes?"

"Take that girl with you. The one you've been pretending not to notice. Fluffy. Give her to that interfering aunt of yours. I'm tired of looking at her."

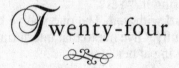

Twenty-four

Kennett House, Mayfair

LOTS OF PEOPLE SOBBED DOWN THE FRONT OF Eunice's dress. Fluffy—Flora, her name was—started doing it the minute she saw her. How did they know?

The Captain fumed the whole way back in the hackney. The minute Flora disappeared upstairs, with a maid helping her on one side and Eunice on the other, Sebastian shoved Jess out of the black and white foyer, into the library. Nice and private, the library, but Lord, it was cluttered. Old books lay everywhere and broken pots wherever there weren't books. She hadn't bothered to look for secret papers in here, it being what looked like a lifetime career sorting through that, not to mention nobody would keep his secrets where Standish puttered around all day.

Sebastian pulled her inside, and found the only piece of bare wall in the place, and backed her into it, and began kissing her.

"Captain . . ."

"Be quiet."

It was glorious. He was a lot better at kissing than Ned had been. Realms better. Guess he'd had about ten thousand times more practice. With Ned, kissing had mostly been bumping teeth, all clumsy and not quite fitting together. Kennett knew what he was about. He kissed her for a while, showing her a whole new way of doing it. There were depths and complexities she hadn't known about. There was this business of doing things with your tongue, for instance.

Sebastian couldn't be Cinq. Couldn't be. Couldn't be.

She said, "Look, I think—"

"Just . . . bloody . . . stop . . . thinking."

Shivers took over her body. Hot shivers that jostled and quivered under her skin and tried to jump right out. Nothing helped but getting closer and closer to him. He'd been waiting for that.

He couldn't be Cinq. Cinq wouldn't come to the padding ken to rescue her. Wouldn't face Lazarus to buy her back. That had to be proof. Had to be.

Kiss by kiss, her mouth got more numb and tingly. He tasted like wine. She held on and kissed back and it felt wonderful. Felt wonderful with her whole body. Felt like being rubbed with velvet over every inch of her.

His boots shoved her feet wide. Wider. Ready for him. He treated her like someone he was about to make love to. He ran his hand all the way down her stomach. Stroking. Assessing. It was a shock, feeling him touch her there, between her legs, vulgar and confident.

"I don't . . ." She had something she wanted to say.

When he pulled her against him, he was ready and hard, pressing eagerly. Feeding hunger and heat into her. He wanted this swaying back and forth. Wanted her rubbing herself against him. His hands told her what to do. This way, then back again. Till she was doing what he wanted. By this time, it was what she wanted, too.

There was a glow on him, he was so alive. It was like there was lightning under every inch of his skin, striking at her in tiny sparks. Made her twitch and jump every time he touched her.

Then he stopped and held her tight. Held her wanting and aching, open against him, and not able to get to him because they had too damn many clothes on. "I didn't mean to come this far." He stroked her hair, which seemed to have come undone all on its own. "You don't know anything at all, do you? None of it. I should have been gentle."

"I'm not a damn virgin." She was embarrassed all of a sudden. He had her wedged in between one lot of dusty old pots and another. No room to move. She was halfway to making love with him right here, and there wasn't a square inch for it.

He said, "We'll go slowly. I promise. Much, much more slowly. I'll go slow as grass growing with you, Jess."

She didn't want to hear that. Didn't want to think about it.

"I can always tell when you've been to the warehouse. You come home smelling of spices."

"Not always. Sometimes I go look at wool cloth and come home smelling like sheep."

She reached up and ran the edge of her thumb along his cheek. Scratchy. This was where he shaved. His face was darker, here on his jaw. She touched the corner of his mouth. Smooth there. That was what had been giving her so much pleasure—his mouth. It was the color of madder, the shade they made in Lyon, in that silk factory where they dyed it twice. That was the color of his mouth. A dark undercoat with a sheen on top, just a shade lighter.

He turned toward her hand and set his mouth against her knuckles. Disconcerted the hell out of her. While she was wondering what to do next, he pulled her hair forward, around her face, and kissed it. She couldn't feel his mouth there, but it made her tremble anyway. Someone kissing her hair. So strange.

He said, "I like your hair."

"I like yours, too." Those Greek boys who dived in the sea and brought up sponges had the same jet black hair. It was soft when she put her hands up in it, the color and texture of Russian sables. If Badger had stabbed her this afternoon, she would have missed all this—the feel of a man's harsh shaved chin, the black hair slipping through her fingers.

He played with his mouth on her earlobe. So damned skillful. It was all meant to be enjoyed.

There'd never been a man who made her want to close

her eyes and let him take over. Not ever. Not even Ned. But here she was trembling, letting Kennett wash over her like a wave, drowning her in pleasure. If she let go, he'd pull her under. The pleasure would be worth it. To forget for a few minutes . . .

So much she wanted to forget . . .

She pushed away from him. About an inch away. "Bloody damn cripes. I can't do this."

It was the right thing to say. Instead of trying to convince her that she could, indeed, do this, Sebastian threw his head back and laughed. "All right Jess, then you don't have to."

He didn't let her go. Whatever he planned to do with her next, having her backed hard against the wall seemed to be the starting point. "Why did you walk into that place? You almost got yourself gutted in front of me. Do you want to die?"

"It was one of those calculated risks."

"Calculated madness. Did you really kill somebody for him when you were eight?"

"Not exactly. Look, I don't want to talk about that." There didn't seem to be any pins left in her hair. She shoved him away some more and bundled her hair back over her shoulder. "I'm cautious, generally. Ask anyone. You barging in there and asking Lazarus for me—now that was daft."

She'd watched the two of them, Lazarus and the Captain, trading for her. Dickering. Somehow, Sebastian said the right words and she walked out of there. There wasn't another man in London who could have managed it. Only the Captain.

She'd never meet another man in her life like him. It hurt, how much she wanted to make love to him.

"If you're going to look at me like that, we might as well get back to what we were doing." His hands just took up where they'd left off. He started kissing her eyebrows, for pity's sake. Whoever heard of someone kissing eyebrows?

It worked, though. He went back and forth across her with his lips and his fingers, and it was like he was weaving some complicated spell with her flesh. When she said, "I think I want to stop doing this," he sucked the words right out of her mouth as she spoke them. She might as well have kept quiet. She shook her head back and forth. It didn't budge his hands any at all. They just played across whatever was going by—cheek, lips, hair. It all worked fine for him, whatever part of her he touched. "It's not going to work. I'm not going to make love with you."

"Some people enjoy just kissing." He breathed it warm into her ear, casual and innocent, as if he didn't know how that felt to her. He was going much, much more slowly, just like he said he would.

"I don't want to enjoy it."

"You are, though, aren't you?"

She was meshed up in what he was doing to her. Burning, every place he put his hands on her. He was so wise with her body, there didn't seem to be any way to stop him. He must have done this to a hundred women. Velvet, his lips were, all over her face.

"I'm a damn fool." She said that because she was sucking on his hand, where he'd set it to her lips. That was worse, somehow, than kissing him, this wanting to know what his hands tasted like. "I'm not going to bed with you, Sebastian, no matter how well you're seducing me. Remember that."

"I'll remember that." He spoke down into her hair.

"You didn't expect to get me all the way upstairs like this, did you?" she said. "I'd have got my senses back somewhere in the front hall probably. Or on the stairs at the latest."

"Certainly on the stairs." His smile sank into her bones. He did it on purpose. "My very dear Jess, I'm not trying to get you to my bedroom. We have all the time in the world. There are many, many things to do before we go to bed."

"I don't want to do any of those either."

"You don't even know what they are. You don't know anything."

She shivered for him. He watched her do it and his eyes turned to black, hot lava.

"You liked seeing me do that, didn't you?"

"Immensely. Don't be so nervous. When we go to bed together, you'll want it as much as I do. I don't take anything by force from women. Not even a kiss."

"You talk them into it. It's more fun that way." He'd ask nicely. So very nicely . . .

"Much more fun." He said it like it was an old joke between the two of them. "Since you're not going to end up in my bed tonight, you can just relax and see what happens next."

"I don't want to relax. Can't anyway." She wanted to unbutton his shirt and put her cheek on his chest and smell his skin. She wanted to taste him. That was what came of not being innocent. If she'd been innocent, she wouldn't know about naked chests.

"You're waiting to see what happens next, aren't you?" He ran his hands up and down her back, all friendly. "Maybe you're curious."

"I doubt that's it." She swayed into him, where he was touching her. Sort of putting herself into his hands. It felt wonderful. "Dunnoh why I'm letting you do this. Generally I have more backbone. I think it's being terrified for an hour straight. Loosens you all up inside, somehow. Makes everything hit harder afterwards."

White teeth flashed in his dark face. Oh, but she was amusing him, wasn't she? "When you brush up against death, you want to couple afterwards. I found that out years ago. I didn't know it worked the same with women. Does it?"

"Does this time," she said frankly. "Mostly I was real young. And the last couple times I was so seasick I didn't want to do anything but curl up and die. I'm glad Lazarus didn't kill you."

"I'm glad he didn't kill either of us." The Captain seemed to find that funny, too. Outside, in the hallway, somebody clopped rapidly down the stairs.

"It would have been a great waste." She slipped her hands under his jacket, on his shirt. "Do you know, you are the most alive person I've ever seen. I can't explain it. I was looking at you back there when I thought I might be going to die, and it was like there was fire everywhere inside you." Wherever she touched his body, the fire crossed through their flesh, till she was burning with it.

She didn't drop her hands away. She held on.

He must have seen the pleading in her eyes. He kissed her then, giving her what she'd wanted. When she kissed back, her lips and tongue scraped on that stubble of beard along his jaw. She got rubbed sensitive by it. He ran his tongue over her lips then, and there was hardly any skin between them. Just feelings brushing against each other.

She'd go upstairs with him in a few minutes and they'd make love. When they couldn't stand this kissing anymore, they'd stop lying to each other and get into bed. That was where this was leading, and they both knew it.

"Ah, there you are." Standish stood in the doorway, looking pleased to have found them.

The Captain's mouth lifted from hers. "Yes. Here I am."

"I wish you'd be more careful of the pots, Sebastian. That's a Minoan dolphin beaker next to your elbow. Eunice says, will you please go get the midwife for . . . Dear me, I've forgotten her name."

"Oh my God," Sebastian said.

Had to happen sooner or later. "Flora. That's her name. Lazarus must have really liked her. He cut this one close."

Twenty-five

Hungerford Market

DOYLE WAS EXACTLY WHERE HE WAS SUPPOSED to be, where she'd arranged to meet him. He was standing on the bridge, a fishing pole out over the canal. Jess stopped two feet away and set her basket on the footpath.

"Nice day for ducks, miss," he said respectfully and pulled at his cap.

She grinned and leaned her elbows on the stone rail and looked down at the ducks so nobody could see her lips when she spoke. "Hello, Mr. Doyle. How's the fishing?"

Doyle peered down into the water and twiddled with his line. "Good enough, me not having any particular need for fishes today. We got ourselves what you might call a special agreement, me and the fishes. I don't put anything on the hook, and they don't bite it." He was frowning like he had bad news to deliver, but he didn't spit it out. Instead he said, "You're being followed. Four men." He looked up the road, the way she'd come, then, casually, back along the canal. "British Service. They're being sloppy."

"They aren't trying to hide. They're intimidating me with their official demeanor. Makes me feel like the Pied Piper of

Hamelin, leading a pack of rats around." They were ugly ducks in the canal, patched up from a couple different lines of ancestry. When they saw her, they swam over quacking, raucous, milling around and nipping at each other. Cockney ducks. She'd brought bread. She started tossing bits at them.

"The Service put a couple of men to watching you, right from the first. Adrian wanted you safe." Doyle twitched the fishing rod. "Safe as you could be, all considered."

And that was the bad news. She thought it over, trying to decide how she felt about it, and tossed more bread into the water. Wherever it landed, the same ducks always got it. There was a lesson in that, she thought. "The men watching me . . . you were the first of them."

"With orders to keep you safe. Give you the information what you asked for. Give you advice, if you'd take it." He glanced at her, sharp, quick, humorous, tough. "Adrian told me to keep you outa trouble." The scar on his cheek creased. "Not likely."

She didn't seem to feel anything. Not anger. Not betrayal. She'd got used to the world falling down around her ears. Maybe she didn't have any more shock left in her.

Doyle was British Service. Adrian had sent him to her. To protect her.

She rolled it around in her mind, and nothing changed. He was still Doyle. If sea monsters climbed out of that canal, this minute, he'd put down the fishing rod and fight them off with his penknife, telling her to "hop it." He'd do the same for the fishmonger's daughter. Working for the Service was irrelevant to the likes of Mr. Doyle.

"Adrian wouldn't just do it straightforward and have me followed. He has to be sneaky about it."

"That's him."

Adrian, plotting and plotting to make sure she was safe. He'd sent the very best he had. She was sure of it. Doyle would be an important man in the British Service—he'd be a general manager if he worked for Whitby's. Adrian had set him to running errands for her.

And all of a sudden it was funny. She'd sent Doyle out to hire dozens of men to follow villains and break into offices all over London. He'd probably just set Service agents to doing it. This last month, she'd been funding British Service operations. "How long have you been British Service, Mr. Doyle?"

"All me life. Started telling lies to pretty girls like you when I was a nipper."

She leaned out far and got rid of the last of her bread. "I never knew. Not the least niggle of a suspicion. Not once."

"Well, I'm good, see. Around Meeks Street they call me Doyle, the Secret Shadow. I got me a reputation."

She didn't laugh. Or maybe a little.

He looked at her keenly, bushy eyebrows and lined face serious. "I have a daughter your age, Jess. She's out in the wilds of Spain, last time I heard from her, making life difficult for the French. I hope somebody looks after her if she needs it. I was doing this for your father, as much as Adrian."

Papa, being two pins in a paper with a man like Doyle, would agree. Knocked the legs out from under her being angry. "I am just replete to the gills with everybody taking care of me and figuring they have to lie to me three ways from Sunday to get it done." She reached down to pick up her basket. "You know what this means, don't you? Means I'm not going to pay you for last week. I'm damned if I'll put a Service agent on the payroll."

"I can see the sense of that. 'Ere now. Let me, miss."

Anyone watching would have seen the amiable, rough-looking man set his fishing pole down on the stones and stoop to pick up the basket for the lady. He handed it to her and she thanked him very prettily. He raised his cap to her as she left.

SEBASTIAN followed her and watched her do it right before his eyes. Talking to Doyle on the bridge, she'd been every inch a respectable young matron on her way to market. By the time she turned down Brantel Street, he was following what was unmistakably a pert servant girl on orders from the cook to do the shopping and get back to the kitchen smart, if you please.

Hungerford Market fronted the river. The market men landed their wares at the stairs on the Thames and wheeled them up in barrows. It was ordinary, just fresh vegetables and plump geese laid out in rows. It was small, a mere long block with a market house. The Ashtons sent the cart to Covent Garden at dawn twice a week to do the main shopping. Hungerford Market was just for what they needed fresh each day.

They needed fish, evidently. Jess was eyeing a pile of mackerel laid out under the awnings on damp burlap. She'd given her basket to one of the market boys.

"I dunnoh," she was saying. "I thought maybe a bit of haddock would go down nice." Then she listened with patent disbelief to the claim that the haddock at the next stand had been lying there nigh onto three days, but this here mackerel were fresh caught this morning.

"I dunnoh." Jess prodded a largish specimen. "Haddock's cheaper, too."

The conversation deteriorated into minutia of one and six for three medium mackerel or four bigger ones for two shillings, thr'pence. He propped himself on a stall heaped with cabbages and turnips and listened for ten long minutes while Jess resolutely reduced the price of two mackerel and five tiny, anonymous, silvery-gray fishes to two shillings, ha'penny. The market woman wrapped the fish in a broadsheet and stowed them in the basket with the satisfaction of a woman who'd been willing to go to two shillings even.

"Oysters," Jess murmured to herself as he approached. "Hello, Sebastian, why are you following me?"

"I like following you." The ragged boy carrying the basket, about half full of fish, eyed him balefully. Evidently Jess aroused protective instincts in his young breast. "Must you do the shopping? I haven't checked lately, but we usually have half a dozen girls sitting around the kitchen doing nothing in particular. One of them could do this just as well."

"If you will bring women home to pup in the guest bedroom, you must expect some disorder. Your cook is drunk.

You're having fish stew for dinner. It's about the only thing I know how to make."

"Anything is better than letting Aunt Eunice loose in the kitchen. Where to next?"

"Onions. No, not that kind." She ignored the baskets they were passing. "Spring onions. Over with the greens. Why don't you go . . ." she waved him away from the stall, ". . . look at things or something."

So he wandered around. The ground was covered with floating feathers from the geese they were plucking upwind. The man selling dried fruit and nuts had some almonds, so he bought a handful, wrapped up in a twist of paper, and carried them around, eating as he went. He liked the look of the oranges, too. They were probably some of his. He whistled to the boy Jess had picked out and, when he trotted up, dropped the almonds on top of the oysters and started loading oranges in.

He kept a pair of oranges, one in each jacket pocket, and walked back to where Jess was, at long last, concluding the contract on a handful of spring onions and a tiny bunch of what looked like weeds. This involved counting out much very small change.

She peered in the basket. "Oranges. You know you already have a basket or two cluttering up your pantry. Or you don't know, I guess. And almonds. Oh well, they don't go bad. Take it to Kennett House, please. You know it?"

The boy indicated he did by rolling his eyes heavenwards and murmuring, ". . . where they keep all them doxies . . ." He grabbed the penny Sebastian offered and disappeared.

"He's supposed to get a farthing piece," Jess said.

"I've set him up for life then, haven't I? Do you enjoy this sort of thing?"

"Buying fish? I do, actually. Most places I live they don't even let me in the kitchen. It must be three years since I bought fish. I mean, one fish, not a boatload, dried." She began threading her way briskly through the stalls, around piled vegetables and crates of live chickens and the baskets of fish that spilled out into the narrow walkways between the vendors. "You've ruined my reputation in there," she said. "I'll never be able to go back. You have them all convinced I'm your dolly mop."

"That'll teach you to chatter broad Cockney to them."

Jess had dark circles under her eyes again. They'd both been up all the night. Flora's baby, a boy, had been born with the sun. Healthy chap. Loud pair of lungs on him.

A little girl sat with her tattered skirts spread out, selling violets at the edge of the market. He flipped her a sixpence and picked a bunch and presented them to Jess. She slowed down after that. They walked along and she turned them in her hands and didn't seem certain what to do with them.

"You didn't need to give her sixpence," she said at last. "Pointless, too. The old lady who runs her will just take it away from her."

"You're supposed to say, 'Thank you very much' and hold them to your nose and smile. Hasn't anyone ever given you violets before?"

They were out of the market, heading down one of the side streets that led to the river. She smelled the flowers. But it wasn't a smile, more a considering and puzzled frown. "I don't think anyone ever did give me violets."

He thought about that bunch of dried flowers he'd found when he searched through her clothing. Daisies. Her angel-faced lover had given her summer flowers, all those years ago. They'd been nuzzling each other like puppies all through haymaking, he supposed.

She said, "I never sold flowers. Picking pockets was so much more profitable."

"I have the most enlightening conversations with you. Where are we going?"

"I don't know where you're off to. I'm going to the office. I have a hundred and thirty cubic yards of empty cargo space for Boston next Wednesday and nothing bought for it."

"What will you buy?" They were down to the quay. The street was broad and quiet here, with only a few passersby. Wind blew off the river and the poplars planted in a row beside the Thames turned silver green leaves back and forth. A barge glided steadily downriver. A waterman in a long, shallow black boat sculled across higher up, near Westminster Bridge. A calm, sunny day.

"That is the question, isn't it? Tea, I think. I can trust myself to negotiate a deal in oolong. You cannot imagine how difficult it is to have my father locked up like this. I'm not a tenth the dealer he is. If he'd been buying those fish, we'd have got them for sixpence."

She said this with perfect seriousness. The wall along the river was a broad, smooth stone ledge here. She ran the bunch of violets lightly along it, thinking about getting the fish a little cheaper or breaking into his office or buying a hundred thirty cubic yards of tea.

A pair of stone lions guarded the flight of steps down to the river. His Jess was absorbed, gazing up into the sky, a faraway expression on her face. Dozens of swallows wheeled and swooped above the river, riding the warm winds. He slowly edged her to the wall until she sat, practically in the lap of the nearest stone lion.

"Those aren't sparrows, are they?" she said.

"Those are swallows, Jess."

She was still being a servant girl or a pickpocket or some other Cockney thing inside. She sat on the ledge and drew her knees up close, letting her chin rest on the back of her forearm. This time, when she lifted the violets up and smelled them, her lips curved. "Swallows," she said, memorizing. "What do you do with violets after someone gives them to you?"

He took the violets from her hands and slipped the string off the stems and let the flowers loose in her lap. "You enjoy them."

She grinned at that, happy and relaxed for a change. That wouldn't last long. Not with what they had to say to each other.

He pulled the oranges out of his pockets and tossed one to her. She caught it neatly and broke into it with her thumbnail and began to peel it, looking at him with her usual level regard.

"Do you know, you can do the same thing my father can. Bargain with people. Make them do what you want. I mean, look at me . . ." She held up her hands, with the orange and orange peel, and wordlessly indicated her lap, filled with violets. "I have three thousand and six things to do today and I'm already late. Why am I sitting here eating oranges with you?"

"No breakfast?"

She shook her head. "Sheer persuasiveness on your part."

She was so beautiful sitting there. He'd have to be made out of stone like that lion behind her not to be aroused by her. She was taking such delight eating that orange. She'd picked up one of the violets and was staring into it. He could see her discovering all the separate streaks of color in the heart and the oblong dots there. If they'd been in the middle of a field somewhere, with all the time in the world, she'd have told him about it, as if it were the first time in history anyone had noticed what a violet looked like. He'd have showed her there were just as many things to discover in her own body as in the heart of any flower.

"Tell me why you went to see Lazarus."

The brightness of her closed up, like a flower closing. Her mouth got obstinate. She was beautiful when she was soft, looking at flowers and smiling. He liked her like this, too. Mulish.

"What did you ask Lazarus for? You came all that way and you risked your neck. What was it?"

She didn't want to say. At last, she shrugged. "Sailing dates. Lazarus keeps records of all that. Everybody who pays the pence gets writ down. It's all there—names, ships, dates."

Every ship, large and small, paid the pence to Lazarus, from the schooners anchored in the Pool of London to the coal barges in Stepney. "He keeps records?"

"Of course. He'd get stole blind otherwise. There's just nobody honest." She brooded on that. "I'm not saying he keeps banker's records. Every couple of months they toss them in a back room. Some get lost. But he has accounts going back years."

And that was the last, missing piece. Lazarus kept the records nobody else did, the listing of all the ships in London. Amazing. That was why she'd walked back into the padding ken and bargained with that monster. "Get word to Lazarus. Tell him to send them to the Admiralty tomorrow. You'll find out for sure whether I'm Cinq, then."

"Guess so." Her eyes were gold, like old coins, when she looked at him.

"I wish you believed me today."

"That's the trouble. I do believe you." An organ grinder a few streets away was endlessly repeating a short, discordant tune. Jess looked away and plucked at the fabric of her dress. "Feels like betraying Papa, when I trust you this much." She still had a lapful of flowers, but it seemed she didn't want them there any longer. She began picking them up and letting them fall, one by one, into the river. "I'll know tomorrow, won't I?"

They sat and watched the river about three barges' worth, saying nothing. There was a coy, unreliable southwest wind winding past them and a high tide, just turning after the slack. Far downriver, near the Tower, amid a forest of tall masts, a square stern brig upped anchor and let the tide pick her up. They'd dropped the foresail to catch wind enough to maneuver. Without a glass it was too far away for him to read her name.

Jess broke the silence. "Lazarus would have found some way to keep me if you hadn't come. I like to think he wouldn't have, but . . ." She shrugged, looking uncomfortable. "He's strong. And the old life tempts me. It wouldn't have been easy to get away from him a second time. I owe you myself."

"You wouldn't have worked for him again, but you might have suffered for it. And I would have come to get you out. Jess, why did you sell yourself to Lazarus?"

"I wish I could figure out how your mind works. How did we start this?" She scrubbed a hand across her face, looking perplexed. "That was a long time ago. Let's talk about something else."

"You're supposed to be grateful to me. Prove it. Tell me."

She gave that little quirk upward at the side of her mouth. There wasn't a more expressive face in London. "You're doing it again, Sebastian . . . getting me to do things. Sometimes you sneak them out of me artful, and sometimes you just ask. I never know which it's going to be."

"This time it's just asking. I'll be artful later."

"It's all very sordid. You don't want to hear about it."

"If I didn't want to hear, I wouldn't ask."

"Oh Lord, if you want to know . . ." Twenty feet away, a seagull swooped down and scooped up one of those violets floating out to sea. A second later it dropped the flower and flew off, looking disgruntled. Jess watched, while she mulled everything over and decided to tell him. "I was real young. Eight, I guess. My father went off to France and got himself arrested. We didn't know that. We just knew he didn't come back. I did my best, but the money ran out. My mother and I ended up . . . there." She jerked her thumb over her shoulder, downriver, toward the worst of London's slums. "There was a pimp who came to get my mother. I ended up killing him."

This graceful girl in front of him, the reflective, intelligent face, the subtle, simple dress. He tried, but it was impossible to match her with any part of this—not with pimps, not with killing, not with Lazarus.

"You cannot imagine how much trouble I was in that night. He got the knife away from me and fell on the stupid thing, and I was covered with blood everywhere. He had about a million cousins. I was going to get me and Mama killed real, real bad."

He could see her hands trembling where she had them fisted in her dress. "I knew Lazarus. Knew him face-to-face. I'd been picking pockets to feed us, and Lazarus made me pay the pence right into his hand. He does that with some of them he's watching, though I didn't know it then." Her hands opened and closed again, clutching at the cotton of her skirt. "He was taking about everything I lifted, too, which isn't like him. I don't know what he thought we was living on."

He snarled. He heard himself do it. She didn't notice. She was a dozen years in the past.

"He wanted me to work for him. All the kids I knew dreamed about that—working for Lazarus. But I didn't want

any part of it. Every week, he kept talking about me being a
Runner." She sketched a motion in the air. "And I just danced
away."

Eight years old, and setting herself against Lazarus. She
never had a chance.

"When I killed Lumpy—that was the pimp . . . Sebastian,
do you know what it's like when you look and look and the
world has got so narrow there's only one thing to do? I went
to Lazarus for help. Only he wouldn't let me just be a Runner. He said I had to take his shilling. He bought me. Bought
my soul, he said."

"You killed somebody for him?"

Unexpectedly, she grinned. "That was just him playing
with you. He took Lumpy's death. Made up some story and
stuck a knife into the table, the way he does, and took the
death as tribute. He never made me do things like that. Knew
I was dead soft. Used to scold me for it."

There was a scrap of orange peel on her skirt. She picked it
off and flicked it over into the water. "I bought sausages with
it. With the shilling he gave me. I was so bloody hungry."

He thought about chopping Lazarus into fish bait. He'd
use a dull knife.

"It was good with Lazarus, after I stopped fighting him."
Jess stared into the past. "That place behind Lazarus, where
the boy was—that was mine. I was Hand. You don't understand. That's like being vizier or something. I could go anywhere. Do anything. It was wonderful."

That, he could picture. Jess as a child, watchful and
silent, sitting at the wall behind Lazarus, running his errands
all over London. After she stopped fighting him, of course.
What an absolute, bloody monster that man was.

"Hard for me at first," she said. "Nobody'd ever run me
before and I wasn't used to it."

Lazarus knew exactly how to control someone like Jess.
He'd owned her soul, all right. "I can see it might be difficult."

She looked at him then, really seeing him for the first
time in a while. "It wasn't like that—what you're thinking. I
was . . . special. He used to just laugh at me when I cheeked
him. He'd do things for me, almost anything I asked. And

when I fell, he kept them looking for me till they found me. And he came and got me out. Had 'em kidnap some nob doctor to set my arm. He sat up all night, talking to me, to keep me from knowing how much I hurt."

The man had sent her scrambling across roofs. Lazarus should be divided into many, bloody pieces.

"I was with him three years. I would have died for him."

It was a miracle she'd survived at all.

People strolled by along the river walk. Jess straightened her dress over her knees and kept her eyes down at the printed pattern in the cloth when she said the next thing. "I have a favor to ask, since we're just sitting here and I'm already thirty foot deep in debt. I want to give you a shilling, in exchange for that one you gave Lazarus. I want to . . . buy myself back from you. I know it sounds stupid."

It made her uncomfortable, him owning her soul. Good.

She said, "It's just passing a shilling piece from hand to hand. Call it superstition."

When he didn't say a word, she glanced up and bit her lip, wondering what he was thinking about, probably. And there she was, leaned back on the stone lion, her skirts rucked halfway up. Any other woman in London would have realized how accessible she looked.

"Do you think I own you because of that shilling?" He leaned forward. Very gently, he ran the back of one finger in a smooth line down from her neck, across her bodice. He slowed when he got to her breast, but he didn't stop. "If I own you, I can do this."

She got quiet. She looked down to where his hand was, not quite believing what he was doing. "For God's sake, Sebastian. We're in the bloody street here."

"Somebody I own doesn't get to object to anything I do. Remember all those years in the East. Lots of women for sale in the East." He slipped along, headed for the crinkle of her nipple. It rose up under the fabric as he approached. He didn't touch, just circled round, softly, with the tip of his finger. She was lovely. "Generally they cost more."

It would be interesting to see what she did. There was a

good chance she'd break his nose and heave him in the river. She could do that, if she wanted.

She batted his hand away. "Stop this. Will you stop this? There must be fifty people can see you."

"Nobody's looking." He didn't give a damn who was looking. She'd run herself snug up to that stone lion. No retreat in that direction, unless it got up and walked off.

"This isn't Paris. Nobody in this town makes love in the open but pigeons." Her voice was all beautiful and tense with what he was doing to her. She clutched at his arm. No. Not fighting. Getting closer.

It seemed a good time to kiss her. As always, she was an intriguing combination of ignorance and some theoretical knowledge and a high level of native skill. After the first shudder, she just held on to him, getting softer and more willing every minute. With Jess you knew when she was willing, because you didn't get your teeth knocked out.

She pulled away and licked her lips. Lovely lips, fuller than usual, from the kissing. "This is going to be a report on Adrian's desk in an hour."

"Should be more interesting than what he generally reads. Are you letting me do this because I bought you for a shilling, Jess? Is that why?"

Dazed eyes. Unfocused. Vulnerable. She put her hand up on his cheek, feeling the texture of him there. It was all new to her. She had no practice with the way a man feels. Her angel-faced martyr boy probably hadn't even shaved yet.

"Forget the damned shilling," she whispered.

Triumph streaked through him, stronger even than the lust that was running amok in his blood. *Mine. Not bought or stolen or taken. Just mine from the beginning of time. Mine even before I met her.*

He kissed her deep, entering in slow as if he were going into her another way. She didn't recognize that yet. There was so much for her to learn. She vibrated under his hand everywhere he touched her. "Owning's for objects. I don't make love to objects."

Her mind was taking its merchandise inside and closing

down the stall. Only a few thoughts left. Jess, thinking, with all the force and calculation of her damnably cunning mind, was a formidable opponent. Jess, twitching each time he caressed that sweet nubbins on her breast, was just a woman. He liked dealing with her as just a woman, once in a while. It gave both of them a rest.

This wasn't Paris. It wasn't so usual to see a couple locked together like this in London town. They got stares and giggles from people walking by. And the hell with them. He kissed her a while, and it just got better and better.

Then they stopped kissing and sat there breathing deep at each other, and she outlined his lips with her fingertips. It was as if she were worshipping the flesh and bone of him.

"You picked a silly place for this, Sebastian." He could see in her eyes she was letting herself fall in love with him. She was about three-quarters deep so far and sinking fast. He wondered if she knew. Almost too late for her to stop. It had been too late for him for a long time.

"This is a fine place." His hand was on her thigh. She picked out soft fabric for her dresses. Like so much about her, you couldn't tell how good it was till you looked at it closely. You didn't know even then, unless you were canny as hell, the way she was. "Beautiful view, for one thing."

She looked him full in the face. "I like it." There was no man alive who deserved what was in her eyes, least of all him. But he'd take it all. This was Jess. He could no more let her go than he could stop from breathing.

He cupped the back of her head, into that hair all gold and brown, and fitted her close to him and held her strong and comforting till her body stopped quivering. The whole noisy world stretched out on every side, and he had the most important part of it right in his hands.

"Who do you belong to, Jess?" he asked, real quiet.

"I belong to myself."

"Good. That's a start. Do you have a shilling on you?"

She looked up at him. "Yes."

"Hand it over."

She fumbled in a pocket among the farthings and pence

and picked one out. Not as new and shiny as the one he'd given for her, but a perfectly workable shilling.

"There," he said. "You've bought your soul back. Take better care of it next time." He tucked the shilling away safe in his watch pocket.

She said, "Don't spend it all on sausages."

Twenty-six

Kennett House

FLORA'S BABY WAS FINE, BUT HE WAS STARTING to get hungry. They were getting a little goat's milk down him in the kitchen, but Eunice wouldn't let them get a wet nurse in. She just kept sending him back up to Flora, who left him in the cradle.

Flora wasn't doing well at all. She'd been lying all day, staring, answering direct questions, but otherwise not saying much. She ignored the baby.

Eunice evidently thought Jess might help. Anyhow, she'd sent her up to sit with Flora as soon as she got home from the warehouse.

There was a chair by Flora's bed. Jess sat there and put her feet up on the rung of the chair and looked out the window and tugged at a strand of hair. So many people were expecting her to find an answer tomorrow. Maybe she wouldn't find anything. Maybe she wouldn't like the answer she found. She closed her eyes, feeling hollow.

"You ran away from Lazarus. No one does that." It was about the first thing Flora had said to anyone, just on her own.

"It's complicated." She went back to pulling hair through

her fingers. She wasn't feeling terribly talkative, herself, right then.

"I heard about you. From when you were Hand. Jess the Hand."

She shrugged. The baby was making weak sounds in the cradle, like a kitten or something. They sounded like that the first couple weeks. "That was years back."

"You tunneled into a bank once, and everybody almost drowned when it started to rain. They still laugh about that."

"Always rains in this town. I'd go about it different if I was doing it now." People had been patting the woman's hand all day long and encouraging her to talk. Maybe a little quiet was what she needed.

Flora sat up in bed. She was older than Jess had thought. Twenty-six or twenty-eight. Eunice had put her in a huge white cotton nightgown that buttoned up the front with about sixty little buttons. Her hair was scraped hard back from her face, and she looked exhausted. But she was beautiful. Lazarus always picked pretty girls to play with.

"He was always telling Twist how you did everything better. He said you could plan a caper so it ran like a gold watch."

"That's just him talking. Me, he used to tell about this kid named Hawker. Before my time. Seemed Hawker could do anything but walk on water."

Flora twisted her hands in the quilts. "They're very kind here. But they don't understand. I have done such things. You know the kind of things I had to do."

"Nobody'll know if you don't tell them."

"There are whole pieces of myself I can't find anymore. I became . . . I cannot believe what I have become."

"You get over some of it, I think. You don't go back to what you were."

"You understand, don't you? The rest of them just say I can do whatever I want and not to worry. But you understand." Flora lay down and looked at the ceiling again. "I can't go home."

"Up to you, really. You can be whatever you want to when you don't have anything to lose."

That made Flora look thoughtful. She wondered if she'd said the right thing, then decided in the long run it probably didn't matter what she said. Flora would work it out for herself. Everybody did.

She sat beside Flora for a while, planning what she'd do tomorrow. She'd use the cargo manifests, if she had to. It depended how much information Sebastian had managed to find for her.

A maid pushed through the door, carrying a tray. It was fish stew. That meant it was time for her own lunch.

The baby was lying in the cradle, waving his hands around, looking fairly unhappy as she walked by. "Better make some arrangement for this one if you don't want him. Another couple hours, and he'll start getting scared, all alone, when it gets dark." She thought that covered it.

Either that worked or something else did. Anyway, Flora fed the baby, and they fell asleep in bed together that night.

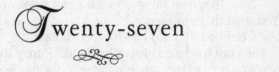

Twenty-seven

Garnet Street

"TRY TO KEEP THE STACKS IN ORDER. THEY'RE sorted and I know where everything is. Nine-tenths of my problem tomorrow's going to be finding things."

"MacLeish brought boxes. Over there." Pitney didn't look happy. She could see he was worried right to his guts about Papa. It hunched his shoulders and put another twenty years on his face.

"Everything on my desk. The rest of the ledgers, too."

By this time tomorrow she'd know what ships carried treason across the Channel. Papa would be home and safe the day after. She had to believe that. "Put the files in the wagon tonight and set a guard sitting on top. It goes to the Admiralty about three tomorrow afternoon. They'll have a room clear for us."

The Whitby warehouse was deserted. Nobody left but her and Pitney and three guards patrolling downstairs. Empty.

"This is damned dangerous. Jess, you should talk to Josiah."

"No point in it. I already know what he'd say. I don't want to have to go against his orders." Kedger's cage was empty. She checked the food bowl and water dish. Both full. There was a pile of notes she'd left on top of the cage. She picked them up, tapping them neat. "Everything in my desk drawers, too. There's notes I may need. Ships sighted. Ships not sighted where they should be. There could be one line in there that makes the difference."

"Jess, they can hang you with any page in those books. You trust them too much."

"Could be. It's too late to stop, though."

"It's not too late to leave England." Pitney looked sick. He was brave as a tiger when it came to facing the Revenue cutters. Papa getting arrested shook the order of his universe. He'd be all right when Papa was cleared.

She took one last look round at all her charts and lists. All her letters and reports. All her planning. "I'm going to know Cinq's name tomorrow. I can do this. I can really do this. You would not believe how much paper they've pulled together for me to sieve."

"Think about what you're doing." Pitney took the papers from her like he was getting an order for his own execution. "There has to be another way."

That was the problem with life. Sometimes there wasn't.

Twenty-eight

IT WAS SHORT OF NINE O'CLOCK IN THE MORNING when Sebastian rang the bell at Meeks Street. Doyle met him and unlocked the door to the study and let him in to see the old man.

Whitby was writing letters. He had three pages in a neat row to the side of the desk, drying. The Service would look those over before they went out, just as they opened the mail before they handed it over to him. The *Times* was folded and laid aside with a bright red apple holding it down.

He had French silk brocade swathed around his middle today, cream and crimson stripes. Expensive fabric for a waistcoat, but he could afford it.

"Ah." Whitby looked him over without getting up. "A new face."

Sebastian took his time crossing the room. He set his knuckles down on the wood of the desk and bent over, face-to-face, level with the man. "What the hell kind of father are you?"

"Not a good one, I'm afraid." Whitby leaned back and rubbed the side of his nose. "You're a friend of Jess, then."

His hands closed into fists. The urge to hurt this old man was strong. Whitby let Jess grow up in the worst slums of the East End. Let her fall prey to men like Lazarus. When he got himself into trouble, she went out climbing roofs and accosting strangers in the street, and he didn't put a stop to it. "She's living in my house."

"Then you're Bastard Kennett." Whitby indicated the chair. "Sit down." His face was all bland good nature. "Nobody tells me anything. What's my Jess been up to?"

"Romping through my halls in her dressing gown, searching my private papers. Did you tell her to do that?"

"No. You don't have to loom over me like the dome of Saint Paul's to ask."

"What I'd like to do is break your neck."

"In a few weeks, you can watch Jack Ketch do that. You and half London." Under bushy eyebrows, hard, shrewd eyes studied him. "It's a nice little company, Kennett Shipping."

"Whitby's Trading is a nice company, too. Mostly Jess's work, isn't it?"

"Almost all of it. Not many men canny enough to believe that. Sit down and tell me what Jess is doing."

"Rifling through my shipping records. Picking the lock on my strongbox. You made her into a first-rate thief."

"Not my doing."

"The devil it wasn't. Where were you when Jess was learning to pick locks?"

"Here and there." Whitby's mouth set flat. He pushed back in his chair and opened a drawer in the desk. The cheap clay pipe he took out was white and new looking. "I know summat of your aunt, Lady Eunice. We met once—she won't remember, but I do. She has a name in London. My Jess is safe with her." The next drawer down, he found a tin of tobacco and shoved up the lid with his thumb. "Safe as she's likely to be anywhere. What's Jess to you?"

"She's mine." He sat in the chair by the desk and stretched his legs out.

The brown eyes went opaque. For an instant, Whitby looked every inch as dangerous as his reputation. Then it passed, and he was a tun-bellied old merchant in a striped waistcoat, filling his pipe. "Mr. Pitney tells me you claimed my girl in front of Lazarus. They're saying you bought her."

"So I did." That was what he'd come to tell Whitby. To see the man's face when he said it.

"I wouldn't try enforcing that." Whitby began packing the bowl of his pipe. Tobacco grains scattered across the papers on the desk. Whitby wasn't as calm as he pretended. "Has claws, my Jess does. She thinks you're the spy, Kennett."

"She's risked her life trying to prove you're not. I hope it was worth it."

The old man stood up. He wasn't well. His clothes had been tailored for the man before he'd taken off a stone or two. But he moved like a piece of granite getting up and walking around. Heavy. Dangerous. Solid. Whitby didn't bend to get a coal from the fire. He sat down on his haunches, like a man who'd grown up without much furniture.

He made a lengthy business about picking the coal up with a pair of thin sticks and lighting the pipe and getting it to draw. He glanced up. Whitby had Jess's eyes—steady, brown, self-possessed, unafraid. It was disconcerting to see Jess's eyes looking out at him from this man's face.

"Maybe she's risking her neck to prove it's not *you*. Did you think of that, Kennett? We're two men letting a woman do the dangerous work." He pushed at his knees and stood. "I'm locked up in this cage. What's your excuse?"

He pushed anger away. "A disinclination to clap the woman in irons. I doubt anything less would work."

"Happen tha's reet." Whitby pulled the decanter from a nook in the bookcase and poured one glass. "They keep a damned mediocre port for me. I'd offer you some, but I doubt you'd drink with me."

"You're right about that."

A chewing sound came from under the desk. It could have been rats, of course. "She's left that goddamned rodent with you, hasn't she?"

"Aye. Jess thinks I need the company. He steals things from the desk and gnaws them to bits. That's a pencil he's got hold of." Whitby made a slow business of settling down at the desk again. "And nothing poisons the beggar. Now tell me without more rigmarole what you're doing to my Jess. You've come a long way to see an old man if you've got nothing to do but brag you've debauched my girl."

"The *Neptune Dancer*. My ship. I had friends aboard."

"That'd be one of the ships sold out by our traitor. A Kennett ship." Whitby sighed. "I'm sorry, man, but it's nowt to do with me."

"I traced two hundred pounds from the French Secret Police, to the go-between in Naples, and then to your London drawing account. You were paid by the French. There's no doubt."

"That's to say, you have no doubt. Fair enough. Some of the evidence would convince me, if I didn't know better."

"You're guilty as sin."

The old man sucked on his pipe, looking thoughtful and absurdly ordinary. "Wish I'd had a few more minutes with Jess instead of a great hulking lout like you," he said, at last. "Still, glad to have a look at you, I suppose."

"I wanted to have a look at you, too."

"Already had that, I should think." Whitby poked his pipe toward a painted landscape that hung on the wall nearby. "Through yonder peep or t'other ones. I'm asking myself what Bastard Kennett is doing with my lass if he thinks I'm guilty of murder. I never heard you took revenge against women."

"It's nothing to do with Jess."

"But she's caught in the middle, isn't she? You're taking vengeance for an act of war, man, and that's pure stupidity. The captain who sank your ship's probably a likeable enough chap. You plan to gut him someday when this is all over?"

"Not him. Just Cinq."

"More power to you, then, finding him. He might even be the villain you think he is." Whitby took a drag on his pipe. "Or he could be an honest enough man, fighting for a cause he believes in."

"I don't care what he is." Sebastian gripped the arms of the chair, feeling his breath wrench and haul inside his chest. This old man sat here puffing on his pipe, being philosophical. Fifty men on the *Neptune Dancer* had been robbed of all their years. They'd never be old. "In a few hours, Jess is going to give me Cinq's name. If you're Cinq, that's the Furies' own revenge. You're going to die at the hands of your own daughter."

He stood up. There was nothing he could say to Whitby. Nothing he could do to him. The man was twice his age and cornered up like a rat. ". . . and she's going to have to live with killing you."

"Kennett."

He jerked around to face Whitby.

"There's planted evidence aplenty."

"Or proof."

"You bought the girl. Now she's your responsibility. If the evidence falls against me, I expect you to get her out of England. Get her safe. You owe her that much."

Sebastian set his teeth. He nodded tightly.

"And don't marry her. I don't care what you feel for her. Don't make her live with a man who hanged her father. She deserves better than that."

What Jess deserved was a different father. "I hope you rot." He banged on the door to be let out.

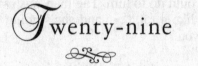

Twenty-nine

Kennett House, Mayfair

JESS WAS IN THE RAGGED GARDEN BEHIND THE Captain's house, lying on her belly on a blanket on the ground, poking around in the grass. Eunice sent her here. She was supposed to be resting, getting ready for the work tonight.

Sun spilled down through the trees in thousands of shilling-sized drops on the grass. She picked a tiny plant with three leaves. She recognized it from the playing cards. "It's a club."

"It's clover." Claudia's feet, in dark green leather slippers, were to her left, in the grass, an inch from touching her elbow.

"Clover."

"It gets flowers on it. About this big." When she looked up, Claudia was showing her with two fingers. "Purple. Shaped like balls. You are the most deplorably ignorant person I've ever met."

"I just haven't been in England much, mostly." She tried to imagine purple flowers shaped like balls all over the grass and couldn't. She would have noticed if something like that was going on, wouldn't she? Life just got stranger and stranger the more you thought about it.

"You'll get brown if you sit out in the sun," Claudia said.

"I had a governess once who said things like that. I got brown in Egypt. Never got unbrown again, really. I didn't care much at fourteen." She thought for a bit. "Don't care at twenty-one, either."

"You're showing your ankles."

The pretty muslin print of her dress was kicked up to her knees. "Showing considerably more than my ankles."

"I'd advise against attracting masculine attention in this house. But then, you consort with weasels, don't you?" Claudia's feet shifted. "Quentin's waving at me from the window. I'm going inside." And she swished away. Unaccountable woman, Claudia. She stood there for ten minutes, just heavy with something she wanted to say, and never did decide to say it.

Jess had never taken the time to have a good look at grass. Always been too busy. Now that she investigated, she found it wasn't just grass. It was a whole town down there, like London, full of every kind of inhabitant. Clover. Ants. Bugs. Made you wonder what you were stepping on when you walked around.

She'd come out here to be alone to think. Hadn't been alone yet. But then, did she really want to think? Probably not.

She picked out one of the plants that was velvety and tough at the same time and had blue flowers on it like bells. Flowers smaller than her fingernail. When she crushed the leaves, they smelled like mint.

A deep voice behind her said, "That's horehound." It was Sebastian.

"You have something to do on a ship someplace. I'm almost sure of it." She didn't look up.

"They make a cough mixture out of it." He sat down beside her on the blanket.

She twirled the little plant in her fingers. The stem felt bumpy.

"It's square. Look." He took it from her and pinched off the end of the stem and showed her. "I remember Standish showing me this when I first came to live with him. I was seven or eight."

A plant with a square stem. Why would you have a plant with a square stem? So you could pack them more closely?

"You can eat it if you like," Sebastian said.

She rolled over on her back and looked up at the sky, biting the stem. It tasted like the red-and-white sweets they sold in shops. Sebastian came closer till he was above her, lean and intent, smiling down on her. His eyes held the knowledge of all that kissing they'd done and what she'd felt about it. He knew he could do it again to her, whenever he wanted to. Made it hard to meet his eyes.

She'd spent some of last night, when she wasn't sleeping, wondering whether Sebastian might take it into his head to climb up those stairs and make love with her. He didn't though.

It wouldn't take a clever man like Sebastian more than two minutes to get her out of a nightgown. He'd slide it away and do some of those things he was so good at. It set off an odd, hot excitement in the pit of her stomach, looking up at him and thinking about him that way. She wanted to make love to him. No moral backbone at all, that was her problem. Came of all those years thieving.

"I finally tracked you down," he said. "Too bad we're not out at sea somewhere. One of the good things about a ship is you always know where to find people."

"One of the advantages."

The Captain had pulled off his neckcloth—it was over there on the railing—and opened his collar, showing some brown skin. His face was like those bluffs in the desert in Egypt where the wind scoured away till there was nothing left that wasn't strong. Every jut and hollow was harsh. He hadn't had an easy life, to have a face like desert rocks. Sometimes when she looked at him she wanted to kiss those edges and hollows, just to show him there was some gentleness in the world.

Silly thoughts to have about a man like this. She shivered. A warm sort of shiver.

"You look tired," he said. "Why don't you go up to your room and take a nap. It's hours before Adrian will be ready for us."

"I should put in time at the warehouse, actually. There's

still a business to run. The *Northern Star*'s sailing tomorrow. Naval supplies to Lisbon."

"The tide doesn't stop because you're not sweeping at it. Relax. You have good men in charge. Pitney knows who to bribe. But the *Northern Star* isn't naval supplies. That's contraband into Brittany, isn't it? Tea?"

"Indigo and tea. It's brandy coming out. Once they transfer that, the *Star*'ll go on to Lisbon. We might even move some naval supplies. Who knows?" Crikey. Once, just once, she'd like to have an ordinary conversation with this man. About the weather. Or horses. Something terribly, terribly British. "I should be there."

Looking up past Sebastian, she could see the sky was full of clouds scudding along from left to right. Almost, it felt like the sky was standing still and the earth was moving, carrying them with it. Made her dizzy, thinking things like that.

Sebastian began stroking her forehead with the tips of his fingers. He made it feel wonderful. She should tell him to stop, since anyone could look out the window and see them, and this wasn't exactly proper.

She said, "You planning to do all that stuff to me out here in the open? Kissing and so on. It's another silly place to get started on that sort of thing."

He said softly,

"Whoever loves—if he does not propose
love's right and proper end, he's one that goes
to sea for nothing but to make him sick."

It didn't rhyme much that she could tell, but there wasn't very much of it. "That's poetry?"

"That's John Donne."

"Never read much poetry. I always meant to, but I never got it done somehow. What you're saying is you've got more ambitious thoughts in mind than just kissing. Right?"

"Exactly right, Jess."

"Might as well just say so." She yawned into his face, not commenting on the poetry, just tired. She'd drink some tea before she started sieving all those records tonight.

"Remember when I was looking in your study the other night?" That was a polite way of saying picking three locks and sneaking around in the dark. "You remember?"

"I remember." He wasn't annoyed. Good.

"I found a letter. Giovanni Reggio. You know the one I mean?"

It took him a minute. "Maps of Florence and plans for some fortifications in Tuscany. They're almost certainly fifteenth century, but whether they're by DaVinci is anyone's guess. I passed them along to a dealer in Paris. Jess, why are we talking about maps of Florence when I want to be making love to your eyebrows?"

"Because your damn letter didn't say maps in 1550 or plans of what. It just gave a whalloping great price for them. In francs. You have to watch that."

He laughed at her. A pirate, burned all brown with the sun, laughing at her. "You've decided I'm not Cinq?"

"Dunnoh who is, yet. I know you're not."

"Good then."

He started stroking along her eyebrows, using the side of his thumb.

"I have funny eyebrows. They don't curve. Makes me look angry all the time."

"They're fine." Sebastian just kept on finding her amusing. "You worry too much."

What black eyes he had. Hungry, keen, obsidian eyes.

He paid attention to her eyebrows some more. His fingers were getting in the way of seeing things, weaving back and forth between her and the light of the sky. So she closed her eyes. He drew lines on her forehead, back and forth. She should tell him to stop. Felt nice, though.

Hours later, when Sebastian woke her up, it was to tell her it was time to go to the Admiralty. She knew he'd been beside her all afternoon, watching her while she slept.

Thirty

The Admiralty

"THE FIRST LEAK WE KNOW ABOUT WAS MARCH, five years ago." Adrian stood in front of the long bank of windows, facing her. "The most recent was two weeks back. Where do we start?"

Jess didn't know who'd been ejected from his office at the Admiralty. Somebody important. This was a huge room with a commanding view over the parade ground and a globe the size of a wheelbarrow in one corner.

A pair of armed marines stood outside the door, looking tough and alert, guarding things.

She unrolled the first of her charts. These were tides, weather conditions, winds, and the phases of the moon for every month, every year. Give her a ship, and she'd tell you how far it could travel on any given day, all up and down the Channel. It had taken a while to put this together. "We'll start with the oldest and go on from there."

"I knew you were going to say that." Sebastian started restacking books. He had Kennett ledgers and Whitby ledgers. Some from other shipping companies. To his right was what looked like the shipping books from Lloyds. She wasn't going to ask how he'd come by those.

The Service had torn London apart, giving her all this. Spread out on the tables was an amazing collection of ship manifests and paper from the Customs, Board of Trade clearances, naval logs. There must be two hundred pounds of government paper that didn't have any right to be here. There was a fine selection of British Service agents to help her sieve it. They stood at the long table, twenty of them, each commanding a small kingdom of paper, waiting for orders. Trevor'd put himself beside her, behind a stack of clean paper, ready to make notes.

"It's your show, Jess," Sebastian said. Adrian brought her the big, red leather chair from behind the desk. She was in the center of the long table. Best seat in the house.

The pompous young man from the Admiralty hovered protectively over his own stacks of records. "May I say it's an honor to meet you, Miss Whitby. I've been working with Captain Kennett on the Whitby ledgers since they were brought in. I'm thoroughly familiar with the Whitby system. I'll explain anything you don't understand. Your father's accounting methods . . . even under these circumstances, I have to say they're tremendously exciting. I only wish I were half the accountant he is."

"If you're half the accountant my father is, God help us all." If he started explaining the mysteries of bookkeeping, she'd scrag him. "Can we send one of those monkeys at the door to bring us tea?"

The men from the British Service were watching her. The room got quiet.

This was going to work. She'd make it work.

She rested her fingers on the tabletop and looked from man to man, up and down the room. "March twenty-fifth. A memorandum on troop movements slipped out of the War Office. It surfaced in Boulogne on April third. Let's see who sailed."

A tall man, thin as a scarecrow, unsmiling, was already deep in the files Lazarus had sent over. Trevor picked up the pen and took ink.

A man to her left said, "The *Pretty Henrietta*, owned by George Van Diehl, sailed on March twenty-sixth. Bound for Bristol."

Another voice, "The *Parrot*. March thirtieth. But that's just a coastal lugger."

She said, "Put her down."

Sebastian angled a Whitby ledger out of his pile and slid it in her direction.

From the end of the table—"The *Nancy Lee,* seventy tons, bound for Bristol. March twenty-sixth. No cargo listed here. Owner is . . . I can't read it."

She knew that one. "Michael Sands, owner and captain." It was time to add the Whitby ships. She leafed to March. "*Northern Spirit,* for Lisbon. She didn't weigh anchor till April first. That's cutting it close, but put her in. *Northern Destiny* sailed March twenty-seventh."

"*Island Dancer* on March twenty-sixth, bound to Cagliari," Sebastian was started on his own ships, "which would put her well past the coast of France before April. I suppose she could have hove to in a bay somewhere and waited a week. The *Belle Dancer* didn't sail till April seventh." He closed the Kennett books and picked up another ledger.

"*Red Tempest* from the Red Star Line, bound for Boston, April first," someone said. Trevor wrote it down.

"Cross *Northern Spirit* off. She put into the Isle of Thanet on April second and set two sailors ashore. Measles. Didn't leave there till the fifth."

"The *Manatee*, owned by Gregory and Fitch, April first for Boston. Likewise the *Haughty Girl,* registered at Plymouth."

She could eliminate some of these. The Van Diehl books were down the table. She headed that way and leaned over a shoulder to check an entry. And here it was. A fine bit of memory on her part. "It's not *Pretty Henrietta.*" She'd had her hands on these books for about an hour, three weeks ago. "Hunt bought a crate of Sheffield knives, in Bristol, on April fifth. Had to be off the *Henrietta.* Here it is." She watched Trevor strike out the name.

"The *Crystal Jane,* out of Bristol. She left . . . No . . . *didn't* leave March twenty-eighth." A rustle of papers. "She sailed April first, instead. Delayed for refitting."

"Cross that one off, too." Sebastian said it before she could. "That's Pettibone. They went out of business the next year."

Mr. Admiralty was still playing bump on the log. She fixed her attention on him. "You need help with those naval vessels?"

"I am perfectly capable of addressing the naval vessels." Admiralty was talking around that wad of annoyance he was keeping in his mouth. "The ships of His Majesty's Navy, unlike merchant vessels, weigh anchor on time. They go exactly where they are told, and they stay there. They most definitely do not carry illicit memoranda, and they do not—"

She said, "You would not believe what naval vessels get up to." He didn't know much about lace smuggling, did he? "Get to work or get out."

"Another ship for Boston, the frigate *Oak Tree,* registered in Baltimore to McFarlane, sailing April first. The sloop *Betty of Newark*, registered in Plymouth to . . ." He'd uncovered a whole flock of them, Boston bound.

"You can cross every one of those off. This isn't going to be a ship moving all chummy in convoy." The Service didn't know a thing about shipping, did they?

Adrian set a cup of tea by her elbow.

NINE hours and twenty-three minutes later, she closed the Whitby ledger for August. Her eyes stung. She put her head down into her hands and pressed her fingers tight to the bridge of her nose.

"We'll finish tomorrow," Sebastian said.

"Jess, we can stop this now," Adrian said.

The Admiralty man said hoarsely, "I'll get you some tea."

Sebastian snapped, "She doesn't need any more of that."

"No tea." All kinds of pain shot through her back and her legs when she stood up. She hurt everywhere. A clean sweep, when it came to pain. "I don't need to finish tomorrow. You know that as well as I do. We're done here."

The agents from the British Service stood up when she did, every man jack of them. Adrian opened the door for her without saying a word. Only Sebastian followed her out.

They walked past the marines and through the corridors of the empty building and out into the night. The big court-yard was shadowy with distant lanterns. Out on the street, Sebastian had a hackney waiting. He opened the door and flipped down the steps and helped her in. No comfort and explanations from Sebastian yet. He was just getting her away from the Admiralty.

Twenty feet farther along the street, the Whitby small wagon was pulled to the side of the road, the horse and driver dozing. A man sat huddled up in his coat on the back, wait-ing.

It was Pitney. She'd known he would be here. If anyone had asked, he'd say he was here to pick up the Whitby books. But he was here to see her.

"Stop. Over there." It was the first thing she'd said to Se-bastian. "I need to talk to him."

She opened the door of the hackney and put a knee down on the floor and leaned out. "Pitney . . . I'm finished in there."

Pitney saw everything in her face. Had to see it.

"I found . . ." *It hurts, it hurts, it hurts.* Her throat closed tight as a fist. "I traced everything . . . to the Whitby ships. I know . . ." *Breathe in. Breathe out.* It cut like knives. "I'll see Papa tomorrow. I can't face him tonight."

"Jess . . ."

"I can't . . ." She'd run out of words. Pitney looked flat and unreal, like he could tear into strips and blow away. "I have to get out of here. Are you going to be all right?"

He shook his head. There was nothing to say. Nothing to say. He'd been Papa's friend for thirty years. "Jess—"

"Leave her be." Sebastian pulled her roughly back to the seat and reached past her to pull the door closed. The coach started.

It was Whitby ships. The secrets crossed the Channel with smuggled goods, carried by crewmen under orders, who didn't even know what they passed along. Whitby ships. It was in the records, again and again and again.

The design on the leather walls of the carriage was fleurs-de-lis, imprinted in worn gold leaf, one about every four inches. Sometimes the pattern made diamonds, sometimes squares, sometimes long, slanted rows. It depended on how she looked at it. The horses clattered through St. James Park and into the silent streets of Mayfair. Nobody was out at this hour. The wide, dark spaces between the streetlamps were empty. Once, a cat darted across the road in front of them.

At some point Sebastian put his arm around her and pulled her against him, and she started crying, noisy and wet, gasping into his jacket like she was choking on something. If he hadn't been holding her, she would have broken into three or four pieces.

They pulled up in front of his house. After they'd waited there a while, she wiped her nose on her sleeve and drew herself up stiff and held her breath. A couple more sobs got out. It was hard to stop.

"I'm . . ." It scraped the inside of her throat. "I'm sorry. I'll be out of your house tomorrow."

"You'll stay. You have nowhere else to go. Jess, we have to talk about this."

"I don't want to talk. Let me go inside, Sebastian. I'm so tired I'm shaking with it." Of all the useless emotions of her whole life, being in love with this man was the most hopeless and useless of the lot.

"Listen to me. Your father—"

"I'm about to start crying again. Will you please, please, let me go do it someplace that's not in front of you."

"Fine. We'll talk when you're not exhausted. Go to bed."

She let him climb out and lift her down from the coach. Someone was waiting in the lighted doorway. Eunice. How did she always know?

She was crying again even before she got up the stairs. Eunice didn't say a word. Just held her.

Thirty-one

Kennett House, Mayfair

IT WAS EASIER AFTER SHE'D SLEPT A WHILE. Nothing changed, but events got separated somehow. She went to sleep and woke up and everything had happened yesterday instead of today.

She wouldn't think about yesterday.

She lay in bed looking at the slanted ceiling. She could get a man out of England. No problem with that. A Whitby escape route was always laid out in every city where Whitby men worked. The London route would be in just quivering readiness. Pitney'd made sure of that himself. The Swedish sloop, *Ilsa Lindgren*, with no ties to Whitby, lay anchored in the Thames. A dory was tied up at the Asker Street docks, manned day and night, ready to row somebody out to her.

She'd help him escape. She didn't forgive—no one could forgive what he'd done—but she wouldn't let him die. She didn't have the iron heart and metal guts for that kind of justice. She'd get him away safe. She'd make sure she never saw him again.

She didn't want to think about any of that.

The night outside her window was thin and gray at the

edges, with light as weak as seawater. It was so early the women hadn't started bringing milk around. No hubbub of voices. No clanking pails. It was the private time of night when no one was up but thieves and women with light morals. She was both of those. No wonder she was awake.

When she stole Cinq from the gallows, it made her guilty, too, didn't it? That's how Sebastian would see it. He was a man who had a good call on vengeance and the steel innards to enforce it. He wouldn't pardon what she'd done, when he found out.

And that was another thing she didn't want to think about. There wasn't space enough to turn around in her head, she was avoiding so many subjects.

She'd leave England soon. Nothing left for her here anyway.

Outside, one bird woke up to sing ten or twenty notes and then rolled over and went back to sleep. Still early.

This was another long, hard day in front of her. There were going to be some good parts to it, though. She'd best get started.

She padded down the stairs barefoot and opened the door of his room a crack.

"It's me," she said softly. "Don't throw a knife at me or anything when I come in. All right?"

His voice came from the bed. "I'm fairly careful about that."

He slept nude. She'd been right about that. It was a nice warm night for it. Warm dawn, actually. She pulled her nightgown off and dropped it next to the bed and climbed in with him.

Naked slid on naked. It was startling, touching her whole skin against him this way. Like jumping into a warm sea with every nerve surprised at once. She hoped he'd give her a few minutes to get used to this.

He might not. He was very interested in her. On the other hand, he was also laughing. A complex person, Sebastian.

He leaned up on one elbow and ran the tips of his fingers down her side, reassuring like. "Would you mind telling me what you're doing here?"

There was just enough light to see him. The hair on his

chest gathered into a line and grew right down across his stomach. It got thick down between his legs. She didn't quite look there, feeling shy. That was something else she didn't expect. Feeling shy. "What I thought was, I'd get in bed with you and let you decide what to do about it."

"Well." He sat up and started undoing her braids. Either he liked her hair or he was giving himself time to think. "So here you are."

"You keep talking about how much we both want this. Turning into gold, you said. I'd like to try that."

"I did say that, didn't I." He unwound her braid, pulling the strands out between his fingers.

She was going to put Cinq beyond his reach forever. She was going to steal his vengeance. This morning, before she betrayed him, was her only chance. "If you could forget who I am for a while—"

His fingers were on her lips. She wasn't used to how quick he moved sometimes. He was just one place and then another without any time in between. "It's not that. Jess, let me tell you what we—"

She didn't try to match his speed, but she covered his mouth with her hand. "Don't. Please. If we talk about it, I'm going to cry again, or we'll fight. That's not what I want to do right now. Please."

He kissed her hand, where it was pressed against his lips. "Then we'll talk later."

There isn't any later. That was part of what she wasn't going to think about. She put her mind on how fingers felt when a man was kissing them. She didn't want to miss any of this, because she only had the one time. "Have you decided?"

"Jess, I'm still trying to wake up. Can we go at this a little slower? Decided what?"

"Whether you're going to make love to me or not."

He took up where he'd left off, kissing the palm of her hand. "I decided that long ago."

SEBASTIAN listened to a horse and cart clatter through the square. When they passed, it was quiet again. Jess lay beside him in the dawn, wearing a pale, silk ribbon around her neck and the locket on it and not a blessed thing more. Pretty soon he'd lay her down underneath him and take her.

Nothing could have been more natural. It was as if they'd been married a dozen years and she'd come back from checking up on the kids. She let her nightgown slip down around her feet and took the empty spot in the bed. In all creation there was no woman so right for him. She was his.

She loved him. It was written in her eyes for him to read, her loving him and hurting about it and planning something hazardous to her safety fairly soon. She'd try to break into Meeks Street or storm Parliament. He'd talk to her and put a stop to it. Adrian was sure he could get Whitby transported to Australia, not hanged. He'd explain that, and some of the desperation would go away.

Right now, she didn't want to hear anything he had to say. She was hurting and afraid, and she'd come to him to hide for a while.

Lovemaking is a good place to hide. "What we will do," he said, "is take a little trip."

He kissed her fingers, one by one. She was watching him, interested. This was the very beginning. Soon, she wouldn't watch him do anything at all. She'd feel it. He said, "Look over the edge."

Perplexed, she looked where he pointed, over the edge of the bed.

"Rug sharks." He shook his head sadly.

"Rug sharks?"

"Lots of them. Hungry looking, too. Can't get out that way." He crawled across the bed to the window, motioning her to follow. It was only just first light. "See that?" he pointed to the garden in the middle of the square.

"Yes . . ."

"That's the island. I imagine we'll drift up against it sometime or other. Probably in a day or two. Till then . . ." He put his hands on her shoulders. That was a good place to start, the shoulders. "We're stuck here. On the raft."

She smiled, tentative. "It's a nice raft, though."

"A fine raft." She had lean, elegant muscles, tense as carriage springs. He kneaded up and down her neck, loosening them up. "There's just the raft. No past. No future. Only the ocean around us. Nowhere to go and nothing to do but make love to each other."

He watched her let go of them—past and future. "I'd like that," she said.

"Lie down then. No. On your stomach."

She lay down, willing, but puzzled. When he got on top, straddling her thighs, her skin startled. Little ripples of shock spread out.

So this was new. Her first lover, that boy, had taken care with her. Been gentle. But he hadn't known much. There'd be lots of surprises for her this morning.

He patted her rump, *Hello, rump. Aren't you a pretty thing,* and introduced himself to the muscles up and down her back . . . fingering his way along . . . stroking them the way they liked . . . getting them on his side . . . telling them they were safe with him. He knew what he was doing. It was a beautiful, beautiful body she had.

She had her head to one side, looking around his room, glancing back to see what he was about. "Shouldn't we be doing something?"

"Can't do anything. All those rug sharks. We just have to stay here and amuse ourselves."

"I meant, amusing ourselves. I've done this before. I know there's more to it."

"Indeed there is. But we're not in any hurry. Got a couple of days to fill up before we get to the island."

After he'd been working a bit, she forgot to worry. Her eyes closed. A little while onward, she whispered, "This is what it feels like afterwards. Like I'm melted."

So that was enough on those back muscles. She'd loosened up nicely. When he got off and rolled her over, she almost flopped.

He started in on her hand. Many bones and muscles to make friends with there. Then up her arms to her shoulders. Her eyes were half-closed when he went down to get acquainted with her feet. Jess could relax and enjoy herself. It just took a while.

"That feels good. I didn't know." She spun the words out of a soft breath. "Didn't know." Her eyes closed. "Are you sure there isn't something I should be doing? It doesn't seem fair."

She was breathing deeply, letting his hands tell her when to breathe. This was where he wanted her to be. This was what he wanted her to feel.

"You truly hate to lie back and do nothing, don't you?" he said.

"This isn't doing nothing. I don't know what it is, but it's not doing nothing."

He knelt between her legs. So beautiful. It took all his strength to hold himself in check, thinking what it was going to feel like . . . Jess, closed around him.

SHE liked what Sebastian was doing to her. Kissing her knee. Made it hard to get her breath. Hard to stay still. But, oh, she liked it. Was this what people generally did in bed together? She hadn't known it took this long. She was almost certain you could get to it faster if you wanted to.

Then he kissed her breast, and it was like being plunked down over a fire. Heat everywhere.

He put his mouth on her, eating her with noisy sucks and bites, like she was a melon or something, and he was hungry. He pressed his teeth against her nipple. She would have sworn she was drawn too tight to move, but she thrashed like a hooked fish when he did that.

"I want . . ." She wanted to grab him and crawl through his skin. Into him. She wanted him *there*. She held her legs open for him because that was what this was all about. She wasn't ignorant.

"You never do anything by halves, do you, Jess?" He stroked from her shoulder to her breast and down her belly, between her legs. She jerked and jerked in the wake of his hand. "No defenses at all. Nothing held in reserve."

That probably all meant something. She'd think about it later. "Could we . . . could we do the rest of it?"

"We are."

"I mean a little faster. Now."

"Why would we want to go fast? Remember? No place to go. Nothing to do." He wound some of her hair around his fingers. "I like this. It's the color of the ropes on a ship, when they're dried out in the sun." He played with her hair, doing something to it. "You watch for that color because the ropes lengthen up, and you have to send the boys about tightening them to trim the sails. It's a good color. It means fair weather."

"I don't think I can stand much more of this."

Damned if he wasn't pulling one strand through the other, like he was braiding it somehow. Braiding her hair. "This is a reef knot," he said. "That's the first one you learn on a ship."

He was tying knots in her hair. Sailor's knots. The man was insane.

"You use it for holding ropes together," he said.

"I don't care if you . . . dance jigs in it. Look, can we talk about this some other time?"

He took her hair apart. No more reef knot. He stroked her again, oh, slow and strong down her belly, and she pushed her whole body up underneath his hand. He let her press herself up into the heel of his hand four or five times, till she was dancing for him. She whimpered when he took his hand away.

"Please . . ."

Kneeling over her, he played with her hair some more. "This one's called a sheet bend. It's another one you use for joining ropes."

She watched while he undid her hair. She was tensing and untensing, rhythmically, waiting for him to finish with the damned knot nonsense. He was waiting, too, being stern with himself. When she set her fists on his chest, he was iron. He was oak-hard flesh, quivering. He wanted her.

He said, "The joy at the end takes only a minute. Pleasuring can last as long as you like."

There was a logical fallacy behind those words. She was sure of it. When they were through in bed, she was going to kill him. "I don't like this."

"What part don't you like? This?" He trailed his thumb, soft, across her, where she was open.

Her eyes spasmed shut with the poignancy of it. She was shaking now, continually. "It's not being able to . . . stop. I don't belong to myself when you do that." She lay panting. She hadn't known she'd have no control at all.

She wasn't the only one. He was gasping for air. Shaking. He kept his hand cupped over her there, at the center of all that pleasure, all that urgency, and looked down at her. She saw it in his eyes. He was caught, too. Famished. Fascinated.

But he was the one who knew what happened next. That made him so damned powerful. He could do anything to her when he touched her there.

"It's just me," he whispered. "Just me. I like luring you along till you can't think anymore. No harm in it, between the two of us, here in bed." Another kiss. He had a thousand different kinds of kisses. This was the brush of lips on the inside of her thigh. "Let me pull your sails into the wind. There's nothing you have to take charge of."

She couldn't have taken charge of a folded napkin. She felt him, warm as water, licking her between her legs. Madness was what she felt. Oceans of madness.

He didn't stop till she was gasping out his name. Till she was shaking.

He propped himself on his forearms, above her, looking down. "Do you know, Jess, a while back I swore to myself I'd have you like this, underneath me, with not a stitch on you, begging and incoherent. It's as good as I thought it would be."

"Not quite incoherent yet."

"We will arrange that. Open your eyes. I want to see in."

He lay his length upon her and came into her. She didn't know what he saw in her eyes when he entered her. Surprise maybe.

What she saw was Sebastian filling up the whole world above her and then filling up the whole world inside of her, too. He was exactly what she needed—strong and powerful and not gentle at all. Her pleasure started with the first thrust and kept on as he thrust into her again and again and again.

"STAY with me," he said.

Sebastian lay in bed and watched Jess slip the cotton nightgown on over her head with that same simple grace he'd seen when she was taking it off. In the first light, her hair was a fall of tawny silk. Her body was alert as a tiger, happy, suave muscle gliding easily under her skin. The way she was meant to look. But her eyes were so sad.

"Stay," he said.

"The maids are up. I'm not going to make a scandal in your aunt's house. I know better than that."

"I need to tell you what's going to happen—"

"I can't." She was already at the door. "Let me go do what I have to do. We'll talk about it later."

She was going to her father. She needed to do that alone. There was nothing anyone on earth could do to make that easy for her.

He'd met with Adrian, hurriedly, last night. Between the two of them they could save Whitby from the hangman. Whitby would spend the rest of his years as a convict in New South Wales. Not easy for an old man. He'd suffer. Maybe that would be enough.

Her father's life would be his wedding gift to Jess. He'd set aside his vengeance. Josiah Whitby, damn his soul, was right. That was the only way he could have a life with Jess.

He said, "Marry me, Jess."

For an instant, she stopped. She laid her forehead to the wood of the door. "Sebastian . . ." She didn't look at him. "Ask me tomorrow." Then she fumbled with the doorknob, those clever hands of hers clumsy as paws.

Thirty-two

HER NAME WAS BRIDGET AND SHE CAME FROM County Mayo in the west of Ireland. She was a whore, a good one, and as shrewd and grasping as a magpie. Even respectably dressed, she looked like three pence against the nearest wall or ten pence upstairs in a bed.

She drank ale from a large pewter tankard and wiped her mouth. "She's gone. Girl slipped out at first light and left those lumbering fools behind."

"Alone, then." The Irishman set his elbows on the sticky table. "Was she carrying a bag?"

"You think I pranced up and asked her? Jaysus." She drank again. "And you bastards owe me a pound, even."

"Later."

Next to him on the bench, the other man said, "If she's leaving England, we know where she'll be." He shoved to his feet. "Let's go. Out the back way."

"You could pay for me drink," the woman muttered. "Pigs."

* * *

PITNEY wasn't at his house. His housekeeper, all flustered, said he'd come in late last night and packed a bag and left. He wasn't at the warehouse either. When Jess checked the safe, the ready money was missing, so he'd been there and gone. But he wouldn't have been fast enough to sail out on last night's tide. He was still in London.

She took a hackney to Commercial Road, which was as far as the jarvey wanted to venture into these waters. A sensible man. She counted coins for him while her bodyguard assembled at a discreet distance.

She'd dodged Sebastian's men, but not the Service. That was the next item on her agenda. Cutting loose the Service.

She slipped around the corner and down the alley, listening to heavy boots hurrying after her. At the end of Goose Lane she climbed a rain barrel and went over the palings into the narrow, crooked pathways nobody ever got around to naming. They were in her part of town now.

CLAUDIA sat in the ugly front parlor at Meeks Street, red-eyed, clutching her reticule in her lap.

". . . his clothing gone from his room. All his things. The door to your study was open." She swallowed and went on. "The drawers of your desk have been pried out. The miniatures are missing from the upstairs hallway, and some of the other paintings. My jewel case . . ." She kept her face averted from them while she talked. Her eyes stayed fixed on some knob or curlicue on the hideous sideboard to the left of the door. "My jewel case was extracted from my room last night, while I slept. I found it in your office, on the floor, broken open and emptied. Eunice's jewels were—"

"He's run for it." Sebastian stopped her. There was no need to make her count through the whole wretched list of what was stolen. He felt sick. "It was Quentin all along. Quentin and Whitby. It adds up."

"Quentin." Adrian was doing some adding of his own. "But not Josiah."

Doyle didn't move from his position near the window. "It's Pitney." Doyle met his eye, soberly. "Your cousin knows

Pitney, not Josiah Whitby. It's Pitney who carries paperwork to the Board of Trade."

"A conspiracy of small fishes," Adrian said. "That's why we missed it. Sebastian, I'm sorry."

Service agents were silent at the edges of the room, watching.

Adrian said, "Your cousin had access to secrets. Pitney could use Whitby company ships any way he wanted. Josiah wouldn't question him."

Quentin had done treason. Quentin lived in his house. He'd sat beside him, eating dinner every night. He'd offered sympathy, damp-eyed, when the *Neptune Dancer* went down. His cousin had been playing a part for years. "Quentin is in charge. His ideas. He needed a man with access to ships, so he pulled Pitney into it somehow."

Adrian was up, pacing off the room. "Jess knows it's Pitney." After a minute. "She knew it when she left last night. She warned him."

"Pitney was waiting at the gate when we left the Admiralty." He remembered what Jess had said. He remembered their faces—Jess resolute and frozen, Pitney gray as death. "She told him right under my nose. I watched her do it."

"Mr. Pitney." Claudia's voice was tight. Her hands twitched in her lap. "From the Whitby company. When he came, they'd leave the house and walk along the street, to talk. Quentin made certain they wouldn't be overheard. I knew something was wrong. I saw Quentin, once, hand money to him."

She had the attention of every man in the room.

"I have known, for some time, that Quentin was engaged in something shameful. I had hoped it was . . . an unimportant corruption. My father committed numberless depravities without becoming a traitor." Her face was proud. Impassive. "My brother has not succeeded in even that."

"Claudia . . ." This was his fault. He should have seen what was happening in his own home. He'd ignored Quentin because he disliked him. What could he say? She'd never wanted friendship or comfort from him before. He didn't know how to offer it now. "Where has he gone?"

"To Hades, I devoutly pray." Claudia rose and shook her skirts out. "It's as well the Ashton name will die in this generation. The bastard shoot is the best we've produced. Have a care to your Jessamyn, Sebastian. I've seen how Quentin looks at something he plans to steal. He watched your Persian miniatures that way. That's the way he looks at Jess." She smoothed her glove. "And he likes to hurt things."

Jess was headed to Pitney, wherever he was hiding. To Pitney. And to Quentin.

FROM the outside, all rookeries look the same, but some are more dangerous than others.

Ludmill Street was peaceable in its rough way. Safe enough, if you knew what you were doing. When a pair of Irishmen approached, making monetary offers, she snapped back, sharp, in Italian. They left her alone, thinking she belonged to the Italians. There were lots of hot-tempered Italians in this section who didn't like even their whores approached by Irishmen. A few hundred yards farther on, she sent an Italian boy on his way with a Gaelic curse. Lots of hot-tempered Irishmen in this quarter, too.

When she got to the Limehouse, to Asker Street, it would be considerably more dangerous. She'd be unwise to visit alone.

The Reverend's soup kitchen was open, and the door to his office unlocked. Guess he felt the same way she did about locks. An invitation to thievery, locks were. Being the Reverend, though, he probably came to the same conclusion in a more roundabout way.

When he walked in a few minutes later, she had his communion chalice down. "I should get you something better than this," she said. "Something that's real silver, at least."

"I don't own anything worth stealing, Jess." Which was more or less what he said to her the first time they met, when she was eight and planning to lift that particular cup.

She set it back on the shelf. "Reverend, you would not believe the trouble I'm in." Which was exactly what she said to

him on another memorable occasion, a couple hours before
she sold herself to Lazarus.

WHEN Sebastian came into the study, Josiah Whitby was
staring into the fire. The old man didn't look up. Not making
a point, just not much interested. Some rumor from last night
had reached him. He knew it'd been Whitby ships.

Sebastian collapsed into the chair. "I'll take that port you
didn't offer me yesterday."

That got Whitby's attention. A cool, shrewd look, and
Whitby read everything he was saying. Confirmation of his
innocence. The *amende honorable*. Apology.

Whitby responded with his own set of messages. He
brought the bottle and two glasses to the desk and poured for
them both. "Looks like you could use it."

"Why the hell didn't you get Jess out of England the day
you were arrested? Anybody but an iron-plated bastard like
you would have kept her out of this."

Whitby saluted with his glass and drank. "You'll find,
Kennett, that there's a fine art to giving Jess orders."

Time to tell him and pray the man knew something
that could help. "An hour ago your daughter ran into the
Whitechapel rookery as if all the Hounds of Hell were after
her." He waited for that to sink in. "Unless you can think of
some way to get her back, she'll be in a brothel by tomorrow
morning. Learn to take orders there, I should imagine. *Salut.*"

The old man's eyes turned to brown rock. This was the
Josiah Whitby who'd faced down the mob in Izmir and
plucked a crew of men back from hanging. This was the king
smuggler who ran his gang of cutthroats under the noses of
the customs. "The Hounds of Hell being yourself, I take it."

"Being the British Service." He didn't try to hide the
anger that filled him. "She gave the slip to men who were
supposed to protect her. Fast as a greyhound, your Jess.
Comes from all those years doing your dangerous errands.
And Lazarus's. She must be used to running scared."

Whitby slapped his drink down, rattling. "No games,

Kennett. I don't need to be rooked into helping Jess. Why'd she run from you?"

"We would have stopped her going to Pitney."

There was not the smallest change in Whitby's eyes. "Pitney."

"The part of Cinq that used your company to commit treason."

A minute passed. Whitby gave a nod. "I wasn't sure myself, till they told me it was Whitby ships. Then I knew." He wiped at the spilled drops of port with the side of his hand. "I wish it hadn't been Jess who found this out. She'll take it as her fault somehow."

"He has a dangerous partner—the man who was behind this all. If Jess shows up, Pitney won't be able to protect her. I have to get to her. Where are they?"

"What happens to Pitney?"

He didn't answer. They both knew there'd be no amnesty for Pitney.

Whitby sat back in his chair and stared out the window, past the bars. Three sparrows were on the windowsill, tucking into crumbs of bread. It'd be Whitby who set that out for them.

"I've known Pitney for thirty years." Whitby drank and set the glass down. "Jess is headed for the docks. There's a warehouse. The old Belkey warehouse on Asker Street. That's the conduit out of England."

Asker Street. Jess had lost her bodyguard near Commercial Road. That was a long, treacherous walk for a woman. He stood up. "I'll find her."

A sleek gray muzzle poked out from behind the curtain. The beady nose sniffed in his direction and slithered toward him. Jess's vermin.

He said, "Touch my boots and you die."

There was no fear in the ferret. It was like Jess, that way. It stood on its hindquarters to snuffle up his leg to the thigh. Then it set a clawed foot on him, for balance, and started sniffing across his hand.

"He smells Jess on thee," Whitby said.

"If it bites, I'm going to wring its neck."

"I've thought of fricassee ferret, myself, from time t' time."

"She can't walk through Limehouse alone. Who will she go to?" The ferret made an odd half scramble, still sniffing, following him to the door.

"It's been too long, Kennett. Her old friends have gone. Everything's changed. She doesn't belong there anymore."

"Then she should damn well stay out of there."

The study door wasn't locked. That was Adrian's acknowledgment of Whitby's innocence. The ferret, damn its furry soul, scuttled along at his bootside like a pointy-toothed dog.

"Take him. There's a carrying cage in the hall." Whitby stood to watch him go, his hands on the desk, balled into fists. "Take him along for luck, Kennett. He won't get in the way. And if you get close to Jess, let him out, and he'll find her for you."

It was easier to bring the vermin than argue.

"She'll get to Pitney, wherever he is," Whitby said. "Whatever he's done, she'll get him out of England, and safe. Loyal to the death, my Jess. That's another reason you have to be careful, giving her orders. If you belong to her, she'll move the foundations of the earth for you."

PITNEY dropped the seabag at his feet. It was the same one he'd carried thirty years ago when he signed on with Josiah. Nothing in it but some handfuls of money and a few changes of clothes. Not much to show for a lifetime. He was old now and a pariah and he'd sold his soul for a mass of pottage. It'd be hard to start over in some seaport in the East.

He said, "I left a letter."

"Inevitably," the smooth, cold voice beside him said. "The tool turns against its master. Napoleon himself was betrayed by Barras."

"I named Buchanan. I told them he planted the false evidence and where and how. I named the Frenchmen. And you. I've left more than enough proof to hang us all. Josiah's going to walk free before this day is out and he'll come looking for vengeance. He won't come after me, because we were friends, once. But I wouldn't want to be in your shoes."

"I've arranged my own protection against Whitby. He won't touch me."

"Maybe not." It didn't matter. There wasn't much that mattered to a man after he'd betrayed his friends. He couldn't even say why he'd done it. The company felt like his own, after all these years. The warehouse and the ships. It hadn't seemed wrong to do some smuggling on the side and keep it off the books.

It had fallen apart. He'd done treason. He still didn't know how he'd come to it.

The voice behind him just wouldn't stop. "The Republic doesn't forget its heroes. There's a place prepared for me. I go into honorable exile, and only for a time. When the emperor rides in triumph down Pall Mall, I'll be one of the men behind him. They'll need Englishmen to lead the new government. I have experience."

Pitney heard the cocking of a gun. He allowed himself one final look at the brown water of the Thames and the clean blue sky above it. He turned.

He didn't want to be shot in the back.

LIMEHOUSE was full of sailors and stevedores of every country and race known to man, most of them rolling drunk, even in the middle of the day. It was a gauntlet she wouldn't have wanted to run alone.

Belkey's warehouse was a quarter mile farther on, in Asker Street, in a row of falling-down waterfront warehouses, slated for destruction. Most were empty now or holding bulk storage.

The Reverend kept beside her. His black jacket and white collar cleared a path for them through the sailors and whores. Men respected his cloth or wanted to avoid the sermons men of religion passed out in this part of town. The locals recognized him and knew he was under Lazarus's protection.

Asker Street, by the docks, was mostly deserted. The Belkey warehouse, halfway along, had been closed up for a year. Grass grew in the spaces between the cobbles of the loading yard. The windows were broken, even up on the third and fourth story. Must have taken weeks for the local lads to throw rocks that high and break out every blessed pane. Nothing like a challenge.

No sign of life. Nobody had made himself at home in that rubble on the far side of the yard or in some cozy corner of the fence. That alone meant somebody stayed here regular to rout the squatters out. Dogs had set up housekeeping, though. There were a dozen of them, mean and hardy and wise, crouching behind the broken boards of the fence. They watched strangers cross the open space, staying safe in the shadows. The boys in this district taught dogs to be wary of humans.

The river smell was strong. Just the other side of the warehouse wall lay the stinking mud of the Thames. Cold, damp air blew off that water, leaving a bad taste in the mouth. At the wharves, just out of sight, ships creaked and snapped and banged. Chain rattled and there was a sudden loud pop, like a distant gun. It was never quiet down at the docks.

Pitney might still be here, waiting, out of sight, or he might have come and gone. Either way, there'd be a man inside the warehouse, alert and capable, with a boat ready any hour of the day or night. Papa always had a back door out of any city they lived in. Nobody more careful than Papa.

The door in the side of the warehouse was an inch open.

"This is unlocked," the Reverend said.

"I expect the locks got pulled off some time ago."

At first, when she walked in, the place looked empty. Gutted. The storage racks had been pulled down and the wood stolen for fuel. Bars of sun slanted through the broken windows.

Somebody was living here. She smelled beer and piss and charcoal and stale food. There'd be rats. There were always rats. "You better stay outside, Reverend, till I see what's what."

"I won't leave you alone. I've seen worse, Jess."

On the far side of the open floor, below the windows, a bedstead was shoved up against the brick wall. Beside that was a charcoal stove with a kettle on it. Good signs. Whitby's man would show up soon enough.

She led the way inward, past dark, empty arches where they used to store cargo, toward that patch of domesticity. She didn't see what stepped out behind her and looped a cord around her throat. The world was gone, sudden as snuffing out a candle.

"IT's the Reverend," Adrian said.

Sebastian rolled him over. The man groaned and his eyelids fluttered. There was blood on his forehead where he'd hit the floor.

Jess had been here. The ferret chittered in its cage, lashing its body back and forth.

"He was hit from behind. Here." Sebastian's hand came away bloody. "This just happened. A friend of Jess's?"

"Friend of all the world. Jess must have gone to him. Smart, smart girl."

"Two men . . ." the Reverend's eyes opened, "took her."

"Don't move. Trevor, stay with him. When he can walk, get him to my aunt." Sebastian laid the man gently back on the floor. "Pitney didn't order this. Quentin has her." *She could be anywhere on the docks. On any ship.* "I need to see Lazarus. I need men to search the docks."

Adrian stood up. "When's the next tide?"

"Three hours." They didn't have much time. Maybe no time at all.

Doyle's face was grim. "The Reverend's under Lazarus's protection. So's Jess. He's going to kill somebody for this."

Good. "Let's get moving."

DARKNESS brightened first at the center. Not with light. With pain. That's how she knew she was alive. Being alive hurt.

She was wrapped in sailcloth, being carried like a bundle over somebody's shoulder. He sang. He crooned to himself. She thought it might be Gaelic. Her head flopped again and again against his back. Through a gap at the end of the smothering folds she could see the black wood planks of the dock and blinding sunlight glinting off the river. She was being taken to a ship.

She fought to wake up, sick and terrified. If they got her on board, she'd drop out of sight like a stone in the ocean. Maybe exactly like a stone in an ocean.

One chance. She worked her hand up to her throat and snagged the ribbon at her neck. Got it off over her head and pushed her hand out of the cloth . . . and she let her mother's locket go. She let it fall on the dock.

Find somebody. For God's sake find somebody and tell them where I am.

It might work. Folks didn't leave gold lying in the dirt.

She set to making herself conspicuous, yelling and flopping and trying to kick the cloth off. It didn't make any difference, as far as she could tell. The bloke carrying her didn't speed up. Nobody stopped him to ask why his bundle was making a fuss. It wasn't three minutes later she felt the change in his steps that said he was going up a gangplank. The slosh and clank said ship, and she was carried aboard. Ship smell surrounded her. Nobody would find her now.

She was tossed down and spun out of the wrapping. She landed with a thud that knocked the breath out of her. Shock stole her sight.

Her eyes cleared. She lay on her back, on deck, faced up to the sky. Above her was dazzling blue sky with a mast in it. She let her head roll to the side and saw Blodgett. Captain Blodgett. So she knew where she was. This was the *Northern Lark.*

Lark was old and lumbering and always in need of repair—a poor excuse for a ship, but she stayed just barely profitable. *Lark* carried dirty cargo she didn't want fouling better vessels—horse hides and dried fish and such.

Strange how it didn't come as a shock to see Quentin here, his back to her, arguing with Blodgett. It was like her brain had kept working and calculating, and it'd already come up with Quentin's name and was just now getting around to telling her about it.

Quentin and Pitney. Quentin was the schemer. Pitney would never have come up with this on his own.

Lark's crew was aboard. She could feel their footsteps on the deck boards. Fine weather for sailing, and it sounded like they were getting ready to do it.

"Jess . . ."

She turned her head. Light on the water blinded her. Then the shapes sorted out. It wasn't a pile of dirty cloth next to the rail. It was a man, tossed down and twisted unnatural.

"Jessie . . ."

She rolled to her belly and crawled to him.

Pitney had been shot. Blood pooled on the deck under him. He had red at the corner of his mouth. It was blood with bubbles in it, and that meant he'd been hit in the lungs. Men didn't live when they were hit in the lungs. "Pitney."

"Jessie girl. I didn't . . ."

His mouth was full of blood. He couldn't finish the words. She could. "You didn't mean this. None of it. You wouldn't hurt me. Wouldn't hurt Papa. I know that. I never thought anything else, not for a minute."

She managed to sit and pull him up, into her lap, so his head lay against her. His clothes were sticky wet. So much blood in a man. The tears coming down her cheeks fell on his face.

His breath sucked and bubbled. ". . . just letters, Jess. Letters to France. I didn't know . . ."

"You didn't know they were treason."

Easy to see how he'd been tricked into this. Just letters. That's how it started. He'd taken a coin or two to send packets of letters, secret, to France. "To my sister." "To my business in Lyon." All those years smuggling lace and brandy and tea in good faith, he wouldn't think about treason. Not till he was in too deep to stop.

". . . I wouldn't . . ."

"You never would. Not treason."

"Thought Josiah would get away . . ."

"He doesn't blame you."

"I tried to . . ." His breathing took on the rattle that meant death was coming. ". . . stop . . ."

"You stopped them, Pitney. You did fine." He was still breathing, but his eyes didn't see anymore. He could hear, maybe. "Yer always saving me neck. You remember the time you come in arfter me, when I fell out of that damn dory off Hythe? And we neither of us could swim a lick. Papa was so bloody irritated. He yelled at me about it, off and on, for a year. You would not believe . . ."

There wasn't any more life in him. She could tell the change, holding him.

LAZARUS held court in the same house, in the dim, vulgar parlor. In the back, four men piled the tables with swag from a large robbery. Two others talked to an old woman hunched over an account book. Most thieves paid their penny to the local Runner, but if you took gold, you had to come to Lazarus, to the old woman, to pay your pence. There wasn't a fence in London would touch it otherwise.

Sebastian strode up the center of the room, Adrian beside him. None of the thugs lounging to the left or right said a word or tried to stop them. All those cold, violent eyes followed them.

Lazarus was holding a fine sable robe, admiring it. He ignored Adrian and cocked his head toward Sebastian. "What the hell's going on, Captain?"

"We know who Cinq is. He's got Jess."

ON the far side of the deck, Quentin wound his way through a long, arrogant, complicated complaint. Blodgett was answering. None of it meant anything. She lay Pitney's body back to the deck and closed his eyes. When she turned, Blodgett was saying, ". . . shoot him here. Then you bring me Whitby's daughter. Get her below, for God's sake."

Quentin was different, here. He stood proud as a rooster. Swaggering. "I said to cast off."

"We will, Mr. Ashton. We will. Nobody's going anywhere on the slack of the tide." Blodgett spat, showing his opinion of landsmen. "Billy, clear these boxes out of the way." He kicked a valise.

"Take her to my cabin," Quentin ordered a passing sailor. He sounded excited, like a kid going on holiday.

Blodgett snarled, "Not *now*. You, Henshaw, wrap some chain on that body. We'll roll it overboard, downriver. And get the damned girl belowdecks."

"Aye, Captain."

They caught her before she made it over the railing. A pair of them slammed her to the planking, hard. One added a quick punch to her stomach to make her think twice about trying that again.

When the red faded out of her vision, Quentin stood over her, blotting out the sky. "You have given no end of trouble. And for nothing." He poked his boot into her ribs. "You waste your time. You waste my time. You cause me expense and danger. It's ridiculous. You two, hold her. I cannot understand why—"

He'd killed Pitney. She lunged for him. A sailor kicked her down and held her.

"Coward. Sodding, poxy, slimy, lying—"

Quentin leaned down, nagging. "You will learn to do what I tell you. There are good reasons for everything I do. Matters of state beyond your comprehension. If you would stop and listen to me for a minute—"

"I said to get her under cover." Blodgett shoved Quentin aside and grabbed her by the hair and jerked her to her feet. "We're at dock in the middle of London. Every ship has some fool with a spyglass. You can play with her when we're out at sea." Blodgett pushed, and she fell, staggering, against the belly of a huge sailor. "Stow her."

She fought while they dragged her off and screamed every time she got her mouth loose. It took two of them to haul her away. She hurt them some. But not as much as they hurt her back.

Down below, in the cargo deck, they twisted her arms behind her and pushed her into a locker built tight to the hull. They kicked it closed and locked the door behind her and left her alone in the dark.

"HE wants her for ransom. And to give to the French." Sebastian paced the carpet. "She's only valuable to him alive.

He has to keep her alive." He was trying not to think about all the ways Jess could be hurt, and stay alive.

Beggars, thieves, cutthroats, and pimps detoured around him, making their way to Lazarus for orders. Word was spreading out. Every minute, more and more of the scum of the earth were looking for Jess.

Somewhere out there, she was afraid. Maybe hurt. He wouldn't believe she was dead.

He stepped over the ferret. Adrian had let it loose in here for some goddamned reason. It kept getting underfoot. "Quentin won't risk moving her twice. They'll take her directly to the ship." What else? There had to be more he could figure out. "It'll be a small ship. Fifty tons or less. Small enough to have a crew that can be trusted to keep quiet. They're smugglers or worse. He wouldn't try this with an honest crew. We're looking for a small ship with a bad reputation."

From the corner of his eye he saw Lazarus signal his boy, Twist, to his side, and whisper orders, ". . . tell the Measle . . . Bernardo . . ."

Quentin had been listening to Jess at dinner every night. He had to know the net was closing. Quent had laid plans for his escape. "Look for a ship's been sitting idle a week, with the crew aboard. They'll have some excuse."

Lazarus said, "Take those words with you. Pass them along. Don't stand there. Go."

Twist sprinted down the room. Adrian wandered over to stand next to Lazarus. "He's slow. You can't get good help."

"Some of you turn out better than others." Lazarus eyed him. "Some even go honest, like Jess."

"Using the broadest possible definition of honest, yes. Is Twist the best you could do?"

"He's new to it. It'll be another couple months before he stops thinking he's smart." Lazarus contemplated the doorway. "You been careless with my Jess, Hawker. I expected better of you."

"I made a mistake."

"Too bad for Jess."

"Sebastian will get her back. If she's alive under the sun, he'll get her back."

"I hope you're right. But part of her never healed up from being scared so bad, that last time, when she got hurt. She's fragile inside, in the heart of her. Like eggshells. If we're too long about it, I don't know what we'll get back."

Doyle was talking to a pale-haired woman with a baby in her lap. She sat cross-legged on a small rug, wrapped in the long sable coat. Her hair was a snow-colored curtain, loose around her, spilling over her shoulders and down her back.

"That's the girl you sent to Eunice, isn't it?" Adrian said.

"Fluffy. She showed up at the door last night, saying she was my responsibility, if you please, and I wouldn't get rid of her that easy. I don't know what to do with her," he scowled at her a minute, ". . . or that damned smelly bundle she's so fond of. She's named it after me." He pushed to his feet. "I'd better stir her up to get us some tea. It's going to be a long day. And you can tell me why you brought that bloody ferret with you."

DARK was solid as the wood around her. She could reach out and touch every edge of the locker they'd put her in. It smelled of old contraband . . . tobacco, brandy, tea. Water slapped just on the other side of the planks, cold and angry-sounding. When she put her hand down to hold Mama's locket, she remembered it was gone. She'd thrown it away. The last thing gone.

She curled up in the Dark. She could see Sebastian in her mind as clear as if he was next to her. See him the way he looked this morning, in bed, with the sun on him in long streaks.

Sebastian would think she'd left with Pitney. He'd think she went to Pitney right from his bed without saying good-bye, not intending to come back. He might even think she'd been part of Cinq all along.

He wouldn't come looking for her. No one would come.

Dark wins, in the end. The last candle goes out and Dark wins.

A rat scuttled in the passage next to her. Rats. She made herself into a tight ball and put her hands over her face. Somebody nearby began moaning a single note.

No. Not nearby. She was the one doing it.

"WILL you stop that! Bloody blazes." Sebastian plucked the bedamned ferret off the table. "Get your nose out of that."

The old woman who kept Lazarus's records hissed like a stray cat and scraped her bangles and gold chains back into a pile. The ferret had collected himself a ribbon and was too busy holding onto its booty to bite him. He tugged the ribbon away from the pointy white teeth.

The thin blue ribbon had a gold coin hanging on it.

Not a coin. He was holding a plain gold locket, buffed smooth against flesh, worn to a soft glow. He opened it with his thumbnail. A design was etched inside, delicate and perfect. A flower.

"This belongs to Jess," he said.

Lazarus took it from him. "You're right. Jess wears this. Who brought it in?"

JESS lay on her side in the cell. If she was quiet, maybe the rats wouldn't come. But they smelled you. Even if you held your breath, they smelled you and found you.

I can't get out.

Bad dreams. She was caught in bad dreams. She was back to being a kid, that last time on the roofs, when she fell. Rotten timbers gave way. The air shaft in the old warehouse collapsed around her, and nobody came. Nobody knew where she was. Nobody could hear.

I can't get out. Bricks and wood and plaster came tumbling down on top of her, pinning her down. Burying her alive.

She got so thirsty. When she couldn't scream anymore, she made a sound like air squeezing out of a bag. Then the rats came.

"You can't have me." She told the rats that. She kept telling the Dark that, hour after hour. Telling the Dark, "Leave me alone." The rats didn't listen. Her hands got slick with blood, fighting them off.

The Thames River was at her back, on the other side of the boards. Dark as blood, that river. Old dreams crawled out of it and sucked at her. The worst dreams. She knew how they ended and she couldn't get out of them.

The smell of shattered wood and plaster and mold filled her lungs. She was so thirsty, and she couldn't get out.

The Dark won. She gave up and didn't remember doing it.

She wasn't fighting anymore when Lazarus crawled in and woke her up and dragged her out. He hurt her. Pain washed, red and black, again and again, when he uncovered her. The Dark tried to get him, too. Timbers caved in. Lazarus kept the falling bricks off her with his own body. He jostled and pulled and carried her through the Dark, pain after pain.

"Hold on, Jessie. One more stretch and we're out."

Then they were in the padding crib. In the dream she heard herself say, "I'm cold."

"You'll be warm in a little while." Lazarus held her wrapped in a blanket against his chest. He was bothering her with a cup. "Drink this."

It was an order. She tried to make her mouth obey. "Don' want it. Wanna go to sleep."

"You can't go to sleep till you drink it, Jess." So she tried. She couldn't make her lips work.

"Here's the man who's going to fix your arm. You finish drinking this, and you'll go to sleep." Dark laid layer after layer around her. Buried her. "When you wake up, it'll be over."

Cold fingers closed on her arm. Exploring fingers, like evil icicles.

"It 'urts. It 'urts bad."

Men whispered. More hands came to hold her still. Agony hit like black lightning. She screamed and fell into the Dark.

In the hollow aftermath, Lazarus said, "Go ahead and cry, Jess. That's right. Nobody here to see you but me and Black John. Just your friends. Nobody else."

Lots of nightmares hid inside her, waiting to come out. They were with her in the whispering Dark.

There's always something to do.

Shaking, she pushed herself up to her feet, hunched over. Not much room in here. The wood was damp and chill, slimy to touch.

It wasn't just nightmares in her. There were good days to remember. Think about . . . the Greek islands. Flowers. Air clear as glass. And she'd seen the northern lights over the snow fields in Russia. Think about that. She'd named a Whitby ship *Northern Light.* Pretty little sloop.

The hull was at her back, only the cold water of the Thames beyond it. What about this overhead? She braced herself on damp wood and pounded with the heel of her hand, trying to jar something loose. Solid as the earth, this wood. They just had to build this damn locker like it was going to hold wild bears.

Remember good days. Think about Sebastian leaning over her in the garden, dark as the devil, laughing at her. "It's square. Look," and he showed her the stem of the horehound. She could smell the clean, green smell of it like it was in here with her.

She kicked at the doorframe, where it swung closed. Weakest point.

She could see the purple of those flowers Sebastian held. Delicate as butterflies, they lay safe inside his hand, in a circle of muscles like steel.

Sebastian was going to find her. Any minute now, he'd come. Or next week or in six months. That was one of those things you could count on. The sun would rise. Sebastian would come for her.

Dark chuckled down the back of her neck like a drip of cold water. Always wins, Dark does.

SEBASTIAN stalked down the wharf, assessing ship by ship. Some of them were already casting off, drifting into the current of the Thames. These were coast huggers here below Asker Street. Scows and dirty fishing boats and coal barges. There were too many to search, and Jess could be in any of them. There was no time.

"About 'ere." The young thief swept an expansive hand. "Somewheres along of 'ere, more er less. Found it onna ground."

Dozens of ships on the wharf ahead. More farther down. There were too many. They'd never find her. "Let it loose. Do it."

Adrian set the cage down and pulled back the bolt and opened the door. The ferret spilled out like it'd been poured from a cup. It circled and looped, back and forth as if it wanted to test a smell from all directions. Then it put its nose to the ground and dug excitedly.

"Now, ain't 'e the smart little ratter." The boy walked over and squatted down on the muddy boards. "It were roight 'ere. Picked that bauble up roight 'ere. Good as a dog, ain't 'e?"

Kedger took off, flowing over the rough, uneven planks. Sebastian paced after it, pulling a pack of silent men behind him.

He was a fool to follow a bloody furpiece. But it was the only chance he had.

GOOD Lord, but it stank. Quentin pressed a scented hand-kerchief over his nose and tried not to breathe.

"She's in 'ere." The sailor held the lantern up to a section of wood. Behind the panel, the Whitby girl didn't make a sound. She was in there planning something.

"If it's alla same wif yer . . ." The sailor hawked and spat on the deck. "I'd jest as soon 'ave a man at my back if I open this up."

She'd shot a bandit in Turkey, once. He'd heard the story, but he'd never believed it. Not till now. Not till he'd seen with his own eyes what she could do. She'd punched a sailor in the face and broken his nose, shrieking like a fishwife. Clawing and kicking like an animal. What was Whitby thinking, raising his daughter to be a savage?

A day or two in this foul hole without food or water would go a long way toward making her sensible. Naturally, he didn't want to hurt her. He wouldn't do anything to hurt her. Not willingly. But sometimes a man didn't have a choice.

"Jess." The wood felt clammy on his cheek when he pressed himself close. "Answer me, Jess."

Silence.

"If you're good, I'll let you out. But you have to behave yourself. I'm not going to hurt you if you behave yourself."

He'd let her out when she was weaker. She had to be in a state to listen to reason. He'd open the door then. Not yet.

But it was . . . disturbing to hear nothing at all.

"You're in no danger, Miss Whitby. You won't be hurt if you cooperate." He couldn't hear her breathing. Had she died in there? They'd hit her hard. Maybe he should check . . . "You'll be perfectly safe. You have my word of honor. I'm asking for nothing but rational cooperation." She was his prize. His gift to Napoleon. The Whitby heiress. A man who moved in the first circles of government, the way he did, understood these matters. This insolent, bumptious girl was the vessel of power. Power in the East. He'd give that power to France. "You'll be perfectly comfortable. I'm a decent man. This doesn't have to be frightening for you."

He'd take her to the house on the coast and keep her there till she was a fit gift to the Republic. Weeks. Or months. It might take months till she was humbled and cooperative. He might even find a way to collect ransom from her father. That would be clever. That would be best. Yes.

No sound came from the storage locker. She was playing with him, trying to trick him into opening the door. He wasn't that stupid. Let her lie in her own filth for a while. She wouldn't be so damned superior then.

"Don't force me to be . . . stern. It'll be your choice if I have to hurt you. Remember that."

Why didn't she answer?

The sailor pulled at his sleeve. "We're casting off, sir. I gotta be on deck."

"You'll leave when I say—" The sailor just walked away, taking the lantern with him. "Now, wait a minute. I didn't give you permission to leave. Do you think I can be flouted by a . . ." He had no choice but to follow the lantern. There was no other light in this filthy hole.

Did this dolt think he could get away with this insolence?

Blodgett would deal with him. He'd tie this blockhead over the yardarm and beat him till his skin peeled off. That was justice at sea. Manly justice. The ship was a microcosm of the rational social order. Everyone working for the good of the whole. Like the Republic. When he explained it to Jess, eventually she'd understand. The social order was too valuable to allow one person's selfishness to threaten it. Jess would learn not to fight him. If she got hurt, it was really her own fault.

He climbed out of the companionway into the sun-light . . . and tripped over Blodgett. The captain of the *Lark* sprawled limp across the ladder, his eyes staring, the handle of a knife sticking out of his throat.

A dozen men moved across the deck, perfectly silently killing people. One of them was Sebastian.

It was happening so fast. Why hadn't anyone come to warn him?

This was horrible. Horrible. Ten feet away, a man thrashed on the deck, his throat slit. That could have been him. He had to get to his cabin and barricade himself in there till the fight was over. If he stayed on deck, somebody might kill him by mistake.

Sebastian didn't slow down, didn't speed up, just came inexorably toward him.

It wasn't supposed to be like this. Everything was falling apart.

"Don't come any closer." He pulled the pistol out and backed to the railing. He'd have to run for it. A great man knows when to cut his losses. He'd leave it all behind. He still had the bank account in France and the guineas in his money belt. They'd welcome him in France. He'd be a hero there.

Sebastian said, "Where's Jess?"

"Somewhere safe. Get out of my way, Sebastian. I don't mind shooting you." *I'll enjoy it.* He'd reloaded, after dis-posing of Pitney. The gun filled his hand. Heavy. Solid. A Bourdiec pistol, the best gun ever made. Accurate to a hair. He'd force Sebastian with him, past the other men, to the gangway, and kill him there, and escape in the confusion. "Nobody's going to get hurt if you let me pass."

"What have you done with Jess?"

Jess was Sebastian's weakness. And the man with the gun was always in control. "Nothing's happened to her. Yet. I'll tell you where she is when you let me go." *Wait. Wait for it. You only have the one shot.*

Sailors were being herded into a ragged, terrified line at the stern, surrendering. But he'd escape. He'd use Sebastian to get him off the ship. He was in command. "When I'm on the dock, I'll tell you—"

One of Sebastian's mongrel friends ran up. Hawkhurst. "She's below."

They were gone, running across the deck. They acted as if he wasn't there. "Stop. I'll shoot—" *There are two of them. If I kill one . . .* They ducked down the ladder to the hold before he could do anything. He had a pistol, damn it. He had his finger on the trigger. They couldn't ignore him.

On both sides of him, sailors were leaping from the ship, swimming in the toxic waters of the Thames, trying to climb the pilings to the dock. He backed to the rail and threw one leg over. He'd get the guinea belt off and abandon it. All that gold. It'd weigh him down. He pulled his shirt out to get to the tie. Was there some way to take the money with him—

A long, gray streak of rage ran right at him. That ferret. He pointed his pistol. He had only one bullet. If he shot the animal, then he couldn't—

Claws raked his eyes. He screamed and felt himself falling. The water closed over him.

Thirty-three

❧

The Northern Lark

WHEN HE OPENED THE DOOR, JESS CAME OUT kicking and clawing. She knocked them sprawling on the deck, with her on top.

His Jess. He fended her off, getting clawed up. His wonderful Jess.

She lifted her head. "Sebastian?"

Her hair straggled over her face. Somebody had given her a bloody nose at some point. She was filthy. She was infinitely beautiful. He said, "I'm glad to see you, too."

She let her breath out, miles and miles of it, slowly deflating till she was limp on top of him. She lay her head down on his chest and began to cry.

"It's all right." He held her. He could have held her for a hundred years. "Shhh. It's over. It's all right now."

"I knew you'd come for me."

"Of course."

"I knew you'd come. I left because I had to get Pitney away. Pitney is . . ." She shuddered and held on to him harder.

"I saw." Had she watched Pitney die? She had blood all

down her front, so probably she'd been there. He would have given a lot to change the world and spare her that.

He lay on the dirty planking and closed his arms around Jess and pulled her in and let her cry. She was safe. She was alive. Everything else he could fix. He'd get her off this filthy scumbelly of a ship and into the sun. He'd take her to bed and kiss every sweet inch of her. But first he'd let her cry.

Something small and sneaky brushed his arm. Kedger, smelling to high Hades and soaking wet, nosed in between them.

"Kedger?" She pushed herself up. "You brought Kedger *here*?"

Ten thousand words would not be enough to explain. "Yes."

"He coulda been *hurt*. He coulda got 'imself lost. Are you out of your sodding *mind*?"

Kedger—he'd swear this—made himself look hangdog and orphaned and pitiful. Jess fell for it at once. She got to her knees and swept the vermin in and cuddled the smug bugger of a weasel. If the ferret thought he was sleeping with them after they got married, he could forget it. Maybe they'd find a lady ferret for him.

"Let's get out of here." She scrambled ahead of him along the black corridor, heading topside. "All this dark, I'm going to break my fool neck."

Adrian had drafted Lazarus's men to cart away trunks and boxes of Quentin's ill-gotten gains. Agents from the British Service were guarding prisoners and checking the dead. Somebody—Adrian—had put a coat over Pitney's dead face. Trevor was helping move the bodies, pale but not getting sick.

Quentin, and his gun, were gone.

"Overboard." Adrian tossed the news as he walked by. "I've sent my men searching the wharf. I told them to find him dead."

Nothing could save Quentin from the gallows. If he died in the Thames today, Claudia wouldn't see her brother stand trial. "Good."

"I'll go home and kick Josiah out of Meeks Street. What we save in hemp alone on this operation . . ." Adrian wandered off.

He followed Jess and found her near the wheelhouse, sitting on the railing, her feet tucked in to keep her balance. She was at home on a ship. She'd look good on the *Flighty Dancer*.

"There's blood on you." She jumped down and let the ferret plop to the decking and walked toward him. Always the same simplicity about her. The same directness. "I didn't notice before. They told me Quentin's gone. Oh, Sebastian—the Reverend." Her face was suddenly stricken. "He was with me at the warehouse—"

"Eunice has him. He was awake and talking when I left him."

She sighed, and the clutch on his arm loosened. "I'm filthy. You would not believe how dirty that locker was. All this water around, you'd think they'd wash the place." She tapped the rail. "I'm going to scuttle this pig. I'm going to haul it out into mid-Channel and set it on fire and burn it down to the waterline. It's an evil ship." She gazed soberly across the deck, across the dead men, to Pitney's body. "And it's full of ghosts. Sebastian, I have to tell you something. I don't think it'll make any difference, but I have to tell you."

Somebody had hurt her. Maybe raped her. *If he's alive, I'm going to kill him slowly.* "Whatever happened—"

"My father probably won't like you much," she said soberly.

The sun brightened up again. He didn't laugh. She was being serious. "I don't suppose he will, much. Jess, you're going to be my wife. I don't give a damn what your father thinks. You better not either."

"I don't. Anyway, he'll be so glad to have grandchildren he'd put up with you if you were a Bactrian snake charmer. What I'm saying is, I'm going to deed everything I have of Whitby's back to him before I get married. If I don't, I'll get ground to pieces between the two of you. So if you want me, you're going to have to take me without a farthing piece, because that's how I'm coming."

A woman of magnificent gestures. He and Whitby were going to have some grand battles over her before they got the two companies consolidated. Afterward, too, probably. He'd take Jess out to sea when he and Whitby were disagreeing, so she wouldn't be bothered. He foresaw lots of time at sea for Jess. "I'll give you Kennett Shipping to run. You can reorganize my bookkeeping in your spare time . . . when we're not in bed."

Jess grinned up at him. "You would not believe how much I'm looking forward to that."

It felt like it was about time to kiss her, so he started doing that some. "Which one, Jess?"

"Both."

Don't miss the enthralling second novel
in the *Spymaster* series

The Spymaster's Lady

An elusive French spy known only as the Fox Cub.

A British spymaster who might finally be her match.

Two enemies thrown together to forge an uneasy alliance.

In desperate times, is a forbidden passion possible to resist?

'Love, love LOVED it!'
Julia Quinn

Don't miss the intoxicating fourth novel
in the *Spymaster* series

The Black Hawk

An agent stalked mercilessly through the grey London streets.

An assassin who strikes shamelessly under the cover of rain.

Her only hope is the man she once loved and now hates.

Can passion overcome the past and defeat the hidden menace?

'Every word, every page, is a wonder'
All About Romance

Don't miss the magnificent fifth novel
in the *Spymaster* series

Rogue Spy

A British agent must prove his loyalty in one final assignment.

A French spy must rescue a victim from a ruthless fanatic.

Old colleagues collide on a case and love simmers.

As dark secrets surface, where will loyalties lie?

'A lusciously sensual love story'
Booklist

headline
ETERNAL

FIND YOUR HEART'S DESIRE...

VISIT OUR WEBSITE: www.headlineeternal.com
FIND US ON FACEBOOK: facebook.com/eternalromance
FOLLOW US ON TWITTER: @eternal_books
EMAIL US: eternalromance@headline.co.uk